Liam's Lady

D1522698

J.C. Adams

For Naz—my Dulcinea. An artist of exquisite taste.
(present company excepted)

1

Publishers Note:

This is a work of fiction. All names, characters, places, and events are the work of the author's imagination. Any resemblance to real persons, places, or events is coincidental.

Solstice Publishing
www.solsticepublishing.com

PART I

1

"Out! For God's sake get out!"

Liam O'Connor ran, stretching his legs further than seemed humanly possible, pounding the pavement to a mantra recited at the top of his lungs. People were used to seeing this gangly six-foot-five man loping along, lost in his thoughts, but now those thoughts were being broadcast for all to take in.

"Out! Out of my life! Out of my head! Go!"

The curious glances became more obvious. *Jesus Christ, Liam thought, What is this fucking power she has over me? I can't shake it. I miss her. Got to find out what happened. Maybe she lost my number? Maybe she's trying to reach out. Maybe....*

Liam hatched a plan. Surely Sharon would have the answers. Sharon was his long-time shrink, and her office was close by. *I'll just casually stop by. Yeah. She'll tell me what to do.* He picked up his pace like a horse nearing the stable.

Sharon answered the doorbell through a crackling intercom. "Yes?"

"Sharon. It's Liam."

Silence.

Finally, more crackling.

"Liam. I'm with a patient."

"Oh." That wasn't in the plan. "Um... how long will you be?"

"I have twenty minutes left in this session. Is this an emergency?"

"Define emergency. Oh, never mind. How long?"

"Can you come back in a half hour? I can squeeze you in but I have other patients this afternoon."

After literally running around the block for the half hour, Liam presented himself at Sharon's door, panting and out of breath. "Is this good?"

Ushering Liam into the office, Sharon shook her head.

"You don't look so good, my friend. It's been what, at least a couple months since your last session? And, by the way, it helps if you schedule them in advance—just saying. What's going on? Obviously something isn't quite right."

"I met a woman."

"Liam. You meet women all the time, don't you? I've always figured there was a waiting list out there somewhere. Anything unusual this time?"

"I came home and she was gone. She's totally disappeared. I can't find her, can't reach her, and no one will tell me why or what's going on. It's driving me nuts, and I can't get her out of my head. Help me."

"Whoa. 'Came home'? There's a lot going on there. So she's gone. You go through women like Santa goes through milk and cookies. This isn't like you. I have so many questions. Let's start from the beginning. What's her name and who is she?"

"Sylvia. She's an Amtrak agent. Works baggage at the Dells Station. A bit rough around the edges, drinks Pabst."

Sharon exhaled. "Okay, so she's out of your usual lane. I take it she's not the ex-wife of a doctor or dentist, then?"

"Cute, Sharon. No, she's not one of the ladies at The Porter House bar."

"So, do you want to tell me the whole story?"

"Not really." The dance began.

"Well okay. You do recall therapy's a two-way street? You know—a dialogue. I ask questions, you answer. You give your thoughts, I help you work through them. Sound familiar?"

5

"It's really embarrassing, Sharon."

"Kind of sounds like it. Let's take it one piece at a time. How and where did you meet her?"

Liam took a deep breath, sat back, and considered how best to tell the story. Sylvia had shown up innocently enough, a casual introduction by a friend at a dinner party. Absolutely not his type, but nevertheless intriguing. He was a writer of some note, author of a best-selling novel, and owner of a small bookstore near Madison, Wisconsin called the Owl's Eyes. His bookstore catered to and attracted the more literate townsfolk and visitors, which was strike one against Sylvia (and vice versa). Sylvia hung out in blue collar bars and had never heard of, let alone patronized, the Owl's Eyes. Rather plain in appearance and demeanor but not unattractive, she had a spark in her eyes and ease in her manner that attracted Liam and made him a surprisingly easy mark.

"I met her at a dinner party. She was someone's cousin or something."

"That's it? Was there anything that attracted you to her?"

"She wasn't from here. She looked different. She acted different. Her eyes. She made me laugh. I dunno. She said she'd just broken up with her boyfriend."

"What happened at the end of the dinner party?"

"Nothing. I went home."

"Then what happened?"

"I called her the next day and asked her out. I had tickets to a poetry reading, so I asked her to go."

"A poetry reading."

Liam looked surprised. "Yep. Why not?"

Sharon shrugged. "Tell me more."

"We agreed that she would meet me at my house, which was close to the venue, so she wouldn't have to go home first and I wouldn't have to travel to pick her up."

"And did that happen?"

"Yes."

Sharon looked at her watch. "Was there anything striking about her when she arrived? Anything that caught your attention?"

Liam thought for a moment. "Well, she had on an unusual tee shirt."

"Unusual?"

"Yes, but keep in mind she's a railroad worker."

"And…?"

"Well, it was a bright red shirt with a large locomotive coming out of a tunnel on the front."

"That's it?"

"No. There was an Amtrak logo on the back."

"Well, I suppose that makes sense. So that's it?"

"No."

"Oh. Something else?"

"Well, yes. But I didn't see it until later."

"That's okay. What did you see later?"

"She had a tattoo."

"A tattoo?"

"Yes. Just below her belly button."

Sharon sighed. "Okay, I'll bite. What was it?"

"It said 'All Aboard'."

After a long silence, Sharon blinked her eyes. "So was the reading good?"

"I thought so, which is a good thing since the store sponsored it."

"And Sylvia?"

"Yes?"

"Your date. Did she enjoy it?"

"I think so. She *seemed* to have a good time."

"Did you ask her?"

"I don't remember."

Liam appeared simultaneously confused and chagrined.

"What happened after the event?"

"I took her back to my place, to her car," Liam replied.

"Did you have expectations?"

"What?"

"Did you have any romantic expectations?"

"Oh." A glimmer of recognition. "Yeah, I suppose."

"You suppose?" Sharon started writing.

Catching himself, he forced a smile. "Of course! I always have expectations."

"So you took her to your house. What then? Did you invite her in?"

"Sure. I asked her if she wanted to come in for a nightcap."

"Then what?"

"She told me to go ahead, that she had to grab something from her car and she would follow."

"Tell me more…"

"The next thing I knew she came in the front door with a suitcase, licked her lips, and sat down."

Sharon stopped writing abruptly and looked up. "A suitcase?"

"Um, yes. A suitcase."

"Did she tell you why?"

"She said she thought she might stay for a bit."

Sharon set her pen down. "A bit?" This was starting to go sideways. "You of course know my next question— How did this make you feel?"

Liam paused, for perhaps a bit too long. "I don't know."

"You don't know? Really? This woman who you just met announces she's moving into your house, and you don't know how you reacted? Did you, say, ask why she was doing this?"

"No, I guess I didn't. I figured if she went to all the trouble of packing a suitcase, it was only polite to let her bring it in."

8

Sharon laughed out loud, then looked away for a moment. "I'm sorry. I didn't mean to laugh. But how did you feel in the moment?"

"It kind of weirded me out."

Sharon exhaled slowly. "Why did it weird you out?"

"I didn't see it coming." He spoke the words in the manner of a question, as if asking for permission to admit he was blindsided.

Sharon wrote down a few lines, then looked Liam directly in his eyes, which were no longer averted but rather wide open and clearly rattled.

"Sounds like there was quite a bit you didn't see coming. Let me ask you this—was it an unusual event for you to be sexually pursued, and not the pursuer?"

Liam shook his head, as if to clear the cobwebs.

"Not really, at least not since my book hit the *New York Times* list. That brought them out of the woods, from far and wide."

"Okay, fair enough. Did Sylvia know your book, or who you were?"

"No. Nor did she care, apparently."

"So let me rephrase my question. Have you been sexually, and aggressively, pursued before by someone who had no idea who you were?"

"I guess not."

"And how did it go?"

Liam, lost in thought, missed the question. "What?"

"How was the sex?"

"Oh. It was terrific!"

"Okay, so we've established the sex was good. Again, nothing new for you. Did she bring anything special to the relationship?"

Liam thought for a moment. "Why yes she did."

"And what was that?"

"Equipment."

"Equipment?"

9

"Yes. A trampoline. A small, portable one."

Sharon closed her eyes. "I know I'm going to regret this, but why?"

"It's the damnedest thing Sharon. I'm always open to new adventures, but she took sex to a new level. Easily pulled a swan dive onto the bed, but it was the double backflip into the spread eagle that got my attention."

"Yep, I was right. I'm sorry I asked."

Sharon looked at her watch again. "I'm sorry Liam, but we're out of time."

"You're kidding. We're just getting to the good stuff. Man, she was something. Surely you can understand why I want her around, and why I've tried so hard to find her. Did I mention I'm broken?"

"We can pick up on this next time. I want you to give some thought to whether there were clear signs that could have saved yourself from being surprised that she disappeared—anything you either didn't see or chose not to see. Also, think about what else has been going on that might have contributed to your funk."

Liam was nonplussed. "Okay."

"Before you leave, I'm obligated to ask you a couple of questions. First, have you stopped trying to contact Sylvia? Please tell me you have…".

"Of course." He lied, not daring to mention the flowers he had ordered that morning.

"It sounds like you've been badgering the woman, and she's not receptive to your approaches. It's very important that you not try to contact her, in any way, shape, or form. Do you understand?"

Liam, feeling defeated, nodded. "Second, have you had any thoughts of harming yourself physically, or suicide?"

"Why would I do that? Oh. …I don't think so."

"If you should have those kinds of thoughts at any time at all before next week's session, I want you to call me,

10

any time of day or night. You have my private number—use it. Do you understand?"

Liam knew that this was no time to bullshit, and he shook his head.

"Was that a 'yes'?"

"Yes."

And so it happened. As with so many of his sessions with Sharon, Liam walked out the door knowing a little bit more about himself, but feeling cheated that there was no conclusion. Counseling was just like that. A tease, followed by a door slammed in your face.

2

After he left Sharon's, Liam walked to the park next to the river and sat on a bench to get his bearings. Her words rattled around. Not the ones about not calling Sylvia—those had been pushed aside for future reference. Maybe he was going mad. What if he ended up in the nuthouse? But then Sylvia popped up again. Why was he so bothered by her disappearance? Why was Sharon taking so damn many notes? Where were his cigarettes when he needed them? Why was he talking to himself? *Who is that girl over there? She's pretty cute.* Then, standing up, he shook his whole body, like a wet dog climbing out of a pond. *Well, okay then. Time to get to work.* Liam walked briskly through town until he arrived at the Owl's Eyes.

Liam was happy to see John working today. He had two primary employees, John and Marianne. John was in his twenties, a new college grad with a bachelor's degree in English literature. He kept to himself—no personal questions. Liam liked that. Marianne, on the other hand, was a lot more inquisitive, and irritating as hell. In her mid-thirties, she had a degree in art history from Bryn Mawr, and had traveled throughout Europe following graduation and before meeting and marrying Earl, a civil engineer. She had jumped at the chance to work for Liam and had been with the shop for five years. An excellent employee, detail oriented and industrious, she had one huge flaw: she felt compelled to insert her wisdom into others' lives. Everyone's, but particularly Liam's. This was an ideal day for John alone to be on duty. He mentioned that Liam's agent, Janice, had called earlier.

"Did she say what she wanted?" Liam was hoping it was to tell him he had a story picked up, but that was not to be.

"She was inquiring about the status of your new book, and she wanted you to get right back to her. Something about your editor getting impatient."

He decided to punt that call for a while.

Liam went into his office in the back of the shop, and, hesitating, dialed Sylvia's number. As it started to ring, panic set in, as well as Sharon's words:
"It's very important that you not try to contact her, in any way, shape, or form."

As sweat formed on his upper lip, he slammed the receiver down.

"Where's that son-of-a-bitch O'Connor?"

Liam looked toward the front of the store and froze. *Joanne—shit!* The last thing he needed right now was another visit from an old girlfriend. Particularly this one. Joanne had unresolved issues and had started to stalk him, often spewing profanity, yelling publicly about just what a complete jerk he was.

"He's not in right now, ma'am." Thank God John was on it.

"Not in? My ass! I know he's in there. I can smell his goddamn cigarettes. Get out of my way, you little pr— ."

"I'm sorry, ma'am. You're wrong. I'm going to have to ask you to leave."

"Bullshit, you are."

Liam needed an escape plan, but there was no back door. He could make a run for the front door, but she could cut him off. He slipped between the stacks into the psychology section. Surely Joanne would never look there. She saw no use for that science, since in her mind she held the answers to everything.

And so began a very long fifteen minutes. At one point, he had to use the bathroom but thought better of it and just crossed his legs. Finally, as he was starting to count to a thousand, Joanne harrumphed one last time.

"You tell that son-of-a-bitch his time is coming. Oh yes. You tell him that."

She left. It was over.

Stepping back into his office, Liam picked up the phone again, but this time called his agent. "Hi, Janice! So glad you called." He hoped she wouldn't get the irony in those words. "Liam, your editor's calling me. A lot. It's 1992. Do you know what that means?"

"What?"

"It's been six years since *In the Realm of One* was published. It's been four years since they paid you the advance for your next book. You're forty-three, for God's sake. You're not getting any younger, and neither am I. Jesus, Liam, they're looking for at least an estimated completion date. Is that too much to ask?"

"What did you tell them?"

"I said you're well into it, and that these things take time."

"Did they buy that?"

"Of course not. But at some point they're going to get more serious. You gotta get this done. Tell me what I can tell them?"

Liam had to buy time without having bullshit called. "Six months." He could almost see Janice grimace.

"Is that realistic?"

"Sure." It was a bold-faced lie, but if he could get even six months, maybe he could pull something off.

"Let me see what I can do. Are you going to be around?"

Liam smiled. "Where else am I gonna go?"

Maryanne had come into the store while Liam was on the phone with Janice. Hearing her voice, he called out to her.

"Hey Marianne. Could you do me a favor and call the florist to see if Sylvia got her flowers?"

"No need, Boss. They called here earlier."

14

"And?"

"The flowers were undeliverable."

"How could that be? I gave them her address."

"Well, yes you did. But she apparently refused them."

"Refused?"

"Yeah, well actually, she took them and shredded them in front of the delivery guy. Threw them on the ground and stomped on them. Tore up…"

"Okay, okay! That's more than I needed to know." Although crestfallen, Liam recovered quickly. "Well, at least I know she saw how beautiful they were."

"Yep. If that makes you feel better, I'm sure she did."

3

"You're lookin' glum. What's wrong, cowboy?" Ruth was Liam's favorite waitress at the Early Bird diner.

Liam glanced up with a half-smile. "Nice to see you too."

"So what is it?"

"Bad date. Real bad date."

She laughed. "I thought all the girls loved Liam."

"You'd think so. But apparently not."

The door opened and Doris walked in, wearing a lime-green running suit, a sweatband holding back her blond bobbed hair. Noticing Liam, she scowled. Two fingers in a *V*, she pointed at her eyes, then at Liam's, then back at hers. The *malocchio*.

"I'm watching you, asshole." She brushed past Ruth and went to the back of the diner.

Ruth chuckled. "Another satisfied customer?"

"Yep. That one didn't go so well either."

"You wanna talk about it?"

"Oh, hell no. But thanks for asking."

"So, you need anything from me?"

Liam grinned. "Yeah. My damn coffee."

***

Back at home, Liam sat down in his study and started to type. He had told John and Marianne he wouldn't be in, that he wanted the day to write. "No calls unless it's an emergency. Got it?"

The phone rang. *Damn.* He tried to ignore it, but the rings continued. Exasperated, he picked up. "Yes?"

"Liam, it's John."

"This better be good, John."

"Your agent called."

"Crap! I told her to stall."

John chuckled. "No, no, not that. You got a story picked up."

"Where?"

"*The New Yorker*!"

Liam held the phone away from his face and stared at it. "Really?"

"I wouldn't lie about this."

"I'll be damned. I submitted that piece eight months ago. I'd written it off." He thanked John and told him he'd call Janice later.

Liam felt vindicated. His shelf life hadn't expired. He'd get a nice check just when he needed it. The store was barely covering expenses, and he'd grown fearful he might have to lay someone off. He could exhale.

He turned back to the typewriter, but caught himself and stood up. His endorphins were kicking in. The book could wait. He laced up his running shoes and headed into the late summer air.

Liam had several running routes. He chose a long one. He savored being totally unreachable. Isolation presented a great opportunity to empty his brain and recharge his batteries.

One problem with an empty brain was its capacity to refill with all manner of thoughts. Say, perhaps, Sylvia. Sure enough, a stray thought hit.

Why would she dump me? I need to do something. Yeah, I need to turn this around. Maybe if I wrote her a letter?

As if a reminder of this foolishness, he tripped on a broken piece of curbing and launched, sprawling on his face in the weeds. Pain shot up from his ankle and he screamed out loud.

"Goddammit. Shit!"

This was not good. He got up on his knees, then went for it. As soon as the weight hit his ankle, he fell back to the ground, writhing in pain. The pleasure of not being reachable evaporated. He couldn't get home on his own power and had no way of contacting anyone to help. *Well, this is awkward.*

Liam figured he should stay put and see if things improved. He knew better but had no choice. After what seemed like an eternity, he heard a putt-putting sound. Around the curve came Marianne on her dull-green motor scooter. Liam had mocked her for riding that Vespa, but in this moment he was ecstatic to see her. She quickly pulled over and ran to him.

"Oh dear. Are you alright?"

"Apparently not. I think I did something to my ankle."

"Can you walk?"

"I don't think so. Do you think you could get someone to come pick me up?"

Her face lit up. "I can handle this!"

"What?"

"If I can help you up, I can take you home or to the hospital."

"You want me to ride on that thing?"

"What are you, chicken?"

The gauntlet thrown, Liam motioned her over and took her hand. She helped him to his feet. His ankle was shot, but he wasn't about to admit it—particularly not to Marianne. She walked with him as he hopped to the scooter, telling him to hold onto the back of the seat for balance while she got on. Once she was seated, she pointed at him. He positioned himself behind her, putting his arms around her. Then he tried to put his feet on the pegs, but all hell broke loose. He couldn't bend his ankle and put weight on it.

Marianne appeared to think for a minute.

"Okay. Put the other foot on the peg. Extend your bad leg straight forward and put it in my lap."

"You're kidding."

18

"Do you wanna get somewhere, or do I just leave you?"

Obeying, he extended his bad leg forward, wrapping it (sort of) onto her lap. As they wobbled off toward the emergency room, it was a sight to behold: six-foot-five Liam hanging on for dear life on the back, one leg out front at a crazy angle, and five-foot-four Marianne grinning and gunning the throttle.

"Jesus, Marianne!" Liam, falling back, steadied himself and clenched his teeth.

They made it to the hospital. The ER doctor gently manipulated the ankle.

"Shit!" Liam grimaced.

That was enough to send him off for X-rays. Feeling better when he got back to the exam room, Liam figured he'd be sent on his way with instructions to stay off it for a few days.

After what seemed like an eternity, the doctor returned. "You're lucky, but not completely."

"What does that mean?"

"The good news is you didn't break it."

"And?"

"The bad news is you have a sprain. I'm going to wrap it for you, and I'll send you home with a pair of crutches. You may only need one to get around."

"Crap."

"If you behave, you should be able to put weight on it in a couple of weeks. That's if you follow instructions."

By that time, John had shown up to relieve Marianne. Liam hobbled out of the hospital and into John's car.

John dropped Liam off at his house. "You want me to bring you anything before I head back to the store?"

"I don't think so. I'll be okay." Hobbling in, he started for the study but collapsed in the nearest chair. He propped up his leg and leaned back. Within minutes, he was asleep.

19

Liam woke abruptly to ringing. By the time he realized it was the phone, his answering machine clicked on. There was silence on the other end as the tape ran.

Shit. Maybe it's Sylvia!

Liam struggled to get up, grabbed a crutch, and painfully made his way to the phone.

"Sylvia? Hello? Hello?"

Nothing.

"Sylvia?"

"You've gotta be kidding me, boss."

"Goddammit, Marianne."

"Oooo yes, it's Sylvia! As if …. I'm just checking in to see how you're doing. You asleep or something?"

Liam took a breath. "Of course I was asleep. But thanks for calling. Don't tell anyone."

"Wouldn't think of it."

4

"Well, well, well …. What have we here?"

Liam lurched into Sharon's office, hopping on one foot and clinging to a lone crutch for balance. He dropped into a chair.

"My ankle. Sprained."

"How'd this happen?" Sharon asked.

"I tripped. Running."

Sharon looked at him, head cocked.

"Don't ask," Liam added.

Sharon shook her head.

"Are you doing better, Liam?"

"I don't know. I'm still a mess."

"Is Sylvia still on your mind? Have you tried contacting her?"

"Maybe."

"You know that's not a great idea, don't you?"

"Of course. But that doesn't mean I'm not going to do it."

"When was the last time you tried?"

"Two weeks ago."

"Liam. Look at me. We just spoke about this last week. It couldn't have been two weeks."

"This morning."

"Okay." She sighed. "Have you given any more thought to why this woman affected you that way?"

"Yeah, but I'm not making any sense of it. Help me out, Sharon."

Sharon took a moment to look over her notes from the last session.

"Okay. Let's explore some things. What'd you talk about while she was there?"

"Mostly sex. And beer. She really, really liked her PBR. Some guy named Slash. Trivial stuff. Nothing deep."

Sharon glanced at her notes. "Did you sense any common ground with her? I mean, any common interests, any points of intersection in your lives, any educational or intellectual parallels? I know that's asking a lot for first impressions, but go with me on this."

"Truth? I mean, besides sex?"

"Truth."

"Not a goddamn thing."

"When you asked her out, how did you see her?"

"Why does that matter?"

"If—and I'm not saying this was the case—but if you saw her as a one-night stand, the lack of anything in common between you was irrelevant, wasn't it?"

"I suppose so."

"And it wouldn't matter if she liked the poetry reading either, right?"

"I guess not."

He asked if she minded if he smoked. She told him to go ahead.

"So, when she walked into your house with a suitcase, it scared you. The jig was up."

Liam fumbled with his cigarette. "What do you mean?"

"Just what I said. You realized in that moment, this woman, who you didn't know and didn't really care about, had just turned the tables on you. She was now the aggressor, and potentially in for the long haul. You had no idea how to get out of it."

"Yeah, but the sex was good. Man, was it good. Okay, my turn to ask the question. If I was so surprised and scared that she was determined to stay in my house, and I was uncomfortable with that, why am I upset now that she's gone? Wouldn't I be happy?"

"Think about it. Why do you suppose?"

Liam looked at her, obsessively rubbing his hands together as if trying to get the dirt off without using soap.

"Help me."

"Liam. She dumped you before you could dump her. Here was someone you looked down on, and she dumped you without compassion or regret. Just as you were getting used to her being there. She left you powerless. How'd that make you feel? Do you suppose you might want her back now so that you can dump her? Put you back in control? Just a thought."

After what seemed like an eternity, he spoke. "Did you hear me say the sex was great? Okay, let's say you're right. Is that it? Is that all that's going on?"

"No. I think we both know you aren't in this state from this one episode alone. That would be incredibly unlike you. Something else is going on. I want you to think about what that might be over the next week. We'll pick up on it then."

Liam nodded slowly, without speaking.

Sharon changed the subject. "I know we've discussed hypnosis before. This may be a good time to try it. The goal would be to help you modify destructive behaviors. What are your thoughts?"

"You saying I have destructive behaviors? Oh my God. Are you saying sex is destructive?"

"Come on, Liam. Forget the sex for a moment. Consider your obsession with Sylvia. Constructive or destructive?"

"Okay, okay. So hypnosis would cure that, make her go away?"

"I don't know that it would make her go away, but what it might do is help you to let her go and feel better about it. It's not so much Sylvia as it is your reaction to Sylvia."

"What do I have to lose?"

"Exactly. So is that a yes?"

"I suppose."

"Okay. I'd like you to sit back and get comfortably settled. Can you do that for me?"

Liam rustled around but finally leaned back in the chair. Sharon waited until he was still, then spoke in a soft voice.

"Liam, I want you to find a spot on the ceiling and focus on it."

He looked up and spotted a cobweb.

Ha! Somebody forgot to clean.

"Now please stay focused on that one spot, and lift your arms together so that you are sighting that spot between your hands. Your arms should be straight out and your hands maybe six inches apart. Like you're reaching out and ready to applaud, only you keep your hands apart. Focus your eyes through the opening."

A song, "One Tin Soldier," floated into his head.

Jesus. Stop thinking!

Sharon continued. "Now, I want you to put your hands together, but there's a problem. There's a force field keeping them apart. It's difficult, but please keep trying. You can overcome the resistance, but it will take some time. Slow but steady. All the while, keep your eyes focused on the spot."

Liam tried, but his hands wouldn't touch.

What the fuck?

He got them closer and closer.

Sharon continued in the same quiet tone. "You're almost there. When your hands finally touch, close your eyes."

He was getting drowsy. His hands touched and his eyes closed. Sharon was still talking, but it sounded like she was in a different room.

"You're standing at the top of a stone staircase. You start down, slowly and carefully. It feels like there's a weight pushing down on your shoulders, so it's hard to move. You look down and see a figure below you on the stairs. It's a woman. She looks like Sylvia. Maybe she is, maybe not."

Dammit. What's she doing here?

24

"You want to catch up to her, but that heaviness is unbearably slowing you down. You don't want to stumble, so you take one painful step at a time. It's so hard to move. The woman is moving much faster than you. She's getting away."

Shit!

"But the further she gets from you, the lighter the weight bearing on you. Finally, she's completely out of sight. The weight disappears, and you are free to descend without any hindrance. She's gone, and you are feeling light as a feather."

Liam's body went limp. He couldn't tell if he was awake or asleep. Sharon continued to speak. She seemed to be at more and more of a distance, but then it seemed she had turned around and was getting closer.

"I'm going to start bringing you back now, Liam. I'm going to count from one to ten. You will feel yourself becoming more and more aware of the room. When I hit seven or eight, you will slowly open your eyes. At ten, you will be fully awake and present."

When she hit ten, Liam shook his head to clear the fog. "Wow."

"Are you okay? How are you feeling, Liam?"

"I'm not sure. Can I get back to you on that?" He stood up and walked to the window. He spoke without turning to face her. "Generally speaking, I guess I'm more relaxed than I was when I came here. What's next?"

"That's all for today, but I made a tape for you to use at home. I think it might be beneficial. We can talk more next session." She handed him a cassette.

Liam slipped the tape in his pocket. "So is this something we have to repeat? If so, for how long?"

"I think that's going to depend on how you react in the following days. Some people require more sessions than others. Let's just play it by ear."

Liam sat down. "So we're done?"

"Yes, but I'd like you to think about going somewhere for a bit. Get out of town. Just a suggestion."

"Not a chance." He stood up, grabbing his crutch, gave a dismissive wave, and hobbled out the door and down the street.

***

When he got home, Liam tossed the cassette tape on the kitchen counter. He grabbed the phone, and dialed Sylvia's number. This time she picked up, or at least someone was breathing on the other end. "Sylvia? It's Liam." The sound of the train whistle hit him square on, almost knocking him off balance. "Jesus Christ!" He dropped the phone and stumbled away.

Falling into a chair, he threw the crutch across the room. Goddammit. Fuck her.

He sat in silence. A vision of Sylvia disappearing down the stairs passed through his head. He started to smile, a shallow chuckle originating in his chest. It grew into a laugh-out-loud roar.

No. Fuck me!

5

Lying in bed half awake, Liam heard the rumbling of an approaching storm. Maybe he had time to get up and retrieve his paper before it started. Donning his robe and sneakers, and grabbing the crutch, he rushed out the front door, smack into his neighbor, Mrs. Sommers. She went sprawling.

"Oh my God. I'm so sorry."

Getting up onto her knees, she held up his newspaper in triumph. "I was bringing this to you so you wouldn't have to go to the box with your bad leg."

He reached to help her up. "Are you okay?"

"I think so!"

"Can you get yourself home, or do you need help?"

"No, no. I'll be fine." She headed home slowly and with a decided limp.

It was still drizzling when Liam left for the store. He developed a rhythm walking with the crutch, and made it safely into town. He stopped at a convenience store for cigarettes. A voice called out. "Hey, Liam—congrats on *The New Yorker*."

"Thanks."

Who the hell spilled the beans? Goddammit—can't keep anything quiet in this town.

Liam entered the bookstore and glanced around. He saw Marianne trying to catch his eye. She rolled her eyes toward the back of the store. "Vera's here. She's in your office."

Vera was Liam's bookkeeper. A sight to behold, she stood a solid five feet eight, with short, unkempt hair framing a perpetually worried look on her face. She always wore the same outfit, a blue jumper with a loosely hanging open-weave cardigan sweater that was several sizes too big. When she got nervous, she would sweat profusely, accompanied by

27

an overwhelming odor. To compensate, she wore cheap cologne and carried a large aerosol can of deodorant, which she sprayed liberally, right over her clothes. Then she would lift her arms to sniff the results. At the end of the day, though, she was a capable enough bookkeeper, fiercely loyal to Liam.

With an air of resignation and no small trepidation, Liam walked into his office, forcing a smile. "Good morning, Vera! How …" He caught her in mid-sniff, and quickly averted his eyes.

"How are you this morning? You have everything you need?"

Flustered, Vera stowed the deodorant can in the oversize canvas bag that passed for her purse and cleared her throat. "Hi, Mr. O'Connor! I'm great. Yep, I'm up to my elbows in numbers."

Liam searched for a way to disengage.

"That's great. Do your thing, and just let me know if you need anything. I'll be around."

Vera made the gurgling, phlegm-filled noise that passed for her laughter.

"Oh, that's okay. Marianne gets me everything I need. I probably won't bother you."

Liam smiled, gave a mock salute, and left the room. He still had a score to settle.

"John! Marianne! Can I see you?"

There was enough urgency in his voice that they both showed up quickly. Before Liam could say anything, Marianne made what appeared to be an attempt at misdirection. "Marlene Maybach called. They're throwing a party in your honor Sunday night at the country club!"

"Why on earth would they want to do that?"

Marianne beamed. "To celebrate your news!"

Awkward silence.

"Isn't that great?" Marianne added.

"And just what news is that?"

John jumped in. "*The New Yorker.*"

"And just how'd they know about *The New Yorker*?" Another awkward silence followed, broken only by the hissing of Vera spraying her deodorant in the back room.

After what seemed an eternity, Marianne spoke. "I may or may not have mentioned it to Mrs. Maybach."

"You may or may not have?"

"More likely than not, I did." Marianne was crafty. "Wasn't there something you wanted to talk about? You called us here."

Liam's color was returning to normal, but he was still shaking his head. "Yep. I wanted to know who blabbed."

"I'm sorry, Liam. I didn't know it was a problem."

He nodded and walked out the front door. He needed a cigarette. Lost in thought, he felt a tug at his sleeve. Marianne was standing in front of him.

"I'm sorry, Liam. Really. I was just so excited about the news that I told Mrs. Maybach without thinking."

He was over this conversation. "Marianne, stop. What's done is done. What's the deal with the party?"

"Like I said, it's at the country club Sunday night. I think she said seven o'clock. Just a small gathering."

"How small?"

Marianne paused. "Um. Oh. No more than seventy-five?"

"Seventy-five? Jesus Christ, Marianne. That's not a small gathering."

She smiled. "Just think of it this way. In San Francisco, it would be several hundred. It's all a matter of perspective."

"What the hell does that have to do with it?" Liam was resigned. Besides, he did enjoy a party. "I give up."

"I knew you would."

Liam made his way back to the office, but saw Vera dancing, swaying as she read a spreadsheet. It was more than he could handle. He pivoted and retired to the science fiction section. It seemed appropriate.

***

At home later, Liam was antsy to go out for the evening. Sylvia was not an option, and things being as they were with Joanne and Doris, a solo night seemed best. He'd heard good things about a gothic horror movie playing in Madison. Given the state of his life right now, he figured it was a perfect choice. He had time to kill and noticed the cassette tape from Sharon on his counter, right where he'd dropped it after their last session. He picked it up and looked at it.

What the hell ... can't hurt.

Stretching out on his bed, he waited a bit to settle in.

Relax, Liam. Give yourself a break.

He started the tape. Sharon's voice drifted over him just as it had in her office. With no distractions this time, he let himself go into the suspended state he ultimately found in her office. He concentrated on the rhythms of her speech. He felt himself nearly dozing off. Maybe he did. She took him down the stairway at the same measured pace, as the Sylvia figure raced ahead. He felt released from the weight that was holding him back. Sharon's words started to speed up and slow down, her voice wobbling and sounding strained. He didn't remember that part.

THWAP!

What the hell?

He shook his head to clear his thoughts.

Silence.

Shit.

The tape had snapped.

Well, guess that wasn't meant to be.

He put the tape player away and cleaned up for his night out.

30

The drive later into Madison was uneventful until he got to the theater and found no parking spaces nearby. He clambered out of the truck, his crutch breaking the drop to the ground. Swearing, he half-hopped, half-pivoted his way down the sidewalk. Feeling odd being by himself, he was thankful when the lights dimmed and the movie started. Until he was startled by a grotesque image on the screen—a wrinkled old man with sheep horns on his head. Or was that his hair? Whatever it was, he seemed to leap out of the screen. Liam could feel a rush of frigid air as the image moved on past him.

Shit. What the hell was that?

He was pummeled by one dark scene after another. Phantasmagoric creatures, who morphed from women, young and voluptuous, into blood-soaked vampires.

Double shit. Wow.

Afterward, images from the movie roiling in his head, Liam stopped at a nearby bar before heading home. The bar was loud. Loud talking. Loud music. Bright lights— the colors bombarded him.

I'm gettin' too old for this shit.

He drove home slowly and carefully. He was sure he wasn't drunk. Hell, he only had one beer. But things weren't right.

At home, he couldn't shake the disorientation. The hallucinations, if that was what they were, continued. Finally, out of desperation, he called Sharon. It took forever for her to answer.

"Sharon?"

"Uh. Liam? I was asleep. Do you know what time it is?"

"No. But I'm guessin' it's late."

"Yes, it is. What's going on?"

"I'm a mess. I went to a movie and it scared the shit out of me. Lots of bizarre stuff coming out of the screen at me. Blood. Monsters. Grotesque girls with huge tits. Felt like

31

a nightmare. I went to get a beer, but everything was strange. Am I going insane? I swear I didn't think about Sylvia. Well, maybe a little, but …"

"Calm down, Liam. Was there anything unusual about today that might have triggered this? Think hard."

"No, not that I can think of. I went to the store. I came home. I did the hypnosis tape. I had dinner. I drove to Madison."

"Wait. You did the hypnosis tape? How was that?"

"I guess it was okay. I got mostly through it before the tape broke."

"What? The tape broke?"

"Yeah. I heard a big 'thwap!', then silence."

"And when was this?"

"Like I said, I'm thinkin' it was almost over."

Sharon took a breath. "Are you sure it wasn't over?"

"Oh, it definitely wasn't."

"Oh, Liam. If the tape broke before you were finished, you didn't come out."

"Out of what?"

"Out of hypnosis. Until I go through the withdrawal sequence and bring you back to the room, you're still under the trance."

Liam panicked. "Are you fucking kidding me?"

"No, I'm not. I'm so sorry. We've got to fix this."

"Oh … shit."

"It's not awful. Well, not good. I want you to sit back and relax, just like you did during the tape. I'm going to try to go through the end of the session and bring you back. Are you okay with that?"

"I suppose. I'm kinda messed up right now."

"All right. Close your eyes. You're alone, at the bottom of the stairs. You're at peace, the weight of your worries has vanished. I'm going to count to ten …"

"Can you hurry it up? I'd kinda like to get this done."

"Please, Liam. Please let go. I'll bring you home."

"Oh, okay. I'm light as a feather."

Sharon took a breath, then continued. "One … two …"

"Three four five!"

"Liam. Stop. Let me do this. Three … four …"

He took a deep breath and opened his eyes. He spoke, half to himself.

"Nevermore."

6

Liam had mixed feelings about Saturday breakfast at the Early Bird. He valued his time alone, but the subdued atmosphere of its weekday business clientele was replaced by the raucous chatter of families with young children and friends having a morning out. Not a good trade-off. Liam disliked little kids and inane conversations, both in abundance. He compensated by sitting near the front window and keeping a newspaper close by.

"Usual, Liam?" Ruth was scurrying from table to table, her disgust for the demanding, low-tipping crowd in plain view on her face. Liam nodded yes as she rushed off.

Liam gazed absentmindedly out the window. A green Vespa parked at the curb caught his eye. He knew of only one in town.

"Hi, Liam! Imagine seeing you here."

Dear God, let it be a dream.

Head down, silently praying, he heard it again.

"Liam! Are you awake?"

He looked side-eyed at the source of the words. "Why are you here, Marianne?"

"I just wanted to—"

He cut her off. "Are you stalking me?"

She laughed, nervously. "Not at all. It's just that Mrs. Maybach asked me to see if you needed anything for tomorrow night."

"So you are stalking me."

Ignoring him, Marianne slid into the booth and signaled Ruth for a cup of coffee.

Liam was resigned to the intrusion. "What on Earth would I need? You're just afraid I'm not going to show up, aren't you?"

34

"Frankly, yes." Marianne could be maddeningly honest. "You've been known to bolt from social events, haven't you?"

"I'm just fine, and I'm going to be there. I've been practicing walking without my crutch, so I don't trigger any sympathetic thoughts."

Marianne chuckled. "How's that going?"

"Just great! I can put weight on it without any problem."

She glanced under the table and saw the crutch. "And what is that?"

He was caught. "Oh, that's just in case I need to rest. But I swear I haven't used it."

"So you walked all the way here, with a crutch thrown over your shoulder, just for effect?"

"Of course."

Liam changed the subject. "I've been thinking about taking some time off, going away."

Marianne raised an eyebrow. "How long, and why?"

"Maybe a week or so." A lie. He was considering heading up north for up to a month. It was nearly September, and he loved fall in the northern woods. "It's been quite a while, and my writing's getting stale. I'm thinking I could clear my head and work without interruption. Maybe get some fresh thoughts."

"Why are you telling me this?"

He paused. "I wanted to get a sense of whether you and John would be comfortable handling the store." Just then, Ruth arrived with Liam's breakfast and a coffee for Marianne. *Good. A diversion.*

Marianne stifled a laugh. She and John pretty much ran the store all the time. Liam was a distraction—a mostly good natured, benign one, but nevertheless a distraction. She sipped her coffee. "I would have to talk with John, but I'm pretty sure we can handle it."

Assuming a serious expression, Liam slowly spoke. "Good. Please discuss it and let me know." He picked up his coffee and took a sip—cold. *Dammit.* He waved to Ruth and held up his cup. She nodded from across the room.

"So where are you going?"

Liam had lost track. "What?"

"You said you're going away. Where?"

"I'm not sure." He was lying again. He had already spoken with Madeline Frost. She had some cottages about an hour outside of Marinette. Liam had rented from her several times before, and they had a good relationship.

"When?" Just then, Ruth showed up with a fresh cup of coffee.

"You set for now? One check or separate?"

Before he could say "separate," Marianne pointed to Liam and said, "One."

Ruth laughed. "You're good, aren't you?" She left the check with Liam and moved quickly away.

Liam looked at Marianne and shook his head. "What was your question?"

"When are you going?"

"I'm thinking in a week or so. I need to get some things settled before I leave."

Marianne nodded. "Well, Liam. Glad we had this talk." She grinned. "See you tomorrow night!"

"Wait." Liam looked startled. "You're going to be there?"

"Wouldn't miss it!" Marianne for the win. Game over.

In no rush to leave the diner, Liam settled in with the newspaper. As he paged through it, something caught his eye. A photo. The "pet of the week" from the animal shelter. Liam was a sucker for dogs, and something about this dog, in this photo, on this Saturday morning, grabbed him. He read the little blurb under the picture. "Lady. Three-year-old mixed breed. Great disposition. Loves long walks and car

36

rides." The look in her eyes. Her long, wavy coat. He was stopped in his tracks. He motioned to Ruth for a coffee refill, and mouthed, "I'll be right back," so she wouldn't clear his table. He took the paper with him and walked without his crutch to the pay phone at the back of the diner.

"Shelter. Good morning, this is Lucy."

Liam took a deep breath. "Hi, Lucy. This is Liam O'Connor."

"Oh, hi, Mr. O'Connor!" The staff loved Liam. He was a frequent visitor and volunteer. He spent hours there, talking to the dogs and taking them out for exercise. Occasionally he would sit and read to them. He lent his name to fundraisers and gave them autographed copies of his book as raffle prizes. "What can we do for you today?"

"Is that dog Lady still there?"

"Yes, she is. She's a beauty, isn't she? We're pretty sure she'll be snapped up quickly."

Liam took another breath. "Can I come right over and see her?"

"Sure. Should I put you down for her exercise time today?"

"I'm not coming just to visit. I'm interested in her. Can you hold her for me?"

"Of course. Mr. O'Connor, for you, we would do anything!"

Normally annoyed by enthusiastic people, Liam welcomed her excitement this time. "I'm just finishing breakfast downtown. I need to walk home and get my truck. I'll be there as soon as I can."

Shedding his pride, he grabbed his crutch and leveraged his way home as fast as possible. By the time he got there the doubts had set in. For all his bravado, he was defenseless looking into the eyes of an animal. Only his closest friends and the folks at the shelter knew this. The thoughts ricocheted in his head. What was he doing getting a dog when he was about to leave town for who knows how long? His ankle started to ache. Sitting down, he lit a cigarette, took a long drag, and put his head back. He stared at the ceiling. He pulled out the paper. There she was, staring right at him, drawing him in. He was pretty sure he saw the beginning of a smile on her face. He finished the cigarette with one last exhalation.

Oh, hell … I'm doin' this.

Liam threw his crutch into the back of his pickup and, taking a deep breath, hoisted himself up into the cab. When he got to the shelter, he slithered from the cab to the ground, hoping against hope that the maneuver could be accomplished without pain.

"Liam! So. Is this the day?" Emily Stoddard, the shelter's director, embraced him. His face betrayed his coolness by turning crimson.

Shedding the hug, he grinned. "It could be. Where's this Lady dog?"

Emily beamed. "Follow me!"

As they walked into the kennel area, Liam paused to speak with each of the dogs, a ritual he initiated long ago. Even the excitement of today's mission couldn't take its importance away. At the end of the corridor, they came to a kennel with a neatly printed sign affixed: "Lady. 3 Years. Mixed." Kneeling, Liam came face-to-face and nose-to-nose with the most beautiful dog he'd ever seen. Tall, with a wavy red coat that glowed, she weighed maybe sixty pounds.

"What do you know about her?"

Emily smiled. "A farmer picked her up about fifteen miles from here, loose in the fields, no collar, no identification. She was skinny, her hair all matted. We think she's about three, and a mix of collie and Irish setter. She's very quiet but has a mischievous streak."

Liam was smitten. He hobbled outside as best he could, Lady following close behind. She appeared to sense that he was hurting, and made no move to run. He sat down, and she sat next to him. Cocking her head, her eyes locked on his face, she climbed into his lap. He hugged her and she relaxed completely. He spied a tennis ball nearby, picked it up, and threw it. She seemed to smile, then took off and retrieved the ball, dropping it next to his foot. He threw it again, and again. At some point, she simply climbed back into his lap. Liam held her tight, and she rested her head on his shoulder.

By the time they got back to Emily's office, she had already started the adoption paperwork.

He hesitated a moment. "Could you do me a favor, and keep her until Monday morning? I have an event tomorrow night and don't want to leave her alone that soon."

Emily nodded. "That works. I'll have everything ready for you on Monday when you pick her up."

Liam leaned down and gave Lady a hug. "I'll see you soon, my friend. Soon." Lady put her paw on his leg and cocked her head again, her eyes seeming to plead for him to stay. He melted.

Liam tried to walk nonchalantly back to his truck, but his ankle was hurting. His pace slowed and the limp returned, but he was determined to pull this off. Leveraging himself into the cab, he lit a cigarette and smiled.

7

Liam arrived home to see Mrs. Sommers standing at his door, holding a plate of something. With a huge, toothy smile, she held it out. Liam looked at her with a pained expression.

"What have we here?"

"It's brownies! Don't they look delicious?" Mrs. Sommers beamed. "Some nice lady brought them by. Said she baked them just for you! She said to tell you there are more where these came from."

"What'd she look like?" Liam was suspicious. He couldn't put his finger on any woman he knew at the moment who would do anything nice for him.

"She had a hat and big sunglasses on. I couldn't see her face."

That clinched it. Liam bit his lip. "That's wonderful Mrs. Sommers. Thanks so much for bringing them over. What a treat…"

He heard the phone ringing. Seizing the opportunity to disengage, he pointed inside. "I'm sorry, but I'm expecting an important call. Thanks again."

As he walked in, the ringing stopped. *Thank God.* Reaching the kitchen, he threw the brownies in the garbage. There were few candidates, none of them good and each of them capable of trying to poison him. The ringing started again and he picked up.

"Liam, it's Janice."

Double dammit. "Hi Janice. What's up?" He was hoping it was something new and helpful.

"Checking on the new book."

He tried a misdirection. "Where are we with *The New Yorker*?"

"I told you that's all set. Now, about the book...."
She was relentless.

"I think things are really poppin' now. Yeah, just poppin' all over the place!" He rolled his eyes even as he was speaking the words.

What the fuck? Poppin'? Jesus.

"I've stalled about as much as I can. You need to produce something. Something tangible, that they can hold in their hands and examine. They've heard this bullshit from countless writers over the years. They could probably just give you the script. Be honest with me. Where are you, really?"

Liam was a fighter. He wasn't going to accept defeat. Could not accept defeat. He was a best-selling author. The New York Times reviewer called him "Brilliant. A nascent star with a great future". "Okay, okay. Here's the picture: I'm about two-thirds through and starting to pick up momentum. I've had more than one period of self-doubt, but I think I'm getting over it. In fact, I'm going out of town, somewhere remote, where I can work without distractions. Guaranteed. You know that's how I work best. I promise you I'll have a complete manuscript soon."

"How soon?"

"I think I can finish within two months. Three at the most."

Janice laughed. "So—- six?"

Liam feigned hurt. "What— you're doubting my word?"

"Not doubting your intent, just the likely outcome. I know you very well Liam O'Connor."

"Laugh if you must, but you'll see. I'll pull this off." Liam knew she was right. "Mark my words."

He had intended to do some writing, but after talking with Janice his passive aggressive side kicked in. He'd be damned if he was going to do something just because she told him he needed to. He picked up a book, sat down and started reading. Soon he was asleep in his chair.

***

Ben, the owner of The Porter House, greeted Liam warmly. "To what do we owe the honor of your writership's presence tonight?"

Liam smiled. "I'm here to soak up the adoration of all my fans."

Ben laughed. "So. Your usual table for one?"

"You mean my fan isn't here?"

Ben looked over at the bar and winked. "Oh, I think they all await you over there."

Liam cringed. The singles scene was playing out on this Saturday evening. Probably about twenty people around the bar, mostly female, all in one stage or another on the make. He tried to avoid eye contact. He had dated most of the women who were standing dangerously close to him now. Some once, some a few times, some longer, but all with the same result. He would walk away. They were all nice enough, but almost to a one they were divorced from the town's various professionals, most all of whom now had trophy wives. Those left behind were by and large angry, and there was always an edge in the dating process. On one of his initial dates, the candidate *du jour* looked into Liam's eyes and with steely countenance said "I understand you've dated everyone in town."

Liam, amused by the accusation, responded with a smile. "Yes. I believe you're number thirty-one." That was an early evening.

Grimacing, Liam turned back to Ben. "Yes, a booth for one. Preferably in a dark corner. Far from the bar."

Ben led Liam to a booth out of the bar's line of sight. Liam lit a cigarette and sat back, slowly drawing and exhaling. He couldn't stop thinking about Lady. What a sweet dog.

"I thought you were going to call me."

Shit.

That grating, sarcastic voice, like scraping a rake across concrete. "Oh. Hello, Doris."

"You lying piece of shit. You told me. Three times."

"Why Doris. So good to hear your voice." He looked up at her, smiling. Not unattractive, she nevertheless typically missed the fashion mark, and tonight was no exception. Dressed in a short-sleeved white satin blouse and a straight, tight-fitting red skirt, a navy scarf around her neck, she looked more like a discount-airline stewardess than the hip socialite she thought herself to be. Her bobbed, blonde hair was set-off by the contrasting red pallor of her face, accentuated by the bulging vein in her forehead.

Exhaling smoke in his face, she quietly grunted. "Tinydick."

"What?"

"Oh, nothing. I said you make me sick." She turned and sauntered away.

***

The next morning, the realization hit that the country club affair was that evening. Embarrassment and revulsion in equal parts overcame Liam. He knew the celebration of his upcoming publication was a ruse, an excuse to party. On the other hand, unlike the bar at The Porter House, there would be no singles to contend with. The country club crowd was all couples. Pretentious and self-absorbed small-town notables. Ironically, the crowd would include ex-husbands of the women who dallied at The Porter House bar. Ex-husbands with their midlife crisis trophies on their arms.

He put that all out of his mind, and let his thoughts drift to Lady. Soon he would have a dog to hang with. He visualized the two of them, playing, frolicking in a field, tennis balls all around. He wondered how Lady might react

43

to Sylvia. On cue, a drunken Sylvia stumbled into the visualization.

"Who's mutt is that?"

Lady looked up at Liam and cocked her head, as if saying "Is she talking about herself?"

Then she turned and faced Sylvia, who was pointing at Liam and laughing derisively, a breach of dream etiquette and an obvious mistake. Lady snarled and lunged at Sylvia, who turned tail and ran out of the vision.

Good girl! I knew I could trust you.

***

Liam headed to the hardware store to get supplies for Lady, then over to the Owl's Eyes. When he got there, Marianne and John were in a heated argument over the new display for the young adults section. He tiptoed past them, picked up the Sunday *Times*, and closeted himself in his office. He considered barricading the door but opted for holding the paper high in front of his face. He resisted the urge to light up as the smoke would drift into the main part of the store and blow his cover. He settled in, with the self-satisfaction of a young boy who had found the perfect hiding place in a game of hide-and-go-seek.

Liam spent the afternoon reading the *Times* and annoying Marianne by quizzing her about inventory and supplies pending his trip out of town. At about four he realized he needed to get home to get cleaned up and dressed for the evening's event. On the way out of the store, he had to face one last inquisition from Marianne.

"Are you sure you're going to show up?"

"Marianne. How could you doubt me?"

She snorted. "How could you think I wouldn't doubt you?"

***

44

The Country Club was about a twenty-minute drive from his house. He timed his departure to assure he'd be fashionably late and make a more impactful entrance. When he got to the door, the doorman opened it and ushered him in, where the president of the club and his wife stood beaming.

"Liam! We're so pleased you'd join our humble gathering tonight. We are so looking forward to catching up on all the excitement in your life."

Liam smiled. "Me too." He was certain they missed the joke.

A glass clinked as he entered the room, followed by a smattering of applause before the crowd returned to their own conversations. Liam bit his lip as he feigned a smile.

Not celebrating old Liam, are we?

A hand gripped his shoulder. He turned to see a young woman, half in the bag, smiling and slowly nodding.

"I just loved your interview in *Playboy*. So insightful… " She said.

"What?"

The young woman continued to nod, like a horse trained to count to three.

"So deep."

Liam, dumbfounded, nodded in return.

"That wasn't me."

She turned to her husband, who was standing behind her, and shrugged. After a moment, she turned back to Liam.

"Oh. Are you sure?"

Liam saw Marianne across the room and excused himself. When he reached her, he escorted her aside.

"Can I go home now?"

8

"How was the Liam O'Connor Fête?" Sharon could lay down a question in such a way that you couldn't tell if it was a genuine inquiry or an ironic bit of rhetoric.

Liam responded in kind. "It was wholly and completely adequate."

Sharon laughed. "Up to your usual standards then."

"This one exceeded even my lowest expectations. You know these people, Sharon. They're stiffs even when they're smashed. How is that possible? I tried to leave, but Marianne wouldn't let me."

"But you were the star of the evening. I'll bet you dazzled them with your erudite banter, didn't you?"

"Ha! My attempts to plumb the depths of that crowd's interests were like throwing a stone into a pond only to have it skip along the surface and disappear into the horizon. I would've been better off just holding up a mirror so they could admire themselves."

She smiled. "Well, I'm glad you got that off your chest." She quickly pivoted and became all business. "So. What's new since I last saw you?"

"Well, a couple of things, I guess." He paused, either to think or simply for effect. One could never be sure with Liam.

"Would you care to elaborate?"

"Well, I've decided to get away for a while."

Silence.

"Okay, when and where?"

"I'm headed out next weekend. Going upstate to those cottages near Marinette, the ones where I've stayed before. I'm thinking I can isolate myself and work without interruption."

"Good for you. How long will you be gone?"

"Probably a week or two, maybe more if it's going well."

"How're you feeling, Liam? You still seem a bit hesitant. What's your mood right now?"

Trapped, he reverted to staring at the carpet.

Crumbs. Some idiot was eating in here and she let them.

"Liam? Are you there?"

He jumped a bit, his momentary trance broken. "What?"

"How are you feeling in this moment? What are you feeling?"

With a forced smile, he chirped: "I'm just great."

Sharon's expression softened. "It's okay if you're not, Liam."

"Okay, okay. Feeling a little down, I guess."

Sharon nodded. "Is this the same old feeling or something new?"

"No, it's the same funk I've had for over a month, maybe more."

"Have you been thinking about Sylvia again?"

"No… Maybe."

Sharon wrote in her notebook for a good minute or so, then stopped. She looked at Liam with a calm but concerned demeanor.

"We've been through a lot of discussions recently that don't seem to add up. This whole Sylvia thing is so very unlike you, and you know it. You've never had a problem walking away from a brief and meaningless fling gone badly. I'm going to ask you something that may be very painful if I may. Are you alright with that?"

He looked at her and squinted his eyes, thinking. Finally, he swallowed.

"Okay. Fire away."

"When's the last time you thought about Marguerite?"

An iceberg formed in the pit of his stomach. He hadn't spoken of her, or even mentioned her name, to anyone in well over a year.

Sharon reached over and touched his arm.

"I'm sorry Liam. But I had to know if I'm going to help you."

He stared past her.

"You know that, don't you?" She continued.

Silence.

Finally, with no change whatsoever in his expression, Liam nodded. This session just took an abrupt left turn, and what was started had to be finished. He said nothing.

She sat quietly for a few minutes, then stood up.

"I'm going to step out for a bit, but I'll be back. Take your time. I don't want to overwhelm you."

Marguerite. Why here? Why now? He was unprepared for this conversation and would rather have been anywhere else than in Sharon's office. He had moved to New York after his book was published, and met Marguerite there, during the original tour for *In the Realm of One*. She was an established novelist, a couple years older than him. She lived in the West Village and taught creative writing at Columbia. A stunning blonde, with piercing green eyes, she was the very model of intellectual style, and ran in lofty literary circles. She was everything he wasn't yet but hoped someday to become. Awestruck and flattered when she introduced herself and told him how impressed she was with his work, her words still resonate in his memory.

"If I were being honest with myself, Liam, I'd have to admit I'm envious of your talent. Your writing is exquisite, right down to your sentence structure and phrasing. The images pop off the page. How do you do it?"

At the time, he was suffering the insecurities of a new writer suddenly thrust on the stage of success, and felt the warmth of validation from her praise.

48

Sharon re-entered the room.

"Do you want to talk now? It's okay if you don't. I'm sorry to hit you with this one."

Liam deflated, the memory snapping shut.

"I really don't know the answer, Sharon. I don't think I've consciously thought about her or considered the subject recently. That ended what, five years ago?"

"Think hard, Liam. Is there anything in your situation with Sylvia that might have touched some deep-seated nerve?"

"Oh hell no. There's no similarity whatsoever between the two of them."

"That wasn't my question. You've never to my knowledge been serious about anyone since Marguerite, and you've been consistently quick to find something wrong with and blow off your conquests and those who've pursued you. You're an equal opportunity jilter. To my mind Sylvia's the least desirable of anyone you've dated in all the years I've known you, and yet you haven't let go of her."

She had him on this one, and it was something he hadn't seen coming and for which he had no good answer. Liam was deep in thought, painfully dredging up the entire year he spent with Marguerite. They seemed so completely compatible. The sex was incredible, but so were the nonstop conversations that could go on for days when they were together. He returned home to New York as many times as he could manage amidst the stops on his ongoing book tours. She also flew in to meet him on his tours, so they could spend time exploring new places. Ultimately, she moved in with him. It wasn't till well into their affair that the little digs and criticisms started to show up. At an event sponsored by *The Paris Review*, she put her arm around him and smiled.

"So proud of my Liam. He got a great mention in *The Village Voice* last week. Oh… Wait. That was Roth, wasn't it?" Everyone chuckled. Everyone but Liam. "It's okay dear, someday you'll get one." More laughter. He smiled as if he were in on the joke.

Yet Liam remained in love with her and didn't hesitate to tell her. In the beginning, she was quick to say "I love you too", but at some undefined point she either said "thank you", or nothing at all.

"Liam?"

The spell broken, he returned to the present.

"Sharon, you know I broke up with Marguerite."

"Can you tell me again why you broke up with her? What happened?"

His face reddened. "Look. We both know what happened. I don't want to go over it again."

"Okay. That's enough for now. We're almost out of time. Before we wrap up, let's talk about how you want to proceed while you're out of town. Do you want to continue? I'd strongly urge you to keep at this with me."

He took a few moments to calm down and regroup. Sharon had stripped open an old wound.

"There's a very practical problem with that. There's no phone in the cottage."

Sharon sighed. "Do you have access to a phone anywhere nearby?"

He shook his head no, then stopped.

"There's a pay phone outside in the middle of the little town about three miles away. You literally have to stand in the street and wait for it to become available. Everyone uses it, so there's often a line."

"Not ideal, but you have my number. Please call me if you want to talk. You can set up a time with my secretary, but in an emergency, you have my home number."

She paused, then almost as an afterthought spoke. "Anything else you want to tell me today?"

Liam managed a smile. "Yeah. I'm gettin' a dog."

"What? How'd that happen?"

"Yes. My new friend Lady. She's beautiful. Headed to the shelter now to pick her up."

It was Sharon's turn to smile. "Well congratulations. Enjoy your time. I'd love to see pictures when you get a chance, or bring her around when you get back."

Liam was tense, but at least the ghost of relationships past was back in the closet for now. "Oh, I will." He stood up and stretched.

"See you in a couple of weeks?"

He walked out the door without responding.

***

Liam was shaken. The saving grace was that Lady was waiting for him, but even that seemed small consolation.

"Unconditional love."

He spoke the words out loud but to no one in particular. He walked to his truck and climbed in. He looked over at the passenger seat and saw the new collar and leash he bought yesterday. He patted them both.

I'm on my way, my friend.

Emily smiled warmly as Liam came into the shelter.

"Are you ready for this, Liam?"

"Absolutely."

When they had finished the paperwork, he opened the door of his truck and Lady jumped in, tail wagging. Panting with excitement, she pivoted between looking out the windshield and the side window. As they drove away, she lay down and put her head in his lap. Liam started to tremble. All the pain and anger that came with Marguerite's ghost. Just hearing her name spoken by Sharon was all that it took to throw him into a tailspin.

Dammit.

He just wanted to go away and hide.

"Lady—Here we go. You and I are gonna be a team. For better or worse, we've got each other."

Hearing his voice, Lady sat up again, looked at him with what he could swear was a smile, and started to pant.

9

The rest of the week was not one of Liam's best. The only thing that got him up in the morning was Lady. She woke each morning with an infectious joy. When he didn't get up immediately, he was subjected to warm breath and wet licks all over his face.

The resurrected memories of the worst time of his life were too much to escape. The day he thought he had finally let go forever came back, front and center.

***

Marguerite was out and about, and his morning promised to be a quiet one. He'd hoped to spend it writing. As he sat down to have his coffee, he spied the new issue of *The Atlantic* on the kitchen table. He picked it up and glanced at the table of contents to see if anything looked interesting. There, to his surprise, he saw Marguerite's name. He didn't recall her saying anything about a new piece, but then he really wasn't bothered. He opened to the story and settled in to read it. The first line looked familiar. Then the next line, and the next. He was overtaken by shock and confusion. This was his story, one he had been working on for months. Called "Dublin Delight", it was based on a trip he took to Ireland after college, something only he could relate. She had changed the name to "My Irish Adventure", and the protagonist from male to female, but with scant exceptions the words were entirely his. His hands started to shake as he read on, hoping against hope that it wasn't all there, all under her byline. But it was. She'd stolen and submitted his work, in her own name. She'd betrayed him, his love, trust, and all that he had thought their relationship meant. It was as if he had stepped off a sidewalk and been impaled by a bus he hadn't seen coming. This was the woman he not only loved, but who he looked up to as a model for his career. Of course, he had shared the story with her. He believed her to be a loving mentor. Everything that filled his world, every bit of his existence, was gone as if stolen by some mysterious force he could neither see nor touch, but that emptied his soul.

By the time Marguerite came home, Liam's emotions had morphed into rage. He held up the magazine, waving it in her face. She walked past him, turning at the last minute.

"I needed something to get back into print. It's a shitty piece, but it was publishable." Her voice was flat, emotionless.

"Goddamn you. Goddamn you! This is the worst fucking thing you could do to me, and you did it without even considering its effect on me."

She shrugged. "Oh, I considered that. It meant nothing."

He glared at her. No, he glared right through her. "This is total bullshit. You could've just had an affair if you wanted to get to me." Marguerite started to turn red, and in that moment he knew. "Oh no. That too?"

"How could you be so stupid? Where the hell do you think I went all the nights I told you I had meetings with my editors?"

Liam was incredulous.

"Get. The. Fuck. Out of my apartment. You're done. Or do I throw you out myself? I'll sue your ass."

"Go ahead. I'll destroy you. Do you think anyone will believe you? You, a wannabe writer with one lucky book, who hasn't written shit since? You, a jilted lover? You stand no chance."

He moved swiftly across the room, opened the door, and pushed her out. Her purse, with her key in it, was on the table. He slammed the door shut, grabbed the key and, reopening the door, threw the purse out into the hall.

54

She looked at him. "You stupid son of a bitch!"

Liam didn't calm down for some time after she was gone. The scene was swirling in his head. He replayed it again and again. He didn't see it coming. Now he was blaming himself. Now he was visualizing strangling her. Finally, he put himself to work packing her things. Not carefully. Just throwing them into boxes. When he got to her papers, he gave thought to ripping them into shreds, but somehow even that seemed more a futile gesture than productive retribution. He alternately screamed and cried.

Soon, she was back, banging on the door with her fists and this time yelling.

"Open up you worthless little prick!"

He resisted the temptation to respond, staying silent.

"I'm coming back with the police!"

Even then, he stayed silent. He knew she'd never call the police, so it was a hollow threat. What the hell would they do? This was New York. The NYPD could give a shit what some raging bitch had for a complaint. Shortly after, she gave up and left.

After a couple hours, Liam called the only person he trusted to talk about this whole humiliating mess— Sharon. She picked up as soon as she heard his voice on her answering machine.

He started explaining everything, but in a manner so scattered and confusing that Sharon had to stop him and start asking simple questions. Once he had laid out the whole awful situation, she calmly asked him to stop and take a breath.

"Look. Your rage is understandable. It's a good sign that you're able to focus your feelings. But please don't try physically removing her again. You don't need an assault charge."

He assured her he wouldn't. Finally, they talked about whether he should pursue suing Marguerite over the story. This was a tough call, but in the end, they agreed it would probably not be in the best interests of his career. That was a tough pill to swallow. Sharon convinced him that, as painful as it was to admit, Marguerite had him on this one. He hadn't yet submitted the story anywhere, and only he and Marguerite had read it. He had no way to demonstrate that it was his writing, and Marguerite would simply claim that he was acting from revenge alone.

***

Back in the present, Liam was lost in thought when he was startled by Lady pawing him, tennis ball in her mouth. He shook his head to clear the fog and reached down to pet her. It was time to shake Marguerite, if only for a short time. He got up and went out into the yard, Lady following with her tail swaying happily. They played fetch for a good half hour, until the ball was so gooey with slobber that it was nearly impossible to get a good grip on it.

"You've worn me out, my friend." Lady taunted him and refused to come back into the house. He gave up and went in, leaving the back door open for her.

Liam sat at his desk, staring out the window but looking at nothing. Something raced past him, and all hell broke loose. He could hear pounding steps from the kitchen, as if the cavalry was roaring in. A red form galloped by.

What the fuck?

He scanned the room.

Shit!

Lady in hot pursuit of a squirrel. The squirrel bouncing around the room, up on the bookshelves, leaping to the windowsill, diving under the sofa. Even in its panic, the little furball eluded its big red adversary.

Liam jumped into action, but only added to the chaos as he grabbed a broom and went after the squirrel. At one point he cornered it, but it ran through his legs. In a moment of clarity, Liam ran to the front door and threw it open. The squirrel dove through the opening, Lady in hot pursuit ran smack into a wide-eyed Mrs. Sommers, who was standing right outside the door, snooping through the window. Liam watched with horror as she went tumbling, but somehow she rolled and came up on all fours, face to face with a panting Lady. Mrs. Sommers scrunched her face.

"Liam, how on earth did a dog get in your house?"

"Got me, Mrs. Sommers. I have no idea."

10

"I'm so glad you found a girl who suits you."

"Real funny, Marianne."

Liam knew he'd take abuse at some point. Might as well get it over with now. He let Lady loose and she wandered off, exploring and taking in all the smells a book shop presents.

Marianne seemingly couldn't contain herself.

"So. Did you thoroughly love the party? Wasn't it great? So many people, and they all love you."

"Sure. It was really something." The response was calculated to go over her head.

Marianne looked him in the eye. "How long do you really plan to be gone? Give me the truth—I can handle it."

"Why do you doubt me?"

She laughed. "Why wouldn't I doubt you? Give me one good reason."

She had a point.

"Honestly?" He held her gaze.

"Yes, honestly. If you want me, er, us, to run this place, we need to know what we're gonna have to deal with."

Liam nodded, almost imperceptibly, thought for a second or two, and finally spoke.

"I'm saying one, two weeks, but if I'm really being productive and it makes sense to me at the time, it could be a month."

"Tell me again how we get hold of you?"

"You'll have to call Mrs. Frost. I'll give you her number before I leave town, like I told you before."

"How about now?"

"How about now what?" Liam really didn't want to be bothered while he was out of town.

"How about you give me her number now? Just write it down."

"I don't have it with me."

"Ok, but I'm gonna stay on you. What about Vera?"

Liam cocked his head. "What about her?" He had forgotten this part as well.

Marianne's exasperation was showing. "When is Vera scheduled to be here, and do we have direct access to her?"

"Define 'direct access'."

"You know very well what I mean Liam. Do John and I have authority to deal with her, ask her questions, and give our input on your behalf, without having to get hold of you first? Remember, you're the one who is saying it'll be difficult to contact you. And if you say it will be 'difficult', that's code for 'impossible'."

Just then, Lady grabbed a stuffed animal a young child was cradling and proudly paraded around the room. The kid started screaming. Liam chased after Lady, and in the process knocked over a display rack, books tumbling everywhere. Finally, he cornered her, pried the toy from her mouth, and returned it to the child, who continued to scream anyway. Giving up, he returned to Marianne.

"You were saying?"

"Look, Liam, whenever you've traveled in the past, on all your various tours and vacations, you've always been reachable. This is pretty much the first time you're leaving for an extended period without a phone somewhere. What do you want us to do, send you a telegram? Smoke signals?"

He was trapped. "Okay. Okay. You have authority to talk with Vera, to give her direction and to get her reports. Just remember that Vera occupies a different galaxy, and communication is sometimes... well..... odd."

"Oh, I'm well aware of that."

Liam started to say something but thought better of it. He turned and called to Lady. She ran to him, and they

59

walked out of the store. On the way, Liam looked back at Marianne. "Don't screw up while I'm gone."

Marianne shook her head and said something he couldn't hear.

***

The trip North was relatively uneventful, except for the pinball game called Sylvia banging around in his head. Could he get her back? Maybe just a little shove on one side of the machine—a perfectly timed movement. Just enough not to tilt. He couldn't shake her from his thoughts. What if he was misreading her silence? Maybe if he made a small course correction, a simple detour to the Dells?

"Let's do this!" He shouted to the road.

He got off the highway.

As the road wound on, the self-doubts nipped at him. He started a conversation with himself. "Of course. This is the solution. How could she resist me?" He looked in the rear-view mirror and caught a glimpse of himself. "No. No, no, no! Look at yourself...you're a mess." He shook it off and tried to concentrate on the trees lining the road. "There. That's better. You're hot, O'Connor. You're a star... ."

Lady, watching and listening to him, lay down and sighed. Liam could swear she shook her head.

"You're right girl. I'm an idiot. Not a chance."

He got back on the highway.

***

After what seemed like an eternity, he saw the sign for the little burg near the cottages. It was a one stop town— one blinking four-way stop light. Its population was meager, except during the summer season when it blossomed with vacationers. That season was just winding down, and many of the interlopers had already left.

60

Liam turned down a tree-lined, tar and gravel road. A worn, whitewashed sign read: "Windward Resort", in faded blue letters. A weather-bleached rendering of an unidentifiable fish was painted below the name. Down the road, there was a dirt drive in the trees with a small sign proclaiming "Frost". He reached over and stroked Lady.

"Here we are, my friend. Your palace awaits."

He turned and drove slowly into the drive, past a clearing with a tennis court and shuffleboard, both in disrepair. Straight ahead was a small tree-lined lake. It was a little windy, enough so that there were whitecaps seemingly everywhere. There was a two-track along the lake, running past a series of old but nicely kept cottages. He pulled up at a faded yellow, two-story structure. A sitting porch with Adirondack chairs extended across its front. It was just as he'd remembered it.

Madeline Frost had seen him drive in and was walking down the two-track to greet him. She lived in a large, well-kept white house set apart from the rental cottages by a good hundred yards. About sixty years old, she was dressed simply but with a casual elegance. She was about five-foot-five, with short salt and pepper hair.

"Good to see you Liam."

From her accent, you could tell she was not from Wisconsin. East Coast, maybe Maine. She exuded warmth; a trait necessary to the trade of running a summer cottage complex. Liam genuinely liked her. She kept to herself and left him to himself. She was very good at protecting him from intruders, particularly by keeping the only phone in the resort, screening callers, and "forgetting" to give him messages.

"Oh! Who's this beauty?" Lady had leaped from the truck and ran right to Madeline.

"My new girl—Lady."

"Well, she's beautiful. You'd better take good care of her. Your track record with 'ladies' isn't so good, is it?"

Liam blushed. "No. No, it's not. But she's a keeper."

Madeline pointed at the cottage. "Let's go in. I think you know just about everything about it. Nothing changes from year to year, so there's really nothing new."

Liam looked around. "I'd expect nothing less."

"I'll leave you to get settled in. No pressure, but if you're interested, I have a few people coming over for cocktails tonight at seven. I promise you I've vetted them and they should all meet your standards. No single women." She smiled and winked.

"Thanks. I may take a rain check, but maybe." Liam relaxed almost immediately every time he came to Windward. Something about it took all the pressure away.

Lady exhausted herself following him between the truck and the cottage as he unloaded. He looked at her and shook his head. "My friend, you're working far too hard. We have one more thing we need to do, then we can settle down. We need to run into town and hit the grocery store. I didn't bring anything with us. Okay with you?" They headed back into town. The stop at the grocery store was a brief one. When Liam came back to the truck, Lady was eagerly awaiting his arrival. She stuck her nose into the bag, hoping for treats. She wasn't disappointed. Liam was ready to get back, sit on the front porch, and stare at the lake. By the time they arrived at the cottage, the lake had calmed down considerably. The whitecaps were replaced by gentle, regularly timed swells. Just what he remembered. He poured himself a whiskey, grabbed a cigarette, and walked out to the porch. Lady laid down next to him, wagged her tail one more time, rolled on her side, and fell asleep.

He held the glass high in the air.

"To you and me, my Lady. Here's to us."

11

When Liam woke it was daylight and Lady was sitting next to the bed, staring at him. He patted her head and she lay back down. He drifted back to sleep, and Marguerite appeared, just past Lady, beckoning him. Lady turned to Marguerite and bared her teeth. Marguerite recoiled and disappeared. Just then, Lady nudged him, startling him awake. He shook his head to clear the dream. He needed to talk with Sharon. He was not doing well. His emotions were a mess, and unless he addressed that condition, any attempt to get to writing would be a lost cause. He took a cup of coffee outside.

Dammit O'Connor. Snap out of it.

He stared at the lake. He tried breathing slowly, struggling to rid his mind of dark thoughts. His head pounded.

Damn whiskey.

It was too early to call Sharon. Besides, he would have to drive into town to do it. Sitting down, he closed his eyes. He tried to focus his mind on the book. If he couldn't get the book underway in this setting, he and it were doomed.

After a couple hours of accomplishing nothing, Liam cleaned himself up. Taking Lady with him, he pointed the truck toward town. When he got there, he saw the lonely pay phone standing guard over the empty lot where the hardware store had once been, before the fire that left charred the sides of the two-story brick grocery and the abandoned gas station-turned-flower-shop that flanked it.

Liam placed the call. *Please let her be there.* After a few rings, Sharon answered.

"Sharon, it's Liam."

"Liam. I have an appointment in fifteen minutes. What's up? Where are you?"

"I'm up North, and I'm in trouble."

She took a breath, seemingly counting to five, and responded.

"Ok. I'm not surprised. I left you hanging at the end of our last session. I'm sorry—I was worried this might happen. What's going on? Marguerite?"

Liam steeled himself. "Yes, but maybe more than that?"

"Is that a question?"

"No. Not really. I came close to contacting Sylvia on my way up here."

This time Sharon paused longer before responding. "What?"

"I started to drive to the Dells' Amtrak station."

"And did you?"

"No. But I THOUGHT about it."

"Liam. I'm not a priest, and this isn't confession. I don't care that you had thoughts. The important thing is you didn't act on it."

"Really? So I'm good?"

"More or less. By the way, what stopped you?"

"Lady."

"Who?"

"Lady—you know, my dog."

"How did she stop you?"

"She…. She sighed."

"That's all it took? A sigh?"

"Yeah. She hardly knows me, and yet she figured it out."

"So that's it? You almost did something that would've embarrassed you, but your dog sighed and you didn't?"

"Yep."

"You said you're 'in trouble'. What's that mean?"

"It's all too much. Marguerite."

"That's a whole other subject… What's with that?"

"I can't get her out of my head. It's like she has a spell on me again."

"Again? I was afraid of this when I brought her up. But let's go with it. I think we're on to something."

Liam calmed down a bit. "Please help me. What are we on to?"

"What do Marguerite and Sylvia have in common, Liam?"

"Absolutely nothing, as far as I can see."

"Think again."

Liam was focused on the two women's distinct personalities and background, and just couldn't make sense of her question.

Sharon seemed rushed, but Liam knew she was out of time.

"Ok, here goes. Let's break it down. What did Marguerite do?"

"She stole my manuscript. She had an affair. She betrayed me. What more do you need? She was a complete asshole, as it turned out. I left her—threw her out."

"Okay. But what was the net effect on you?"

"I give. What?"

Sharon seemed impatient.

"She abandoned you and did everything in her power to humiliate you. Do you see that?"

Liam was stunned. He'd spent years focusing on her betrayal and his anger. He didn't see the abandonment part, but here it was, right in front of him.

Sharon continued. "What about Sylvia? What did she do? Forget about the part that she was not your type and you had no business with her. What did she do?"

The light went on.

"She abandoned me, and made herself unavailable, even to talk. No explanation."

Sharon exhaled. "Bingo. Do you see the parallel?"

Liam stood silently, taking it all in. He responded slowly.

"I think so. It's going to take a while to sort all that out, but I think I get it."

Sharon's voice softened. "Liam, I really have to go, but I have another question I need to ask first. We can talk further another time. Here goes: What's been your greatest frustration about Marguerite?"

He thought for a minute.

"I would have to say it's that I didn't sue or even publicly call her out for stealing my work. I've been carrying that anger and frustration with me ever since."

"Exactly. Now, tell me your greatest frustration about Sylvia."

His response was instantaneous. "The bitch left without giving me any opportunity to respond or call her out."

"Yep. Your assignment is to think about how they and your feelings about each interconnect. In so many ways, they are one and the same, even though they couldn't be more different people."

"You mean they're both bitches?"

Sharon chuckled. "Yes they are. Let's find another time to continue this conversation. Take care of yourself."

Liam's head was spinning. "Okay. Sharon?"

"Yes?"

"Thanks."

"No problem. It's why you pay me."

When he got back into the truck, Lady looked up contentedly and nudged him. He sat for a time, staring vacantly ahead. Sharon was incredible. But now he had to process all of this, and that was a daunting task. It also didn't resolve the ultimate question with respect to either of these women: What, if anything, could or should he do about them that would remove their hold on him for good? He had work to do.

He was lost in thought as he drove out of town. He knew it was going to take some time to work through the Marguerite/Sylvia conundrum, but he also knew he had to set that aside for now if he was going to get anywhere with the book. He let himself feel the rhythm of the road again. The bumps from the tar patches, the noise of the truck's tires. He let go of everything and sat back in his seat. He looked over at Lady, and she was sitting up, staring out the windshield. All good. A flash of brown, out of nowhere. His brain took a split second to react. Too long.

Grab the wheel, slam the brakes.

Feeling the skid starting, the sickening crescendo of screeching tires pummeling his ears, he put his arm in front of Lady and grabbed the steering wheel simultaneously. A crash, then nothing.

***

Liam woke up knowing something was very wrong. He had no idea how long he'd been unconscious. The truck was tilted on its side, the front end smashed. The passenger door was open.

Shit! Lady! Where is she? What happened?

He had hit his head on the steering wheel at impact, and it hurt. He felt his face, and his hands came away with blood on them. But he was able to move. Incredibly sore but he could move. Desperate for Lady, he crawled carefully out of the cab and fell onto the ground. The truck was a mess. He looked around, confused and frightened. He heard a whimper, then saw her. She was sitting in the road, next to and looking at the truck. She saw him and, her tail wagging, lifted her front paw as if to show him it was hurt. He stumbled over and hugged her. He took her paw and looked at it. It was scratched a bit, but no blood. She seemed to be okay, but she must've hit the dashboard and was probably shaken up. He sat down in the road next to her.

They sat there for a good half hour, but the road was devoid of traffic. He stood up. He was shaken, but everything seemed to work. Coming to grips that no one was going to come by, he motioned to Lady to follow him. She stood and shook herself off. Together they walked, slowly and with some difficulty, back to the cottages.

When they walked down the drive, Madeline saw and ran to them.

"Oh my God. What in the world happened? Are you alright?" Madeline asked.

"We've had a bit of an accident. Deer," Liam replied.

Madeline looked at them.

"Damn deer. They're everywhere right now. Starting their fall movement. I'm so very, very sorry. You sure you're okay?"

"The accident knocked me out for a while, not sure how long. I'm a bit shook up, but no blood except my face. Lady seems ok, except she did something to her leg. I think we're gonna be fine. The truck isn't."

"I can get you both to the doctor if you want. Why don't you come in and let me do something about those scratches?"

Liam nodded. "Thanks. That'd be great."

Madeline helped Liam clean up his face.

"I guess I'm just lucky."

Liam sat at Madeline's kitchen table, Lady at his feet. If the accident had happened on the way to town, rather than on the way back, he probably would've been an emotional wreck, but he found himself surprisingly calm. The conversation with Sharon had been helpful. Lots to think about, but at least he felt he had some answers.

Madeline asked if he wanted to make a call to get the truck towed into town, and he took her up on it. The filling station said they would go get it and let him know their thoughts after they had a chance to inspect the damage. In the meantime, Liam was without wheels. It looked like he was destined to stay put and get some work done. The gods had spoken.

Liam looked up at Madeline. "You know what? Let's get this girl to the vet. Then I've got some writing to do."

12

Liam woke up the next morning sore. Really sore. *Oh yeah. The wreck.*

Yet he wasn't going to let this get him down. Not today. His writing was on a roll. Nothing could keep him from the ideas that were swimming around in his head. He made a pot of coffee and sat down at the typewriter, Lady at his feet. She was snoring away. The prior day had taken a toll on her as well. Liam soon caught his rhythm. His hands were floating over the keyboard, his right hand rhythmically striking the carriage return in its own cadence. He paused for a moment to collect his thoughts. A grin started to form as he adjusted the paper and started to type:

"Darby experienced his share of relationships in his life, but two women stood out seemingly above all the rest. Marci and Olivia. He spoke their names reverently to himself, then whistled and shook his head. From outward appearances, they couldn't have been more different. Marci was sophisticated and witty, maybe too witty. Olivia was anything but sophisticated, and frankly a bit of a dullard if he were being honest with himself. Yet they shared one striking similarity—they were both a royal pain in his ass."

He stopped and took a moment to reflect on the new paragraph. *Bullshit, O'Connor. Don't waste your time on them.* He tore the page from the typewriter, crumpled and tossed it on the floor.

"I like your dog" echoed out a small voice behind him.

What? What the hell was that?

Liam shook his head, like a horse in its stable. He stopped and looked around. He saw nothing and returned to typing.

"I SAID I LIKE YOUR DOG MISTER!!!!"

The voice, no longer small, made a loud and piercing sound. *What? Shit!* His concentration broken, he turned his chair around. Before him stood a little girl, maybe four or five years old, hands on her hips.

"WHY DIDN'T YOU ANSWER?"

Had it been anyone other than this tiny being, he would have gone through the roof. This kind of interruption was the worst. Yet here he was, confused and disoriented.

"Who are you?" Liam refrained from cursing, given his intruder's age and size.

"I'M SARA."

She said it as if it were the most obvious thing in the world.

"Where do you belong, Sara? Or should I say to whom do you belong?" He remained baffled by this irritant in his midst. Lady looked up without moving. Confusion reigned.

"WHAT'S YOUR NAME?"

Apparently she either didn't know where she was from, or saw no relevance in it.

"I'm Liam."

This seemed to satisfy her for the moment. Then she pointed at Lady.

"WHAT'S HIS NAME?"

Liam figured he might as well play this one out. "It's she. Her name is Lady."

"THAT'S A FUNNY NAME."

She seemed not inclined to lower her voice.

He was giving thought to simply ushering the little girl out of the cottage, but then he had no idea where or to whom she belonged. He had no patience for taking her from door to door to find out. None of this was in his plan for today. Too much to do to be messing around with a kid. He heard steps on the porch.

A voice called out. "Sara! Are you in there?"

Sara shook her head "yes" but said nothing.

"Sara!" The voice got closer and entered the room, spoken by a very attractive young woman with short red hair and bright green eyes. "There you are! How many times have I told you not to go into other people's houses?"

Sara pointed at Lady and looked at what was apparently her mother.

"DOG!"

Liam figured this was probably supposed to end the conversation. It didn't.

The woman looked at Liam, shaking her head. "I'm so sorry. She has a mind of her own. I hope she didn't disturb you. She means well."

Sara wasn't finished. "MOMMA.... IT'S A DOG. SHE HAS A FUNNY NAME."

"Well, that's nice, but you know you shouldn't have come into this man's house, don't you?"

Liam sensed this intrafamily struggle was unlikely to resolve itself quickly and was eager to get on with his day.

"That's okay. She was interested in Lady."

His impatience was tempered by his observation that this was one fine looking woman. He couldn't help himself. He could get very interested. Of course, there was the detail that she not only had a child, but an annoying child at that.

Liam was weighing his choices of next actions when another voice was heard. "Have you found her?"

The beautiful woman answered quickly. "Yes! She's in here."

A man walked in. Handsome, movie star quality, just like the woman. It occurred to Liam they were a couple, likely little Sara's parents.

The man spoke first. "I'm so sorry for all of this. I'm Jack, and this is my wife, Susan. I see you've already met Sara."

Shit. Why are the good ones married?

72

"I'm Liam.   Nice to meet you both.   Yes, Sara introduced herself. Apparently she likes my dog." Liam reached out to shake Jack's hand.

Sara was still pointing at Lady. Susan spoke. "Liam. We're so sorry for this intrusion. It won't happen again. We need to get out of your hair."

He couldn't believe his own ears when he responded. "No, no. No problem at all. She's welcome here. Can I get you anything? Coffee? Wine?" Liam couldn't take his eyes off Susan. He silently cursed the rite of marriage. He also knew better.

"No thanks, but that's very kind of you." It was Jack speaking this time.   "We'll make it up to you. We're only here another couple of days, but we'll figure something out."

Liam bit his tongue. "Don't worry about it. Nothing to make up. Hope to see you around."

Susan took Sara by the hand. Sara pulled away, still pointing at Lady. Ultimately her mother prevailed, but not before one more observation.   "MOMMA.   LIAM IS MESSY. AND HE STINKS LIKE CIGARETTES." Susan, blushing, grabbed Sara and ushered her out.

Liam sat back down at the typewriter. As he started typing, his mind wandered back to his first sight of Susan. He couldn't believe how attractive she was, and how she just exuded, well, a Midwestern kind of sexiness. He got up and grabbed a cigarette. Sitting back down, he stared out the window for a while. Finally, he shook it all off.

Married. Off limits.

He got back to work.

***

Several hours passed, and then Lady pawed Liam's leg. She had a tennis ball in her mouth and was looking up at him as if he was the only thing in the world.

"Okay, okay. Let's take a break."

They went out, walked over to the field by Madeline's house, and a game of nonstop fetch was soon underway.

Madeline saw them from her dining room and walked out of the house, calling to Liam.

"You've had a couple of calls. Do you want me to tell you who they were, or do you want to pretend they didn't happen?"

Liam called back at her. "First tell me who called. Then I'll tell you if I want to know."

She walked closer, so as not to have to yell to be heard. "The first was your employee, Marianne."

"I don't want to know that one."

She laughed. "Okay. Next was the garage."

"Unfortunately, you'd better let me know that one."

He stopped, and walked over to her, still holding the tennis ball high in his hand, Lady jumping and running behind him in hot pursuit.

"The news from the garage is grim. Your truck is done for."

Liam had feared this, but still pressed. "Did they say why?"

"They said that the truck is old, and you did a number on the front end. The cost of repair would far exceed its value. They said they could use it for parts and would pay you salvage value for it."

Liam wasn't shocked, but it was a tough pill to swallow.

"Did they say what that is?"

Madeline nodded. "Five hundred to seven fifty."

Liam's neck turned crimson. "What? Those crooks...."

Madeline held her hand out in defense.

"They said you'd probably react that way. They said you can take it anywhere you want, and check other sources for value, but that's what they think it's worth."

Liam was calculating in his head what it would take to replace the truck. He had to admit it was near the end of its useful life. Also, after the accident, it represented a horrible memory, one that he didn't want to have to relive every time he got in it. He thanked Madeline and told her he would deal with the issue himself. He started to turn his attention back to the dog but stopped short. "Hey Madeline? Can I borrow a bike? I need to get into town to pick up some groceries."

"Of course. Help yourself."

He thanked her and wandered back to the cottage, Lady by his side, tennis ball in her mouth. She had a remarkable ability to stay cheerful no matter what. He needed that in a companion. Grabbing his backpack, he left Lady in the cottage and headed out to pick up the bike.

Arriving in town, Liam went straight to the filling station to see what was left of the truck with his own eyes. After some bargaining, he left with a check for a thousand dollars.

***

Later, standing by the lake with Lady by his side and lost in thought, Liam watched dusk creep over the glassy surface. As the sun set, almost imperceptible waves began to lap against the shoreline, sounding against the old wooden rowboat pulled partially onto the shore. This. This is why he'd driven all those miles to a place that seemed trapped in the early twentieth century. He could see lights flicker on around the lake. From the far shore, a loon called.

13

As the sun rose, Liam felt drawn to the center of his peaceful place, this lake. Steadying himself against a low hanging tree branch, he stepped down into the rowboat. He motioned to Lady to stay, and she laid down on the shore. He pushed off, and when the boat broke loose, put the oars into the oarlocks and started to row. The boat moved slowly at first, picking up momentum as he settled into a steady cadence. Pull, and lift. Pull, and lift. As he approached the middle of the lake, he moved the oars back into the boat and let it drift. It slowed, with only the sound of water against its bow breaking the silence. Once it had come to a near stop, Liam slid to the bottom of the boat and leaned back against the seat. He closed his eyes, without falling asleep. With his eyes closed, his ears became attuned to every sound, large and small, that filled the air around him. The murmur of mallards floating nearby, the rat-a-tat of a woodpecker in the trees near Madeline's house, the splash of a fish looking for its breakfast.

"HEY MISTER! YOUR DOG IS HERE!"

He glanced over and saw Sara standing with Lady. He wasn't ready to let go of his reverie.

"HEY MISTER!"

Shit. This required action. "It's okay Sara." His voice carried over the silence of the lake without any need to raise it. "Stay there. I'll come back soon." He saw her little head nod, and she sat down next to Lady and wrapped her arms around Lady's neck. He tried to return to his quiet state, but the spell was broken.

Crap! What if she falls in?

"SARA!!! DON'T MOVE!!!" Liam yelled.

Panic tore at him. *Oh, dear God, don't let her do it.* He clumsily moved the oars into position and started the slow trek back. When he got to the shore, he jumped out and pulled the boat half out of the water. Lady stood up, tail wagging in that whole body shimmy that was her trademark.

Sara stood as well. "I took care of her, Mister."

Out of breath, Liam said a little prayer—no, a big prayer—of thanks. It was easy to figure her parents had no idea where she was. No way they would have let her wander by herself down to the lake.

By now, Liam was torn between relief that she was safe and irritation that she'd interrupted his quietude.

"All right now, where are you staying?"

Sara pointed down the two-track.

"Over there."

Liam took her by the hand. "Okay. Let's get you home."

"Not my home. It's a cottage."

Liam didn't take well to people contradicting him, but for some reason he bit his tongue. "Why yes, you're right. Let's go to your cottage."

"Not my cottage. Mrs. Frost owns it."

He bit down harder. Okay, a little irritating, but honest and accurate. Sara walked along with him quietly. He suspected she knew she'd be in trouble for disappearing. In any event, when they got to the cottage, Liam went to knock on the door, but Sara beat him to it, pushing it open and walking in. He stayed outside.

"MOMMA! DADDY! LIAM'S HERE!!!"

Crap. He nearly bolted in embarrassment.

Susan came from the kitchen, drying her hands on a dish towel. "Sara. What's going on?" She looked straight at Liam, who shook his head in confused resignation.

"Sorry, I was just bringing her back."

Susan looked at Sara, and then at Liam, with panic in her eyes.

"Where were you and why did Liam have to bring you home?"

Sara, trapped, put her arm out and pointed at Lady. "DOG." It didn't work.

Susan responded severely. "Sara. You know you're not to leave the house without us."

Sara looked at the floor. "It's not a house. It's a cottage."

Even Liam didn't see that one coming. *Man. She's good.*

Unfazed, Susan took Sara by the arm and pointed her toward the other room. "We'll discuss this later, young lady." She looked at Liam with an embarrassed smile. "I'm so sorry you had to get involved. Did she show up at your cottage again?"

Now Liam was trapped. His instinct was to lie. He knew it wouldn't go well for Sara if he mentioned she was at the lake's edge. After a momentary pause, he concluded that the truth had to come out, like ripping a band-aid from a wound. "Actually, she came down to the shoreline. I was out on the lake in the rowboat. I think she just came there because Lady was waiting for me. Probably concerned about the dog." He held his breath and looked at the floor.

Susan gasped. At that moment, Jack came into the room.

"What's going on?" He saw they had company. "Oh hi Liam. I didn't know you were here."

Susan, apparently deciding to kick the can down the road, responded accordingly. "It's a long story, Jack. I'll fill you in later."

Jack had that look that Liam knew only too well—no idea what was going on, not a clue, but knowing it best to nod knowingly and say, "All right". It was a no-win proposition.

Seeming to relax a bit, Susan smiled and looked back at Liam.

"We should explain about Sara. She doesn't talk much. In fact, she never spoke a word until she was three.

She's better now, but she may seem awkward to those who don't know her. She relates best to animals, which is probably why she's taken by your dog. She means no harm."

Liam ginned up a smile and nodded. "Oh, I totally understand. So does Lady, I'm sure. Now, if you don't mind, I need to be heading back to my cottage. Lots of work, no time to spare... ."

Jesus, Liam. Such bullshit.

He left quickly, but had to return to retrieve Lady, who was just settling in.

***

Back at his cottage, Liam sat down to reflect. The day had been a whirlwind and it wasn't even nine o'clock. Grateful for even the limited time he got to spend out on the lake and pleased with himself that he was able to clear his mind of distractions—if only for a short while—he had not had time yet to process the chaotic scene that followed. First, his reaction to Sara. It was well known that Liam O'Connor did not suffer little kids lightly. They drove him nuts. Particularly when they were attached to women who might otherwise be of romantic interest. But his initial reaction to Sara had faded for some reason. Sure, she was potentially a large pain in the ass. But she was precociously honest, without any semblance of a filter. You were going to know exactly what she thought. One thing was certain: she was focused on what she wanted, capable of disregarding any obstacles in her way, and as he had just witnessed, highly skilled in the art of argument and deflection. He could respect those attributes and skills.

And then there was the matter of Jack and Susan. *My God, they're too attractive, and too nice. The All-American Couple.* He had no idea how to process that. Ordinarily people like that turned his stomach. No one could be that nice, and no one should be that good looking. Yet they weren't in the least threatening to him. His mind started to wander as his imagination drew him far astray. Soon he was figuring how he could work them into his book. Just then, there was a knock at his door. The spell broken, Liam shook it off and went to answer.

It was Jack, smiling and holding out a bottle of wine. "A little token of our thanks. Susan told me what happened. We're really grateful that you were there to watch over our little troublemaker."

"It wasn't a problem, although I have to say I was as surprised as you to find her standing there on the shore. But all's well that ends well."

"Very kind of you, but she can be a little shit sometimes."

Liam laughed. "Aren't we all, for that matter? Anyway, can I get you a cup of coffee? Why don't you join me on the porch?"

Jack thought for a minute. "Thanks. I could use a break."

As they settled in, looking out over the lake, Jack asked THE question. The one he tried to avoid. "Liam. I realized we never asked your last name?"

Oh crap.

There it was. Liam hoped it wouldn't register. "It's O'Connor."

Jack nodded in acknowledgment. Then, after a moment-- "Wait. Liam O'Connor. The writer?"

Well, there goes anonymity.

"Yes, but I try to avoid it up here."

Jack laughed. "I get it. But Susan's going to die."

Liam cocked his head. "Why?"

"She's a high school English teacher. She's taught your book. It's her favorite. I'm pretty sure she's had a crush on you for years. She has no clue. I love it!"

Liam didn't know how to react. Was this a good thing or a bad thing?

80

"The worst part is that neither of us recognized you. It's not like you fade into the shadows. You're a Wisconsin legend."

"Oh, I really don't think that's the case."

Jack smiled. "You are in our house."

Liam thought about how hot Susan looked when he first saw her. She thinks I'm a "legend"? Cancel that thought. This is her husband for god's sake.

"Maybe we just keep this our secret. No reason to embarrass her."

Jack laughed out loud, a big booming laugh totally out of place with his All-American-Boy look. "Oh no, this is too good to pass up!"

Liam changed the subject, even as the vision of Susan in his arms, looking up at him with lust in her eyes, passed through his mind. "So, Jack. What do you do?"

"I teach at the same high school. American History. Plus, I coach the tennis teams."

Of course you do… that fits perfectly.

"So you both teach at the same place? How does that work for you?"

Jack became more serious. "We met working there, so I guess you could say it's worked pretty well. We eat lunch together, but otherwise don't see each other much most days. She teaches senior English. I teach sophomore American History."

Liam couldn't imagine sharing a workplace with a spouse. But then, to be honest, he couldn't imagine having a spouse. It was an academic question, so to speak.

"So how'd you become a writer?" Jack seemed comfortable now, genuinely interested.

Liam took a slow drink of coffee. "It's a long story. I went to Northwestern to study journalism. After I graduated, I took a job with *The Philadelphia Inquirer* as a reporter. I was on the crime beat. I had some good years there, won some awards. I began to focus more on the

81

people I encountered while reporting. There were some fascinating folks, good and bad, and their stories were intriguing if depressing. After about ten years I became more interested in writing fiction than reporting facts. I decided to take a flyer and quit the paper. That permitted me to work full time on my first novel, and I was able to finish it in relatively short order. I moved to New York when *In the Realm of One* was picked up for publication. About a year later I had a relationship go bad, and felt I needed to get out of New York. In fact I ran as fast as I could. I was from Chicago but had spent time in Wisconsin and decided to take my chances relocating there. I found a small town and moved there to concentrate on my writing. I ended up buying a little bookstore, to give me a diversion from spending all my time writing. And that's pretty much it."

Jack took it all in.

"Sorry about the relationship, but it seems like it was a positive thing in the end, getting back here? Kind of a circuitous way to follow your dream."

If you only knew.

Shaking off the impulse to think about Marguerite, Liam looked at Jack. "What about you? How'd you end up a teacher and coach?"

Jack looked away, staring out over the lake.

"I did it because I failed at what I wanted to be. It was a poor consolation prize."

Liam was puzzled. "How's that?"

"I played basketball at Wisconsin. I wasn't tall, but they said I had great skills. A natural. I was on the watch lists to be drafted pretty high. My senior year was going great, but a couple things happened. I got hurt. I was driving for a layup and the guy defending me took me out. I hit the floor wrong, my leg got twisted badly, and it snapped. I could've recovered, but I was young and stupid. I was pissed off. I started drinking, and then someone gave me some pills for the pain. Before I knew it, I was in trouble. It hit the

82

papers. The school kicked me off the team. The draft was off the table, and my career was done. I took a year off. I got myself straight and finished up with a teaching degree. That was that."

Liam looked away. "I'm sorry. Don't know what to say."

Jack was silent for a minute or so, then spoke. "It's okay. I have a good job, a great wife, and a wonderful little girl. It's all a matter of changing perspectives. You know the saying…. 'When one door closes….'."

It was Liam's turn to be interested. "So. How is it raising a daughter?"

Jack looked down at the porch floor. "In our case, it's tough. You always imagine your children will be perfect. When she was born, she was the most beautiful child you've ever seen. Perfect in every way."

He paused, and gazed out at the lake as if in a trance.

"Well, you got that right. She's beautiful."

Still gazing at the lake, Jack spoke in almost a whisper. "But then time went on and there was some odd behavior." He turned to Liam. "Pulling away from us when we hugged her. Running from other people. Staring. And the silence. She crawled and she walked, right on time. But she didn't speak. Susan was very upset. Depressed, even. Despondent at times."

Liam didn't know what to say. He couldn't imagine Susan depressed. It just didn't fit what he saw. "Did Sara know you were concerned?"

"Sara wasn't fazed by any of it. She just went on in her own world. We took her to lots of doctors. Child psychologists. Had her tested. Like Susan said, she tested out as being highly intelligent. But she didn't talk. The tests were inconclusive, the doctors pretty much throwing up their hands."

"What did you do then?"

"With some considerable help, we worked with her. Finally, after she turned three, she said her first words. She's come a long way since then, but as you've seen, she can become withdrawn, and speaks sparsely around others. But she loves animals. She seems to have a special bond with them. Your dog's a good example of that."

Liam could tell Sara was different. He just thought she was a child of few words. He liked that.

Liam steered the conversation away from personal subjects into lighter fare. They talked about a wide range of topics, everything from the weather to pro basketball, to baseball, swimming, and running. Lady came out of the cottage and laid down on the porch between them. For the first time since he had arrived at Windward, Liam let the book and his own funk go from his mind. He could get used to this vacation thing.

Then Madeline showed up, breaking the spell. "I hate to bother you Liam, but Marianne keeps calling. She says she has to talk to you."

It was bad enough Marianne was trying to interrupt his work, against his orders, but now she was pestering Madeline as well. Liam felt his anger building but controlled his response. "Thanks Madeline. I'll take care of that. If she calls again, tell her I have the message. I'm really sorry."

"That's okay Liam. I know my job here. I'm the ultimate buffer for all our guests. It's what I do."

Liam looked at Jack. "I'm sorry to have to interrupt things. This has been good. I'm glad you came by. But I have an employee who's a burr in my ass. I'm afraid I'm going to have to deal with her. If anyone ever suggests to you that you should buy a bookstore, that it will be fun, *run*. Run away as fast as you can."

Jack stood up. "Not a problem. I get it. Thanks for the coffee and conversation. I needed it. I can't wait to tell Susan that she dissed Liam O'Connor."

84

As Jack walked away, Liam looked at Madeline. "I like that guy. Didn't think I would."

Madeline smiled. "Guess you won't be after his wife, will you?"

Liam winced. He had been accused from time to time of being, well, shallow. He was proud of that. "Now what would make you think I would do that? I hardly noticed her."

"Right." She waved him off and walked away shaking her head.

Liam took Lady back into the cottage.

"You stay here, girl. I won't be long." He closed the door behind him and borrowed Madeline's bike again. Time for another trip to town. The pay phone awaited. His impatience with Marianne was growing.

14

"Owl's Eyes, this is Marianne. Whooo's there?"

Oh dear Jesus. Tell me she didn't say that.

"Cut the crap Marianne. What the hell's going on that requires you to interrupt my vaca....er...work, again?"

Marianne responded in a low, conspiratorial voice. "It's Vera. She says she must speak with yhoooo. Personally."

His patience was gone. "Oh my god, Marianne. Enough. Put her on."

"She's not here. She left in a huff when I told her you weren't available."

"Let me make this simple. Find her. You have thirty minutes to get her back into the store. I don't care how you do it. I'll call then and she'd better be there."

"But Liam…".

He'd already hung up.

What a fucking waste of time. He paced, up and down the street. Finally the thirty minutes was up. Liam dialed the shop. John answered. Liam was off the charts by now.

"WHERE THE FUCK IS MARIANNE, AND WHERE THE HELL IS VERA?"

John fumbled for words. "They…. they're just walking in now."

Liam stopped to gather himself. "Please put Vera on."

John, his hand over the phone and muffling the sound, told Vera to pick up. There was a commotion, and words Liam couldn't make out. John came back on. "She says she won't talk on this phone."

So much for calming down.

"TELL HER TO GO TO THE OFFICE AND PICK UP THE DAMN PHONE."

More muffled words, then John said he was going to put the phone on hold. After what seemed like an eternity of silence, Liam heard a click. "Mr. O'Connor? Is that you?"

"WHO THE HELL DO YOU THINK IT WOULD BE?"

"Okay. I just needed to be sure."

Liam took a deep breath. "Vera, can you please tell me what's going on? Why do you need to talk to me now? I'm working at the cottage. The idea was that I would not be disturbed."

"Well, Mr. O'Connor…."

Jesus.

"I'm afraid there's a problem here."

"Vera. What's the problem?"

"The books don't balance. There's a discrepancy I can't resolve."

Liam was still aggravated. "Doesn't that happen a lot when you're doing your first runs?"

"This isn't a first run. No matter how many times I check and recheck, it's there."

"What's there?"

"There's money missing."

She had his attention. "How much?"

Vera paused, as if afraid to speak. Finally, she whispered. "A few."

"A few what?"

She started to cry, beginning with a small whimper and growing into a throaty, sobbing moan.

"Vera. Out with it."

"Two thousand eight hundred fifty."

"DOLLARS?"

Vera moaned again. "Yes….. Dollars."

"HOW THE FUCK CAN THAT BE?" As soon as he said it, he knew it was a mistake.

Vera was crying full on now. Through her sobs, her quivering voice spoke in staccato: 'I. D….don't. Know. I. Didn't. Take it."

"I didn't say you did Vera. Can you figure out where it went?" Silence. He went on. "Take your time Vera. I'm not mad at you. But I need to know what happened."

"Thank you, Mr. O'Connor." Vera's voice steadied, although clearly she was still very shaken.

Liam was thinking as fast as his mind would permit. "Vera."

"Yes, Mr. O'Connor?"

"Can you quietly investigate? Keep your eyes and ears open? Don't give away what's going on. Just be my private eye on this."

Vera seemed relieved she wasn't under suspicion, and excited at the prospect of being a Sherlock Holmes.

"Oh, Mr. O'Connor. I think I can do that. I'm so honored."

Liam spoke very seriously and conspiratorially. "I trust you Vera. Please lay low, and report to me."

He could almost see her beaming. "How will I reach you?"

"If you learn anything useful, you can call Mrs. Frost and just have her let me know you called. Better yet, don't use your name. Tell her 'Martha says the coast is clear'. That'll be our secret." This was total bullshit, but if it kept Vera interested and on the scent it would be worth it.

"I won't fail you Mr. O'Connor."

Liam permitted himself a grin. "Thank you, Martha."

Vera started to respond, but Liam hung up.

Starting to walk away from the phone, Liam stopped in mid-stride, then reversed course and dialed another number.

After a few rings, Sharon's voice. "Liam?"

"Yes. I was in town and thought I'd see if you were available."

"Is something going on? Should I be worried?"

"Yes, I guess."

She deadpanned. "Okay. Humor me….. Let me have it." Silence. She tried again. "Is there something you want to tell me? Any new women?" More silence.

Finally, as if it just occurred to him at that moment, he spoke. "Oh, I did meet one. At the cottages. Good looking. Pretty hot."

There was a marked pause. "So, how far did you get?"

"I'm crushed that you would think that of me."

"You didn't answer the question."

He answered, too quickly. "I didn't even try. How's that?"

"Not believable."

Liam knew Sharon wouldn't buy it. "Let's just say there were…. complications."

This time Sharon laughed. "Pray tell?"

"Well, for one thing, she has a kid."

"If I recall correctly, that hasn't stopped you in the past."

"And a husband."

"Neither has that."

Liam was trapped. "Okay, okay. The kid's a little girl. She likes my dog. She's very blunt. I've somehow found that I like her."

"I'm impressed. I've never heard you praise any child."

"Well, there you go."

"And the husband?"

"At first I hated him. Because, you know, he was married to this hot woman."

"So what then?"

"Then I spent some time with him, and he's not bad. Good guy."

"So, after all of that, will you still pursue her?"

Liam smiled to himself. "You never know, do you?"

Sharon moved the conversation back to a tougher subject. "Last time we talked, I recall we reached some conclusions about Marguerite and Sylvia. Have you given that any more thought?"

"Marguerite. I think about her just about every day, and not in a good way. I can't say I've given any more thought to Sylvia. She was just a distraction that brought Marguerite back into the open."

Sharon might well have called bullshit to the Sylvia part, but she didn't. "So what are you doing, and what are you going to do, about Marguerite? Are you going to try to sweep her back into the closet, or are you going to deal with her once and for all?"

Liam was getting irritated, as he usually did with this topic. "I told you, I broke up with her. I think I can let go of her now."

"Do you really? Is there anything in particular you're doing, or plan to do, that would 'let go of her'?"

Liam's bravado vanished. "I have no idea, Sharon. How the hell do I get rid of her without resolving the main thing that's kept her in my mind all these years?"

Sharon softened. "Liam, can you tell me, in under ten words, what that main thing is?" He didn't respond. "I'm going to give you some time. Let me know when you're ready." The silence continued.

Liam looked around and behind him, hoping that someone would be waiting to use the phone. There was no one in sight. Finally, he spoke. Slowly, and with angry determination. "The bitch stole my work. She stole my work and she got away with it."

Sharon paused, then responded. "Anything else?"

90

"She was unfaithful to me. She laughed in my face about that and about stealing my story."

Sharon spoke softly. "The Trifecta. She scored the Trifecta on you. How does that make you feel, Liam?"

"I want to wring her neck."

"Be careful Liam. I get the sentiment, but psychologist/patient privilege doesn't extend to threats of physical harm."

"Damn it Sharon, you know what I mean. And you know how I feel."

"Yes. I do. She emasculated you three ways, and maybe more. That's a heavy weight to carry with you for this long."

Liam's voice caught as he spoke. "Truth is, I have no idea how to deal with it. Never have. What? What do I do Sharon?"

Sharon took a deep breath. "Unfortunately, I have an appointment now and we have to wrap up. I think you have more than enough to think over for now. Let's plan to talk again soon. When are you back?"

Liam was grateful to end this conversation. Normally he would feel cheated by the way Sharon ended sessions with him standing on a cliff, but in this case, there was some comfort that at least he was still standing. "Not for a while, I hope."

***

"WHERE WERE YOU?"

There, on the porch, stood Sara and Lady. Wait a minute... he closed Lady in before he left. He walked over toward them in confusion. "Sara. How'd Lady get out? And where are your parents? Do they know you're here?" He immediately knew that was too many questions for her.

Sara held Lady and stroked her ears. "SHE WAS LONELY. I HEARD HER CRYING. I CLIMBED IN THE

WINDOW." She was pointing at the window on the porch that was open, apparently just enough for her to crawl through. "SHE WAS VERY HAPPY TO SEE ME!"

So the kid broke into his house to "save" his dog from loneliness. He had to give her credit for ingenuity—and for another great, deflective, explanation. She was a master of misdirection. He repeated. "Do your parents know you're here?"

"OH YES. I LEFT THEM A NOTE."

He could only imagine what a "note" from this four-year-old looked like. Knowing it wouldn't go well if he were to walk her, once again, back to her parents, he made a suggestion. "Sara. Thank you for taking care of Lady. I'm pretty sure your parents are missing you. Why don't you go back to your cottage? You can visit Lady another time." He counted to three....

"Not my cottage."

"I know, I know. Mrs. Frost's cottage."

Sara shook her head yes and walked off in the general direction of that very cottage.

Liam headed over to Madeline's house, Lady following close behind. Madeline was sitting outside talking with a few resort guests. He ignored the guests and spoke to Madeline. "Could I have a word with you?"

She stood up and walked over, pointing to a stand of trees about twenty feet away. When they got to the trees, she turned. "What's up?"

Liam smiled. "A couple of things. First, if an odd woman calls and tells you 'Martha says the coast is clear", just thank her solemnly and then let me know."

"What?"

"Don't ask. Also, is there any chance I could prevail on you to take me over to Marinette to find a new truck? I'll pay for the gas and your time, but I have no one else I can ask. Only if you have time..... no pressure. I'll understand if you can't."

"Don't be silly. Of course I'll take you. I could use the trip and the company. Who wouldn't want to spend time with a famous author?"

Liam laughed. "Thanks so much. Who did you think might be riding with us?"

Madeline grinned. "Maybe you could see if John Updike is available?"

Liam cringed. "I'll see what I can do. Just let me know what would be good for you."

Madeline thought briefly. "Tomorrow's as good as any. Does that work for you?"

Liam responded quickly. "Absolutely. Thanks! I owe you."

"Of course you do."

15

Deciding to take the bull by the horn, Liam called to Lady and headed over to Jack and Susan's cottage. If he was going to be away, Sara would be worried about Lady and break back into his cottage. Why not let it play out on her own turf? Before they could get to their destination, Sara was out the door and down the steps.

"LIAM! WHERE ARE YOU GOING?" Well, that let the whole resort know where he was.

"Coming to see you, Sara. Are your parents around?"

Susan stepped outside, shaking her head. "I see the sentinel has found you!"

Liam grinned. "She's a pretty good look-out, isn't she?"

Susan looked at him wide-eyed. "I'm so embarrassed I didn't recognize you. Jack told me. How could I have missed it?" Her cheeks turned pink as she spoke.

Liam used the same calming voice he employed with Sara. "It's okay. Really it is. I have plenty of people who want to be my friend because of my name. It's nice to know someone likes me for myself."

Her blush held. Liam took that as a good sign, then stopped himself.

No, no… she's married you idiot.

Changing the subject, he let Lady run to Sara, and went on. "Madeline's taking me over to Marinette this morning so I can buy a truck. Could I prevail on you folks to keep Lady while I'm gone? I figure, one way or another Sara will be with her, and it would be better if it were here. Just till maybe early afternoon."

Susan relaxed, her moment of chagrin having passed. "We'd be happy to have her as a guest. She's a very well-behaved young lady."

Liam was relieved on several levels. "I owe you guys. I'll make it up to you."

Susan's blush returned. "Oh, don't mention it. We'll just be hanging out anyway. This is one of our last days here, and we want to enjoy the place without rushing around and going anywhere."

Liam patted Lady on the head, then did the same with Sara, who was beaming.

When he got back to his cottage, Madeline was sitting in her car waiting for him. With mock seriousness, she got out of the car and opened the passenger door. "Your chauffeur awaits, kind sir."

"Why, thank you, Ma'am. You know, I'm a big tipper. There's something in it for you."

She got in and looked over at him. "There'd better be."

***

Madeline dropped Liam off at the dealership and left. He was on his own now. He said a little prayer that his new truck would get him back. A couple hours later, as he left the lot, it felt like forever since he had driven. At last he could get around on his own. At last he could take Lady with him as he ran errands.

He reached for the radio.

What the hell?

There was no radio.

Shit. What else is missing?

Liam decided to swing by the pay phone on the way back to the cottage. The business with the missing money was weighing on him, and he wanted to check in to see what was going on. As he pulled into town, he saw a line of people waiting for the phone. He parked the truck and rolled down the windows. When the last person stepped up to the phone, he got out and wandered over. Finally, it was his turn. He dialed and waited for the inane greeting. Fortunately, John answered.

"God, I'm so glad it's you. Is Vera in?"

"Sorry, Liam. She's not here."

"Okay. Get Marianne on."

After a few minutes, which to Liam was a few minutes too long to wait for a response, Marianne picked up the phone.

He spoke. "Hi Marianne. Just thought I'd check in. How's it going?" There was a long silence. "Are you there?"

"Yes. I'm here. I don't mind telling you things are strange around here. I have no idea what's going on."

Not the answer he expected, but then nothing ever seemed to be as expected when it came to that shop and its occupants. "It can't be all that bad. I'm sure you're exaggerating."

"I wish I was." Marianne sounded stressed. "It's Vera. She's outdone her weirdness."

Liam was more intrigued than shocked. "I'm sure it's not that bad. She's just, well, eccentric."

Marianne almost took his head off. "She's hiding. Every time I look around I see her eyes. Looking out from behind bookshelves. Peering around corners. Under the sales counter."

"Under the sales counter?" Even he was taken aback by that one.

"Yes."

"How'd you find her there?"

Marianne was exasperated. "The smell. You know—that....odor. Sweat and..."

"Okay, okay. I get it." Liam choked off a giggle. "I'm sure there's an explanation."

Marianne exploded. "What in God's name could be an explanation?"

"Maybe she needed a nap?"

"Liam. She was peeking out, holding cardboard to hide from view."

"She must have been very tired." He knew he didn't dare give it away to Marianne. He had to let Vera do her thing. "Well, thanks for the report, Marianne. I appreciate it. We'll talk soon."

Marianne started to answer, but Liam had hung up. This was the best thing he had set in motion in years.

Liam headed back to the resort. He was feeling good now that he once again had wheels under him. He parked in front of the cottage and walked over to Jack and Susan's place. When he got there, Sara and Lady were waiting out front. Lady had a tennis ball in her mouth and pulled it away every time Sara tried to grab it. It seemed to give them both endless pleasure.

Sara saw Liam before Lady did and came running over. "LIAM! LIAM! WE HAD A GREAT TIME! WE WENT SWIMMING."

Liam stopped short. "Lady swam?"

"YES SHE DID! SHE LOVED IT!"

That was a new one. She'd never shown any inclination to get into the water, let alone swim in it. He didn't know if this was a good or a bad development. Now he would have to keep an eye on her. "That's great Sara." He didn't want to send her the wrong signal. He walked up to and knocked on the door. He heard Jack call to come in

"Well? Did you get a truck?" Jack was sitting in the front room, reading.

"Why yes I did."

"What kind?"

"Blue." Nothing else seemed relevant.

Jack, bewildered, nodded.

"So. I understand Sara and Lady got to swim while I was gone?"

Jack's jaw dropped. "They did what?"

This was one of those moments when Liam wished he could step back and undo what he'd just said. He decided to keep it light, in fervent hope that it would blow over.

"Sara said they both swam."

Jack walked over to the door and looked out. "SARA! Did you and Lady go in the water?"

Obviously it hadn't occurred to Sara that this was information that shouldn't have been shared. She must have seen it as a factual report to Liam about a nice event she had enjoyed with his dog. She pointed to Lady. "Swimmed. She swimmed."

Liam could see that Jack was the parent trying to keep from looking like a raging madman.

"Sara. I'm going to ask you again. Did you go in the water?"

"Lady swimmed."

Jack was now losing it. "Sara, one last time. Tell me the truth. Did you go in the water? You. Not Lady. You."

Liam could almost see the wheels spinning in Sara's head. "DADDY! I SWIMMED TOO!" She said it with such earnest excitement that anyone who heard it must be excited as well.

Anyone, that is, except her father. He clearly was not impressed.

"Sara, please come in now. You and I and your mom will discuss this later."

Sara walked past Jack and Liam and turned at the last minute to look at them. "I swimmed!"

16

Safely ensconced at the typewriter, Liam settled in for a solid morning of writing. He figured he'd solved the "Sara Surprise" element by inviting her to come down and spend the day with Lady. Jack and Susan had told him this was their last day at Windward. They'd be heading back to Milwaukee in the morning to get ready for the start of school. Sara, obviously delighted, promised her parents she would be very good, usually an iffy proposition at best. All was quiet, and Liam dug in contentedly. This was going to be a very nice day.

"LIAM! WHAT'S THAT THING?"

So much for quietude. Before he knew it Sara was standing in front of him, pointing. Ignoring her would be futile.

He mustered a calm demeanor and responded. "This is a typewriter. See? I put paper in it, and when I push down these keys, letters appear."

By the time he finished the sentence, Sara had wandered off. She was staring out the window. "LIAM. WHAT DO YOU DO?"

He lost track of where this might be headed. "I can hear you Sara. You don't need to shout. What do you mean?"

"MY DADDY AND MY MOMMA ARE TEACHERS. THEY GO TO SCHOOL."

"I'm a writer."

Sara was still staring out the window. "WHAT'S A WRITER?" She was pointing at a squirrel on the ground outside.

"I write stories."

Silence.

Finally, Sara turned around. He could see the light bulb go on in her head.

"TELL ME A STORY LIAM!"

He wasn't expecting this. He reached for a logical response. "I write stories for adults." He missed the target completely. Logic wasn't the answer.

"TELL ME A STORY."

He didn't know any kids' stories. After a few desperate minutes, Liam recalled one his grandfather had told him when he was little. It was an Irish tale.

"There once was a young lad…"

"What's a lad?"

"It's a boy, Sara."

"I hate boys. They're mean."

Time to pivot. "There once was a young lassie (that's a little girl, like you)…".

"Like me?"

Patience, Liam. Patience.

"Yes. Like you. And this young lassie had a very good friend who was a tiny person, called a Leprechaun. She and the Leprechaun did everything together. They laughed and played. Then one day, the Leprechaun asked the young lassie to…." *Shit.* In that instant, Liam remembered the rest of the story. It didn't end well. His grandfather used to do that kind of thing to him, just to scare the crap out of him.

Trapped, he deflected. "Hey Sara…. Do you wanna go for a walk? We can take Lady."

"But what about the story?"

"I'll finish it later. I promise."

This misdirection seemed to satisfy her. Calling to Lady, Liam kept the momentum going and walked outside. Sara picked up one of Lady's tennis balls and followed them.

"Let's go by and ask your parents if it's okay."

Sara nodded but was clearly still thinking about that young girl and her tiny friend.

***

100

After clearing it with Jack and Susan, Liam and Sara headed off on their adventure. Liam knew there was a trail that went around the lake but had never taken it. This seemed as good a time as any. Soon they were in the woods, then headed up a rocky hill. They climbed, making slow progress. Liam was able to get footing in the tree roots and vines that interrupted the path, but Sara's little feet struggled. He carried her over the toughest parts, but she was vocal about wanting to do it herself. Finally, he just let her scramble on her own. They reached a crest, and he looked out over the lake.

What a great view.

"Sara. Isn't this beautiful?" He stopped and took it all in, lost in thought.

Lady whimpered, then barked, nosing Liam's leg.

"LIAM! LOOK AT ME!!!"

Liam snapped back into the present and panicked. He looked over to see Sara, standing on the very edge of the rock face that dropped vertically to the water far below.

Oh Dear Mother of God!!!

"SARA! NO! STEP BACK!"

She grinned mischievously and leaned out over the edge. Liam saw his life pass before him. Pulling himself together, he spoke, very softly.

"Please Sara. Come over here. Lady is scared and needs your help."

She leaned out one more time and laughed. He gasped. She turned and walked toward him as if she didn't have a care in the world. Liam held his arms out. Sara continued right past him and kneeled down next to Lady. Lady licked her face.

Sara laughed. "THAT WAS FUN!"

Liam had to sit down. The stress of the moment still held him in its grip. "Sara, please don't do that again. I promised your parents I'd take care of you."

She took off running along the trail. As she did, she turned her head and said "Okay" with a big smile. Lady ran after her.

Liam stood and started to walk. "Please slow down Sara. Wait for me." Sara stopped, turned around facing him, and stuck her tongue out. But she stayed put. He reminded himself she was four years old. As he caught up to her, she took his hand and smiled up at him.

***

By the time they got about halfway around the lake, Liam realized he'd underestimated the distance and difficulty of the journey. Sara had slowed her pace dramatically and was starting to complain. He looked down at her. "Have you had enough, Sara? Do you want to go home?"

Sara thought for a moment. "Not home. Going home tomorrow." There was that literal interpretation, that rigid logic, that seemed to define her approach to life.

"No. I meant, go back to your cottage." Mistake.

"Not my…."

Liam put his finger to his lips. "You're right. Not your cottage. Mrs. Frost's cottage, where you are staying."

Sara nodded. "Yes."

Liam picked her up and set her on his shoulders. "Let's take a horsey ride." He knew before he finished saying it where this was headed.

"Where's the horsey?" Sara was really excited now.

"No, no. There's no horsey. That just means riding on my shoulders."

She looked down at him with a puzzled expression. "No horsey?"

"No Sara. No horsey."

She sighed. Off they went. Liam was out of shape, and it was no easy task to carry Sara all the way back, but he promised he'd take care of her.

When they got close to the cottage, he set her down. She reached up and took his hand. He could see Jack and Susan outside, sitting in the shade near the water.

Sara broke loose and ran to them. She put her arms around her mother. "I CLIMB A ROCK!"

Liam looked to the sky and prayed that statement would just pass. When Susan just said "You did? That's wonderful!" Liam said another prayer, this one of thanks. That could have gone very badly.

Jack stood up and walked over to Liam. "Did she wear you out? I'll bet you could use a beer."

This posed a conundrum for Liam. He really wanted and needed to get back to work. At the same time, a beer sounded pretty damn good. And then there was Susan. He hadn't had a real chance to chat with her since she found out he was the famous author she treasured, and maybe even coveted. That little voice whispered (no, it shouted), in his ear:

You're so full of shit! Give it up O'Connor.

Still, there was that beer thing.

Work. Beer. Susan.

His head was spinning.

Just then, Madeline walked up. "Liam, I thought you should probably know that your employee called again."

Back into the real world. "Who? Marianne?"

"Yes, Marianne."

"What the hell…". He caught a glimpse of Sara in the corner of his eye. "Er…. What does she want this time?"

"She said to give you a message."

"And what was that?"

"You want the exact quote?"

"Oh, why not?"

"In the tree. Outside the store."

Liam cocked his head. "That's it?"

"Yes. Word for word."

When it came to Vera, nothing was surprising to him, but this one took a moment to digest. A vision flashed into his head, and he started to laugh. Now everyone was looking at him oddly. He finally choked the laugh. There was no way he could explain this one. "Never mind. It's a long story. Thanks Madeline." He looked at Jack and Susan. "I'm afraid I'm going to have to pass on the beer. My typewriter's calling me. But thanks." Waving goodbye to Sara, he walked back to his cottage with Madeline.

***

Much later, Liam was lost in thought. Dusk was beginning to take over the sky, but he was unaware of its approach. In that moment he was startled by a noise, as if awakened suddenly from a dream. He didn't want to let go, but there it was again. Finally, he was able to grasp that it was a knock at the door. He stood and slowly walked toward the noise, clearing his head as he went. He shook off the fog and opened the door. There, in the semi-darkness, stood Susan. She had a bottle of wine in her hand.

She smiled with some embarrassment and spoke quietly. "I hope I didn't wake you up."

Still a little shaky and confused, Liam tried to process what she might want and why she was there. "No, no. I was just working."

"Can I come in? I brought you a little token of our thanks."

"I'm sorry. I'm a little out of it. Please do. Come in." He followed her into the room and gestured toward a chair. "Have a seat." He took the wine and thanked her. "Would you like a glass?"

She nodded shyly. "Sure!"

He poured a couple glasses. Susan avoided his eyes, but it was clear she wanted to speak. "Jack and I want to thank you for all you've done for Sara. Also, I haven't had a chance to talk with you since I learned who you are." More awkward silence. "That sounds silly. Since....."

Liam smiled. "That's okay. I get it. But I'm not sure what I've done for Sara."

"You have no idea, Liam. Sara is.... Well, she's special. She's not like other kids. She doesn't have many social abilities. She doesn't talk to other people, particularly adults. She doesn't like anyone... including us... to touch her. Yet there's something about you that has made her connect in a way she hasn't with anyone else."

Liam laughed. Susan got very quiet. He quickly caught himself. "I didn't mean to laugh, but it really is funny. No one has ever accused me of connecting with children, nor them with me. In general, I despise them. I think Sara may like me strictly because of my dog."

Susan shook her head. "No. I don't think so. If it were just Lady, she would have been totally focused on her, and not speak with you. There's something else there."

"You flatter me. I'm not a nice guy."

It was Susan's turn to laugh. "You underestimate yourself. You are a nice guy. At least with Sara. In any event, we're very grateful for all you've done. She's going to miss you."

Liam couldn't bring himself to say that he was going to miss her, mostly because it had never until this moment occurred to him that he would.

Susan paused, then looked away again. She started to blush. "I'm so sorry I didn't recognize you. It never crossed my mind that we would run into Liam O'Connor, particularly up here. It was totally out of context."

"You have no idea. After all the attention I've gotten over the last six years, I welcome the times I can be anonymous." He hoped she wouldn't see through this bit of

105

bullshit. He loved the adoration showered on him by his fans. It helped blunt the sting of Marguerite's abuse and belittlement. He wanted to hear more from this beautiful creature.

She continued. "I can't tell you how in awe I am of your work, Liam. I've taught your book each year since it was published. I've had to fight with the school board a couple of times because they don't think it's 'appropriate' for high school students, but each time I've won out."

"Let me guess—they don't like my descriptions of the dead body, and probably blush over the sex scenes."

"Well, yes. But you write beautifully and powerfully, and in the end that wins out."

"Hey—death happens. Where there's a murder, there's usually a body. And if I remember correctly, high schoolers kind of know about sex."

Susan laughed. "Exactly."

Liam was taking this all in. He watched her face, her glistening lips, her eyes, as she spoke. His hormones started to mobilize. "I'm glad you like the book. That means a lot to me." He was starting to pour it on. Maybe it was the wine talking, but he was enjoying this a lot.

She glanced at the typewriter in the other room. "Is there any chance you could give me a hint about your new book?"

"I'd love to, Susan but it's just not something I'm ready to talk about. Maybe when I get closer to finishing it."

She nodded. "I get it. I shouldn't have asked."

He sensed some vulnerability. "No, no. It's okay. You didn't know. I'll tell you what. I can answer questions about *In the Realm of One*. If you want."

Her face went from shame to enthusiasm in a heartbeat. She paused, as if to gather her thoughts. "Okay. Were your characters drawn from real people?"

"My job put me into close contact with a broad variety of humanity from which to draw impressions. Add to that the criminal element in their midst, and the stuff of fascinating stories was there for the picking. Having said that, my characters were purely fictional, even if they resembled in some aspects real people I'd met. Does that make sense?"

"Sure. What was the biggest challenge you faced writing it?"

"The biggest challenge? That's a good question. I was pretty hardened from my time in the trenches, so the rawness of the murder scenario came relatively easily. The trick was in crafting what was in the end a love story, with characters that by all initial appearances were unsympathetic, and making it believable."

Susan was totally focused on what Liam was saying, her eyes locked on his as he spoke. "But you did that so seamlessly. That's what made the book so magical. You built the love story quietly and unobtrusively. The reader doesn't see it coming. I loved that about it."

"Thank you. I'm flattered."

He topped off their wine glasses, then raised his in the air. "Enough about me. Here's to the new school year, and to my buddy Sara!"

Susan smiled and held her glass up. "Yes. And here's to your new book!" She set down her glass. "Liam, I need to get back. I told Jack I'd only be a few minutes. And you probably need to get back to work."

His hormones were still raging, but in a way he was relieved. "I think my work for today is done, but I'm glad you stopped by. I'll come by in the morning before you leave."

He walked her to the door.

Before she walked out, she paused, turned, and embraced Liam.

"Thank you so much Liam."

She leaned up and kissed him.

Their lips touched just for a moment, and a warmth raced through his body. He started to lean back in but caught himself at the last moment.

I can't. Wrong. Whoa Liam.

He gently broke free and took her hand. "It was really nice meeting all three of you."

Susan blushed as she walked away. Liam returned inside. Lady had been sleeping but got up and came over to him. He looked at her and stroked her head.

That was too fucking close. Too fucking close.

Lady licked his face.

17

The morning brought cool air, hinting at autumn's approach, as Liam walked down the two-track toward Jack and Susan's cottage. He saw their station wagon out front. The tailgate was up, and they were busy stowing suitcases. Sara came running down the path toward him. She had papers of some sort in her hands, waving in the wind. Liam smiled and held out his arms. She blasted past him and embraced Lady. Lady rolled on her back for rubs, to which Sara gave her focused attention. When she was finished, she walked over to Liam, holding out the papers. On one was an approximation of a dog. On the other, a stick figure seated in front of a crude table with a box on it. What looked like a cigarette was dangling from the figure's mouth.

Liam looked directly at Sara, who was staring off to the side.

"Thank you, Sara. These are wonderful. Who are they?"

She turned and pointed, first to Lady, and then to him.

"Oh. Why they're Lady and me?"

She shook her head yes.

"Why they look just like us!"

Sara beamed but said nothing. Then she took his hand and pulled him over to her parents.

Jack looked up and smiled. "Hi Liam. So glad you came by."

Susan had not noticed Liam was there. When she heard Jack's greeting, she was startled, then looked at Liam. Actually, she looked a little past him, color rising into her face.

"Good morning, Liam. Thanks for being here. Sara was concerned she might miss seeing you."

Liam, also a little uncomfortable, turned to Sara. "Sara. I wouldn't miss seeing you for anything. Are you all set to go home?"

Sara pointed at the car. "Home."

Liam nodded. "Yes, this time you're really going home, aren't you?"

Sara wrapped her arms around his leg and squeezed, without saying a word. Then she let go and ran to her mother. Susan embraced her and picked her up.

"Sara is sad to leave you."

Sara pointed at Lady.

"And of course the dog."

Jack spoke up. "What Susan means to say is we're all going to miss you. You'll have to come and visit us in Milwaukee."

Susan blushed even more. "Yes. Please come."

Liam smiled and walked over next to the little family. "That's very kind of you. Of course. I'll try to find a good time. I would love to see you all again." He emphasized the word "all".

Madeline had joined them. Sara hopped down and ran back to Lady. She sat down and started stroking Lady, singing a little song.

"Lady, Lady. Goodbye Lady. You are my friend. I love you—" Lady nestled her head on Sara's shoulder, and Sara put her arms around Lady's neck.

Madeline looked at Liam. "I hate to tell you this, but your girl Marianne called again this morning with another odd message."

Liam rolled his eyes. "Okay. Get it over with…. What did she say?"

"She said…. and I quote….'Black sedan, across the street, binoculars.' "

Liam choked back a guffaw. "Thanks. Someday I'll explain. For now, if she calls again, tell her thanks for the information."

Everything in place, Jack shook Liam's hand. Susan started to hug him, then stopped and shook his hand as well.

Jack broke the ice.

"All right Sara. Let's get going. Home's calling us!"

Sara started to get into the car, then turned and ran back to Liam, holding her arms out. He grabbed and lifted her up.

"I love you Liam." She was crying now.

Liam held her tightly, rocking her back and forth.

"I love you too Sara. You be good!" He gently set her back down, and she ran back to the car. He could see her waving as they pulled slowly away. He raised his hand and waved back.

Madeline turned to Liam as they stood watching the car leave. "Sweet family. You going to be okay?"

Liam stiffened and stood up tall. "Now why the hell would you ask that? Of course I will. Looking forward to the quiet. I can get some damn work done."

She let that bit of bullshit pass. "So what do you have planned for today?"

He looked blankly. "Why, writing. What did I just say?"

She smiled. "Let me rephrase my question. I know what you have planned, but what are you going to do?"

Still staring at the now vacant two track, Liam spoke quietly. "I think I'm going to go for a run."

"Good idea. Now, since you're going to have a quiet day, how about if you come over for dinner tonight? Nothing fancy. Just a chance to kick back. The guests are pretty much all gone, and I'm facing another long off season with the locals."

Liam started to decline but stopped himself. Madeline was good company, and no threat to him at all. He was not looking forward to cooking and had no desire to go to the bar in town to eat.

"Thanks. That would be nice."

111

"Okay. Come by about seven?"

"Deal."

As they walked back, she looked at him with raised eyebrows. "You sure you don't want to tell me what's up with Marianne?"

"Not a chance."

***

"Thank God you're there."

"Yes, I'm here." Sharon's voice was bemused.

Liam was flustered. "I honestly don't know where to start."

"Okay, then let me start. Does it concern a woman?"

"Maybe."

"I think the correct answer is either 'yes' or 'no', Liam."

He thought for a moment. "In part."

"Yes or no. Which is it?"

"Well, to start with, it's more than one woman."

"Why am I not surprised?"

"No, really. I guess you could say there are two, although one's a little kid."

"Let me guess. It's the hot young mother and her kid. And tell me the kid isn't a love interest… please tell me that."

"Of course not. The kid's a pain but I like her a lot. She left today, and I already miss her bugging me. How can that be? I hate kids."

Sharon sighed. "Well, that's a relief. Every once in a while, you're going to find a child that isn't bad. You just got lucky. Now, is it the mom?"

"Yes."

"Has something more happened?"

"Yes. I think."

Sharon went silent for a second. "What do you mean, you think?"

"She came to my cottage last night."

"What's so strange about that?" Liam's turn to go silent.

"Shall I ask again?"

"She kissed me."

"She kissed you?"

"Yes."

"You didn't kiss her?"

"No."

"Did anything else happen?"

"No. I couldn't go through with it, so I stopped her."

Sharon seemed stunned. "Wait. This has never happened before, has it?"

"Not that I can recall."

"Why couldn't you go through with it? That's so un-Liam."

"I told you, her husband's a nice guy. I also like her daughter. Her daughter needs her. She needs both her parents."

"Who are you, and what have you done with Liam?"

"I'm not kidding Sharon. I couldn't bring myself…."

Sharon paused. "Why do you suppose you couldn't?"

Liam was confused. "I don't understand. What are you thinking?"

She took a deep breath. "Is it possible you've developed a sense of empathy?"

"Oh hell no."

"Are you sure?"

"Come on, Sharon. It's me. Liam."

"I don't know. It sounds suspiciously like empathy to me."

"Oh my God. How?"

"Well, you seem to have embraced the whole family."

"So?"

"Could it be you've put yourself in their shoes and can sense how awful it might be for them all if you were to move in on the mom?"

"Oh shit."

"It's called a conscience, Liam."

"Can't be."

"I may be going out on a limb here, but has Marguerite been in your head again?"

"Dammit, there's that name again."

"Have you felt or taken into consideration the feelings of any woman since Marguerite's betrayal?"

Silence.

"I'll give you a few moments. Take your time."

"I'd like to say yes, but I can't think of any."

"Why, do you suppose?"

"If I don't, I can't get hurt. I get all the benefits of a relationship without any risks."

"Any risks other than hurting the other person?"

"That's why it helps to have no conscience."

"So what happened with Susan?"

"I guess I saw more than just an easy score."

"Thank you. I have to go now, but you may just have turned an important corner."

"Shit. I'm doomed."

"Have a nice evening Liam. We can pick up on this next time."

***

Madeline greeted Liam with a warm smile. "Come on in! Why don't you go sit in the living room while I get you a drink? Wine or cocktail?"

"Wine, please."

114

Madeline winked. "Oh, a fine choice, Sir."

As he passed the dining room, he noticed three place settings on the table.

She wouldn't. Please, tell me she didn't.

As he was sitting down in the living room, Madeline returned with two glasses of wine. As she handed him one of them, a second woman entered, also carrying a wine glass.

Crap. She did.

Liam stood up and gave a side glance to Madeline, raising one eyebrow.

"Liam, I'd like you to meet Helen Woodson. Helen, this is Liam O'Connor."

Helen was the first to speak. "Nice to meet you Liam. I of course know who you are."

Liam glared at Madeline as he turned to Helen. "Likewise, although I don't know who you are."

Well, that was smooth.

Madeline glared back at Liam with a "don't do this" look, then spoke graciously and without skipping a beat. "Helen's a good friend of mine from Back East. She's an artist, and a very fine one, with quite a following. I'm surprised you don't know of her."

Well, that was a dig. Liam fixed the smile he had learned to gin up during his book tours. "Very interesting. So Helen, you're from the East Coast?"

Helen had been warned by Madeline to expect reluctance from Liam, but she had also been assured that he would ultimately behave. "No, actually I'm not. I'm from a suburb of Detroit—Troy. Madeline and I met one summer in Provincetown when I was studying at Rhode Island School of Design."

Liam chuckled. "So you're Helen of Tr…".

Helen held her hand up. "Stop. Not an original thought. You have no idea how many times I've had to listen to that since high school."

He retreated. "Sorry. Clumsy of me. You still living out East?"

Madeline interrupted, in an obvious move to defuse the tension.

"Please, why don't we all sit down? It'll be a bit before dinner. Let's just chill and drink some wine."

Liam relaxed. "Go on, Helen, you were starting to say where you are now."

"I'm teaching at Ohio Wesleyan. Art and art history—20th Century."

Madeline jumped in. "Helen's an extraordinary artist. Oils, acrylics, and mixed media. You'll have to see her work to fully appreciate just how good she is."

Liam glanced at Helen. He figured her to be around forty. She was petite, with a ruddy complexion, her face framed by long brown hair, pulled back. She was wearing a bandana around her head. She wore a long white linen skirt, with a flowing tunic over a cream camisole. Stunning. She looked like an artist. "Are you a lecturer?"

Stupid question. Why did I ask that?

"No. Associate Professor. I got tenure last year."

Liam searched for a question that wouldn't make him look like an idiot. "What brings you to Windward? Pretty remote up here."

Helen pointed at Madeline. "I'm here to see her. It's been several years."

Madeline smiled. "But that's not all. Tell Liam the rest."

Is this a setup? Tell me this isn't a setup.

"I was in Madison for meetings at UW. I'm taking a visiting professorship there. Spring Term. While I was in the area, I thought it would be great to visit Madeline and kick back a bit."

"How long are you here?"

"I got in last night. I head back to Ohio the day after tomorrow. It's a brief stop."

116

Madeline excused herself to tend to dinner.

Just as Liam started to frame another question, Helen stood up. "I think I should help Madeline out in the kitchen, if that's okay with you?"

Liam was relieved. "Absolutely. Do you need me to help as well?"

That was stupid.

Helen looked a little panicked. "No. No. We'll do fine. But thanks."

After what seemed an eternity, she came back and announced dinner was ready. Liam followed her into the dining room and sat down, leaving Helen standing. It hadn't occurred to him to help her with her chair. Madeline brought out the food, which was a simple but nicely presented spread of grilled lake trout, caprese salad, boiled redskin potatoes, and garlic toast. Liam leaped up and pulled out Madeline's chair, making his omission of the same courtesy for Helen even more obvious.

Liam's interest was piqued. Just who was this mystery woman? He smiled. "So, Ms. Woodson... or should I say Professor Woodson? Would you say that you are primarily an artist, or an educator? How does that work?"

Helen returned the smile. "I would say it works very well, Mr. O'Connor. I'm an artist. Always have been. I kind of fell into the teaching part when a friend left a university position and recommended me as her replacement. I was intrigued by the opportunity, and found I enjoyed the work. Not as a replacement for my art, but as an aligned activity that supplemented my income."

"How did your parents feel about you going to art school? Were they supportive?"

"Not particularly. My dad was a senior accountant with one of the auto companies, and thought I'd follow him into a business career. When it became clear that I wanted to pursue art, he lobbied for me to go to a state school where

117

I could get both art and business. I chose RISD both because it is a great school and because it made my point with Dad that I was going to be an artist."

"Did he come around to your way of thinking?"

"Eventually, but that's another story for another time." She threw the questioning back to him. "What about your parents, Liam—Do you stay in close contact with them?"

Liam looked at his plate. "No. My parents are gone."

Helen recoiled in horror. "Oh Liam, I'm so very sorry. I didn't mean to…".

His shoulders started to shake and he slowly nodded. "No, they're not dead. I just said they're gone. When I started college, they told me I was on my own, that I had freeloaded off them for eighteen years, and they were out of there."

Helen seemed perplexed. "Where'd they go?"

"To a commune near Sedona. Following the Universe's vibes. It was the last I saw or heard of them. I've no clue if they're still there. They disappeared from my life."

Madeline's jaw had dropped. She looked over at Liam. "You've never told me about that."

Liam winked. "That's because it's bullshit. They're alive, still living in South Chicago. It just makes a better story!"

Helen threw her napkin at him. Madeline roared.

***

After dinner, Madeline told Liam and Helen to go to the living room while she cleaned up. "And no, you can't help. I'll be along shortly." She handed them another bottle of wine. "Just to tide you over while you're waiting for me."

They did as she instructed. Each went to sit in the same spot on the sofa; Liam chuckled and yielded. Helen

118

was down to earth, without pretense. "I have to apologize for my gruffness earlier. I wasn't expecting company tonight. This's been an odd time for me."

Helen nodded. "Oh, I get it. I've been living on my own for so long now that I don't relish being in close quarter social situations. I'm better in crowds, where I can get lost."

"Sometimes I wish I could get lost in crowds. Between my notoriety as an author and my height, I stand out, and everyone thinks they know me. Or at least they've formed an opinion about me, for better or worse. These days it's often for worse."

Helen looked him right in the eyes. "As far as I'm concerned, my measure of a person is what I observe myself. So far, you're doing fine. A little clueless, but then you're a guy."

Liam took note that she didn't look away when she spoke. She drilled down into his mind, right through his eyes.

You've been fooled before, you dumb shit. Why should you believe this one?

Still, he didn't feel threatened at all, so there was that. "I appreciate that Helen."

"Except for that crap about your parents."

He laughed again. "I'm a writer. I make stuff up."

Helen grinned. "So, Mr. Writer—Is there anything else you're making up that I should know about?"

Madeline came into the room. "I've done all I'm going to do tonight. What's up next?"

Liam started to respond, but Madeline interrupted him. "I should tell you I just got another really strange call for you."

He groaned. "I'm so sorry. Now what?"

"Some really odd woman called. Her voice was muffled, I suppose, so I couldn't recognize it. All she said was 'Martha says the coast is clear'. Then she hung up."

Damn. Not now, Vera.

119

He looked at Helen, and then at Madeline. "Madeline, thanks so much for tonight. Great food, great company. But I'm afraid I need to get back to the cottage." He took Helen's hand. "This has been an absolute pleasure. I'm glad Madeline brought you here. Hopefully I'll get to see you before you have to leave."

Helen appeared perplexed, both by the telephone message and by Liam's sudden decision to leave.

He stood and started to walk toward the door. He didn't see Lady lying on the floor and tripped on her. She yelped, and Liam went sprawling. He started to get up, then the pain shot up his leg.

Shit! Dammit all to hell.

"Oh crap."

Lady got up slowly, shaking. Helen went to her and held her until she calmed down, a kind gesture not unnoticed by Liam.

Madeline and Helen then grabbed Liam's arms, gingerly helping him back up and settling him into a chair.

"Are you okay?" Helen kept her hand on his shoulder.

"I sprained my ankle weeks ago. I'm hoping I didn't mess it up again. Dammit."

Madeline spoke. "Can we see if you can put weight on it, or aren't you up to that?"

Liam was rubbing the ankle, hoping it was going to be okay. What an embarrassing way to end an evening. Finally, he looked up. "No time like the present. Let's see."

Helen and Madeline each took an arm. Liam slowly stood. The ankle was painful, but not excruciatingly so. "I think I can get home."

Madeline shook her head. "Not by yourself you can't. Don't be silly."

Helen spoke up. "I need to get back as well. Let me help you. It may be slow, but let's see if we can make it happen."

Liam just nodded. "Might's well try."

Helen had Liam put one arm around her shoulders and held his other arm. He was able to move if he didn't put full weight on the bad ankle.

Helen nodded. "Here we go Liam. One step at a time." They slowly, carefully set out. Helen looked at Liam and smiled impishly. "This is a helluva way to get yourself alone with a lady."

PART II

18

"So. The great novelist Liam O'Connor couldn't get a date for New Year's Eve."

Turned out the bar at The Porter House wasn't a safe haven for Liam tonight. He shuddered as if a cold breeze had landed on him and spoke without turning around. "As always, Doris, you're a veritable breath of stale air. Care to introduce me to your date?" He pivoted and smiled. "Oh, I'm sorry— you're alone tonight? How unusual."

Doris stammered but had nothing. She walked unsteadily away.

He looked around and saw the usual assortment of singles, some paired up and others arranged individually or in packs.

God, this is depressing.

He had no more desire than usual to be around these people. The only difference was that for this event they were more dressed up and even more in the bag. They spoke cheerfully amongst themselves, raising glasses for toasts, the contents spilling to the floor and making walking dangerous.

"Hey, handsome. Whaddya say you and I have another go?" Joanne was smashed. Five foot two and dressed in a red sequined blouse and an almost but not quite matching red mini skirt, she looked like a cheap ornament that had fallen from the Christmas tree.

"No, Joanne. Not a chance. Why don't you get some coffee and chill. Better yet, find some other schmuck to lay your bullshit on."

"You know you want me."

"Please. Just go away." He walked away from the bar and sat down at an empty table.

Ben joined Liam. Liam looked at him. "How do you stand this?"

Ben shrugged. "My people.... They're a sorry lot, but this is my best night of the year. I'll forgive them for the over-indulgence, as long as they don't kill anyone on their way home."

"I guess you do need to cut your bread and butter some slack." He winked. "And Lord knows, there's some serious slack here."

Ben laughed. "I haven't seen you here in a while. You swearing off dating, or have you just picked the town clean?"

"A little of both. I've kinda taken myself out of the pool."

Ben raised his eyebrow. "Really? That doesn't sound like the Liam O'Connor I know. Is it possible you've found someone?"

Liam paused, musing. "I'm not sure I'd say that. I did meet a woman while I was up North, but we seem to have fallen out of touch. I haven't heard anything from her in some time, so I'm not sure there's anything there. It's too bad—I liked her."

Ben nodded but didn't speak.

Liam continued. "You never know, do you? I've learned not to have expectations. I can tell you there's no one in this room who interests me in the least."

"I get that!"

"In fact, I see it's after eleven. I think I'm gonna drift home. Thanks for the company."

"You mean you're not gonna wait for midnight?"

"Nope. It'll happen whether I'm here or not. I need to get home to my dog."

Liam walked out into the cold and snow. He was feeling the effects of the alcohol, but they were fading. He'd cut himself off relatively early. He had no desire to be one of the sloshed souls at the bar. He lit a cigarette and took a long drag.

"Got a light?"

He was caught off-guard. Turning around, he saw a stunning, tall blonde in a fur coat about three feet away. She held up an unlit cigarette.

"Oh. Uh. Sure. Absolutely."

Where the hell'd she come from?

His thoughts raced as he fumbled with his lighter. Success.

"Thank you. Know what? I'm kinda cold."

"Well, you *seem* to have a nice warm coat. Doesn't that help?"

You dumb shit. Is she coming on to you?

She smiled and exhaled the smoke. "I'm afraid I don't have much on underneath. Silly me."

Liam was at a loss for words, but his body was calling to him.

Holy shit she's hot.

"Do you want to go back inside?"

Stupid, stupid, stupid!

"Not really. I was thinkin' maybe you could help me warm up." She nuzzled up to him. Her perfume enveloped him, turning him on even more.

Gucci? Oh, I'd say so. Damn. Am I dreaming? Holy shit.

It was time to go for it. He grinned. "Well, whatcha have in mind?"

She pointed behind the restaurant. "Why don't we go over there and see what comes up?"

Ohhhhh. Shit. This is it, Liam. This is it.

She took his hand and led him behind the building. She looked him in the eye, blew one more puff of smoke his way, and dropped the cigarette. "Whaddya say we look under this coat?"

"Well all right! Your wish is my command."

I don't even know what her fucking name is. Oh, who cares?

Liam leaned in to kiss her as she started to shed the coat. One arm around her back, pulling her close, his other hand slipping effortlessly under the coat and cupping her breast, he heard a vague rustling behind the trash dumpster. He shook it off. Nothing was going to get in the way of this.

The giggling started, followed by cat calls. "Your wish is my command! Oh, that's rich!" More laughter.

"What the fuck?" The blonde stepped back and started giggling as well. Liam moved her aside and strode over to the dumpster. Doris and Joanne were kneeling behind it, beside themselves with their prank. Standing up, they bolted toward the blonde, who by now was doubled over with laughter.

Doris was cackling as she spit her words. "You stupid shit! What an easy mark. Meet Mary, our BEAUTIFUL "Queen of Sots". And YOU, Liam 'I'm-a-Stud' O'Connor, are the BIGGEST sot of them all."

Liam steeled himself. "Well, this is awkward, isn't it? Here we are. I blew both you losers off tonight, or were you too drunk to notice? And yet….. and yet, I was more than ready for this lovely, depraved creature. Or did you miss that part? You're pathetic."

"You… you… you… ." Doris wagged her finger at Liam as Joanne turned away and threw up.

He looked at the blonde, who seemed torn between savoring the joke and realizing she'd missed an opportunity. "And you, Miss "Queen of Sots", are just a tool, aren't you? Your loss." He waved her off and walked away.

What a dumb shit. Shoulda seen that one coming.

He was both embarrassed and really pissed off, at them and with himself. He figured they were already back at the bar, regaling anyone who'd listen with their antics. Trashing him.

Oh well. I hate that crowd anyway. Fuck 'em.

***

Liam was plotting his revenge when he got home. He wasn't certain how, but the tables would be turned. Lady jumped up and stretched as soon as he came in. She walked quickly to him, tail wagging.

At least someone thinks I'm special.

"I think you need to go outside, my friend, so we can hunker down for the night."

He opened the back door and Lady ran into the yard. Just then, there was a loud KA-BOOM!, as one of his neighbors set off fireworks to mark midnight. Startled, Lady bolted.

Goddamn it. Fucking fireworks!

It took a few moments for him to gather his thoughts. He started calling her name.

"LADY! LADY! COME HERE!"

Nothing.

He took off after her.

He was able to follow her tracks in the snow, but at some point she crossed into the plowed street and they disappeared. Panic set in. Nothing worse than losing a spooked dog. Awful images raced through his head. Drunk drivers everywhere, and a dog darting, scared, through the night. He took off running toward town.

No. No. No…….!

This couldn't be happening.

Liam became more and more desperate. He had to find Lady. He ran through the park along the river, hoping she might have sought shelter in the trees. He saw figures in the distance, moving unsteadily through the snow. He took off and raced to reach them. As he got close, he called out. "Hey! I need some help—lost my dog. Thank God you're out here."

One of the figures turned.

Shit! Doris.

"Liam? Ish that you? Ha, ha ha… You're a loosh-er."

"Jesus Doris, you're sloshed."

"Szho I yam…. Whatsh it to you?" She called out to the others. "Hey guysh… L…look who'shere!"

Another one turned.

Oh Christ…shoot me now.

"Joanne?"

Joanne grabbed the other two and pulled them toward her. "Hwhat the ff…uck are you doing Liam?"

"I need help. My dog ran away."

"Ha! Lookee who'sh wishus. This ish Timmy, and that'sh Tommy. No. Wait. Thish is Tommy, and he'sh Timmy."

The men looked at Liam and squinted. "Wheresh thish dog?"

"She's missing. I need your help."

Timmy looked at Tommy. "Did he k..k..kill hish dog?"

"No. No! She's alive. Can you help me?

Timmy held up his hand. "Yesh. I believe we c…c…can."

Liam had to take whatever help he could get. "Okay. She's tall and has long red hair. Can you fan out and let's cover as much area as possible?"

The men nodded and stumbled off toward the trees. Doris squinted at Liam and wobbled away in no particular direction. Joanne stepped toward Liam but face-planted in the snow. Lying on her stomach and giggling, she made snow angels.

Liam pulled Joanne upright and pointed her in the direction of town. He looked at the rag-tag group and shook his head. *Dear Jesus.* He went back to calling Lady and looking around the park.

"I FOUND HER! THERE SHE ISH…." Timmy was standing near a sidewalk, pointing.

128

Liam arrived just as Timmy was kneeling, looking like he was about to be sick. "Over there!"

Liam pointed. "That?"

"Yesh."

"Goddam it. That's a fire hydrant."

"Oh. I wondered why it was sho shtill. But it'sh red!"

"Jesus, man. Give me a break." Liam looked for the others. Doris was squatting next to a building. He shook his head and cautiously approached her. "Did you find something?"

"Go away Liam O'Connor. Can't you shee I'm indishposed?" She was peeing in the snow.

"HERE SHE ISH! I'M HOLDING ON TO THE DOG!" This time it was Tommy. Liam ran to him. He was straddling a wooden bench, holding on for dear life.

"She'sh goin' nowhere!"

"You dumb shit. That's a bench. Get up..."

Joanne ran up to Liam, out of breath. She raised her hand as if to speak, paused, and passed out.

Liam threw up his hands and started to walk away. He stopped and turned back to survey the scene. Joanne was out cold on the ground, Doris standing over her and looking confused. Timmy had his arm around Tommy's shoulder, waving his other arm and calling out to Liam.

"Happy New Year! God blesh ush, effery one."

***

Liam had to admit it was best he went home, if only to catch his breath and warm up before heading out again. He hoped Lady had already found her way there, but as he approached the house, he could see she hadn't. The reality of her absence hit hard, falling tears freezing on his cheeks and his hands trembling uncontrollably. Standing on the stoop and fishing in his pockets for keys, he heard a noise.

129

Looking around, he saw something moving toward him, oddly lit with flashing lights.

What the fuck?

It was Lady, running at a gallop. As she got closer, he could see that someone had put a party hat on her head and draped Christmas lights over her. She was carrying something in her mouth—a can of pickled herring. She dropped it at his feet, then jumped up on him. He wrapped his arms around her, then took her front paws and danced with her. "You crazy dog! Have you been off partying while I was worrying about you? Next time, take me with you!"

19

Man and dog would've slept for most of the morning were it not for the phone. Its noise came to Liam as pounding in his dreams, until finally it drifted into his consciousness. It took a moment for the ringing to register, and by then he was pissed off at the intrusion. He got up and stumbled into the kitchen.

"Hello."

Silence.

Now he was more pissed. "Goddam it Doris. You're a jackass."

More silence, then a small voice. "Happy… ."

Oh shit.

"Sara? Is that you?"

He could hear a distant voice. "He can't see you shake your head, sweetheart."

After a couple beats, the small voice returned. "Yes."

"Oh, I'm so sorry Sara. I didn't know it was you. Happy New Year."

The voice grew. "WHERE'S LADY?"

Liam laughed out loud. That was more like it. "Why she's still in bed. She's tired."

He could almost see the wheels turning in Sara's head. "Breakfast."

"What?"

"Tell her to get up. It's time for breakfast!"

"Why yes, it is. I'll let her know. And how are you, Sara? Are you having a good morning?"

"Eggs."

"Oh. Did you have eggs?"

"Bacon."

"Well okay. That sounds really good."

"TELL ME A STORY LIAM!"

Shit.

Liam's mind was racing. He had nothing. "I'll tell you what. Let me think about that and maybe I can call you later and tell you one. How's that?"

"Snowman." Sara had moved on.

There was a rustle on the other end of the phone. Finally, Susan's voice. "So sorry for the intrusion Liam. Sara's been wanting to talk to you. We held her off this morning as long as we could. I hope we didn't wake you up? And who's Doris?"

"No, no." He lied. "And Doris is... oh never mind. I was up. We're just a little tired over here. Lady got spooked by some fireworks last night and we had an unexpected adventure. All's good though. How are you all?" He flashed back to Susan and that moment when she kissed him at the cottage.

Stop, you idiot. Let it go.

"You know, we're pretty good. We had a very nice Christmas. Sara's been great. She talks about you a lot— well, maybe she talks more about Lady, but you're right up there. Jack says hi. We miss you. We were thinking maybe we might take a trip to Madison this winter and stop by to see you. Madeline told us you're not so good at visiting so we'll do the traveling."

Madeline was right, of course, but it still stung to hear this. "That would be really nice. Just give me some advance notice so I can be sure to be available." He was lying again. What the hell did he have to do around here that would make him unavailable?

I really do need to get a life.

"Great. Let's see how the weather does, and we'll find a good time for all of us. In the meantime, would you mind if Sara calls you again? She really misses Lady. Sorry, just kidding. That was a joke. She misses you."

132

"Not a problem. I like hearing from her. You guys have a great day today. Let's talk again soon.'

Liam sat down at the table, Lady at his feet. She wasn't about to let him out of her sight. This had already been a helluva New Year, and other than the pleasant surprise of Sara's call would be just one more bad memory to cement his dislike for the holiday. It would be a great day for writing, except he was in editorial purgatory on his book. He'd finished *Darby's Gift* at the end of September, much to the surprise of his agent and, even more, himself. He made his final tweaks to it, and mailed the manuscript off to his editor, Harold Simon, on Halloween. He let himself relax for about a week before the doubts started setting in. He finally heard from Harold the day before Thanksgiving. His report was positive, but now Liam had to settle into the editing process, which could take months.

Liam sat for a while, more staring at than drinking a cup of coffee that eventually grew cold. Finally, he sat on the floor with Lady. She put her head in his lap and he relaxed. A knock at the door.

What the fuck? It's too early in the morning for this.

He flung open the door. "WHAT?"

It was that leggy blonde from last night—Mary, Queen of Sots. "I thought maybe we could start over?"

"Start over what? Are you kidding me? How stupid do I look?"

"No, really. I didn't know who you were. Those two women gave me a hundred bucks to set you up."

"So you're a hooker?"

"No. No I'm not. I was just visiting a friend and we came to the bar. I'm going back home tonight and thought I'd take a chance."

"How the hell'd you find me?"

"That woman Doris gave me your address."

"That seals it. It's another set up."

"No. it's really not. Just me."

133

He motioned her to come inside. She was damn good looking. She had that perfume on again, and was standing close enough to him that he was getting turned on. His mind started to drift.

Lady pawed his leg, breaking the spell.

Mary moved closer, but it was too late.

Liam pulled back. "You know, Mary, I may regret this for the rest of my life, but this isn't gonna happen. I want you to do this for me—and for yourself. Go back to Doris. Give her back the money she gave you. Or keep it. I don't care. But tell her it didn't work. And please tell her Liam said she can go fuck herself."

Mary looked surprised. "That's it?"

"Yeah. That's it. Have a nice life."

***

After Mary left, Liam stood for a while looking out the window, wondering what he'd just done. Lady pawed his leg again. He knelt beside her and hugged her. "Some days are just hard to explain, my friend."

Liam grabbed a beer and lit a cigarette. He sat down at his desk and stared at the typewriter keys. Maybe he could start something new. It was a new year, so why not a new piece of writing? The phone rang again.

Shit. Are you fucking kidding me?

He picked it up.

"Liam, it's Helen."

An awkward pause followed while he reoriented his thoughts. Relaxing, he tried not to be too eager. "Well I'll be damned. You are a breath of fresh air this morning."

Helen seemed relieved. "Wow. To what do I owe the compliment?"

"Let's just say I'm coming off an odd night. And an odder morning."

"What was the odd night?"

134

Liam had no desire to elaborate. "Mostly horseshit that has nothing to do with you and me. How've you been?"

"I've been fine, just a bit overwhelmed. Merry Christmas and Happy New Year."

Liam smiled. "Right back at you."

Helen took a breath and chuckled. "I'm packed up and leaving for Madison in the morning. Classes start in a week. My van's stuffed to the gills or would be if vans had gills."

Liam grinned. He had reason to be excited about something again. "That's good news. Welcome to Wisconsin! You gonna need help moving in? I could use a distraction." As soon as he said it, he kicked himself for his insensitivity.

What an idiot.

"I mean, I'd love to see you."

"Absolutely. If you have time and inclination. I've got a lot of stuff. I'm bringing most of my studio with me."

Liam loved it. "Just call me when you get in, and we can figure out when you need me. And be careful driving. The roads are kind of a mess."

That call was exactly what he needed. He even let himself laugh a bit about the absurdities of the night before. And the timeliness of him blowing off that woman Mary.

But damn. She was hot, wasn't she?

20

The next dawn was sunny and bright. Rejuvenated by Helen's call, Liam left the house with Lady by his side, and walked to the Owl's Eyes, which was closed for inventory. He knew better than to get involved in that process and had left it in the hands of Marianne and Vera. They were a deadly combination, but he trusted they would figure out a way to cooperate.

Things were different at the store since John left unceremoniously after Labor Day. After Vera's call to Madeline's the night he met Helen, he'd driven back to meet with her. The evidence she gave him was telling. The money that was unaccounted for had been taken by John. She had tied the timing of the several withdrawals to nights he had closed the store. He had covered by adjusting sales totals but had done it in a way that made little sense when more closely examined. Liam waited until John came into the store the next day, then called him back to the office. When confronted with the evidence, John caved immediately. He had started with small sums that he had planned to pay back as soon as he could, but as he found it an easy process to pull off, he took more and more. He didn't keep any of it for himself. He gave some to his aunt, some to his friends, and even some to random homeless people.

Liam was beside himself. He'd been betrayed by a young man he felt was honest and industrious. As it turned out, John was more industrious than honest. Liam fired him on the spot. John begged him not to file charges, that he would repay all the money within six months. Liam ultimately gave in and worked out a payment schedule, with the proviso that if he missed any payments, Liam was free to file a police report. He also got John to give him a full written admission of his guilt, which Liam would keep in the store's safe. Marianne refused to even look at John as he walked out of the store.

Vera was subdued but seemed proud of the work she had done. Liam decided to reward her by giving her a title and her own office. She would be "Chief Bookkeeper", and the office would be a small space that had originally been a restroom before the store had been remodeled a few years back. Unfortunately, the room had a residual disinfectant odor that simply wouldn't go away. Fortunately, with the combination of Vera's own rather musty scent and the billows of aerosol deodorant that accompanied her, she was totally unaffected. He bought her a small desk and chair, plus a filing cabinet, and stenciled her new title on the frosted glass in the door. She seemed delighted.

***

When Liam and Lady arrived, Marianne and Vera were hard at work on the inventory, accompanied by the temporary employee *du jour*, a young woman who looked to be about twenty, with big brown deer-in-the-headlight eyes. Her name was Nancy, or at least Liam thought it was Nancy, but who knew? Ever since John had left, Liam had tried to hire a suitable replacement, with varying degrees of success. The candidates lasted anywhere from one hour to two weeks before fleeing in the head-shaking panic of one who, when faced with Marianne's strict yet bewildering instructions, had no chance whatsoever of succeeding.

With each departure, Marianne would come to Liam and say: "I just have no idea why we can't get a good employee. The job isn't that hard."

He would say nothing and put another want ad in the local paper.

The inventory seemed to be proceeding apace. Liam asked Marianne and Vera to join him in the office. "Okay

137

ladies. Are we gonna get this done by the close of business tomorrow?"

Vera said "yes", shaking her head vigorously and with unbridled enthusiasm.

Marianne looked at him. "What do you mean, 'we'?"

Trapped, he relented. "Why, I mean my talented and industrious staff. Is that staff going to get this done on time? I want to reopen the store the day after tomorrow. Is that gonna happen?"

Marianne pushed Vera aside. "I believe so, but of course it would go much more quickly if the owner of the establishment were to get involved."

Liam looked at her. "Do you really mean that?"

Marianne's bluff failed. "Oh God no. Go. Get out of here."

***

Liam escaped the store as quickly as he could, headed for an appointment with Sharon. On the way there, Lady rolled in the snow. A lot. By the time she got up, she was good and wet. They got to Sharon's office early. Her door was open, but she wasn't anywhere in sight. He took Lady into the office and started to sit. She was shivering.

Silly dog. Next time stay out of the snow.

He realized he needed to use the restroom, so he closed Lady in the office and walked down the hall.

He could hear Lady barking. He laughed to himself.

She's such a happy dog... I love that.

She was still barking and he could hear her jumping around when he returned. Something wasn't right. There was—an odor—and then...

Oh no!

Something squished under his foot. He looked down and saw it. Dogshit. Mushy piles of it, splattered all over

Sharon's priceless Persian rug. To make matters worse Lady had stepped in it while she was prancing around the room., tracking it everywhere. When she saw Liam, she ran to him and jumped up.

Noooooo!

Now it was on his pants as well. And the putrid smell, filling the room.

Liam panicked for a moment, then leaped into action. He ran back to the restroom and grabbed as many paper towels as he could carry, plus a bottle of hand soap. He got back to the office and dropped to his hands and knees, doing his best to wipe up the mess from the rug. It wasn't helping. Now the stuff was all over his hands. The smell was overwhelming.

What the fuck am I gonna do now? I've gotta get this cleaned up before....

"Oh my God Liam. What's going on?"

"Um—Oh-- I'm gonna make it up to you."

"What happened? Did you have an accident?"

Now he was really embarrassed. "No! Ohmygod no! Not me. My dog." He pointed. "See? She's over there. You two haven't met."

This ain't a social occasion, you moron. Jesus.

Sharon kept staring down. "My rug. My rug. Ohhhh—"

"Like I said, I'll make it up to you. I swear. I'll get this cleaned. No problem."

Sharon was shaking her head. "It's not that easy. It requires special care."

"I'll get it. Don't worry."

"Okay. For right now, could you please move it out into the hallway? It smells awful in here."

With impeccably bad timing, Lady tore across the room and jumped up on Sharon. Now Sharon had dogshit on her clothes. "Ohhhh—No—"

Liam grabbed Lady and made her sit. "I suppose maybe this isn't the best time for a session?"

"No, no. We have some time. If you can stand the smell, so can I. Let's see what we can accomplish. In the shortest time possible."

Liam went to sit down.

"Wait!!! Just a minute. Let me put something on that chair before you sit." Sharon grabbed a blanket from a closet and draped it on Liam's chair. "Okay. Now you can sit."

Liam was still wiping his hands on a paper towel as he dropped into the chair.

Sharon wrapped another blanket around herself before she sat down. "Okay. Let's try to get started. Anything going on with you? Besides an unruly dog?

Liam had that blank look on his face that meant either he couldn't think of anything, or he was trying to figure out whether he dared tell her what was really happening. Finally, he spoke. "Well, that artist called yesterday."

"And what artist might that be?"

"You know, that one I met up North, right before I left to come home."

Sharon deadpanned. "Oh. *That* artist. As I recall, she had a name, didn't she?"

He was trapped. "All right. Helen."

Sharon raised her fist in the air, a celebration of the minor victory.

"Yes! Helen. Now, as I recall, you and I have discussed her a few times since then, haven't we?"

"Yes." Liam wasn't going to make this easy.

"And what did we discuss?"

"I think I may have mentioned that she was okay."

Sharon bit her lip. "Really? She was 'okay'? I think I remember it a little differently. Wouldn't you agree?"

140

"All right. I liked her. Anyway, she called." One small piece of information at a time. A tiny morsel, deposited on the ground to savor.

"Okay. I'll bite. She called. What did she say?"

Now Liam was looking out the window. "What?"

"What'd she say?"

"Well, she said she was leaving this morning and driving to Madison."

"And what was she going to do in Madison?"

"She's moving there to start teaching this term. I think she's an artist in residence."

"You think? Or you know?"

"Okay, I know. She's an artist in residence."

Sharon appeared to be trying very hard to keep a straight face. "Anything else she might have said?"

Liam wasn't going to give anything up easily. "She may have said that I could help her move in if I wanted."

"And are you going to do it?"

"Do what?"

"Liam, are you with me? Are you going to help her move in?"

Oh, how he didn't want to answer this one. "I guess so. I mean, I don't see why I wouldn't."

"Well, that would be a nice thing to do, wouldn't you say?"

Liam nodded. "I guess it would. At least I think so."

"All right, then. We're out of time. Perhaps you could take my rug and your dog and get them both cleaned up."

***

When the phone rang, Liam was deep in sleep. He didn't wake up until he heard the answering machine click on, and then Helen's voice.

141

"Liam? It's Helen. I'm …."

He raced to the phone. "Hi! Where are you?"

"I'm here, in Madison. Just got in a few minutes ago. It was a long day's drive. The weather around Chicago was bad. I'm going to crash. Are you still willing to help me move in?"

Liam tried not to sound excited. "Of course. I'd be glad to help. When should I come over?" Helen's voice sounded wonderful.

"Why don't you drive over in the morning? Any time that works for you. No need to rush. I've got a full van, so I could use any help you can give me."

He stayed cool, or at least hoped it sounded that way. Not too eager. That would be bad form. "Okay. I have a few things I need to take care of, but I can get away by mid-morning. Or probably by then. Can I bring my dog? I'd rather not leave her home all day." He didn't want to say the obvious next phrase— "and all night." That would be presumptuous, but he had hopes.

"Sure. Lady's always welcome."

He had pulled it off without appearing the eager schoolboy. "Great. Then I'll see you tomorrow. Get some sleep!"

Liam sighed in relief as he hung up. He leaned down and hugged Lady. "You stink, but we're going on a road trip, my friend. This is going to be fun."

21

Up early, Liam was full of anticipation blunted only by his poor history with women. Today could be the beginning of a new chapter in his life. Lady hopped into the truck and they headed out of town. Liam pictured a passionate reunion scene. The closer he got to Madison, the more that image faded. What if she didn't feel the magic? Hell, what if he didn't feel the magic? What if there was no magic? By the time he pulled into the driveway of the old grey house Helen's apartment occupied, he was a ball of nerves. He parked the truck and let Lady out. She ran off with Liam in hot pursuit. "Get back here Lady! Now!" Lady saw this as an opportunity to play, something he didn't share or appreciate.

Helen walked outside. She looked even better than he remembered. Her hair again tied back with a bandana, she was wearing khaki pants with a blue denim work shirt. Paint-splattered work boots completed the ensemble, and she glowed. Or at least that's what Liam saw. He wanted to seem self-assured but properly deferential. He held back and waited for her to come to him. He put his arms around her in an embrace that he realized was too enthusiastic when he saw a moment of panic in her eyes. She embraced him far more gently.

"It's good to see you Liam. Thanks so much for coming." She was smiling, which Liam took to be a good sign.

"Why wouldn't I have come?"

Boy, that was a stupid thing to say.

"It's good to see you as well, Helen. I've looked forward to this day."

Stupid again. I overplayed that, didn't I?

143

He could've written better dialogue than that. Maybe he should rewrite this scene and present it to her later.

"Come on in. I'm afraid there's plenty to do. You may wish you hadn't been so quick to get here!" Maybe she didn't notice what a putz he'd been.

"Lead the way, my lady."

Helen laughed. "Me or the dog?"

Crap.

"Let me rephrase that. I will follow you, wherever you may go."

Oh brother. Just keeps getting worse.

Helen took him by the hand. She led him into the living room, which appeared to be her staging area.

"With the exception of the kitchen stuff, I think we should bring everything into here, to sort. That should make it all easier."

Liam nodded. "Makes sense to me. Do you want me to start unloading, and then you can sort it out while I'm bringing it all in?"

"I guess that works, but there'll be some things you'll need extra hands with."

Liam smiled. "You underestimate me. I'm strong. Like a bull."

She laughed. "I'm sure there's some bull in there. Let's see how you do."

Liam started unloading. Lady kept close-by, and he had to work carefully to keep from stumbling over her. Liam carried the boxes in, and Helen pointed where they should go. He was surprised how much she'd brought, given she'd only be in Madison for one term.

Finally, the art works and supplies. Helen made clear this was the most precious of her cargo, and insisted she be involved in unloading it. Liam got it. This was her livelihood. There could be no mistakes. Liam felt he was under constant surveillance, understandable because he was. He marveled at the completed canvases. Her work was powerful and abstract. Reminiscent of cubist but with larger, bold shapes and colors—almost as if Picasso and Rothko had collided. He was overcome by the depth and breadth of her work and told her so. She blushed but had an air of quiet confidence that spoke volumes. It's what she did, and he could tell she knew how good it was.

"These are some of my most cherished canvases. Can I trust you to get them into the house safely?" Helen was grinning. "Have you tripped over any dogs lately?"

Liam shook his head and smiled back. "Why no, I haven't. That little incident was staged, didn't you know? How else was I going to get alone with you? I'm rock solid." As the words left his lips, he walked right into a packing carton and stumbled, catching his balance at the last moment.

"Oh, the irony!" Helen doubled over in mirth. Liam couldn't help but laugh at himself. Any remaining tension left the room.

***

Liam and Helen were deep in conversation when there was a knock at the door. Helen went to check. Liam could hear voices in the hallway. She returned, followed by a man. He looked to be about fifty, with graying hair and horn-rimmed glasses.

Helen smiled. "Liam, this is Stephen. He lives upstairs. Stephen, this is my… friend…Liam O'Connor."

Liam went to shake hands, but Stephen ignored him and addressed Helen. "I'm so glad to meet you. You seem a breath of fresh air after some of the losers that have had your apartment before. I want to welcome you to UW!"

Liam moved closer to Helen, but Stephen's eyes were glued to her. "I'm in the history department. What about you?"

145

Liam stepped between Helen and Stephen, so that she had to peer around him to respond. "I'm visiting this term. Painting and Art History."

"Oh, that's great! I can see we'll have much in common. I'd love to show you around campus."

"Why thank you Stephen. That would be nice. Liam and I are kind of tied up right now, but I'll be sure to check in with you later."

Liam looked at Helen after Stephen left. "Well there goes a pompous asshole if I've ever seen one."

Helen smiled. "Oh I don't know. He seems okay. How about I get you a beer, and we take a break from this unpacking thing?"

She returned with a beer and a glass of wine. "The beer's semi-cold. Is that going to be okay?"

"Anything you bring me will be just fine."

They sat on the floor. Helen leaned into Liam, and he put his arm around her. It felt good. He couldn't recall the last time he was this comfortable with a woman, and wanted to know more about her. "So. Are you excited about teaching here?"

"Very much so. I've enjoyed my time at Wesleyan, but it's such a small school. Wisconsin gives me an opportunity to present myself on a whole different level. I have no idea where the visiting position might lead, but it's an open door."

"Do you see yourself as primarily an academic, or an artist?"

"Do I have to choose?" Helen pulled away, just a bit. *Uh-oh. Better reel that one back in.*

"No, just curious."

"Let me throw it back at you then. Have you ever taught, or considered teaching?"

"Oh hell no. I'm a writer. That's all I've got. I don't think I could stand lecturing or dealing with academics."

"What about the students? It's not all lecturing. I find them interesting, by and large, and eager to learn."

"I guess. But you didn't answer my question: artist or academic?"

Helen looked at Liam and laughed. "Both. Different but each rewarding in its own way. How's that for an answer?"

Liam realized he'd been checkmated. He liked this woman. A lot.

Damn. She's good.

***

Liam realized it was nearly six o'clock and he was getting hungry. He brought up dinner, and Helen pointed to the kitchen.

She laughed. "I'm thinking there isn't anything in there worth taking the time and effort to put together for a meal. How about we walk over to campus and find a bar with food?"

Damn near anything she could suggest would be fine with Liam. "Sure. Let's go for it."

The campus strip was raucous, filled with students back from break. Helen and Liam wove through congregating clumps of bar-hopping kids, until they found a bar that wasn't packed. They went in and sat down. A live band was setting up, but it was going to be a while before they started to play. It was an ideal place for a quiet dinner.

Liam put Stephen out of his mind and concentrated on talking with Helen. She was so unpretentious and unaffected. "Outside of concerts and lectures, I spend surprisingly little time in Madison, and I sure as hell haven't been in campus bars since I left Northwestern. Having said that, I kinda like this place. Maybe it's because you're here with me, but I feel really at home."

Oh boy. Was that too forward?

147

Blushing, Helen took his hand. "I'm glad you feel that way. I had some concerns about introducing you into this madness, but if you want to be around me, I'm afraid this all goes with the territory. Welcome to my world!"

Liam was ecstatic but played it cool. "Well, let's just see how I do." He couldn't wait to tell Sharon. This one was looking up.

Before they knew it, it was nine-thirty. Helen looked at Liam. "I think we should get back. There's still a fair amount to do before I can call it a day. Maybe we can have a nightcap—I've got a nice Benedictine packed away."

They walked back to Helen's holding hands. They were laughing when they got to the front stoop. Helen held a finger to her lips. "I don't want to be that loud woman to my new neighbors." She opened the door to her apartment quietly.

An ominous scene greeted them. Little pieces of canvas all over the floor, painted colors gleaming in the overhead lights. One or two canvas stretchers and frames, chewed, broken and scattered about. Lady was nowhere to be seen, but she crept into view, slinking along the floor with her tail between her legs. Helen shrieked, running from room to room yelling "No—No—No!!!"

Liam was stunned. "Oh shit!"

Helen's face grew red and tears glistened on her cheeks. She picked up a few pieces of canvas and stared at them in disbelief. "My work. My lifeblood. My soul. You have no idea—" She started to shake as the initial shock wore off. "I don't think I can be with you right now. This hurts so much."

Liam stammered. "Bu..bu..but." Out of words, he grabbed Lady's leash. As he stood over her, she puked on the floor…little pieces of colored canvas and saliva. Pulling Lady toward the door, he turned to Helen and tried to take her hand. She recoiled and looked the other way.

148

He picked up Lady and put her in the truck. She threw up a little more. He was absolutely, totally devastated. He got on the road toward home. It was late, and it was starting to snow. Not a blizzard, but heavy enough to make the roads challenging. Shoulders drooping, hands trembling, he drove on. Lady snuggled close to him, and put her head on his lap. He looked down at her. "Well, we screwed up this time, didn't we girl? I really thought this was going to be the perfect night. What were you thinking?" Lady whimpered a little. "I know, you feel bad." She coughed up another bit of canvas. "Really?" He started to get angry at her, but couldn't. "You're just a dog, aren't you? My fault for leaving you alone." He stroked her head and she whimpered some more. "And now we're both alone… together."

22

The shock of the Great Art Disaster became despair. Liam spent the better part of the next two days just going through the motions. On the third day he rose, the urge to act swelling up in him. After staring at the phone for a good ten minutes, he dialed.

"Hello?"

He took a deep breath, exhaled, and spoke. "Doris? This is Liam."

Dead silence.

Finally, an irritated voice. "What the hell do you want?"

"I thought maybe we could get together and catch dinner. Maybe a movie? Might be fun."

"Are you bullshitting me O'Connor?"

"Why no, Doris. I'm asking you out. What do you say?"

Doris's voice sounded suspicious yet hopeful. "Ok. I've got nothing else going on. Where and when?"

Liam was feeling a little better. "How about tonight? I'll pick you up at six and we'll go from there."

"All right. But no diner food. Got it?"

Liam laughed. "Yeah. Got it. See you then." He hung up the phone. He called the store and told Marianne he'd stop by later in the afternoon.

***

Liam took Lady for a walk. When they returned, he saw the red light flashing on the answering machine.

A familiar voice. "Liam, this is Helen. Please call me."

He played it again, not believing it was her. What did she want? Was this a good call, or a call to completely

150

break things off? He had to find out but was afraid. In the end, he picked up the phone and dialed, his hand trembling as he punched the buttons. Three rings. One more and it would go to her machine. Just as he was ready to hang up, she answered.

"Helen. Liam." It was all he could muster.

The silence seemed to last hours. "Oh Liam. Thanks for calling me back. I want to apologize for how I acted the other night. I was in shock."

He was shaking. "No, no, Helen. I was at fault. It was my dog and I should never have left her alone in a strange house. I feel like shit. I'm so very sorry."

More silence, before she continued. "I've replayed the evening constantly. It took me a long time, but I realized it was just an unfortunate incident. No one's fault, really. And, by the way, your dog has lousy taste in art. She only got one painting, and the one she picked I've hated since I did it. It was a throwaway as far as I was concerned, so please forgive me."

"Forgive you for what? I don't know what to say."

"You don't need to say anything. Next time, we'll just close off my studio room."

Liam's heart leaped. "Next time?"

"Yes. I hope there's a next time. In fact, how about tonight? I still have that fine Benedictine. We can share it after I make you a proper dinner. I didn't tell you, but I'm reputed to be an excellent chef."

He didn't hesitate. "Yes, yes. I'd love to see you tonight."

Helen paused. "Just one request, if you don't mind. Do you think you could leave Lady home this time? I think it would reduce risks dramatically."

"Absolutely. I can get Marianne to watch her." As soon as the words left his lips, the dread hit.

Shit. Doris. What the fuck am I going to do with her?

151

Dismissing that thought, he re-assumed an upbeat tone. "What time do you want me? What can I bring?"

"Why don't you get here about five-thirty? You can bring the wine. I can trust you to do that, can't I?"

Liam smiled. "Oh yes, that you can. I'll see you then. And Helen? Thanks. I appreciate you so much."

"Maybe you'd better hold off on the appreciation until after the evening's successful."

He couldn't have written a better resolution himself. He patted Lady on the head. "Well, my friend. We dodged a bullet on this one. Can I trust you not to pull something that silly again?" As he said the words, he felt like they were self-directed. They both had been incredibly fortunate. Someone was smiling upon them. Then he panicked. He had almost no time to take care of Lady and deal with Doris. He jumped into action, heading with Lady straight to the Owl's Eyes.

***

Liam saw Marianne by the check-out counter and rushed to her. She looked up in surprise. "So just where have you been, Mr. 'I Think I'll Disappear'?"

"I've been tied up. Listen, Marianne, I have a big favor to ask."

Marianne looked at him sideways. "And just what might that be?"

"I need to go out of town tonight. Could you keep Lady?"

"I suppose so. What time?"

"How about now? I should be back sometime tomorrow."

Liam became aware of a presence just past Marianne, staring over her shoulder.

Shit. Doris.

The words and accompanying cold air hit simultaneously. "What? What the hell?"

The shipwreck had happened and there was no way he could blunt it. "Oh hi Doris. I was going to call you. Something's come up. A....yeah... a reading. I got called to fill in for another author at a bookstore in Barrington. I'm really sorry. I'll make it up to you."

The fist hit his face out of nowhere. Doris had nailed him, right under his eye. As he blinked and raised his hand to check the damage, she moved in on him, punching him in the chest.

Unfortunately, it was the store's annual after-inventory sale, and it was filled with shoppers. Hearing and seeing the commotion, some fled the store, but a few, realizing it was that famous Liam O'Connor, created a circle around the action.

Liam, still wincing from the blow, tried to help himself. "Gee, Doris. Can I give you a rain check?"

Marianne had pulled Doris away from Liam, but she broke loose and came right back into his face. "You son-of-a-bitch. You're the lowest of low. You can just go to hell." She stormed out the door.

The remaining customers were standing in awe, dead silence in the store. Liam looked at Marianne. "I think that went well. Don't you?"

Marianne quickly turned to the assembled crowd and announced that the owner wanted them to know the store was giving everyone an extra five percent off the sale price of every book purchased that afternoon. Liam watched her in action.

Damn. She's good.

When she turned back to him, Liam dissembled. "Thanks so much for watching Lady. You're an angel."

Marianne looked at him and shook her head. "You owe me."

***

Liam was flying high when he got to Madison. The darkness that had held him in its grasp the past few days had been tossed aside like a bad piece of fish. The campus area was full of life. Energized, he pulled up to Helen's place. Taking a few minutes to make sure he was properly composed, he looked again in the mirror to make sure everything was in place. This was an auspicious moment, one he'd remember the rest of his life. Unless, of course, the night went badly. In that case, he would forever block this moment from his recollections.

Helen walked out of the house and wrapped her arms around him. They stood, facing and looking into each other's eyes. Helen leaned in and kissed him. He felt the warmth rise all the way from his feet throughout his body. He felt like he was sixteen and being kissed for the first time. He held her kiss, and it seemed as if time had stopped. This really was a new experience for him. He was used to his mind being occupied by nonstop thoughts and musings when he kissed other women, but it was unconditionally blank this time.

When the kiss ended, Helen smiled. "I've missed you."

"I've missed you too."

As they walked into the house and down the hall to the door to Helen's apartment, Liam saw Stephen standing at the door, getting ready to knock. He looked up at Liam with obvious disgust, then turned to Helen. "Hi Helen. I was just bringing you a book."

Helen nodded. "Thanks. How kind of you. I'll catch up with you later."

"May I come in?"

"I'm afraid not, Stephen. Another time."

Liam watched Stephen as he walked down the hall. *This guy's gonna be a problem.*

154

23

Once they were in the apartment, Helen noticed Liam's eye. "Oh my. What happened to you?"

Liam had no plausible response. "I.... well... I must've run into something."

Helen touched the spot and he winced. "It must've been something substantial."

"Nothing I couldn't handle."

Helen chuckled. "Would a beer ease the pain?"

"Oh I think so."

Helen disappeared into the kitchen. Liam checked out the room. The lights were dimmed, and there were lit candles all over the place.

Oh, I like this. Nice touch Helen. Nice touch.

She returned with the beer. He handed her a bottle of wine he had picked up on the way to Madison.

Helen looked at the label and cocked her head. "Well, this is an interesting choice. Let's get it opened so it can breathe. You wait here. I'll be right back."

This promised to be a very nice night, if only he could keep from blowing it. He vowed to stay focused and keep his manners. On the other hand, Helen's greeting had turned him on in spectacular fashion and he was starting to sweat.

Helen returned with a tray of appetizers. "Sit down. Make yourself at home."

Holy shit.

The tray held an assortment of scallops and oysters on the half shell, glistening in the light of the flickering candles. Helen set it down and returned to the kitchen. She came back with a glass of Chardonnay.

"Helen, this is spectacular."

"I told you I was good."

Liam shook his head in wonder. "What's next?"

155

"The main course will be an Osso Buco, with a nice risotto. I think you'll like it if I do say so myself."

"So you're an artist of food as well as painting?"

"I went to culinary school after RISD. Cooking had been a hobby, and I decided to take it to the next level. Something to fall back on if my art didn't take off."

Liam couldn't believe his good fortune. "Dare I ask what's for dessert?"

"I have to save at least something as a surprise." She winked and stood up. "I need to check on the main course. Don't go anywhere…."

Liam managed to sit still for about ten minutes before his curiosity took over. He ambled into the kitchen, beer in hand. Helen was at the stove, her motions culinary choreography. He snuck up behind her and put his arms around her waist. She moaned.

Turning her head and smiling, she looked directly into his eyes. "I think…. I think maybe you should go back to the living room. I have to make love to the food now. I'm afraid you'll just have to wait."

Arghhhhhh….. so close!

Liam dropped his arms.

Please Dear God, don't let me mess up.

He returned to the living room.

Helen stuck her head out of the kitchen. "Dinner's ready. Would you care to join me in the dining room?"

"Oh hell yes."

Helen brought in the Osso Buco and the risotto. She lit candles and excused herself. Music filled the air as she returned and took her seat.

Liam looked at her in awe. "What's the music?"

"Debussy. I don't think there's a better landscape for art and food. Just let it fill your mind and your soul."

Liam knew bupkis about classical music, but he did know Helen was going all out to set a romantic mood. "I agree. It's perfect."

156

She stood up and served the dishes. As she leaned over him, the scent of her perfume hit the "go" switch again. He wanted nothing more than to ravage her right there and then, on the table, in the midst of all the food.

Helen's eyes met his. She looked down at the food, then back at him. She licked her lips as she spoke. "Please eat. I think this is going to be a wonderful experience…"

Oh my god, was that what I thought it was?

"Oh, I intend to do just that."

Helen and Liam held each other's eyes as they took each bite. Liam sighed and Helen followed. Helen picked up a shank and sucked the marrow from the bone. Liam followed suit. She grinned and tore a bite off the bone with her teeth. Liam closed his eyes and did the same.

They seemed in a lovers' trance. A trance broken when they took their first sips of the wine Liam had brought. He spit it out. "Jesus Christ this is awful."

Helen laughed out loud. "Yes it is. Could be the worst ever."

"How can I make it up to you?"

"How about next time you let me buy the wine?"

"I guess I suck at this."

"I don't like you any less for it. But yes, you do."

They tried to recapture the moment of lust but couldn't stop giggling. Finally, Liam picked up his shank and, looking into Helen's eyes, held the shank up to her lips. She closed her eyes and licked it, then picked up hers and entwined her arm with his, offering her shank to his lips. He groaned and took a bite, then leaned over and kissed her.

***

After dinner, Liam asked Helen if she'd show him more of her art. He hadn't had much opportunity to see it on his first visit.

"Oh, I don't think so. I'm not going to bore you with my work."

"No, really. I want to see it. Madeline told me how good it is. I want to see for myself."

"Okay... if you insist. Follow me. And promise you'll tell me when you become bored."

Liam put his arm around her shoulders. Helen turned on the lights in the studio to reveal a remarkable array of canvasses. She led him to a large one with bright orange, blue and brown somewhat random forms, with a splash of bright red.

"This one was inspired by a gentleman I saw in Barcelona. He had waded into a fountain and wrapped his arms around it. He was soaked but seemed oblivious. He called out to anyone who would listen. I think he was saying that he was tasting the water of life. The colors represent the sun, the water in the fountain, his brown coat, and the red scarf tied around his neck."

Liam wasn't sure if time was flying or standing still, but after a good hour, Helen grew quiet. She held up her hand as if gently stopping traffic.

"I almost forgot. I promised you dessert."

Liam cocked his head. "Oh, don't worry about that. I'm full."

Helen smiled. "Oh, I don't think you're full yet. Follow me." She led him back through the living room toward the dining room. "Just a minute. Let me get something." She ducked into the kitchen and returned with a bottle and two glasses. "I told you I had a good Benedictine."

He was perplexed as she walked right past the dining room. She turned down a hallway and motioned for him to come along. "This way, please...." She led him to her bedroom, also candle-filled. "It's dessert time."

Liam noticed a serving cart with five silver cloches on it. "Oh wow. What's for dessert?"

158

"I thought you'd enjoy… my pie."

She poured two glasses of the Benedictine, handed one to him, and then lifted four of the cloches to reveal bowls overflowing with strawberry pie filling, banana cream, butterscotch, and whipped cream.

"They're deconstructed. So you can have them just as you like."

"I've gotta say, that's quite a spread."

"Oh… you haven't seen my spread yet. Watch and learn."

She slowly unbuttoned her blouse, then Liam's shirt. She put her arms around him. He downed the liqueur in a single gulp, and let out a deep, half-grunted, "Oh my God!".

"Patience, love. Patience." She took off her blouse. "Now, is there something on the cart that interests you?"

"Yeah, but there's no dishes, or serving spoons."

"Hmm…. Take off your shirt."

He did. Helen scooped up a handful of whipped cream and spread it on his chest with her fingers. She added some butterscotch. "I think this looks delicious." She started licking the cream and butterscotch off, stopping to kiss him. "Get my drift?"

"I think I might be catching on." Liam leaped into action, grabbing handfuls of banana cream and strawberry filling, spreading them on her shoulders and licking them off, first slowly then more aggressively. She sighed and slipped out of her bra. He lost all control as his hands scooped up whipped cream and butterscotch, eagerly covering her breasts and diving in.

Helen touched his lips with her finger. "I think maybe we need some more alcohol. Do you agree?"

As she poured the Benedictine, Liam dropped the rest of his clothes, standing naked before her. She groaned as she eyed him up and down. "Ohhhh…" She moved in and touched him. "Oh my… I can see you're up—for my final culinary event."

"Oh, I'm up all right."

"You're sure you're up?"

"Oh, yes.   What's on your palette for my final stroke?"

She smacked her lips and lifted the final cloche.

"Fondue."

24

"Well, I had one helluva night, my friend. Did you have a good time too?" Lady stared at Liam from the passenger seat, panting. "I'll take that as a yes. Good for you!" As they pulled up to the house, he noticed a figure moving toward him—Mrs. Sommers. Holding out a package and moving a little too quickly. She slipped on a patch of ice and went sprawling face-first into a mound of snow. She let out an "oof" sound as she hit, still with a death grip on the package.

"Are you okay, Mrs. Sommers?"

She shoved the package at him. "I'm pretty sure this is important. It's from New York."

Liam dusted her off, then glanced at the package. It had Harold Simon's return address. The first round of edits to his manuscript. It had been opened and resealed with tape. He looked at Mrs. Sommers. "Did you do this?"

"Well, I might have accidentally opened it. I wanted to make sure it wasn't a bomb. It was just papers, but they had all kinds of markings on them."

Liam looked at the package, then at her.

"I thought it was really interesting!"

His eyes narrowed. "You read it?"

"I only peeked a little."

"Jesus Christ! It's confidential. Says so right on the package."

"Why I would never tell a soul. No sirree. I wouldn't do that."

"I know where you live."

The phone was ringing when he walked into the house. He set the package on the kitchen table. As he was reaching for the phone, Lady bolted out the open door. He ran after her. "Lady... Stay!" She stopped and turned around. He could swear she was laughing. He walked up to

161

her but at the last second, she took off. The game was on. He chased her around the yard, finally catching her. When he got back inside, the red light was flashing on the answering machine.

"Liam. It's Helen. I just wanted to see if you were home yet. Actually, I wanted to hear your voice, but I guess that'll have to wait. I so enjoyed last night— I hope you did too. Call me when you get a chance? Bye now."

He dialed her back, but she was already gone.

Damn.

He knew she had a full day at school, so he'd likely missed his chance. "Helen. Liam here. Yeah, I'm home. Here's my voice." He tried to sound cheery, to mask his disappointment. "Oh, I had a spectacular night. Can't wait to see you again!"

God, I'm pathetic. Maybe I should call back and try again. No. No do-overs you idiot.

Liam felt something wet on his arm. He shook it off, but whatever it was came right back. Lady was standing next to him with a slobbery tennis ball in her mouth. "Nope. Not gonna happen."

He opened the badly re-taped package.

Jesus. What the hell Harold? What a fucking mess.

His irritation grew as he started to read the comments. He lit a cigarette and tried to calm down. The phone rang, this time a welcome diversion. Momentarily.

"Boss, you've gotta help me." Liam could hear the agitation in Marianne's voice.

"What's the problem and why can't it wait?" He heard a loud sound in the background, a rasping SPLOOF like an out-of-control Bronx cheer. "Dear Jesus, what was that?"

"Vera."

"What—does she have the croup?"

"Nope. It's her horn."

162

"What?"

"She's blowing a hunting horn."

"Why?"

"Apparently she's trying to get my attention."

"Put her on. Now."

He could hear a muffled discussion. Finally, Vera picked up.

"Hello Mr. O'Connor. How are you?"

"Vera. What the fuck are you doing?"

"Marianne never picks up the intercom when I ring her. So I got this horn. I blow it, and she comes to my office to tell me to shut up. Then I have her and she has to speak with me."

"Oh my God, Vera. Put Marianne back on."

After a few moments, Marianne picked up. "Did you make her stop?"

"Oh hell no. Just ignore it."

"That's it? That's all you got?"

"Pretty much. I'm sure it's just a phase. It'll pass."

"Thanks for nothing."

"You're welcome."

**

After he hung up, Liam grabbed a carton of cigarettes and started a page-by-page review of Harold's comments that consumed most of the day and evening. When he finally looked up it was nine o'clock. He hadn't planned to wait this long to call Helen. He dialed her number. It went to her answering machine.

Where the hell is she? She should've been home from school hours ago. Wait. That little fucker Stephen. Shit! He's "showing her the campus". Goddammit.

163

"Um. Hi Helen. Please call me when you can. I mean if you can. I mean—you know..... I miss your voice!"

Oh no! I didn't say who I was.

Liam went back to reading Harold's markup but had difficulty concentrating. Where was she? What was going on? He didn't trust that Stephen, and Helen seemed to like the asshole.

They're together... Goddamn it, they're together. I'll bet he shows up every single day. How can I compete with that?

His mind conjured up an image—Stephen ushering Helen around an art museum, making bullshit charming comments when she points out a piece.

Oh my God, they're holding hands.

He shook it off. Realizing he wasn't going to be productive, he went to bed, tossing and turning, his stomach churning with distress. Ultimately, with or without trying, he slept. A deep sleep, broken only by the sound of the.... what was it...the phone ringing.

Fuck!

It was light outside. He took off for the kitchen and picked up. "Hello?"

Helen's voice was on the other end. "Are you okay? You sound out of breath."

"No, no.... I just got up.'

"I'm so sorry. I'm embarrassed to say I fell asleep at eight last night. I think our date might've had something to do with that. Plus, I had a full day of boring faculty meetings. So much process and procedure. I slept right through your call and your message. In fact, I didn't even see that I had a message until I got up this morning. Anyway, enough about me—how are you? How was your day yesterday? And how's your dog? Has she eaten anything interesting lately?"

"Oh me? It was pretty routine. A little drama at the store. I got the first round of edits on my book."

"You got edits? I thought you told me it would take a lot longer?"

"Apparently my editor was interested enough in the manuscript to push it ahead of some others. He still butchered it. I've got a lot of work to do. Or, more importantly, I've got to figure out how much of what he did I can even agree to. This book is my child."

"Oh, I get it. My paintings are all my children. But like children, some are good, some are bad, and some are awful. I still love them all. I just have to come to grips with their flaws."

"Are you saying my work's flawed? You wound me to the core, Ms. Woodson."

"Yeah, yeah. You're such a frail flower, O'Connor. You haven't shared it with me, so I don't know. But I do know you're a great writer, so there's that."

Liam figured he might as well go for it. "So when do I get to see you again?"

"Does this mean you liked my… pie?"

"Why yes I did."

"Well in that case, let me check my busy calendar."

"This offer won't last long. First come, first served."

"So… it seems my calendar is open Saturday night. Does that work for you, sir?"

"Let me think it over… Yes."

"Okay then. Let me put this in my book. Shall I use a pencil or pen?"

"A promise from Liam O'Connor is unbreakable."

"Pencil it is."

25

Liam walked into Sharon's office, head high and smiling. Sharon did a double take. "What have we here? Something you want to share?"

Liam cocked his head and put his hand on his chest. "Wouldn't you like to know?"

Sharon smiled. "Oh, I don't really care. You're paying me either way. But if you do want to share, that's certainly fine."

"I saw Helen."

Sharon didn't react.

"I said, I saw Helen."

"Go on."

"I saw her, and I didn't mess up. Well, that's not true. I did mess up, but then I didn't."

Sharon had put on her reading glasses to take notes. She peered at him over them. "Wait. Did you or didn't you mess up? And if you did, how'd that happen?"

The wheels were spinning in Liam's head as he tried to put together a sequence of coherent thoughts. In the end, he just said the first things that came into his mind. "Well, I went to help her move in. Did I tell you she called to ask me to help? Anyway, I went to help her move in, and it all went very well until my dog ate one of her paintings, and…"

"Hold up. Your dog ate a painting. You want to explain that for me?"

"Well, we worked very well together, but then we went out to dinner. When we came back, Lady had eaten one of Helen's paintings, and she was so upset we had to leave."

Sharon wrote something. "I'd have to say that's understandable. How did that make you feel?"

166

"Like shit. It made me feel like shit. We both came home with our tails between our legs. I figured I had blown what could have been the first great relationship I've had in years. I gave up, went into a deep funk."

"The same funk as with Sylvia?"

Liam glared. "Sylvia was nothing. Don't ever compare her to Helen."

Sharon scribbled a few sentences and then looked up. "That sounds like you may be serious about Helen. Am I right?"

Liam was so eager to spill his news that his leg started to shake. "Okay, so after two days in the tank, I finally got to talk to Helen, and it was all good."

"So did or didn't your dog eat her art?"

"You see, that's the thing. Lady ate the art, but she thought about it and decided it was just an unfortunate accident. Well, at least she didn't like the painting Lady ate. And she invited me back. Without Lady, at least this time. Anyway, we had a date. She cooked for me. A masterpiece. Dammit Sharon, she's good. She can do anything."

"Anything?"

"Yes, damn near anything."

"I hesitate to ask, but how was the rest of the evening?"

"It was spectacular!"

"And by spectacular, you mean… ."

"Oh yes. That's EXACTLY what I mean. The most incredible night of …. ."

"I get the picture. So, how'd that make you feel?"

"I really like this woman."

Sharon smiled. "That's what I was waiting to hear. Tell me, do you think she's the real thing, or are you just projecting some ideal on her that she can't live up to?"

"No. I haven't known her long, but my intuition is that she's a wonderful woman. Not like any I've been with before."

167

Sharon took more notes. "I'm not going to comment on your intuition. We know how that's operated in the past. But saying she's unlike anyone you've known before is a big statement. I want to make sure it's realistic."

"I get all that. But I'd like you to give me the benefit of the doubt. Yeah, I've messed up a lot, and you've seen most all of it. But when I tell you this woman's different, I'd like you to give me that."

Sharon set her pen down and closed her notebook. "You've got a deal. I couldn't be happier for you. Of course you know there's a 'but' involved. That's what I do. So here goes: Just keep fully aware of what's going on around you. Let your eyes and ears be your guide, not your imagination. It's your imagination that gets you in trouble with women. Think. Think before you assume anything, good or bad. Can you promise me you'll do that?"

"Of course I'll do that. I always do."

Sharon rolled her eyes. "No you don't 'always do' that. Try again."

Liam knew he was beat. "I promise."

***

Liam left Sharon's office more contrite than when he walked in. It occurred to him that she was trying to make sure he didn't go off half-cocked. She hadn't questioned anything about the genuineness of his experiences with Helen. He decided to head over to the store. By the time he got there, his mood was back in the clouds. It was too early to say he was in love, but oh man. What a night, and what a woman. He couldn't wait for Saturday. Opening the door, he saw Marianne at the counter, as usual. As he walked toward her, he heard a shriek. At least he thought it was a shriek, or was it more a high-pitched wail? There it was again, and it was getting closer.

"OOOOOOOOOOOOH……. IT'S HIM! HE'S HERE!"

A slightly built young man in a purple sweatshirt and tight pants was trotting through the store with his arms held high. He was headed straight toward Liam, but Marianne stepped out from behind the counter and almost tackled him. The voice continued, more subdued but just as excited.

"It's him, Marianne. What should I say? What should I do? I think I have the vapors… ."

Marianne stopped him in his path. "Now we talked about this, didn't we? You have to use your inside voice. Take a breath. No, a deep breath, not a pant. That's better. Now, I think you should go to the back of the store and compose yourself."

The young man was nodding but kept panting. Finally, Marianne turned him around and gave him a little push. He moved out of sight. Liam caught up to Marianne.

"Just who and what the hell was that?"

Marianne spoke in a calm voice, as if absolutely nothing had happened. "That. That's just Jeremy."

"Jeremy who?"

"Jeremy, your new employee."

"What do you mean, my new employee? Who the hell hired him?"

"I did. Those losers you hired were useless. So I made a decision."

Liam stood silent. When he spoke, it was about as measured as he could manage. "You made a decision. Who gave you the authority to make a decision?"

"Sometimes you just have to do what's best for your employer, whether he knows it or not."

"Who is this Jeremy guy? I don't want to be critical, but he's a bit odd, and did he shriek? What was that all about?"

"Well, I'll admit he's a bit eccentric, but in fairness he was very excited at the prospect of meeting you."

169

"He shrieked, Marianne. He shrieked."

"Well, yes. We're working on that. But I think he really does have some skills, and he takes direction without complaining."

"Where did you find him?"

"It's more like he found me, or rather us. I met him at a party. Let's just say my feelings about him are positive. And I have to say he was very excited at the prospect of working for you."

"So he's read my book?"

"No, not exactly. He saw your picture on the back cover."

"What does that have to do with anything?"

"I believe his exact words were: 'Oooo... he's hot!'".

"Marianne... ." Liam was trying to formulate an appropriate response when he heard, in nightmarish sequence, Vera's horn, followed by yet another shriek from Jeremy.

"OOOOOOOOOOH! What was that?"

Liam turned toward the back of the store and bellowed. "YOU TWO! SHUT UP!" He turned back to face Marianne, but she was already striding back to the counter.

Just as Liam walked into his office, Marianne rang on the intercom.

"Liam, there's a young lady on line one for you."

"What do you mean, 'young lady'?"

"Just pick it up, Boss."

Liam answered the line. 'Hello?"

"YOU PROMISED TO TELL ME A STORY!"

"Oh my goodness. Is that you Sara?"

"STORY. NOW."

"Well okay then. Let me see." Liam had nothing, but knew she wasn't going to accept that. He was going to have to pull one out of his ass.

170

"There once was a beautiful little girl whose parents loved her very much."

"WHAT WAS HER NAME?"

"Well, I believe it was… Sara."

"THAT'S MY NAME!"

"Why yes, it is. Anyway, her parents decided one day to give her a very special present."

"WHAT WAS IT?"

"It was… a shiny red bicycle."

"NO!"

"What? Why?"

"TOO DANGEROUS. SARA WILL GET HURT."

"Oh, I don't know about that. But maybe they didn't give her a bicycle after all. Maybe it was…a…uh…kitten."

"NO! SARA'S ALLERGIC TO KITTENS."

This was going downhill fast. Liam searched for something easy and noncontroversial. "Okay. Here you go. They gave her a piece of bubble gum."

"BUBBLE GUM ROTS YOUR TEETH!"

Liam heard Sara set the phone down. She must have walked away. He waited for a few minutes, figuring she would return. Finally, Susan's voice, laughing.

"That didn't go so well! But we were calling for two reasons. She wanted a story, but maybe more importantly Jack and I thought we'd pop down with Sara to see you this weekend. We can spend some quality time together. She's really excited about it. We could come in on Saturday and stay until Sunday."

Liam closed his eyes.

Crap.

"Wow. That would be a lot of fun, but I'm not going to be here. I'm going to Madison for the weekend."

"Even better! We could join you there. More things to do. We'd love that!"

"Um… oh… No. You see, I already have plans. In fact, I have a date. I'm so sorry."

171

"Oh, Liam. I'm the one who should be sorry. I…or rather we… should never have presumed. Sara will be disappointed, but we'll just have to tell her we can't go."

"Do you want me to explain it to her?"

"No. We're going to have to handle that." All the mirth had left her voice.

"Maybe another time?"

"Sure. Another time. Thanks Liam. Talk to you soon."

"I can't believe you turned them down." Marianne was standing in his doorway.

"Dammit Marianne. Were you eavesdropping? What the hell?"

"I couldn't help but overhear."

"Yeah, since you were standing two feet away. Anyway, I feel awful. Don't make it worse."

A voice came from the hallway, sounding like a mantra. "Marianne. Marianne. Marianne."

Marianne turned in the direction of the voice. "Yes, Jeremy. What is it?"

"Yoo hoo—Marianne. What shall I call…you know."

"What?"

A figure appeared in the doorway. A figure pointing at Liam. "You know… Him."

"Marianne… why is he pointing at me?" Liam was struggling to keep up.

"I think Jeremy wants to know how to address you."

Liam started to say "Mr. O'Connor", just as Marianne said "Liam, of course."

Jeremy, with a confused look, nodded. "Soooooo… 'Mister Liam O'Connor'.

Liam dropped his head into his hands. "God save me."

26

The moment Liam had fantasized about was coming to pass. Helen opened the door and he swept her into his arms. As he did, he happened to glance over her shoulder. Stephen sitting on the sofa

Christ!!! What the fuck?

"Liam, Stephen stopped by to chat."

Liam managed to keep his composure. "Well, well, well. So good to see you Stephen."

Stephen was cradling a glass of wine. "Yes, Helen and I have been looking at some great pictures of campus and planning our time together to explore it. We think it'll be swell."

"Oh really? 'Swell?' How charming."

Fucking asshole.

Liam stepped closer to Stephen as Helen moved in between them.

"So Stephen, I think I told you I had plans for tonight. It was very nice of you to stop by, but Liam and I are heading out now."

"That's okay. I can hang here and we can continue our chat when you get home."

Liam was fuming.

Oh you little piece of shit.

Helen looked at Liam. "Let me just grab my coat. What time did you say our reservation is?" She winked.

It took Liam a moment, but it dawned on him. "Right. The reservation is in twenty minutes. We're going to have to hustle if we're going to get there on time."

Stephen smiled. "I'll just make myself at home."

Helen turned. "I'm sorry Stephen, but I'm afraid that won't work. Another time?"

"Well, then, I'll just be going. I really enjoyed our time together, Helen. I'm really looking forward to all the adventures we will have—and do give some thought to that conference in Chicago. It'll be a hoot to be there—" He glared at Liam and smirked. "—together." He handed her his wine glass and ambled toward the door. He didn't take his eyes off Liam until he was out in the hallway.

Helen looked at Liam and smiled. "So, Mr. O'Connor… What have you planned for us tonight?"

"Um… Oh…."

"Thought so. Well, I made a reservation. We'd better get going if we're going to make it on time."

"Doggone it, I was going to do that. It just got away from me."

"I'll bet it did. But let's go."

As they left the house, Liam looked up and saw a Gatsby-like figure standing in the dark shadows of the second story window, staring as if at the green light on Daisy's dock. Liam locked his eyes on the figure and made a slitting motion across his throat.

***

With lots of teak, mahogany and glass, the restaurant was something to behold. Liam was impressed.

"Wow Helen. You did well."

She took his arm as they followed the maître d' to their table. "Only the best for my man."

When they were seated, Liam looked at Helen and, reaching across the table, took her hands in his. "This is incredible. Ms. Woodson, you never cease to amaze."

A young woman appeared at their side. "Good evening and welcome. I'll be your server. Would you like a bottle of water to start?"

Just as Liam was turning to answer, the young woman fixed her eyes on Helen.

"Oh my God. You're Professor Woodson! I can't believe it. I'm in awe of your work."

Helen smiled. "Why thank you, Stephanie."

The young woman gasped and put her hand to her chest. "Wow! You know my name! That's so special."

Helen pointed at her blouse. "Name tag."

"Oh. Of course. I'm so embarrassed."

"No, no. Don't be. It's good to meet you. I'm still getting to know names."

Trying to put things back on track, Liam looked up at Stephanie. "May I order a bottle of wine?"

Helen cut him off. "Stephanie. Could you ask the sommelier to stop by?"

As Stephanie left to fetch the sommelier, Helen touched his hand. "I think maybe I should select the wine this time."

Liam, chagrined, nodded.

She continued. "What's our budget tonight?"

"The sky's the limit!"

"No. I don't think so. Apparently, you haven't looked at the list. Can we do, say, fifty?"

Liam was relieved she hadn't accepted his bullshit response. "I think that would be fine."

The sommelier arrived, and Helen made a selection.

"Very good, Ma'am."

Liam looked at Helen and narrowed his eyes. "Tell me how you knew I wouldn't have made reservations."

"Let's just say I had a hunch. Besides, you're in my town now. When we're in your town, you can make the selections."

Liam realized two things in that moment. First, there was no point in trying to bullshit her. Second, she was thinking about coming to visit him.

"When we're in your town…"

This was starting to feel like a relationship, and it felt good. He could let his guard down. Even make fun of himself. Her jabs seemed to be in jest, not meant to inflict pain. He looked into her eyes. "You do know that you're

175

not going to see places like this where I live. It's all pretty much low key. More like low life."

"I don't believe that. I don't think you would've lasted this long in a low life place. You have too much class, even if you pretend you don't."

"You know, when you come to *my* town, I'll show you a spectacular time."

"So, Mr. Bestseller… What makes you think tonight isn't going to be a spectacular time?"

***

It was snowing heavily by the time they got to Helen's flat. It was clear there was a storm bearing down on Madison. She looked at him. "I'm assuming you ordered this snow so you'd get to stay over, right?"

Liam laughed. "You got me on that one. I didn't think you'd notice."

"Well, it worked. Come on in."

Once they were in her flat, Liam helped Helen out of her coat, then grabbed her and pulled her close. "Can we make out now?"

She gave in and embraced him. A passionate…. No, a very passionate…kiss followed, full-on, tongues probing deep. No turning back, and nothing could stop him. Nothing but a loud knock on the door.

The moment broken, Helen pulled away. "Can you get that? I want to hang our coats up."

Liam was almost beside himself. He walked over to the door and opened it. Stephen.

Really? What the fuck?

"What the hell do you want?"

"Get Helen. I need to speak with her."

"She told you earlier we were going out. Didn't you get the hint?"

"Oh come on. I'm sure you've got to go home now. Please do. But in the meantime, tell her I'm here. She'll want to see me."

Liam went off like a firecracker. "Listen, you little prick. She told you she had plans. I happen to be those plans, as you can plainly see. If she wanted you around, she would've asked you to join us. But she didn't, did she? She told you to leave hours ago, and yet here you are again. I'm going to count to three, and you'd better be out of my sight before I get there. Do you understand?"

"I said I needed to speak with Helen." He was holding a small canvas, which Liam instantly recognized to be one of Helen's.

Shit!

"Give me that…" Liam grabbed it, but Stephen was clutching it even harder, smirking.

"She said she'd personalize it for me."

Liam exploded. "One."

Stephen didn't move.

"Two."

Again, no motion, but he was starting to tremble.

"Did you hear me, fucker? Three." Liam raised his fist.

Stephen bolted from the door and walked quickly up the stairs, still clutching the canvas.

"Who was that?" Helen walked back into the room.

"Oh, no one. Wrong address."

Helen turned Liam around to face her. "You do know he's my neighbor, don't you? I try to be cordial with all of them."

"Cordial enough to give him a painting?"

"What—are you jealous?"

She had struck paydirt, but Liam wasn't about to admit anything. "Of course not. Jealous of that nerd?"

"Well, since you're not jealous, there's no reason to worry about what I give him."

177

Liam bit his tongue. She had him. For now…

Still flush from the combination of alcohol, anger and lust, Liam asked Helen if she would like him to build a fire in her fireplace.

"Should I trust you with fire?"

He puffed up his chest. "Lady, I am fire. Watch me burn."

She pretended to swoon. "Ooooo, be still my beating heart!"

Liam piled on some logs and soon had a respectable blaze going. "I told you I was hot."

Helen grabbed him and pulled him close. "You didn't need to tell me. I could feel it. I think it's catching. Now I'm hot too."

27

Liam could see through the front window that Marianne and Jeremy were engaged in an animated conversation. Their arms were flailing about as they exchanged gestures of exasperation. He nearly turned around, but then figured he might be able to slide by them unnoticed. Walking in with his eyes focused on the back of the store, he nearly made it. Nearly.

"Where do you think you're going?" Marianne's voice was firm and unyielding.

Shit. She noticed.

He tried to deflect. "Uh.... I didn't want to interrupt."

Jeremy started to speak, but Marianne clapped her hand over his mouth. Staring at Jeremy, she spoke in a monotone, as if to the wall. "Liam. Jeremy has something he needs to tell you. Will you listen without going off?"

Liam stumbled on his response. "What makes you think I'll go off?"

Marianne took her hand off Jeremy's mouth. "Speak."

"Well, I've been very busy the last couple of days. I've been looking over the store, and I noticed that it was really, well, drab. If you don't mind my saying so. Also, the way you put the books on the shelves makes no sense. I don't know how anyone could find anything. Sooooo.... I had a great idea I knew you would just love."

Marianne cut him off. "Mr. Design here took it upon himself to rearrange all the books in the fiction section. By color."

Liam's mouth dropped as his eyes moved over to the shelves. Sure enough, what he saw was a sea of colors, flowing from reds to yellows to oranges to greens to blues. He closed his eyes and reopened them, hoping it wasn't so.

"What the fuck?"

Jeremy beamed with pride. "Isn't it just wonderful? So harmonious, and yet so vivid. I think it just speaks....."

Marianne put her hand over his mouth again. "You're not going to get mad now, are you Liam?" She stared Liam down, but to no avail.

"Jesus Christ. What the fuck were you thinking Jeremy? Have you ever bought a book? Borrowed one from a library? For God's sake, have you even ever read one?" He turned to Marianne. "Fix this, goddammit."

Jeremy tried to speak but Marianne held her hand even harder on his mouth. With her free hand, she nudged Liam toward his office. "Please go. I'm sure you have more important things on your mind. I'm certain Jeremy will have this restored in no time."

As soon as Liam sat down in his office, there was a knock at the door. He heard the aerosol spray before he saw Vera. She was standing, arm stretched out, spraying herself and the hallway at the same time.

"May I come in, Mr. O'Connor?"

"Sure. Why not?" He didn't see how this day could get any stranger.

Vera sat down right on top of a stack of files. He cradled his forehead in his hands and let his face fall to the desktop.

"What can I do for you Vera?" The smell was overwhelming, so he hoped this would be a quick conversation.

"I've been looking at the ledger books, and I think you're missing ways to increase our bottom line. It's all a matter of cost management, you know."

"Excuse me Vera, but what the hell are you talking about?"

"If you'll permit me, I'll explain."

"Go ahead. Might's well."

Vera walked closer and tried to hand him a poster-size piece of cardboard with numbers crudely written in various colors. His head was still on the desk, and he didn't see what she was doing. She poked him in the head with the cardboard. He looked up with the weary expression of someone who had just had his last reason to live taken away. "What the hell is this, Vera?"

"It shows your revenue and your expenses for the past six months. As you will note, your expenses are rather high, compared to your revenue. This is not good."

"So?"

Vera stopped and sprayed a bit more deodorant on herself. Apparently satisfied, she spoke. "So, I think I can save you quite a bit on your expenses. I would like you to authorize me to implement a plan that will, if I do say so myself, make us a lot more money."

"'Us', you say? Who the hell is 'us'?"

"Well, I suppose you could think of it as 'you'."

"Thank you. Go on."

"Will you give me authority?"

"To do what?"

Vera went to pound the desk with her fist but missed and swung at the air. "To save you money!" She smiled and her head bobbed in self-delight.

At this point, Liam just wanted to get her out of his office. "Okay. You've got it." He had absolutely no idea what he had just agreed to, but it seemed to satisfy her.

As he sat at his desk, reeling from all that had just gone down in the short time since he had walked into the store, the phone rang. He waited for someone to pick it up, but it just kept ringing.

Dammit.

Finally, he answered it. The voice on the other end sounded surprised.

"Liam. It's Harold. Is there something wrong over there? You never pick up. "

"No, no…it seems my crack staff is occupied with more important tasks."

Harold, obviously disinterested, continued. "Where are you on turning my edits? We need to keep this moving."

"Christ, Harold, if you hadn't made such a train-wreck out of my work, I could've had it back to you by now."

"Just tell me when I can expect a revised draft."

"Two days."

"Really Liam? Is this the game we're going to play?"

"Of course not. You'll get it when I finish it."

"Right. Just keep in mind that I've got a pile of other works in progress on my desk. I can't guarantee I'll be able to give you any kind of priority if you get too far behind."

Liam mumbled something.

"What was that?"

"I said I'll see what I can do."

"Good. I'll look for your package. Have a great day."

Liam heard a click. Just like that, Harold was gone. As he was thinking about what he should've said to Harold, the awful sound of Vera's horn rang out.

Marianne's voice was loud and clear. "Not a chance! You want something, you come out here. I'm busy."

The horn sounded again. Shaking his head in resignation, Liam stepped into the hallway. "Ladies! Ladies! Either settle down or take it outside. Your choice."

Vera stepped out of her office, looked around, and walked back in, closing the door behind her.

Marianne held her arms up in victory. "Hey Liam. Can you come over here?"

Over at the fiction section, chaos reigned. As Liam approached, he saw Jeremy sitting on the floor, surrounded by a sea of books. The shelves were nearly empty. Marianne stood over him. "Alphabetical order, Jeremy. Alphabetical order." She picked up a book, and pointed to the author's last name.

182

"But I don't think that works, Marianne." Jeremy picked up two books with the same color spines, put them together and pointed. "See how tasteful this is? So much better."

"Not a chance, Jeremy."

Defeated, Jeremy placed the book on the shelves in the correct position. So far, there were about twenty books restored to their proper locations.

Marianne looked at Liam and smiled. "I think we're making real progress here."

"Did you want something?"

Marianne pulled Jeremy, who by now was standing next to the shelves, over to her. "The boys are having an event and they would like you to come. Jeremy, would you like to tell Liam about it?"

Liam gave her a dark look. She looked back with a glance that said "Don't you dare".

"My roomies and I are having a gala Valentine's party Saturday night. We'd absolutely love it if you would honor us with your presence!"

Still staring at Marianne, Liam said nothing.

"So what do you say, Liam?"

"Jeremy, it's not Valentine's Day. And I can't because I have plans."

Jeremy looked at Marianne in desperation.

She faced off with Liam. "The boys believe every day in February should be Valentine's Day."

Jeremy nodded enthusiastically. "Oh yes! Why stop with one day of romance when you can have thirty?"

"Uh, Jeremy, twenty-eight."

"Twenty-eight what?"

"There's twenty-eight days in February."

Jeremy scrunched his face and started chanting. "Thirty days hath September, April, June—" He nodded as he mouthed a few more words. "Oh. Oopsie!"

Liam, struggling to believe the conversation, was resolute. "Whatever. But I can't be there anyway."

Marianne grabbed his arm and pulled him down the hall. "Why can't you be there? Just what plans do you have?"

Liam tried to walk away, but she blocked his path. "You don't have any plans, do you?"

"I'm planning to ask Helen to come here on Saturday. I'll be damned if I'm going to walk her into a circus."

"Look, Liam. All you have to do is show up, make an appearance and some small talk, and leave. What harm can there be? Anyway, Earl and I will be there. You'll be fine. I'd love to meet Helen."

"I don't know. I have a bad feeling about this. Look at him. What the hell?"

Now Jeremy was holding up three books, once again matching the colors of their spines and shaking his head.

Marianne resorted to pleading. "Do this for me, Liam. If I can go, you can go. It's the least you can do."

"I'll give it some thought."

"Great! I'll tell them you'll be there."

"Wait a minute…"

**

Back home, Liam's mind drifted back to the spectacular weekend he'd had with Helen. By evening he could wait no longer and called her. The phone rang for a while, and when she finally picked up, she seemed a bit out of breath. Liam was quick enough to pick up on this.

"Uh-oh. Did I catch you in the middle of something?"

Shit. She's with Stephen. I knew it!

"No, no. I just walked in the door. Long day of classes and meetings. But I'm fine. Actually, I'm better

184

now, hearing your voice. To what do I owe the pleasure? Did you forget something at my place? Or did you just miss me so much you couldn't wait to talk?"

"I was wondering if you might like to spend next weekend over here? I could pick you up Friday night."

"Unfortunately, you can't."

"Goddamn it. Are you with Stephen?"

There! It's in the open now.

"What? No. I agreed to have dinner Friday with the department chair and a couple of other faculty members. Not my first choice, but academic politics being what they are, I really couldn't say no. How about I drive over Saturday afternoon? I have some errands to run, but I could be there by about five."

Liam was suspicious, but at least he got Saturday night out of it.

"Five works."

Helen's voice reflected a smile he couldn't see. "So, stud—What do you have planned for me?"

"Well, first we can catch dinner at my usual restaurant. It's not in the same class, or for that matter the same universe, as what you took me to in Madison, but it's passable."

"A great endorsement."

"I knew you'd figure it out for yourself, so why not tell you in advance? But the company will be great."

"Of course! Do go on. What's next? I mean, after the mediocre meal and great company?"

"Well now. Um. Oh... . There's this party I agreed to stop by. It'll only take a few minutes. Say hi and move on."

"Is it a special occasion? Tell me more!"

"Um. It's a Valentine's party."

Silence.

"Liam? It's not Valentine's Day."

"Yes, I know. I know. It's not easy to explain, but just go with me on this. I swear we won't have to be there long."

"Sounds like it might be fun. Kind of mysterious."

"You have no idea."

"So. Who'll be there?"

He mumbled. "Don't know."

"What? I didn't catch that. Who?"

"I have no idea who'll be there. It's at a new employee's house. He and his two roommates. I suspect it might be a bit strange. I think they're inviting anyone who will come. And by 'anyone', I mean *anyone*."

"I love that. Don't you?"

"If you only knew."

28

It's a Gala Valentine Party!
Come one, come all!
Bring your Sweetie!
8:00 to ?

Handbills were posted all over town. They were on colored paper, with bright glitter-covered lettering. Jeremy's address was below, together with a fringe of tear-offs with a phone number at the bottom, none removed. Liam shook his head in amazement.

Arriving at the store, he saw Jeremy standing amidst books scattered on the floor in the fiction section. Picking them up one at a time, he looked at each, shook his head, and dropped it back to the floor. Marianne was standing off to the side. Liam could see her mouth moving but couldn't make out what she was saying. He took a deep breath and opened the door. Marianne saw him and ran over, trying hard to keep his focus away from Jeremy.

"It's about time you showed your face here."

"I see you have everything under control."

"He says the alphabet is too exhausting, and still insists color coding is the way to go."

Liam looked at her with mock seriousness. "He must have some good traits. After all, you hired him."

Marianne kicked him in the shin.

"Ow! That was uncalled for."

"You want me to do it again?"

"No, no. Listen, I'm going to be out with Helen on Saturday night, and against my better judgment we're going to stop by the party. I would kinda like to know what to expect. Do you think we could get him to tell us?"

"I have no idea. Let's ask."

Jeremy saw them coming. "Liam! I'm so glad you're here. Can you help me out? This alphabetic order thing that Marianne simply insists on is too, too much work. Will you make her stop?"

Liam's eyes caught Marianne's. They stared at each other in disbelief. Liam began. "Jeremy. I'm bringing my lady friend to your party."

Jeremy clapped his hands. "Yay! You're both in for a treat!"

Marianne stepped between them. "So, Jeremy. Let's start with food and drink. What do you plan to serve?"

"We….. and you're going to love this so much… we're going to be serving up something very special! Are you ready for this?"

Liam started to walk away, but Marianne again stepped in the way. "Now Liam, let Jeremy tell you his surprise." She looked at Jeremy. "I don't know. Are we?"

"Oh yes, I think you are. We're thinking we're going to have… wine spritzers! And pigs in a blanket!"

Marianne spoke before Liam could react. "Uh. Jeremy. That's very nice, but I think maybe your guests might want something else. As well. Yes, as well." She looked at Liam. "Don't you think their guests might want something else to go with their spritzers and hot dogs?"

Liam grunted. Marianne didn't skip a beat. "So how about this? I'll make up some additional appetizers. Liam, why don't you stop and pick up a keg on your way?" Liam started to object, but Marianne shot him a look that put an end to that.

Jeremy was joyfully standing by. "Oooooh! Now, why didn't we think of beer? Maybe one or two of our guests might prefer it to a nice spritzer."

Liam was still staring, by now with his mouth open. Marianne saved him again. "Also, can you tell me how many guests you're expecting?"

"Well, I don't know. We've put up posters all over town—have ya seen them? They're marvelous. So bright, so sparkly… . Anyway, I think we could have *hundreds* of people."

Liam pulled Marianne aside. "Dear Jesus. Do you actually believe anyone's gonna show up? Have you seen those posters?"

"Yep. I've seen them. I'm sure there'll be enough people there that you'll be able to blend in and make a safe getaway after not too long."

Liam pointed his finger in her face. "You. You're responsible for getting me into this. You'd better figure out how to get me back out."

Marianne pushed his finger aside. "Look. You can be the center of attention. You love that—admit it." Laughing, she walked away.

Just as Liam got settled at his desk, the phone rang. This time Marianne picked up.

"Owl's Eyes. Whooooooo's there?"

There it was. His worst nightmare, made even worse when Marianne called back to him. "Liam! Harold Simon on Line One!"

Arghhhhhhh.

Taking a deep breath, he picked up. "Hello Harold. What can I do for you? Didn't we just talk a few days ago? Didn't I tell you I was working on it?"

"I had a thought this morning. How long's it been since you were here? In New York? My office? Why don't you come in, say, Monday morning? I think if we sit down together and roll up our sleeves, we can get the next draft well underway."

Liam was shocked and skeptical. "Harold. Are you saying you miss me, or that you don't trust me to do this on my own?"

"Neither. But I do know that we need to turn this one if we're going to stay on schedule. And I'm willing to sit face-to-face with you to get that done."

"Let's say I do. If I fly into LaGuardia, I can probably get to your office by ten. How much time are you willing to give me?"

"I can give you the day, and into the evening if needed. If you're willing to stay over, we can meet again Tuesday morning and try to wrap up what we can. Does that make sense?"

Liam decided to push his luck. "I fly first class."

"That's fine, Liam. I'll have my secretary call you and set it up. Your usual demand for a hotel?"

"Four stars. You know the drill."

Leaning back in his chair, Liam let his mind wander. It would be good to be back in the bigs. He called out. "Marianne! Can you come here?"

Marianne walked in. "What's up Boss?"

"I'm off to New York Monday morning. I'll be back in town Tuesday night. Can you handle the store while I'm gone?"

Marianne stifled a laugh. "Sure. I think I can handle that."

"I'm going to have to pull some supplies together. Can you bring me a box of pens and a couple of legal pads?"

"No."

"What do you mean, 'no'?"

"I mean no. As in, there aren't any."

"How the fuck do we have no pens or pads? It's a bookstore for god's sake."

"Vera."

"Vera?"

"She won't let us order any. She says as long as anyone has a pen, we don't need new ones. Same for the pads."

"That's stupid."

Marianne shrugged. "I believe you're the one who gave her the authority to cut costs."

Liam looked around helplessly. "JEREMY! GET YOUR ASS IN HERE!"

Jeremy came running down the hallway, nearly knocking Marianne into the wall as he flew past her. "Did I do something wrong? Liam—er—Mister Liam O'Connor, please don't fire me!"

"No, no. You're not fired. Jesus, Jeremy. And call me Liam for Christ sake. Here's a twenty. Go down the street to the drug store and get me a couple of pens and pads of paper. Can you do that?"

"You mean—you mean you want me to get you—supplies?"

"Yes, Jeremy. Can you handle that?"

"Oh yes. Yes, sir. I can do that."

"And Jeremy?"

"Yes, Liam?"

"Don't tell Vera."

Jeremy scampered out of his office. Liam peeked down the hall, and saw that he was now skipping, and singing a song.

About a half hour later, Jeremy strode in, beaming. "Here you go! Just what you asked for. And here's your change. I think it's right, but I never was so good at math."

Liam took the bag, and put the money in his pocket. The phone rang, again. Marianne buzzed him.

"It's your agent."

Liam was perplexed. He picked up the phone. "Janice! Good to hear from you. And why am I hearing from you?"

Janice spoke before the words were even out of his mouth. "So why didn't I know you're going to be in New York?"

He was taken aback. "Mostly because I didn't know myself until an hour ago. How the hell did you find out?"

"I have my ways. Don't forget that I'm your ticket."

191

"Yeah. My ticket to the nuthouse. I love you Janice but come on. Look. I'm gonna be tied up until maybe lunchtime on Tuesday. I could meet you then. In the meantime, please chill. Things are moving along. I'll call you. Okay?"

"It'd better be a good restaurant... ."

His concentration broken by Janice's call, Liam looked in the bag Jeremy brought him.

What the hell?

Three glitter ink pens, one each in green, purple and blue. Two pads of "I love you" stationery, with hearts stenciled across the top.

"JEREMY!!!" Nothing.

"JEREMY!!!" Still nothing.

Marianne showed up at his door. "Jeremy wants to know what you want."

He held up the pens and the pads.

"He thought they might cheer you up. He said it's too...."

"I know. I know. Drab. Jesus Christ Marianne. I can't use, and by God won't take, this crap to New York. Fix it."

She started to speak, but he cut her off.

"NOW."

"I'll see what I can do."

Liam reached in his pocket and pulled out the change Jeremy had given him. Two dollars and fifty-five cents. Out of twenty.

I give up.

29

"This isn't so bad. From your description I expected far worse."

"What?" Liam missed what Helen had said. He was too busy looking over her shoulder at the rogue's gallery of ex-dates gathered at The Porter House's bar. They were all staring in his direction, trying to get a good look at Helen.

"I said, this restaurant isn't bad. It's kind of quaint."

He turned to face her directly. "That's kind of you. Not exactly white tablecloth. The food's just okay. It's what we have in this burg."

An older waitress approached the table. "Hey Liam... We've missed you!" She turned to Helen and winked. "We can always tell when he has a new squeeze. He just disappears for a while. But he always comes back."

This was not going well. He was close to bolting, but Helen was smiling. The waitress toddled off to the bar. Several of the ladies closed in on her as she approached. Liam could see them glancing over as they grilled her. He shook his head. This could be a long night.

Liam returned his focus to Helen. "So. How was your dinner with the faculty?"

"It was nice. Stan, the chair, was welcoming, which was reassuring starting in a new environment."

"How about the others?"

"Apparently they couldn't make it for one reason or another, so I was the only one there."

"Wait. It was just you and this Stan person? Did you know that in advance?"

"No, I was as surprised as you are. I got there and it was a table for two. But it all worked out."

Helen reached out and squeezed his hand. "What've you been up to this week? I haven't heard from you, so I'm assuming you've been busy."

193

He smiled. "I have. I've been working on my manuscript, trying to sort through my editor's changes."

"How's that going?"

"Pretty well. I resisted at first, but I have an incentive to get through it. He asked me to come into New York on Monday. We're gonna sit down and work through it together. I'm flying out of Madison early, coming back Tuesday afternoon."

"That's great! I might even be just a bit jealous."

"Maybe next time you come with me."

"That'd be nice, but I'm pretty much full time here for the rest of this term. Maybe when you do the tour for your new bestseller."

"Very kind of you, but that all remains to be seen."

"Oh, I don't know. I have great confidence in you, sir. I've read your work. I don't think you've anything to worry about."

Liam laughed. "We'd better order dinner. I think the drinks are getting to your brain."

At some point, Liam excused himself to go to the restroom. As he was returning, he noticed Doris and Joanne had joined Helen at the table.

This can't be good.

He could overhear snippets of the conversation.

"The man's a schmuck." "Don't trust him for a moment." "He'll sweet-talk you then dump you in a heartbeat for the next young piece of ass that shows up. I know. He did it to me." "Oh, he's a bad one."

Liam noticed Helen was slowly nodding, with a bemused expression, saying nothing. He approached with his arms waving in the air.

"Be gone, evil spirits! Get thee to a nunnery. Oh, sorry, too late."

They glared at him as they slowly rose from the table and walked back to the bar. He grabbed a wine glass and held it up in their direction.

"Nunnery! Oh, would that your mothers had done so."

They flipped him off.

He looked at Helen as he sat down. "Just what the hell was that all about?"

"They wanted to warn me. They said you're a jerk, that you've dumped everyone in town. Can't keep a relationship. Not worth the time or effort."

"Well, that's sweet of them. What'd you say?"

"There seemed no point in responding. Besides, I couldn't get a word in edgewise."

"They're a piece of work, all right."

"Is there anything to it? Something I should know?"

"I think they demonstrated why I'm not with them."

"Fair enough. So is there anything you want to know about me?"

"Nothing I'm aware of, Ms. Woodson. Unless... unless there's something you want to tell me about your neighbor?"

"Stephen? Actually, he's okay. A little misdirected, but he's tolerable if you give him a chance."

"And that's all?"

"Let it go O'Connor. Who am I with?"

"Well... at the moment, the best looking, most well-read, talented guy in the bar."

"You do know that's not saying much?"

Silence.

"Just kidding, stud. Just kidding."

After dinner, Liam escorted Helen out of the restaurant. As they left, he looked over at the bar and gave a sarcastic nod and wave. He could see Joanne mouth "you son-of-a-bitch". He smiled back.

As he helped Helen into the truck, Liam dropped the next surprise on her.

"By the way, I need to stop and pick up a keg of beer."

"I don't think I even want to know, so I won't ask."
"It's a long story."

***

Jeremy's house was well lit, but there were no cars on the street.

Liam muttered. "That's curious."

"What's curious?"

"It's a party, but there aren't any cars. Are we early?"

"I don't think so. It's after nine."

As they approached the front porch, they could hear the beat of disco music. Marianne ushered them in. The music was blaring throughout the house, and there was a disco ball attached to the ceiling.

Liam looked around. "So. Where's everybody?"

Marianne seemed a little concerned. "The other guests haven't arrived yet. I'm sure they'll be here soon."

"So where are the hosts?"

"Oh, they're here. They wanted me to give them formal introductions. I think they were saving that for when there were more guests, but what the heck? They can always do it again."

She walked over to the doorway into the hall leading to the rest of the house. "Are you ready for your close-ups?"

Jeremy's voice called out. "Oh yes. I believe we are! Cue the music!"

Marianne walked to the stereo. Donna Summer rang out. Marianne cupped her hands around her mouth and started the announcements.

"First up, let me introduce you to the one, the only— Jeremy!"

They could hear footsteps coming down the hallway. Jeremy strutted in wearing tight white leather pants, a sequined red shirt, and a gold lame beret. He danced around

196

the room, stopping next to Marianne and dropping to one knee, arm outstretched toward Liam and Helen. Helen applauded and whistled. Liam looked at the ceiling.

Marianne returned to the stereo and the music segued to flamenco guitar. Marianne pointed to the hallway door. "And now, the one, the only, Ronaldo the Magnificent!"

A figure came through the door dressed in a gold matador's outfit, carrying a red cape. He had dark hair greased back, and a mustache penciled on with eye-liner. He wore a stoic expression, a silk rose clenched in his teeth. He walked over to Liam and Helen and bowed formally. Helen curtsied as Liam continued to stare at the ceiling.

Marianne stepped over to the stereo. Gloria Gaynor. Marianne looked around the room before spinning to face the hallway door. "And now, all the way from Des Moines, Iowa—you may have known her as Michael, and though she's no maiden—if you get my drift—in her maiden appearance, the newly-minted Mikaela!"

After a too-long pause, steps could be heard plodding down the hallway. Finally, Mikaela stepped into the room, attired in gleaming red satin and teetering on high heeled shoes, wearing a long black wig. Helen put her hands on her heart, then rushed over and gave Mikaela a hug. Marianne started to applaud, and Helen joined in. Earl stood silently until Marianne shot him a look, at which point he joined in the applause. Helen walked over and nudged Liam, who looked the other way. The three hosts stood together and bowed.

A smiling Jeremy approached Liam and Helen.

"Liam, I'm so glad you could come. And you must be Helen. I have to say you're ravishing! Can I get you two a wine spritzer? We have some pigs in a blanket warming up."

Helen took his hand. "I'm so charmed to meet you Jeremy. Why yes, I would love a spritzer! Liam?"

"Um. No." He took Earl aside. "What the hell's going on here? Where're all the people? I was going to stop by, mingle a little bit, and leave. But there's no one to mingle with. Jesus."

Earl shrugged. "They put posters all over town. Surely someone will come, out of curiosity if nothing else."

Liam looked over at Helen, who was clustered with Marianne and the three boys. Jeremy was spinning in time to the music, his eyes locked on the disco ball, seemingly lost in another world. Ronaldo stood at attention, red cape out to one side, staring, expressionless. Michael/Mikaela was smiling and swaying, heels getting the better of her balance.

The doorbell rang. Liam felt a huge sense of relief.

Jeremy ran to the door and opened it to—-Vera, standing in mid-spray, arms outstretched. She dropped her deodorant can into a large purse and handed it to Jeremy. It looked like she was there to stay.

Helen tapped Liam on the shoulder. "This is fun! I'm so glad you brought me. The boys are adorable. How about we dance?"

"I don't know."

"Oh come on. We're here. I love it. Let's dance!"

He looked to Earl for support, but Earl pulled himself a beer and walked away. Liam gave up and gave in. The song ended, and they looked around the room.

Marianne was dancing with Jeremy, but Ronaldo and Mikaela were standing by themselves. Helen turned to Liam.

"We need to get this party going. I'm going to dance with Ronaldo. You can dance with Mikaela."

"Not a fucking chance."

"Oh, I think you will."

"Oh hell no."

She got closer, inches from his face. "Did you want to have a wild, crazy night with me after we leave here?"

198

"Why yes. Yes I did, er, do."

"Then you're going to go over and dance with Mikaela, aren't you?"

"But I really don't…"

She touched his lips to quiet him. "I said, I think you're going to go over and dance with Mikaela."

"Shit."

They walked over to the boys together. Helen held out her arm to Ronaldo. "Let's dance, Senor." He took her arm and marched her to the middle of the room. Pausing for a moment, and not without effort, he moved her into a tango. She responded effortlessly. It was clear this wasn't her first tango.

Liam and Mikaela stood motionless, facing each other but neither making eye contact. Finally, Liam sighed and stared into Mikaela's eyes. "Let's do this thing." He put his hands around Mikaela's waist and took her hand, holding it aloft, and strode forward in sync with the music. No one could accuse Liam O'Connor of being a bashful dancer.

Mikaela moved backward, teetering on her high heels, and started to shimmy just a bit. Liam pulled up short, shaking his head. "Oh for God's sake, you dance like a girl."

Mikaela, still a bit off balance, looked up at him. "Thank you?"

"No, no. This is a tango, not a fox trot. Be a woman, man—show me you can dance like one. Purposeful movement—got it? Tango. Let's start over."

Mikaela stiffened, took a deep breath, and stepped backward, nearly but not quite following Liam's steps. Liam nodded encouragement and kept the tango going. Without warning, Mikaela suddenly tumbled to the floor.

"Shit! My heel broke." Mikaela started to lose her composure, her eyes tearing up.

Liam leaned down and took her by the hands. "Okay. I don't think anyone saw that. Let's just get you back on your feet."

Mikaela, trying to hold it together, was crestfallen. "I look like an idiot."

"No one's watching. Lose the damn shoes and let's just keep going. Okay? And this time follow my lead."

The doorbell rang. Jeremy shrieked and ran to answer. He opened the door, turned to the room, and yelled. "They're here! They're here!"

Young people streamed into the room. Madison had arrived. Lots and lots of students. Art students, theater students, dance students. The air filled with loud talking and laughter.

Liam felt a tap on his shoulder. Turning around, he saw Helen standing behind him. She touched Mikaela's arm. "We've gotta get out of here. A lot of these kids are my students. I don't think I want to be around them."

Liam scanned the room. "Oh, shit. What'll we do?"

Helen was calm. "It's okay. Let's just say our goodbyes. No need to make a scene. We can slip out."

They found Jeremy with a plate full of pigs in a blanket. "OOOOOOH! Do you have to go? The party's just gettin' good. Um, not that it wasn't good before…. . Anyhoo…. You'll probably want to take some of these delicious piggies home with you?"

Liam had already left. Helen touched Jeremy's arm. "Oh, that's okay Jeremy. You've got a lot of guests who I'm sure will need to be fed. Don't you worry about us."

As they walked to the truck, Helen leaned into Liam and smiled.

"See? That wasn't so bad."

Liam looked at her and shook his head. "Really?"

30

"It's going to be a bit before we push back. Can I bring you a drink? Coffee?"

The voice was too damned cheerful. Liam remembered why he didn't like these early flights. Hell, it was still dark out. He looked up at the smiling young attendant and grumbled. "Bloody Mary."

"Certainly, sir." She lingered for a moment, staring at him. "Hey. I know you…. You're that…"

He looked up at her. "Yes. Yes I am."

Her face lit up. "I knew it! You're that football player from the Packers."

This did not help his mood. "No. I'm not."

She cocked her head, shrugged, and left to get his drink. As she set it down, she pointed at him. "I've got it! Silly me. You're that guy from the Milwaukee TV news!"

This was getting irritating. "No. Sorry."

She bit her lip in thought.

He started to speak. "I'm… ."

She cut him off. "Don't tell me! I'll get it."

As she walked away, he took a swig of the Bloody Mary and closed his eyes. He started to doze off but startled when he felt the plane lurch back.

The cheerful voice returned. "I'll have to take the drink, but I'll be happy to bring another when we get into the air." As she leaned over, she had a perplexed look on her face. "I'm really puzzled. Who are you?"

"Liam O'Connor, the author."

"Who?"

***

Liam stepped out of the elevator directly into the publishing house's reception area. He announced himself at the desk.

The receptionist looked up. "Could you spell your name?"

Not a great start. He sat down in the lobby and pretended to read the *Times*.

"Mr. O'Connor?"

A well-dressed young woman in a business suit introduced herself as Mr. Simon's assistant and escorted him to a conference room that had seen better days.

Harold strode into the room at full clip. "You're late."

"Good to see you too, Harold."

Harold looked past him. "Let's get to work. I don't have all day."

Liam felt his neck go hot. "That's not what you told me when you asked me to come here. Did I waste my time traveling to New York? You just going to insult me or are we gonna get something done?"

Harold dropped the manuscript on the table. "Let's get going."

***

A lunch cart was wheeled into the room.

Harold changed the subject from the book for the first time.

"When are you moving back?"

"Moving back where?"

"New York. Where you belong. Haven't you had enough of being Tom Sawyer? You need the city for your career… if you still have one. You've been out of sight for what, five years now?"

"I'm hardly out of sight."

Harold shook his head. "If memory serves me, your first book was published six years ago. It can't continue to carry you when you've disappeared from the scene, hiding out in Minnesota."

"Wisconsin. I'm in Wisconsin, Harold."

Harold shrugged.

"I'm about a hundred fifty miles from Chicago, for God's sake. You do remember Chicago, don't you?"

"I don't see you in the papers, not even the *Tribune*, let alone the *Times*. When you're back in them, I'll believe you."

"If you stop fucking with this book and get it published, I'll be back." He left the conference room and headed to the restroom. He needed to cool down.

He waited about fifteen minutes and then walked back into the room. Harold was sitting, eating his sandwich. Liam looked at him.

"Let's call a truce and get this son-of-a-bitch done. Are you going to stay with me on it for the rest of the day, or am I going to lose you?"

"Yeah, okay. You've got me, but we need to speed up the process. Sit down."

Outside of a few calls Harold said he had to take, they worked on into the evening. About nine-thirty, they stopped and looked at each other.

Harold spoke first. "I think that's enough for today. You're staying over, aren't you? Let's pick up in the morning. You've got me till noon."

Liam was exhausted but not about to admit it. "I'm reluctant to let you go now, but if you're too tired..."

Harold stiffened. "I'm not too tired, but you look like you're ready to doze off. Let's quit."

***

"I love it when you pant. Can you tell I've missed you?"

Liam cracked a beer and sat back, sighing.

"Oh, that's great… You're the best. Pant for me!"

A voice interrupted. "Are you done?"

"What?"

"I said…are you done? For God's sake, Liam."

"That's not fair Marianne. I miss my dog."

"You do know she walked away from the phone? She's at her food bowl now."

"But did she know my voice?"

"You're pathetic."

"And proud of it."

There was a knock at the door. Room service.

"Gotta go, Marianne. My feast awaits… I could get used to this shit."

"Knock yourself out."

It had been a stressful but productive day. He fell asleep in his clothes.

***

He'd agreed to meet Janice for lunch the next day after his meeting with Harold, at a restaurant close by. He held out his hand, but she knocked it aside and hugged him. A big, false, I-love-you-so-much embrace, which ended with her quickly disengaging and sitting down at the table.

"So. When's our new masterpiece going to press?"

"Jesus, Janice. You know better. Who knows when it's going to be done?"

She sniffed and sighed. Then she looked at him and smiled.

"So tell me what you've been up to? How's Iowa?"

"Wisconsin."

"Oh yes, Wisconsin. I always get those farmer states confused. Anyway, I've got some good news. The *New*

204

Yorker is picking up another of your stories, and I think *Esquire* is ready to commit to one as well. You're going to be in great shape if you can just get the new book on the shelves."

Liam's mood brightened. She was earning her keep after all. Janice looked at her watch. "Oh. Look at the time! I've got to meet someone in ten minutes. Gotta go! Kiss, kiss. Bye!" And with that, she was off, just as his drink arrived.

Liam was left with his thoughts, a drink, and a welcome dose of silence. He decided to sit and enjoy his lunch. He had come to New York with very low expectations. It had seemed more a command performance for his publisher when he got off the plane at LaGuardia. The meeting with Harold was predictably tense, but productive. The edits were well underway. *Darby's Gift* looked more and more like a reality.

"Liam?" The quiet voice paralyzed him. He was afraid to turn around. It repeated. "Liam?"

Finally he looked up and winced. "Marguerite." He wanted to run. He wanted to do anything, be anywhere but there.

She smiled. "I thought it was you. What are you doing in New York? It's so good to see you."

He stood up and stiffened, not knowing what to say or do. She walked over and embraced him. The familiar scent of Chanel, the warm touch of her cheek on his, overwhelmed him and made him sink into the floor.

"Did I interrupt you? Looks like you have company."

"No, no. That person left."

Marguerite stood back. "Let me look at you. You look great Liam. May I sit down?"

He was unable to find words. Before he found them, she had seated herself. The waitress arrived at the same time with another drink. Marguerite pointed to it. "I'll have one of those as well."

He was still standing. His mind wouldn't operate, couldn't grasp what was happening.

She motioned to his chair. "Please. Please sit down. Let's talk. Let's catch up."

His instincts were to run, but his legs wouldn't move. He slouched into his chair, trembling. He'd rehearsed this moment for five years. For five years he imagined the words he would burn into her face, that would bring her to her knees, destroy her. Now she was here, in front of him, within his reach. But there were no words. Something kept him from pulling the trigger, but what was it?

She gazed at him with that charming look he saw when they were first together, like the basket concealing the cobra coiled inside, waiting for the perfect opportunity to strike. "I'm so sorry we left each other on bad terms, Liam."

"You stole my work."

The basket opened, the snake began its dance upward. "That's too harsh a word. 'Stole'. I told you at the time that I was under pressure to produce. I'm sure I would've done the same for you if our roles were reversed."

Don't let her do this. Don't let the snake bite again.

She reached for his hand. Recoiling, he pulled it back.

"Don't be afraid of me, Liam. I've often thought about you. How good a couple we made. How wonderful it would be to see you again, and here you are."

He stared blankly, unseeing, as she continued.

"What are you doing in New York? I thought we had lost you to your midwestern hideaway. Do you have a new book? I've looked and looked, but I've seen nothing from you. Have you stopped writing? That would be a shame."

Her drink arrived. She took a sip and smiled. "Or do you have some new career? I heard you owned a quaint little bookstore. How nice."

"I've got to go. I wish I could say it was good to see you, but I can't. Too much. Just too much."

She was still smiling. "I understand, sweet Liam." She wrote something down on a piece of paper and stuffed it into his coat pocket. "My number. Any time. I would love to continue this conversation. You've always meant a lot to me."

In full flight mode, he stood without speaking and almost ran over the waitress as he asked for the check. He walked out of the restaurant in a daze. He never looked back.

He walked out into traffic to hail a cab, and was almost hit by a car and a messenger on a bicycle, in that order. Mercifully a cab pulled over and the driver helped him in. "Where're you headed, Mister?" He couldn't think. Silence. "The meter's running, pal. Where to?"

"LaGuardia."

31

"I'll leave you alone with your coffee." Ruth walked away, shaking her head.

Liam was having a hard time forming any thoughts. He had gotten in from New York late in the evening, called Helen to let her know he'd landed, and stopped at Marianne's to pick up Lady. Marianne asked what was going on.

"You look like shit."

He didn't have an answer. It was all too much to explain. Hell, he couldn't even comprehend what had happened at that restaurant, let alone put it into words.

"Bad day. I need some sleep."

He had called Sharon's office first thing in the morning. Her answering service picked up. Sharon was out of town for the week, unreachable. The operator asked if it was an emergency, but he couldn't bring himself to mess up Sharon's vacation. He told her he could wait till she was back and hung up.

***

Liam walked into the Owl's Eyes absently, his head still filled with the disorienting aura of the Marguerite episode. Disco music?

What the hell?

The scene was more than he could handle. Jeremy and some random customer, dancing and shaking, prancing around the store, heads bobbing to the beat.

Where the fuck is Marianne?

He heard noise coming from his office. As he got closer, he could see her, sitting in his chair, her feet up on his desk. She was talking on the phone, her free arm moving in exaggerated gestures. He stopped and turned around.

"WHAT THE FUCK ARE YOU ALL DOING? TURN THAT SHIT OFF! MARIANNE. GET YOUR ASS OUT HERE!"

Everything came to a screeching halt. "Okay. Which one of you would like to explain? I leave town for two days and this is what happens?"

Jeremy apparently couldn't help but try.

"Oh Liam. We're so happy to see you! We were just so carried away by the spirit of our little party Saturday night—- and may I say that you and Helen cut quite a vision—that we wanted to... ."

By then Marianne had crossed the room and put her hand over his mouth. "What Jeremy is trying to say is that he was so excited after the party that he felt the need to bring that level of enthusiasm to work."

Jeremy was nodding while Marianne kept a death grip on his mouth. Liam was unimpressed. "Even if that were the case, which I seriously doubt, what the hell were YOU doing in my office with your feet on my desk? I don't see your name on it. Am I missing something?"

"Well. Let me say this. Um. Someone called. Yes. Someone called, asking about an invoice. Yes. There was an invoice, and it was on the floor next to your chair. I had to sit in your chair and leverage myself to reach down to get it, and needed my legs elevated to balance properly."

"That, Marianne, is the biggest crock of shit that has ever passed through your teeth. Get back to work. Both of you. And no disco music. Got me?"

The offenders returned to their stations. The music started back up, but this time it was Verdi's *Requiem*. Liam stuck his head out of his office.

"Real funny, Marianne. You've made your point. Turn that shit off."

Liam took the manuscript from his briefcase and tried to concentrate. About a half hour later, Marianne buzzed him.

209

"WHAT???"

"Vera called."

"And?"

"She's okay."

"What?"

"The burns were superficial."

"Marianne, what the hell are you talking about?"

"Apparently she had an incident."

"An incident?"

"Yes."

"Oh for God's sake, what happened?"

"She was spraying her deodorant. As she does."

"Yeah? So?"

"She tried to light her stove at the same time."

"I don't think I want to know."

"And the aerosol ignited."

"Jesus Christ! That's a bomb."

"That's what she said, but she said she threw the can across the room."

"Then what?"

"It exploded. But it was far enough away that it didn't hurt her."

"So is she okay?"

"Were you listening? She's okay, just superficial wounds. Maybe a couple blisters."

"Does she need help?"

"No. But she wants time off. She says she needs some time to reassess her life. And the relevance of deodorant."

Shaking his head, Liam tried to settle back into the edits. Within a few minutes, the phone was ringing again. Marianne stuck her head in his office. "It's Helen."

He looked up. "Thanks. I'll take it." He waited a moment, sensing she was still standing right out of view. "You can go now, Marianne." When he was sure she had left, he picked up the phone.

"Hi. What's up?"

"I wanted to make sure you made it home last night. You sounded rough when you called from the airport. Are you alright?"

"I'm okay, I guess. New York turned out to be a bit tougher than I expected."

"Did something happen yesterday?"

"I saw a ghost."

PART III

32

"Beautiful day, isn't it? Spring is…"

Standing at Helen's door, Liam's eyes caught something in the living room. Stephen. Sitting on Helen's sofa, shoes off, with an empty glass of wine in his hand and a photograph album in his lap. He looked up at Liam with that nauseating self-satisfied grin.

"Why hello Liam. Helen and I are having a wonderful time looking through her photographs. I was just telling her that I have some of the two of us that I think would complement her collection nicely. But then you arrived. Pity. I guess you'll just have to come back later." He motioned to Helen. "Sweetheart, can you bring me another glass of wine? You were spot on with your suggestion." He looked back at Liam and smirked.

Liam's eyes narrowed. "I'm going outside. You can let me know when your 'guest' has departed."

Helen started to respond but Liam left the house and stood by his truck, trying to maintain his composure. Finally, she came out. "Okay Liam. What's the issue?"

"The 'issue', as you put it, is that prick hanging around you, acting like he owns the place. Does he? What's going on?"

Helen's face reddened. "What is it to you if my neighbor stops by my place to chat? Are you that insecure?"

"Should I be?"

"You're too much, O'Connor. I'm permitted to have a life outside of you—or am I not?"

"So, is he gone?"

"No, he's not 'gone'. I don't just throw people out of my house on your whim."

Liam sensed that this was not going anywhere good, and decided to dial it back. At least for now. "I'm sorry, but there's just something about that guy that creeps me out.

Can we start over? I think we had a date for today. Is that still on?"

"Yes, Liam. Yes, of course our date is still on. Give me some time to gently end my discussion with Stephen. You may come in or not. That's up to you."

"I'll wait here. Try not to be long... ."

When Helen returned, she punched Liam in the arm. He wasn't certain if she was being playful. "Are you better now? So what do you have planned for us today?"

"Oh, we're invited to a barbecue. Does that sound good?"

"I guess that depends on whose and where it is. But I'm game."

"I hesitate to say this, but it's at Jeremy's. The boys decided there was no better way to spend a bright spring day than to gather the bookstore's crew for what they are calling a 'gala picnic on the grounds'."

Helen chuckled. Obviously she was relaxing. "What grounds?"

He shook his head in resignation. "Their back yard. I'm sorry it isn't something more enticing."

Helen spun and took him into her arms. "Nonsense! The boys are fun."

Letting go of his anger, Liam embraced her and gave her a passionate, if short, kiss. She hugged him.

"That's better. Let's get going."

As they approached the boys' house, they could see heavy black smoke rising from the back yard. The scene was chaotic—Jeremy running around, screaming, Ronaldo and Michael standing open-mouthed, a barbecue grill engulfed in flames, smoke pouring into the sky.

Marianne shoved Liam out of the way as she rushed by, fire extinguisher in hand. She pulled the pin and the extinguisher let loose a flow of white foam that went everywhere but toward the fire. Finally, she steadied it and directed the spray at the grill. When the fire was out, all that was left was a charred hulk of metal and plastic in the rough shape of a kettle.

Covered in foam and soot, Ronaldo and Michael had been a little too close, and slow to move out of the way. Jeremy had escaped this simply because he was running around too fast and didn't get near the fire. Steam was rising from the ashes. There were no sounds, except the tick-ticking of the cooling metal.

Helen spoke. "Hello boys! Well, that was quite a greeting. What can we do to help?"

Liam stood without speaking, shaking his head. Marianne looked at Jeremy and motioned to him.

"Can we step aside for a moment? Let's you and I chat."

Jeremy tried to duck, but she grabbed him by the shirt and dragged him away.

"I'd suggest you go get some food. Something we won't have to cook."

"But we wanted barbe.... "

"Not going to happen. Look at the grill. No, look at your friends. I'll get you some money. Go!"

Jeremy collared Ronaldo. "Come on Ronnie. You can help me."

Ronaldo tried to escape, but Jeremy had a death grip on him. They left. Marianne looked around.

"Who wants a drink?"

Michael turned to Liam and Helen.

"If you'll excuse me, I'm going to go change out of these clothes."

Helen took Marianne's arm. "Let's you and I go find some wine. Liam—you want something to drink?"

Liam nodded. "Anything to get through this."

As the women walked away, he turned to Earl.

"Having fun yet?"

Earl wore his usual look of pained resignation. "I couldn't be enjoying myself more if I tried."

215

Liam laughed. "And to think I closed the store for this."

Michael returned, a glass of wine in hand. Liam gave him a casual salute.

"Where's Mikaela?"

"She won't be here. She prefers special occasions. You'll have to make do with Michael."

"I don't really understand, but it's okay by me."

A commotion arose from the front of the house, getting closer. Jeremy turned the corner with two buckets of fried chicken in his hands, followed by Ronaldo, carrying a large bag.

Marianne looked in the bag.

"Not exactly what I would've expected, but at least it's edible."

Jeremy's head drooped. "Well, we first went to another place, but we had some issues there. Soooo, we ended up at the Chicken Koop."

Helen reached out and took Jeremy's arm. "What kind of issues?"

"They made fun of us."

Marianne looked at him and sighed.

"Give me a minute."

She ran into the house and returned with a mirror. Holding it up in front of Jeremy, she pointed at the image.

"What do you see?"

Jeremy stared at the mirror. "Ooooooo…".

Marianne nodded. "Yes. Exactly."

"I look SPECTACULAR!"

Marianne almost lost it. "Jeremy. Here's what I see. Pink short shorts. Gold lame' beret. A tee shirt that says '*I can't even think straight!*'. What did you expect?"

Jeremy was still staring into the mirror.

"I KNOW! Isn't it great? What an ensemble! It just screams 'Look out world!'."

Marianne looked at Helen and shrugged.

"I give up."

Jeremy had already moved on.

"Wait a minute! We planned a special drink for today. Ronnie—go get these people our surprise!"

Ronaldo ambled into the house and returned, carrying a large bottle of cheap whiskey.

Liam whistled. "Looks like you got the student special, didn't you? What're you makin'?"

Jeremy clapped his hands. "Whiskey sours!"

"Okay. But aren't you missing something?"

Jeremy giggled. "We don't actually know how to make them."

Marianne sprang into action. "Boys! Get some lemons, and some sugar."

Michael shook his head. "We don't have any."

"Oh for God's sake. One of you go to the store and get frozen lemonade. Can you handle that?"

Michael grabbed the car keys from Jeremy. "Let me do this. Jeez."

Jeremy had again moved on.

"Let's get some tunes going! We need to dance."

He danced his way back into the house, returning with a boombox. Setting it down on the table, he pushed a button. Show tunes.

Liam looked at Earl. "This is gonna be a long afternoon."

Michael returned, accompanied by Vera. She was, as she told anyone who would listen, a changed woman since the deodorant flambe' incident. When she returned to work after a two-week hiatus, she announced that she had an epiphany. The incident was a message from a higher power that her body should be free of all restraints, including "anything that would clog my pores". Hence, no deodorant. She showed up at the picnic in an enormous halter top, sweating profusely.

While the open air blunted somewhat the overwhelming odor that accompanied her, everyone jockeyed for position, each seeking not to be downwind. Totally unaffected by it all, she joined in the dancing, her legs a tie-dyed blur, her bare arms wildly gyrating, and her enormous breasts building momentum no fabric could contain as they swung up and down and side to side. At one point she got too close to Liam and would have taken him down had he not deftly side-stepped to safety.

Helen and Marianne returned from dancing. Liam was over it all.

"Marianne. Could you, uh, switch up the entertainment?"

Marianne rolled her eyes. "Sure. But look at these guys. You do know their selections are, well, limited?"

"Just lose the show tunes."

Marianne ambled over to the boom box and switched tapes. Motown filled the air. Liam smiled, then noticed Jeremy put his hand to his mouth in shock.

"Ewww! That's so boring. So 60s. Where's the drama? Where's the glamor?" Diving toward the boom box, he pushed Marianne aside and swapped tapes again. Carol Channing filled the air. "Diamonds Are a Girl's Best Friend."

Marianne put her hands on Jeremy's shoulders and looked into his eyes. "Not a chance. Anything. Anything else!"

"Oh, okay. Let's compromise on the 80s?"

"Much better."

Jeremy switched tapes again. The Weather Girls. "It's Raining Men."

Marianne looked over at Liam and shrugged her shoulders. "I give up."

***

218

The rest of the afternoon passed without drama. Liam and Helen said their goodbyes and left. As they drove away, Helen looked at Liam.

"That wasn't so bad, now, was it?"

He grunted. As they neared his house, she spoke softly.

"Liam. I need to tell you something. Just so you know. I've agreed to go to dinner with Stephen."

Stunned, he said nothing.

"Did you hear me?"

"I don't think so. What I thought I heard couldn't be."

"I said, I've agreed to go to dinner with Stephen. He's been a good neighbor and a great friend to me this term. He's been asking me, and I felt it was the least I could do.."

Liam pulled the truck over to the curb. "What the fuck has been going on when I'm not around? I saw that weasel this afternoon. He called you 'sweetheart'! What the hell's that all about? No. He's not going to pull this off. Not if I have anything to say about it. No fucking way."

Helen stared at him. When she finally spoke, she did so without raising her voice, yet the coldness of her response sent chills. "I've always been honest with you. You know that. I'm telling you there's nothing there. Do you believe me?"

"Why should I believe you?"

"I'm not even going to answer that. I'm telling you this so you don't think I'm sneaking around. Stephen's a friend. A dinner with him means nothing."

"Ha! Nothing means nothing."

"What the hell is that supposed to mean?"

Liam of course had no idea what it meant. He stared back. "You can't do this to me Helen."

She took a deep breath. "I'm not 'doing' anything to you. But I'm going to go. You aren't my overlord, and you should know by now how I feel about you."

"I don't accept that. It's him or me."

"Oh, come on Liam." She reached out to touch his arm, but he pulled it away. After a long, awkward pause, she turned her head and looked straight ahead.

"Maybe, just maybe, you and I need to take a break. I'd suggest you take me home."

"But I had things planned for tonight."

"Maybe you should've thought of that before you spoke."

33

"Helen and I broke up yesterday."

As Sharon was taking this in, Liam pulled a pack of cigarettes out of his pocket and fumbled around opening it. She held up her hand.

"You can put that away."

Liam did a double take. "What?"

"I've made my office no smoking." She pointed to a small sign on the coffee table.

"You've got to be kidding. You're a shrink. You of all people should understand."

"I do understand. But my health comes before your emotional crutch. Sorry." She got right back to the matter at hand. "So you broke up. What does that mean, exactly?"

Liam took a moment before answering. "She admitted to me that she was going to go out with that little prick who lives upstairs from her."

Sharon had picked up her notebook but set it down.

"She said that? She said she's 'going out' with this man?"

"Prick. That prick. Yes, that's what she said."

"In those exact words? 'Going out'? Think hard, Liam. Tell me exactly what she said."

Liam looked away. "She said she was going to have dinner with him."

"But she didn't say 'I'm going to go out with'... ."

"That prick. No, she didn't. But that's what she meant."

"Are you sure? What else did she say?" Silence. "Tell me everything, Liam. I want to know it all."

Liam was obsessed with his own interpretation, and not about to let Sharon poke holes in it. He tried a diversion. "Can I get a cup of coffee?"

"Certainly. You know where it is. I'll be here when you get back."

When he returned to the office, Sharon was sitting with her notebook open on her lap. "So. Tell me about this guy. Who is he and what's the issue?"

"Prick. He's a prick."

"I think we've established that. Now, what's his story?"

"He's a nerdy history professor who lives in the apartment above Helen's. He showed up the day she moved in, and he's always around when I go there."

Sharon jotted a couple of sentences. "Well, wouldn't that make sense since he lives there?"

"You don't understand. He's tried to butt in every time I'm there. He smirks. He takes his time leaving. I know he's at it when I'm not there, and who knows what goes on?"

"You know that for a fact, or are you just imagining it?"

"It's obvious, isn't it?"

"Why's that?"

"If he's there when I am, wouldn't he be there even more so when I'm not?"

Sharon leaned forward, hand on her chin. "Let's get back to what Helen said. Beyond that she was going to have dinner with this guy."

Liam knew she was going to keep at it until he told her everything.

"She said he was a 'good neighbor' and a 'great friend', and that it was the least she could do."

"Well, that doesn't sound so bad."

"That assumes you believe her."

Sharon looked up from her writing. "And you don't?"

"No, I don't. I'm not buying it."

"Why?"

222

Liam stood up, fidgeting. "Because I asked her not to do it, and she refused."

"You 'asked her'?"

"Yes. Well, no. I told her. I forbid her."

"Sit down Liam. Are you telling me you actually 'forbid' her to have dinner with her neighbor?"

He didn't sit down. "Goddammit, Sharon. I wasn't about to have one more woman piss on me. The fact she was telling me in advance didn't make it any more acceptable."

"And what did she say when you forbade her?"

He sat down and glared at her.

"She told me it was time for us to take a break."

"Do you blame her?"

"What the fuck, Sharon? If she was bound and determined to do something I asked her not to do, then we're done."

"You didn't 'ask' her, you 'forbid' her. Big difference, Liam. Don't you think you might have taken this too far?"

"Absolutely not. I told you. I won't let another woman.... ."

"Dump on you. I know. But you might want to take some time.... No, I think you need to take some time to consider whether you've overreacted. A lot. I thought you cared about this woman. Believed in her. Maybe, just maybe, you've misread the situation."

Sharon stood and put her hand on Liam's shoulder. "I think we've gone about as far as we can go today. We can pick up on it next week. In the meantime, please think about exactly what she said, not what you imagined it meant. Consider what it might mean if you overreacted. It certainly wouldn't be the first time."

"You're as bad as she is."

"Should I take that as a compliment?"

***

Liam still had a chip on his shoulder when he walked out of Sharon's office. Helen had led him on, only to pull the rug out from under his feet. She and Stephen were probably sitting together at this very moment, laughing and mocking him.

Sweetheart my ass.

He headed off to the store. He knew he'd be in for some abuse, but he needed to figure out a plan, a way to clear his head. By the time he got there, he had something in mind. Unfortunately, it had to wait.

An unmistakable scent lingered in the store.

"Marianne! In my office. Now."

Silence.

"NOW!"

Marianne walked in, smiling. He glared at her.

"This place stinks."

"I know. It's kind of an unfortunate byproduct of Vera's renaissance."

Liam thought for a moment. "I need you to handle it."

"I don't think so."

"What do you mean, you don't think so?"

Marianne sat down in one of his chairs, in no hurry to respond. Finally, she got up and closed the door.

"You know as well as I do that Vera doesn't listen to me. She never has, and never will. She just blows that damn horn in my ear."

He knew she was right. "So what do you think we should do?"

"I think you should handle it."

"Not going to happen. I'll just end up firing her." A thought came to him. "How about Jeremy? They seem to be best buds. Surely, he could pull it off?"

"You've got to be kidding. How's he going to get her to use deodorant? We're talking Jeremy here."

"He's all we've got. I'll leave that to you. Make it happen."

She got up and started to leave without speaking. As if an afterthought, he continued.

"Oh. One more thing. I'm going to take a few days and go up to the cottage. I need a break. Can you watch Lady for me?"

Marianne scrunched her face. "Sure, I'll keep her, but what's going on? I thought Helen had a full schedule of classes?"

"She's not coming." He was hoping this would go without comment. It didn't.

"Wait a minute. You don't do anything without her. It's getting to be sickeningly romantic between you two. What do you mean she's not going?"

Busted, he paused, this time for effect. He needed some sympathy.

"We broke up."

Marianne's jaw dropped. "What happened?"

"I don't want to talk about it."

Marianne turned to leave. When she reached the door, she opened it and looked back.

"You're an idiot."

Liam busied himself collecting the papers he might want to have with him. He had no idea how long he would stay at the cottage, so he wanted to be prepared. The phone rang. Marianne buzzed him.

"Harold Simon on line one." There was only one line, but she seemed to get a kick out of saying it.

Liam picked up. "I'm kinda busy Harold. What's up?"

"I think we're done with the editing, Liam. I'd like you to come up to New York to go over the artwork and other details. When can you be here?"

"I'm just heading out of town for a bit. I've got some things on my mind that I need to work through. I could probably do it in a week."

Harold seemed impatient but resigned. "That's fine. I'll have my secretary call you and set it up."

"Love you Harold."

"Bullshit. But this is a good one, Liam. Congratulations."

Liam hung up.

"You can stop hiding, Marianne. I know you're there."

She stepped into the office, having stood outside eavesdropping.

"So does this mean there's going to be a new book?"

Liam looked at her. "Jeremy. Go get Jeremy to fix the smell. I can't afford to shut this place down."

34

"Oh Liam. Something awful's happened." Liam had called Madeline to tell her he was planning to come up to Windward for a few days. When she answered the phone, he could tell from her trembling voice something was very wrong.

"Oh my god Madeline."

"There's been an accident."

"What? Who?"

"Susan. And little Sara." She broke down.

"Oh my god, no. What happened?"

She spoke through sobs. "Susan had just picked Sara up from a friend's house. They were driving home, and someone ran a stop sign."

She stopped to catch her breath. Liam was in shock but had to know more.

"Are they okay?"

Madeline exhaled. "They were hit from the passenger side. Susan was badly injured but should live. Sara... ." Her voice trailed off.

Liam was beside himself now. "Oh no... ."

"Sara was in a booster seat in the back but was on the side that was hit. She's in a coma. They don't know if she's going to make it. That poor thing."

The words broke Liam. All he could think of was that little girl, that pest, but what a wonderful pest she was. He flashed back to their adventures. How she was curious. How she spoke out, loudly. Even inappropriately. But then, how she held her tiny hand in his as they walked together.

"How'd you find out?"

"Jack called. He's absolutely lost. They haven't told Susan about Sara yet, but I think that's going to happen today. He's been splitting his time between their two rooms. He hasn't slept. I just don't know what he's going to do.

What they're going to do if Sara doesn't make it. She's their whole life."

"What can we do? What can I do?"

Madeline struggled to speak. "I really don't know. Pray. Not sure what else there is right now. Just pray for them all."

"Where are they?"

Madeline shook her head. "I don't know. There are several hospitals in Milwaukee. I can try to find out."

Liam stood up. "I'm going. They can't be alone."

Within the hour, he was on his way to Milwaukee. He'd called Marianne to let her know something had come up. He asked her to call Harold and let him know he might be delayed getting to New York. Everything was on hold right now. Marianne pressed for a reason, but Liam wasn't up to explaining.

"I'll call you later. I can't talk right now."

***

When he walked into Susan's room, she was sitting up in bed. She had scratches and bruises on her face. She had one arm in a sling and a partial cast on one leg. Liam looked at her and took his best shot at smiling.

"You're beautiful as always, Susan. I'm so glad to see you."

"Liam. I didn't expect to see you here. I know you're lying, or you need glasses. I'm a mess in case you haven't noticed." She seemed happy to see him. By her demeanor, he gathered Jack hadn't told her yet about Sara. This was going to be tough.

"I wouldn't miss it. Where's Jack?"

She motioned to him to come closer. "I'm sorry, Liam. I can't move very well. They've told me I have to stay put for a while. They say I was in an accident, but I don't remember anything about it. I've asked Jack to bring Sara

228

by, although I don't know if I want her to see me banged up. He stepped out but should be back soon."

A nurse walked into the room. She looked at Liam. "It's time to check over Susan's wounds. Could you leave us alone for a few minutes? You can just step out into the hall. I'll let you know when you can return."

"I'll see you in a bit. Don't go anywhere!" The joke fell flat, but it was the best he had. He left the room and stood in the hallway. As he did, he saw Jack walking his way, looking down, his face drawn.

Finally, he glanced up. "Liam. Madeline told me you were on your way. I'm so glad to see you. I've been here full time—haven't slept, don't know what to do."

Liam wanted to reassure him, tell him that everything was going to be alright. That's what you do in a situation like this, isn't it? But he couldn't because he knew what was coming next.

"I'm here for you. Tell me—how much does Susan know?"

"She doesn't know much. She didn't remember the accident--totally blanked on it. She didn't and still doesn't remember Sara was with her, and she's asked me several times to bring her by. The doctors didn't want me to say anything, but they told me this morning that I could and should tell her."

Liam could hold back no longer. "Give me the truth about Sara. I need to know, and I want to see her."

Jack motioned to a small lounge nearby.

"Let's go over there. I need to sit down."

The lounge was empty. Liam arranged two chairs so that they faced each other.

"Take your time. Take as much time as you need."

"It's bad, Liam. Really bad. She was in the direct path of the collision. By some miracle, she wasn't killed. The EMTs were amazed. Apparently, she was relaxed because she didn't see it coming, never had a chance to react.

Her body absorbed the blow. She has a broken arm, but her bones seem otherwise intact. It's not clear what's going on inside. She was knocked unconscious. So was Susan, but she came out of it. Sara didn't. She was in a coma by the time she got to the hospital. They've run a lot of tests. There may be some internal bleeding, and they're concerned about her head since it hit something hard. There's no way of knowing if there's brain damage. Only time will tell. But the toughest thing... ."

He broke down. Liam's mind went to the worst case. By now, he was in shock, trying unsuccessfully to take it all in. He had to block the visual because it was overwhelming. Jack caught his breath again.

"The toughest thing is that, since they don't know the extent of the damage, they don't know if she'll come out of the coma, or even if she'll live."

Liam had no idea what to say or what to do. Anything he could come up with seemed a trite or useless gesture.

"I'm so very, very sorry Jack."

"I know. I know, Liam."

Liam could tell Jack needed to talk. He also knew Jack was going to have to face up to the impossible task of breaking all of this to Susan.

"So, when are you going to talk with Susan?"

Jack 's eyes met his. "I was planning to do it now."

"Can you point me to Sara? I want to see her. You can take whatever time you need with Susan. I promise I'll be there when you need me. For anything."

Jack nodded.

***

Sara lay motionless on the bed. She seemed in a serene state. But for the cast on her arm and the tubes and apparatuses hooked up to her, she appeared to just be

230

sleeping. The beat of the heart monitor was the only sound. Her face was pale, her eyelids motionless, hiding that piercing and inquisitive stare that Liam had come to both fear and enjoy immensely. Liam spoke in a whisper, to no one in particular.

"Sleeping Beauty. That's who she is… ."

"I don't know what we're going to do if we lose her, Liam. She's our life, our joy. She means everything to us."

"I'm not going to let that happen."

As soon as the words left his lips, he regretted them. *What a stupid thing to say.*

Jack stared at the wall, without apparent focus. "If you'll stay with her, I'm going to go have the hardest conversation of my life."

Liam sat by Sara as Jack left the room. He took her tiny hand in his and squeezed it.

"Sara? Can you hear me? It's your buddy Liam. You remember me? I'm the guy you wouldn't leave alone. Now I'm not going to leave you alone. You hear? I'm going to stick right here, whether you want me or not. How do you like that? Shoe's on the other foot now, isn't it?" Tears dripped down his face. "Please don't go anywhere, little one. I want to have more adventures with you. You know, next time you step up on a rock and try to scare me, I'm just going to let you do it. Next time you stand by the lake and act like you're gonna jump in, I'm going to let you. Not only that, I'll join you. I'll teach you to swim. You can't even imagine the places we'll go and the things we'll see. Every day will be a treasure hunt." He squeezed her hand again. No response. "I know you're in there, Sara. And you know I'm here. Please don't leave me."

Falling silent, he sat next to her, holding her hand. Every once in a while, the nurse would come in and take her vitals.

Liam didn't know if it was hours, or only moments, when Jack returned. He pulled up a chair next to Liam.

231

"It didn't go well."

35

A nurse was standing outside Susan's room. Liam saw her badge. "Sherrie Scott, RN".

"Nurse Scott. I'm Liam O'Connor, a friend of the family."

"I'm sorry Mr. O'Connor. Susan isn't seeing anyone right now."

"But Jack asked."

The nurse stiffened. "That doesn't really matter. Did he tell you what happened?"

Liam wasn't prepared for an interrogation. "Yes, I know that he and the docs told her about Sara."

Her face was expressionless. "She erupted. She tried to rip the IV and the wires off her and to jump out of bed. She was determined to go to Sara. She attacked Jack. We had to restrain her. She's sedated now. But we can't risk setting her off again, so no visitors."

Liam tried to clear his head. "So what should I do?"

"I only know you're not going to go in there." She motioned to a folding chair in the hallway. "If you want, you're free to sit and wait things out. But if I were you, I wouldn't hold my breath."

Defeated, Liam followed directions. He waited. The afternoon progressed without resolution. Periodically, nurses would enter the room, close the door, and emerge minutes later. Each time, he would stand and try to see in. Each time, he was rebuffed and directed back to his chair. For the first time since Madeline told him about the accident, he felt isolated and alone. Who was he to even bring himself here? What business was it of his?

He could see through the window at the end of the hallway, it was getting dark outside. He noticed Jack at the nurses' station, speaking with Nurse Scott. Finally, Jack approached.

"Visiting hours are ending soon. Why don't you go back to your hotel and get some sleep? Hopefully by tomorrow you'll be able to see her."

Liam could see the distress in Jack's eyes. "You going to be able to get some rest? Anything I can bring you?"

"The best thing you can do for me is show up in the morning, rested. I'm going to need your help."

"I'm here for you, pal."

***

The next morning, Liam met Jack in the hospital's cafeteria. Jack looked haggard but managed a smile.

"Bless you, Liam. Did you get any sleep?"

Liam was amazed. Here was a guy whose wife and daughter were in the hospital, in bad shape, who undoubtedly had pulled an all-nighter, and he's asking if Liam had any sleep.

"I did fine. Anything new on Susan?"

Jack shook his head. "Not really. I sat with her for a while during the night while she slept. I'm going back there this morning if you could sit with Sara."

Liam nodded. "I planned on that. I think I'm ready. When and if Susan's ready, I'll swap with you."

When Liam reached Sara's room, a young nurse was coming out. She glanced up and down at him. Apparently, he passed inspection.

"Are you family?"

Liam couldn't help noticing she was very attractive but held back his habitual temptation to flirt.

"No. I'm a friend of Jack and Susan. I was here for a while yesterday. I'm in town and promised Jack I'd keep the vigil when he can't be here."

That seemed to satisfy her. "Okay. Let me know if you need anything. My name's Jenny."

234

"Thanks, Jenny. I will." He stepped into the room, newspaper under his arm, a coffee in one hand and a bag in the other. He was loaded for bear.

During the night, Liam had hatched a plan. He was convinced (or at least he tried to convince himself) that Sara could hear him, whether she could acknowledge it or not. They were going to have a lot of time together, and they might as well put it to good use. He'd stopped at a bookstore on his way to the hospital and picked up a *Times* and some books. He situated himself next to her bed and opened the *Times*. Glancing through the paper, he started to chuckle. "Oh here's a good one! Some sixteen year old kid stole a subway with two thousand people on it. Can you imagine that?" In his head, he could hear the expected Sara question—*What's a subway?* So he explained. "Why, a subway is a big train that runs underground in New York." He knew what the next question would be and chuckled. "I know, it sounds silly. But they have big tunnels that… Oh, never mind. It's a big train." He looked down at Sara, who lay silently and still.

Moving on, Liam looked over the treasure trove of books he had brought. Steinbeck. Hemingway. London. Conrad. Fitzgerald. Joyce. He thought for a while, and selected *Travels With Charley*. He figured *Charley* would be a special treat for Sara. "I think you're going to like this one. It's by a guy named John Steinbeck, a famous writer… you know, a storyteller. He took a trip all over America, in a truck, with a dog." Liam looked over at Sara, and imagined she was pointing at him. "Yes, yes… just like Lady and me. Anyway, maybe I should give you a little insight into Steinbeck's dog, who was pretty cool. You see, he was a poodle, and Steinbeck joked that he needed to talk with him in French so the dog wouldn't have to translate."

Liam stopped and looked at Sara. He thought maybe, just maybe, he detected the hint of a smile. Or was it just the light and his imagination? Then it hit him—she didn't get

235

the joke. "So, you see, poodles originally came from France." He could imagine the next question—

Where's France?

"Oh boy. Let me see. It's a country far away, where they speak a different language called French. And Charley doesn't speak French. Or English. 'Cause he's a dog—he speaks dog. We've got a lot to talk about today, don't we?"

He felt a presence at the doorway. Jenny had heard his voice and was listening and watching. When he turned around to look, she smiled at him and winked. Then she left. Liam lost track of time as he worked his way through more passages from the book. The act of reading lifted the heaviness. He felt he was doing something constructive, something for her.

He felt a tap on his shoulder. He looked up into Jack's face.

"Susan's awake. I think the initial shock wore off. She told me she would like to see you. Can you go up there? I'll take over here. Just come back when you're ready. It's going to be a lot for both of you, so you may not be able to stay there very long."

***

Susan's door was open. He walked in with a larger-than-life grin.

"How's the prettiest lady in the whole state of Wisconsin?"

She was sitting up in bed. Her face was still red and streaked with tears, but she managed a smile as well.

"You must need glasses."

Thinking quickly, he pulled readers out of his pocket and put them on. He peered at her through them as if sizing her up.

"Nope! You're still the prettiest thing I've seen in a long time."

236

He took the glasses off, stowed them, and walked over to the bed. He leaned down and kissed her on the forehead. She looked up at him, managing to hold her emotions in check.

"My baby's hurt. They can't or won't tell me if she's going to live. And they won't let me see her. I don't know what I'm going to do, Liam."

He thought he was prepared for this one. "I absolutely get it, Susan. You're just not ready to move around yet, but that's coming. I've been with Sara, yesterday and today. I know that's of little consolation to you. In fact, you're probably pissed off right now that I have and you haven't seen her. But Jack's been there since the beginning. The docs are evasive, but I'm guessing that's because they just don't know anything yet. I don't mean to lecture you, but you've got to take care of yourself so you can take care of her."

That set Susan off. "That's if she lives. Isn't it? What if she dies and I'm not there?"

Liam had nothing. Then she pulled out the big gun. "You're not a parent, Liam. You have no idea what I'm going through."

He had no choice but to stand there and take it. He wanted to tell her he was in pain as well, but he knew that wasn't going to help. The silence lasted too long, moving from awkward into agonizing.

Susan started to cry. She reached out to Liam and took his hand.

"I don't mean to take it out on you. It was very nice of you to rush over here for us. Thank you. You hardly know us."

"Of course I know you. All of you. The bigger question, I suppose, is whether you now know who I am! I kind of recall that you hadn't heard of me when we met?"

Susan turned red with embarrassment. "Oh. That. You were just, oh, out of context."

237

He chuckled. She squeezed his hand.

"Ok. You're right. My literary hero, and I stood right there next to you and didn't put two and two together. What a fool!"

He squeezed back. "Actually, it was kind of endearing. I guess you could say it meant my work stands on its own. Once I write it, I turn it loose to have a life of its own. That's kind of cool."

She smiled. "Thanks for letting me off the hook. I owe you."

"And I plan to collect on that. Guaranteed."

Liam and Susan spent the hour or so catching up, interrupted from time to time by the nurses coming by to check on her. Finally, Jack came into the room. His wary expression disappeared when he saw them.

"Thank God you two are doing better." He looked at Susan. "I was worried that you'd throw Liam out of the hospital. I don't know what magic he used, but I could use some of it myself right now."

Susan called him over. He leaned down and she kissed him. "I was gonna throw him out, but I needed you to do it. You were nowhere to be found. I guess I'll let you both stay."

Jack held her hand and turned to Liam. "If you don't mind, I think it would be really nice if you could go down and spend the rest of the afternoon with Sara, while I make up some time with my wife."

"So you're throwing me out after all, aren't you?"

Jack and Susan spoke in unison. "Yes."

***

That night, Liam got back to the hotel in a relatively good mood. At least it was a good one as long as he didn't think about the accident. He had been in accidents that came out of the blue. Even if Susan's mind had protected her by

238

blocking the memory, he knew very well that, in the split-second of impact, both she and Sara felt the violent surprise and terror, heard the metal and glass crashing and grinding, from the forceful and deadly intrusion of the other car into the space that a moment before had been safe and comfortable. That imprint would be unmistakably ingrained, subconsciously if not consciously, for the rest of their lives.

This was going to be one long night. It was early. He needed something to take his mind off the situation. His eye caught a glimpse of the phone. Slowly, hesitatingly, he picked it up and dialed. Ringing on the other end. One. Two. Three. And, just before the click of the answering machine, he heard it picked up. He counted to five.

"Marguerite? Liam."

36

"Well, well, well… I didn't think I'd hear from you. I guess you misplaced my number."

"How've you been, Marguerite?"

She chuckled. No, not a chuckle. That irritating, sarcastic laugh. "I'm just fine. Couldn't be better. My new book is launching next month. I've already set the tour. We're sure it's going to be a monster."

Interesting choice of words—monster.

He was already regretting the call. "If I recall, you said you'd 'love to continue' the conversation from the restaurant. Now's your chance."

"Yes. Yes, I did. And I do. But I'd much rather do it in person. I don't suppose there's any reason for you to be back in the City, though. Is there?"

The edge was unmistakable. If she was fishing for information, he wasn't about to give it to her.

"Oh, I might. You know, I come in from time to time these days. I'm not certain when. I have a life here. But I'll let you know."

"I do miss our late-night conversations, and I miss your brilliant analytical abilities. Maybe when you do get to New York, we can visit some of our old haunts. Also, I've gotten to know Plimpton pretty well. I think you two would hit it off spectacularly, and who knows, maybe *The Paris Review* awaits you?"

Liam was intrigued but caught himself. "Oh really?"

"You know, Liam, as spectacular as my success has been—and it has been spectacular--, I do lead a lonely existence. If you get my drift. I could use a good old-fashioned romp in the hay. Are you game?"

Dammit.

She was soliciting him.

"Are you talking dirty to me, Marguerite?"

"That depends. Do you want me to?" He was equal parts turned on and repulsed. He had nothing better to do, so he let her keep going.

"Can you imagine what I'm wearing?" Now she was purring.

"Not particularly, but do go on... ." He picked up the Milwaukee newspaper and started to scan the headlines.

"Why, I'm not certain if I'm wearing anything at all... ."

The call continued for a while, till she tired of her own game. He just let it play out. When they hung up, he told her he'd call her if he got to New York. He didn't know if he meant it.

***

"Good morning, beautiful! Your ol' Uncle Liam is here for your morning studies. Please feel free to interrupt if there's anything you don't understand, or if you need to take a break."

Liam sat down next to Sara and took a sip of coffee. Setting the cup down, he opened the *Times* and started glancing through its pages but found nothing interesting enough to discuss. He set down the newspaper and peered into his bag of books. He needed something of real substance today. His eyes were drawn to the largest volume in the bag.

Yes! That's it!

What better introduction to great literature than the greatest of them all— *Ulysses*. James Joyce. His idol. Oh, this was perfect. He looked at Sara.

"You're gonna love this one. I promise." He came to Buck Mulligan's verse and grinned.

"...He moved a doll's head to and fro, the brims of his Panama hat quivering, and began to chant in a quiet happy foolish voice:

I'm the queerest young fellow that ever you heard.

My mother's a jew, my father's a bird.
With Joseph the joiner I cannot agree,
So here's to disciples and Calvary."

The hospital's chaplain was walking by at that very moment. With a double take, the priest spun around and rushed into the room.

"Young man. What are you doing?"

Liam turned and looked up at him over his reading glasses. "I'm giving this little girl some culture."

The color rose in the priest's face as he nearly spit the response. "Blasphemer!"

Liam thought it best to try to cool the conversation down. "Oh, I don't know about that Father. It may be a bit disrespectful, but Joyce had real reservations about the Church."

Not about to be placated, and holding his hand to the sky (or at least the ceiling), the priest intoned in a deep voice—"…whosoever speaketh against the Holy Ghost, it shall not be forgiven him, neither in this world, neither in the *world* to come." On a roll now, he slowly and with great emphasis proclaimed—"The Word of our Lord, according to Matthew!"

Liam thought for a moment, then in equally grave tones, pronounced—"When the shark bites with his teeth, dear / Scarlet billows start to spread." Pausing for dramatic effect, he looked directly into the priest's eyes. "The Word of Bertolt Brecht, according to Bobby Darin."

The chaplain looked befuddled. "If you're mocking the Holy Ghost, you're on thin ice."

"I'm not mocking the Holy Ghost. I'm merely quoting a great German playwright."

"Bah! The penalty for blasphemy is…" Now he held both fists in the air. "…death!"

Liam smiled. "Joyce is dead, so I guess he got his punishment. Look Padre. This child's my friend. She's in a coma. She may or may not live. I'm going to do everything I can to stay connected to her, and to help her heal. You can, and please excuse me for saying this, fuck off."

The priest's jaw dropped. He turned to leave but stopped halfway. "Be gone, Satan!"

Liam chuckled. "You talkin' to yourself?"

Liam leaned in toward Sara. "I'm so sorry you had to see that. Some people, huh?" He sat down and opened the book again.

"Now. Where was I? Oh yes…

--If anyone thinks that I amn't divine
He'll get no free drinks when I'm making the wine…"

But the exchange with the priest had taken its toll. Putting Joyce back into the bag, he took out *Travels With Charley* again. "Okay, let's talk some more about Charley. You know—Steinbeck's dog. Another funny thing about him. Steinbeck claimed he could pronounce the consonant "F". Have you ever seen a dog who could do that? I know Lady can't. In fact, Charley makes the sound "Ftt" when he's ready to go pee. Yeah, I know. That's kind of a potty joke, and your mom would be upset if you said it. But it is funny, isn't it?"

Liam heard voices in the hallway outside the room.

"See? I told you. He's spewing filth at that sweet child, God rest her soul."

"I'm not sure what you heard, but what I'm hearing is innocent enough."

It was an older woman's voice. He thought he'd heard it before. One of the hospital's administrators. The voice got closer.

"Excuse me, sir. Can you tell me what you're reading?"

They were in the room now. He looked around and saw the priest, standing with clenched fists, a scowl on his face. The administrator had a kindly expression.

"Why certainly, ma'am. Happy to. It's John Steinbeck's *Travels With Charley*. A wonderful piece. I'm hoping it brings comfort to Sara."

She looked at the priest. "Honestly, Father, I don't know what you're worried about. Let's leave this gentleman to do his good work. Bless you, sir."

***

When Liam walked into her room later, Susan was sitting up, having lunch. He leaned down to kiss her on the forehead. She reached up and pulled his face to hers, kissing him on the lips. He flashed back to that moment at the cottage.

Oh no.

He pulled back.

"Oh, Liam. I'm so sorry. There I go again."

He fumbled for words. "I'm flattered Susan, but you know that's not going to work. Doesn't mean I don't care about you. You know that don't you?"

She turned away, looking out the window. "What a fool I am. Forget that ever happened. Please."

"What? What happened?"

She took his hand and squeezed. Another awkward moment averted. Then she looked at him and smiled.

"Tell me. Please tell me you weren't reading Joyce to Sara?"

Caught off guard, Liam choked back a laugh. "Why, who told you that?"

She shook her head. "Well, I guess it is an important work in Irish literature. And you are Irish, aren't you?"

He grinned. "I may have a little Irish in me."

244

A nurse came in and told Liam it was time to do an assessment of Susan's mobility. He stood up and reached down, giving her a hug. She held the hug, maybe a bit too long.

***

Liam was in his element that afternoon. He picked up *Travels With Charley* once again, and read on and on, for hours. Hitting his stride, he became completely absorbed in his storytelling. That is, until all hell broke loose. He saw Sara's arms twitching. The twitching swiftly moved into full convulsions. Her arms and legs, her hands and feet, started to pulse, alternately shaking and going completely rigid. Her head trembled and shook from side to side. She bit her tongue. She started to turn blue. He heard feet pounding, running down the hallway, breaking into the room. A sea of white coats and green scrubs muscled past him and surrounded Sara's bed. He stood up, scared and confused. One of the doctors grabbed him.

"Get out! You need to get out of the room."

The door slammed behind him as he hit the hallway.

Oh my God. Is this it?

He heard more footsteps. Jack was pushing Susan in a wheelchair, moving at a fast clip, accompanied by one of the nurses from Susan's floor. Their eyes were vacant, their faces grayish white. He held out his hand to greet them, but it was as if they didn't even see him. They pushed past him to Sara's door. The door opened and they were hustled in. He started to follow but the door closed in his face.

Soon, the door opened, and the white and green scrum pushed a gurney with Sara on it out of the room and down the hall, at a full run, Jack and Susan right behind. Neither acknowledged Liam. As near as he could tell, he was invisible.

37

"Mr. O'Connor, Sara's not coming back here."

He looked at the young nurse in panic.

"No, no... She's alive. They've taken her to intensive care so they can monitor her more closely. She's stable for now."

"Can I go to see her?"

"No. ICU's restricted to immediate family."

"Where are Jack and Susan?"

"I think they're with her or in the ICU waiting room, but..."

Liam took off at a run. Jenny shouted after him. "You can't go there... ."

Jack and Susan were sitting by themselves. Jack looked up without emotion. Susan didn't make eye contact. Liam figured she was too upset to talk. He went to hug Jack, but Jack stepped back.

Liam spoke in a subdued voice. "I'm so sorry all of this is going on. It's so much for you guys to handle, on top of everything else."

Jack's head lowered and he seemed to be talking to the floor. "You need to leave, Liam."

"What? Why?"

"The chaplain says you set it off by reading blasphemous and obscene books to Sara. Her system couldn't handle it, and now she's possessed."

"You don't honestly believe that, do you?"

"No, of course not. But the hospital believes you've become a distraction and that you're interfering with their treatment of Sara, and frankly, we can't argue with that. So please, for Sara's sake, leave us alone."

Liam felt hands grab his shoulders, and looked around to see two burly security guards, one on each side of him. He tried to shake them off. "What the fuck?"

***

"It's a mess and I don't know what to do."

"Oh Liam. What is it?" Madeline's voice was calming but clearly concerned.

"I think maybe it's time for you to come over here. If you can. Something's happened."

"What's wrong? Is it Sara?"

Liam had no clue how to explain. "She's okay, although she had an episode today that has the doctors concerned. I've done about all I can do here."

"What kind of episode, Liam?"

"She had some kind of a seizure. Maybe epilepsy? Don't know."

Silence hung in the air for a few moments before Madeline spoke again. "Okay. I understand that part. Now, what is this about you've done all you can do? What's that mean?"

"I've kind of been, well, thrown out of the hospital."

***

Liam went down to the hotel's bar. It was not his finest hour. He awoke in the morning on the floor of his room. There was a pounding that came from deep inside his head. He tried to place it but struggled. It dawned on him that it was the phone ringing. He crawled over to the bed stand and reached up. He fumbled with the receiver, finally snagging it and pulling it down to him.

"Liam? Is that you?"

"Maybe."

A pause. "Are you drunk?"

He looked around, then looked at himself. "I don't know. Why'd you ask?"

247

There was a chuckle on the other end. "Just a lucky guess. Liam, it's Madeline. I'm not even going to ask what's going on. I just wanted you to know that I'm about to head out. I should be there in a couple of hours. Are you going to be at the hotel?"

Liam looked around again. "I don't know. Let me check." He walked over to the window and drew back the curtains. "What time is it?"

"It's about nine thirty. I should be there by noon. Will you be there?"

"Well, I sure as shit don't have anywhere else to be."

"Have you called Helen?"

"Why would I do that?"

"Because you should. You're a fool if you don't."

"What else?"

"Please don't do anything rash before I get there."

"I don't have a rash."

"Of course not. See you soon."

Liam placed a call to Harold's office in New York. The receptionist said he wasn't in yet, so Liam asked to speak to his assistant. She answered the phone in her usual businesslike manner, but as soon as she heard Liam's voice her demeanor lightened.

"Hey Liam. I'm glad you called. Mr. Simon's been getting impatient about finishing up your project."

"Well, he should be very happy. I'm coming in tonight. That is, um, if you could make my arrangements?"

Liam spent some time putting his room back into order and getting cleaned up. A while later, Harold's assistant called back to give him the details for his flight and hotel for the evening. He thanked her and hung up. He sat for a minute or so, then picked up the phone and dialed another number. The call went directly to Marguerite's voicemail. He left her a message, saying that he would be in the City tonight, and would try to call again after he got in.

248

38

Taking a few minutes to re-orient himself, Liam looked around. It was the same upscale apartment building he recalled from years earlier. As he approached the door, he saw the familiar face of the long serving doorman.

"Hello Charles. Long time!"

Charles looked at Liam and cocked his head. His face lit up.

"Well hello Mr. O'Connor. So happy to see you again. Will you be visiting Miss Fairfield tonight?"

Liam smiled at the recognition, not the destination. "Why yes. Yes, I suppose I will."

Charles opened the door and motioned down the opulent hallway to the elevators.

"Enjoy your evening, Sir."

Liam tipped him and walked slowly down the corridor. He waited for the elevator, recalling they were very slow in this old building. That seemed just as well. His sense of anticipation was not what it had been in the early days with Marguerite. Yet here he was, on the same journey once again. As he pushed the button for Marguerite's floor, he took a moment and looked in the mirrors on the doors. He had to admit that he looked damn good for a forty-something. He was very much presentable.

Marguerite's apartment was at the end of a long hallway, directly opposite the elevator bank. He started the walk. It was almost like walking to the gallows. As he approached the door, preparing himself to knock, it opened. Charles had obviously alerted her that he was on his way.

Damn.

He didn't even have that final moment of decision. He smiled.

She spoke first. "Hello, stranger. I'm so glad you could join me."

He mumbled a response. Something between "Oh hi" and "Oh hell". She wasn't listening. A vision to behold, she was wearing an ivory-colored silk kimono. It glimmered in the soft light from the room behind her. Her hair was a bit longer than he remembered, her face flawless. She approached him slowly and took his hand in hers. Closing the door, she led him into the middle of the room.

"You don't know how long I've waited for this moment. I've missed you terribly, my Love."

Liam was turned on but attuned to the wariness he'd instilled in himself over the past few years. Was she a beautiful, passionate lover, or a venomous viper waiting to strike? He looked into her eyes. They were focused on his. She smiled and softly spoke.

"May I get you a drink? I'm assuming a nice whiskey, like old times?"

Liam nodded but didn't speak.

He looked around the room as Marguerite poured his whiskey, and a gin and tonic for herself. She was living high these days. Same apartment, but the artwork and furniture were a huge step up from what he remembered. She wore her wealth in a very visible fashion. She turned on some low jazz, setting the mood and doing it very effectively. He started to relax. Maybe this was going to be great after all. She came over and handed the glass of whiskey to him. She raised a toast.

"Here's to our mutual success. The Team. The Team."

Shit.

That was the rallying call they had made up in the early days, when it seemed like they were meant for each other, and about to take the literary world by storm. He fell back into that sweet mindset of an easier time. She took him in her arms, and started to dance, slowly and sensuously. He stiffened a bit, then grasped her and took charge of the dance.

They were wonderful together. Dancing with her came naturally, like riding a bicycle.

When the song ended, and before the next track came on, Marguerite wrapped her arms around Liam and reached up to kiss him. He leaned into the kiss, but just when he got there, she stepped back. With a flourish, she released her kimono, and let it fall to the floor. She was completely nude. As she stepped back into Liam's arms, an alarm went off in his head. Barely audible, but it was there. He closed his eyes and tried to ignore it, but it was insistent. It was saying something to him.

The Team… it stuck in his craw.

Everything that went down the day he threw her out flooded back into his mind. He listened. "Run."

No. This is bullshit.

"Run, Liam."

Marguerite looked at him. "What's wrong, sweetheart?"

He almost imperceptibly shook his head.

No. No.

"I want you! Don't you want me Liam?"

He took a step back. She moved toward him. He stepped back again. She moved again. He looked at her.

"No. No, Marguerite. I can't. I won't."

He turned toward the door. As he walked toward it, she grabbed his hand and put it on her breast. "Don't leave. Don't leave me, Liam."

He kept walking.

"I said don't leave me Liam!"

He glanced back. She had tears in her eyes. Running down her cheeks. He hesitated, then turned around and kept walking. She kept calling out to him as he walked out into the hallway. He could hear her sobbing. He glanced once more. Her body was trembling, and she was kneeling on the floor, naked. He hesitated momentarily, then turned back around and kept walking. When he got to the elevator, he

251

pushed the call button. The doors opened. He turned one more time to look. Marguerite was standing in her doorway, her face beet red and contorted.

"YOU COCKSUCKER!!!! HOW DARE YOU! I'LL DESTROY YOU!"

She gave him the finger, just as the elevator doors were closing. Liam smiled to himself. He spoke out loud, to the empty car. "Nope. Not a genuine bone in that scrawny body. It was all an act. Goodbye, Marguerite."

Charles held the door for Liam as he left the building and hailed a cab. As he was getting into the cab, Liam stuffed a healthy tip into Charles' hand.

"Goodbye old friend. Have a wonderful life."

Charles smiled, closed the cab door, and tapped on its top to signal to the cabbie to drive away.

39

"I did it!"

"Liam? Is that you? You do know it's midnight." Sharon sounded like she just woke up.

"But I did it. I thought you should be the first to know."

Sharon sighed. "Okay. I'll bite. What did you do?"

"I got rid of Marguerite."

She sounded confused. "I wasn't aware you had her? What's going on?"

He had neglected to tell her anything further after his mention of running into Marguerite on his last trip into New York. In fact, he hadn't even spoken with her in several weeks.

"Oh. I guess you didn't know."

"Know what, Liam?"

"I made a date with her. I'm in New York."

There was a long pause. "Are you sure this can't wait till tomorrow?"

"No. I'm headed back to Milwaukee tomorrow."

"Milwaukee?"

Another detail he had neglected to mention. "Yeah. I've been in Milwaukee."

"I'm not even going to ask." Sharon sighed. "So tell me about Marguerite. Why in the world did you make a date?"

Liam wanted desperately to get to the good stuff, but figured he needed to set the stage. "I had been kind of lonely and stressed. I thought maybe there was something there. She gave me her number when I ran into her before, so I called. I went to New York to wrap up some work on the new book. It went very well. Harold was... ."

"Liam. Focus. Let's stick with Marguerite."

"Oh yeah. Anyway, she invited me to her apartment."

"Oh, Liam. Why?"

He was too excited to reflect on that question, so he continued with his own narrative. "I went to see her. She came on to me. Hard. She had on a silk kimono, and... "

"Stop. I don't want the details. Just tell me the outcome. Did you sleep with her?"

"Oh hell no. I walked away." He knew what was coming next.

"And how did that make you feel?"

He paused for dramatic effect. "Well, at first, I felt really bad. She was crying, shaking, calling out to me. I wondered if maybe she really cared. Did I mention she was naked?"

"No, and I'd prefer you didn't. I need the results, not the pictures."

He was disappointed. He wanted to recount all the good stuff. Sharon could be such a killjoy. "Okay. Your loss. She kept crying out, pleading with me to come back, as I walked to the elevator. I was torn. Almost gave in."

"So what happened? Why didn't you?"

He paused again for effect. "Two little words."

"Two words?"

"Yes. Two words."

She sighed. "Okay, fire away."

"You cocksucker."

Long pause. "My fault. I shouldn't have asked. But now that I did, how'd that make you feel?"

Liam almost exploded with his response. "Great! It made me feel great! That bitch was playing me again. Nothing has changed. It was all an act. Badly played, but an act nevertheless."

"So what's your bottom line?"

"Vindication. When we broke up the first time, the advantage was all hers. I wanted her. I thought I loved her.

254

She did everything in her power to destroy me, and it worked. This time, I rejected her. Victory is mine. I have no feelings whatsoever for her. She has no power over me. She's just a pathetic, aging con. She begged me to want her. I walked away. I can't tell you how good I feel right now."

Sharon chuckled. "I think you just did, Liam. Congratulations. I'm proud of you. You've grown up."

Liam was on a high. His shrink actually praised him. "Thanks Sharon. I couldn't have done it without you."

"I know. Now, can I go back to sleep? We can talk further soon. Maybe, just for a change, you could make an appointment?"

***

"Why are you here? I could get to the hotel on my own."

"Oh, I don't know. I thought you could use some company." Madeline was standing at the gate in Milwaukee when he deplaned. "I may be a poor excuse, but it seems I'm what you've got. Let me drive you back to the hotel. We can talk along the way."

Liam was afraid to ask what had happened in his absence, and Madeline didn't volunteer anything until they got in her car and headed away from the airport.

"How are you, Liam? Was New York everything you hoped it would be?"

He was looking out the side window, watching the scenery pass by. "Oh, I guess you could say it was a success. I think the book's in good shape, and I took care of some old personal business that was long overdue."

"That's good. I'm glad you accomplished what you set out to do there."

They fell into a long silence. Finally, he looked over at her. "What's going on, Madeline? Why'd you come to the airport?"

255

"I think you should come to the hospital with me."

"Why in the world would I do that? I've been banned. They're not going to let me in."

She shook her head. "Remarkably, a lot has happened since you went to New York. Things have changed."

Liam was immediately concerned. "No. Please don't tell me... ."

"No, not that. It concerns the priest."

"What about him?"

"His name is Father Frank."

"Okay, Father Frank. Jerk."

She smiled. "Well, it turns out Father Frank was Father Fruitcake. After he succeeded in getting you thrown out, he decided to flex his muscles more. He started to make pronouncements and give orders."

"Like what?"

"He announced that Sara was possessed by the devil, and that he would 'deal with that'. Then he went on to submit a list of all the other patients he determined were also possessed. At that point, they knew he was a bit off."

"Wow. I guess so."

"It didn't stop there. That night, he was seen walking the corridors with a large silver cross hanging from his neck, carrying a wooden stake. When a couple of security guards confronted him, he became enraged and started shaking violently."

"That must've been quite a spectacle."

"He screamed at them when they touched him."

"What did he scream?"

"I am the Lamb of God..."

"Well, in fairness, he is a priest."

"Yes, but he then he thrust his hands to the sky and bellowed 'I am Oz, the Great and Powerful! Who are you?' Then he took off running. Finally the guards caught and tackled him."

"Holy Shit. Did they get him?"

"Yes, but it took a couple of orderlies piling on to restrain him."

"So, where's he now?"

"I'm not sure. Suffice to say he won't return."

Liam sat back in his seat. After a moment to reflect, he grinned and looked at Madeline. "Come forth Lazarus! And he came fifth and lost the job."

Madeline looked at him and shrugged. "What?"

"*Ulysses*. Fitting, I believe.

***

The tension was palpable as Liam and Madeline walked through the front entrance of the hospital. They checked in at the reception desk. Liam felt his first sense of relief when they were given visitor passes without question or comment. Then a sense of panic when the receptionist called after them.

"Oh, Mr. O'Connor. Please wait."

He froze in his tracks.

"Can you please stop by administration before you go up to the nursing floors?"

Liam looked at Madeline. She shrugged.

"I guess we'd better do as they say."

When they got to the administrative offices, Liam announced himself to the receptionist. She nodded and pointed to a small waiting area. "Please have a seat. Someone will be with you shortly."

Liam glanced at Madeline. "I don't have a good feeling about this."

She held her finger to her lips. They sat down. After a few minutes, which felt like hours to Liam, an older gentleman in a suit walked over to them.

"Mr. O'Connor?"

Liam stood up. "Yes. And this is Mrs. Frost."

The gentleman shook both their hands. "I'm Ted Connover. I'm the patient liaison for the hospital. I wanted you to stop by so I could personally express our sincere apologies for the unfortunate incident you had with Father Frank. I speak on behalf of the entire administration. The Father is not representative of anything this hospital stands for. His behavior was inexcusable, and it's being appropriately addressed."

Liam couldn't help himself. "Yeah, but it was you guys who kicked me out."

"Yes, we made a mistake. A big mistake. We take full responsibility. Please let us know if there is anything we can do to make things easier for you here. We've assigned a new chaplain to Sara and her family."

Liam looked directly at Ted. "Oh for God's sake. Keep the damn priests away. Haven't you done enough damage?"

"I completely understand. Thank you again for stopping by."

Liam took Madeline's hand. "Let's go. No need to waste time hanging around here."

As they started to leave, Ted called out after them. "Oh. One more thing. Legal has asked that I have you sign this paper."

Liam was incredulous. "What paper?"

Ted half mumbled his response. "Oh, it's just a release. It says you won't sue us."

Liam stopped and looked directly in Ted's eyes. "Ftt." The same sound Steinbeck's dog Charlie made. He walked away.

***

"We were such fools." Susan was sitting up in a chair, Jack standing by her side. "I don't know what to say. We never should have let them throw you out."

258

Liam ginned up a smile. "I hope you know I would never, ever, do or say anything to hurt Sara. You do know that, don't you?"

Susan spoke haltingly. "Liam, I..." She caught herself. "We... love you. We were frightened to death about Sara. We still are. But we need you."

She motioned for him to come closer. He stepped over, and leaned in. She grabbed him and hugged him. He let her.

"We have a favor to ask. Do you think you could find your way to read to Sara again? We'd love that. No strings. Whatever you want."

Madeline cleared her throat. "Might I make a suggestion?"

They all looked at her.

"I think Susan and Jack might actually have something particular in mind." She looked directly at them and smiled. "Am I right?"

Jack nodded and reached under the bedside table. He pulled out a well-worn volume and handed it to Liam. Liam looked at Madeline, then at the book. *In the Realm of One.*

Susan spoke up. "It's my personal copy. As you can see, I've read it multiple times."

Liam touched the book, held it up to the light, and flipped through its pages. "I think I can do this. I kind of remember it. No, I'd be proud to read it to Sara."

Susan chuckled for the first time. "Just not the controversial parts, okay?"

"Wouldn't think of it!"

Liam walked down the hall to the elevators. He was going to see his favorite little girl. Life was looking up. Marguerite: out of his life. Sara: back in his life. A very satisfying exchange. As he approached Sara's room, he ran into the young nurse, Jenny. She brightened when she saw him.

"Oh, I'm so glad you're back Mr. O'Connor. We've missed you around here."

"Thanks, Jenny. It's good to be back. How's Miss Sara today?"

"I think she's okay. Her color's good. No more episodes, at least none yet. Her vitals are stable. It's a good day."

Liam walked into the room. He sat down, took Sara's hand, and resumed his interrupted dialogue with her.

"You're looking lovely today, my little friend. I have a special treat for you. At least I hope it's special. You remember when you saw me typing, and you asked what I was doing? You remember I told you about storytelling? Well, I have here a book. It's a long story, and I wrote it. Yep, all by myself. It has a name— called a title in books. I named it. I got to do that because I made up the whole thing. It's called *In the Realm of One*. Now, I don't expect you to understand everything, so if you have questions, you know the drill. Just hold up your hand and I'll call on you. You'll have to speak clearly. I promise to do my best to answer you. All good? Great. Let's get going."

The reading came easily. After all, it was his own words.

"I'm not often at a loss for words, but here I was, standing on a hill and looking out at the magnificence of the Golden Gate Bridge… and I had nothing. On the other hand, I was alone. No harm, no foul, I suppose. If Bridget were with me, I suppose I could have waxed eloquently about the silver mist rising from the water, half obscuring the vivid orange towers that reached toward the sky, as the sun glinted off the cables high above. Yeah, that's what I could have done. She would have leaned in, her auburn hair soft against my shoulder. I would've turned and kissed her, smack on the lips. San Francisco would have us under its spell. But she wasn't."

Sara was the most special audience he'd ever had. He was certain she was hanging on every word. Every once in a while, he would stop and watch her. She would move ever so slightly, her lips twitching almost imperceptibly. Was she just waiting for her prince to come and sweep her away?

At some point, his voice tapered off and his head nodded forward. He fell asleep. He dreamed of playing with Lady at Madeline's. He threw her ball out into the water, and she swam effortlessly out to fetch it. A stranger stopped by him to watch. He could tell the stranger was taken by Lady's graceful motion as she swam. He was bursting with pride. He looked over at the stranger and called out.

"That's my dog!"

The stranger nodded appreciatively. "Magnificent animal." Liam turned back to the water, but Lady wasn't there. He panicked. She couldn't be gone. He just wanted to get out of there. As he struggled to escape, he slowly came out of his sleep. The stranger was calling. "Where's your dog?"

He woke up with a start. "Dog..." He looked for the stranger, but he wasn't there. The voice was familiar. Small, but very distinctive. Was he imagining it? It hit him. Sara. Sara speaking. Sara looking, eyes partly open.

Oh my God. She's awake.

He reached over, ever so gently, took her hand in his and squeezed. She squeezed back.

"Sara. Are you with me?"

She smiled, as if recognizing this was someone she knew. She cocked her head.

"Dog?"

He stood up. "Yes. Dog! Lady. Lady's her name."

She laid her head back on the pillow and mouthed the word. "Lady."

Liam was beside himself. He squeezed her hand again, and she squeezed back, harder now. He fumbled

261

around for the call button. When he found it he pressed it. Again and again. Jenny came running into the room.

"What's wrong?"

"Nothing. Absolutely nothing." He pointed at Sara. "She's back. She's with us."

Jenny leaned into Sara's field of view. "Hello, Miss Sara. It's so very, very good to see you."

Sara's eyes opened. "Who are you?"

That's my girl.

Liam chuckled.

Jenny smiled. "I'm a nurse. Nurse Jenny. I'm here to help you."

Sara looked and pointed at Liam. Liam pointed to himself.

"It's Liam, Sara. Do you remember me?"

Sara nodded and mouthed the word. "Liam."

He nodded in agreement. "Yes. Yes! Liam."

Color returning to her cheeks, Sara sighed and fell back into the pillow, apparently satisfied.

Jenny looked at Liam. "You stay here with Sara. I'm going to call the nurses' station upstairs and let them know. They can get her parents down here." She left the room.

Liam wasn't about to go anywhere.

40

Jack wheeled Susan into the room, Madeline following a few steps behind. Susan took Sara's hand. Sara opened her eyes briefly, saw her mother and smiled before closing them again. Madeline motioned to Liam and pointed to the door. They left the room just as a bevy of doctors and nurses arrived. Jenny came out of the room. "The doctors are going to have to spend some time with Sara now, and she's going to need a lot of rest. She has no clue what's happening, or even where she is. I'd suggest you guys go get some rest. Maybe a nice dinner. Can I let Sara's parents know you'll be back in the morning?"

***

In the morning, Liam and Madeline went together to Susan's room. She was alone, as Jack was with Sara. Susan smiled, then started to cry when they came in, but was able to compose herself. "I'm so very, very glad to see you two. I'm sorry we didn't get to talk yesterday after Sara woke up."

She looked up at Liam. "I would've loved to have been there when she opened her eyes, but I think it's beautiful it was you. What'd she say?"

"Dog. She said 'Dog'. Never mind the rest of us."

Susan shook her head. "No, Liam. She said 'Dog' because she saw you. She's always associated you with Lady. From the first time she saw you. You and Lady are one to her. It's lovely."

That hadn't occurred to him. "I guess I'm just the guy with the dog."

Susan looked up at him. "No. I think you're everything to her. The first adult who's ever taken the time to communicate with her, be by her side. You're very special."

263

Madeline took Susan's hand. "Would you like us to take you down to see her?"

"I'd love that. I just need to get out of this bed and into my wheelchair." She looked at Liam. "Could you excuse us for a few minutes?"

Liam looked confused. Madeline took his arm. "Liam. She wants you to leave. Can you do that?"

It dawned on him. "Oh. Sure. I'll just be… um… outside."

Madeline turned him toward the door and gave him a gentle push.

***

Madeline walked beside the wheelchair while Liam pushed it to Sara's room. When they got there, Jack was sitting at Sara's bedside, head on his chest. Sara was asleep. Madeline spoke.

"Mind if we come in, Jack?"

Jack broke into a big smile. "Yes, please." He motioned toward Sara. "She was awake for a while. She comes in and out, but she definitely knew I was here. I'm sure she'll be happy to see you. The doctors say we need to take things slowly. It's going to take some time to get her fully back."

Susan took Sara's hand and squeezed. Sara squeezed back, then lifted her head. "Momma?"

"Yes, dear. Momma's here. I'm never going to leave you."

Sara smiled, then fell back onto the pillow and closed her eyes again.

Susan motioned for Liam to come close. He kneeled next to the bed and stroked Sara's forehead.

"Sara. It's your Uncle Liam. You've been a very good student, and a great listener. It's been my honor to be with you, and to read stories to you."

She looked up at him. She mouthed his name once, then spoke it. "Liam."

"Yes, yes… Liam."

With some effort, she pointed at him. "Dog? Lady?"

"She's not here, but I know she misses you and wishes she could be."

Sara nodded. "Lady. Love."

Liam hung on each word. "Yes. Yes, Sara. Love."

Sara pointed at him again. "Liam. Love."

He lost it. He nodded yes as the tears streamed down his cheeks.

"I love you too, Sara." He stepped away to pull himself together, and motioned Jack to follow him. Once they were in the hallway, he took Jack's arm.

"I'm going to have to get back home. It looks like things are coming together here. Are you and Susan going to be okay with me leaving?"

Jack looked at the floor while he gathered his thoughts. "We so appreciate you, Liam. I don't know what we would've done without you. You brought us hope, and you brought our daughter back to us."

Liam shrugged. "No, your daughter brought herself back. Liam was just a passenger on the journey. I've been happy to be here to give whatever support I could."

"You've had a huge impact on us all here. But I do understand, and I'm sure Susan will as well. Please don't stay here on our account. You need to get home."

Liam held Jack's gaze. "Okay. Madeline's going to stick around as long as you need her. I'll not be far away. You need anything, just call me."

Jack and Liam returned to the room. Liam went to Sara and took her hand, again.

"I think it's time for me to go home. Madeline's going to stay. I won't be far away."

He squeezed Sara's hand and looked at her. She opened her eyes.

265

"I want you to take care of yourself. You need to get well. Your parents are here for you, and they're going to make certain you're cared for. Are you good with that?"

Sara nodded.

"Good. Now your Uncle Liam is going to go get in his big blue truck and rock the highway. You want anything from me, you just tell your mom and dad." He let go of her hand and turned to leave. As he started to walk toward the door, he stopped and turned around. "Oh. One more thing. Sara—I love you." He turned back around and walked out of the room before anyone could see him break down. He heard a voice behind him.

"Liam! Wait up a minute." It was Susan. He turned to see Jack wheeling her out of the room. She got to him, and waved Jack off. Liam knelt next to her. She locked her eyes with his. "You mean so much to me. I want you to know that. I'll never forget you."

He went to kiss her on the forehead. She grabbed his face and kissed him on the lips. He let her.

41

"I hear you want to fetch your charge?" Earl was smiling.

"Sure do. I've missed her."

Liam heard footsteps. Lady came running around the corner and charged over to him. Her tail was wagging furiously, her whole body wiggling. He leaned down and hugged her. Lady licked him with obvious joy.

"Oh, how I've missed you!" He knelt beside her, and she pressed her body against his, then rolled over for belly rubs.

He looked up at Earl. "She's looking a little chunky—I think she suckered you into too many treats."

Earl laughed. "Oh, she didn't sucker us at all. She deserved every one of them. After all, her dad abandoned her."

"I'd never do that. She's too special." He stood up. Lady stood as well, her body still pressed against his leg. Liam opened the door and Lady ran straight to the truck and sat, waiting for him to open its door. She hopped up and Liam followed. Starting the truck, he waved to Earl and drove off.

"We're going home, my friend. You and I have a whole lot of catching up to do."

***

As Liam pulled up to his house, he could see something approaching out of the corner of his eye. No. Not something. Someone. Mrs. Sommers, pulling a large sack filled with newspapers and carrying a plate of something.

Dear God, please don't let this be happening.

She was inexorably headed his way, with a determined look on her face. She arrived, grunting as she pulled the sack.

"Oh good! I didn't think you were coming home. I was afraid you'd left us."

"What the hell is this, Mrs. Sommers?"

"Why, you never stopped your newspapers, so I kept them all for you."

There was no use protesting. He eyed the plate.

"And what in God's name is that?"

It held five shriveled up, moldy clumps that may have been brownies at one time. Two of them had bites missing.

"That lady made these for you."

"When the hell was that?"

"Oh, a while ago. I thought you'd want them. They were very good, you know. I didn't think you would mind if I tasted them."

Gagging, he looked away. "Get rid of them. Jesus."

She shrugged. "Your loss." She picked up one and took a bite.

***

Later, as he and Lady approached the Owl's Eyes, Liam heard music. Disco music. Coming from the direction of the awning over the front door. He didn't remember having a loudspeaker outside, and he was starting to be wary of what he was going to find when he got there. When he walked in the door, the music was even louder. He didn't see anyone tending the store. Then, the unmistakable sound of Jeremy's voice.

"HE'S HEEEEEERE!... HE'S HERE!!!"

Then, Marianne's voice.

"Inside voice, Jeremy. How many times do I have to tell you?"

They both appeared from the back of the store. Jeremy was twirling, pointing at the speakers in the ceiling.

268

"Isn't it great? Now, everyone can party!"

Liam glared as he pulled himself together. "What the fuck are you doing to my store?"

Jeremy apparently wasn't going to let criticism get in his way.

"Well, we thought... ."

Marianne cut him off. "No. Not 'we'. You thought."

"Yeah! I thought... I thought it was high time for this place to have some great energy. And what better way… ."

Liam walked past them without speaking and went to his office. Or what had been his office when he last saw it. His desk was littered with empty pop cans and empty bags of pretzels. He stopped dead and spun around.

"MARIANNE! GET THE HELL IN HERE. NOW!" Nothing. "Oh Marianne—could you please stop by my office?"

She tiptoed in. "Yes?"

He swept his hand toward the mess. "Why? Why were you using my office?"

"Well, you weren't using it, and I was in charge."

"In charge of what? Mayhem? I'm going to give you about ten minutes. When I come back, I expect my office to look exactly like it did when I left town. Got it?"

She started to respond. "But… ."

"But nothing. Exactly. Got it?"

"I guess."

Liam walked out, pushing past Jeremy, who was dancing in the hallway.

"And Jeremy? With all due respect, could you please turn that shit off?"

Liam took Lady and walked down the street, trying to get away from the store and the aggravation he'd already faced. He ambled down to the riverfront and sat on a bench along the boardwalk. He pulled a pack of cigarettes out of his pocket and started to take one out. He paused and reconsidered. Smoking had lost its appeal. He put the pack away. He thought about his last conversation with Sharon. She said he'd "grown up". He tried to get his head around that concept. Was it true? Was he really being more mature? Maybe he wasn't ready to be grown up. Or maybe he was growing up and just couldn't see it?

Jesus. It's too much.

He stood up, shook it off, and headed back to the store.

He heard the *Requiem* as he approached the front door.

Damn that Marianne. She has to taunt me.

He walked in and stopped in his tracks. Both Marianne and Jeremy had black capes on, and they were moving somberly around the front counter.

"Oh my God. Unless this is a magic act and you're gonna disappear behind the capes, I'd suggest you cut the crap."

They looked up at him and slowly nodded. Then they grinned and dropped the capes.

"Welcome back Captain."

Liam looked around. "Where's Vera?"

Marianne spoke first. "She's not back yet."

Liam was puzzled. "Back from what?"

"She's still resolving some 'issues'."

"And when might we see her again?"

"Not sure."

Liam moved on. "Okay. What else is going on that I need to know about?"

Jeremy held up his arm. "Oooh, Oooh!"

Liam looked at him and shook his head in resignation. "Jeremy? Do you have something to say?"

Jeremy nodded animatedly. "Oh, yes. We've prepared a little event for you. We're VERY excited about it."

"Not sure I should ask, but what is that?"

Jeremy looked at Marianne. "Do you want to tell him?"

Marianne stepped forward. "Okay. Jeremy and the boys have some friends who've opened a restaurant in Madison. They— We— have booked it for a private party for Saturday night. To celebrate your return to town. It should be very nice."

Jeremy had his arm back up. "Oooh! Oooh!"

Liam looked at him. "Yes, Jeremy?"

"It's a wonderful little spot. Our friends are very proud of it. This will be their first event."

Liam looked at Marianne. "And you're satisfied with this?"

She nodded. "I think it's gonna be okay. Just a small gathering. The boys, me, maybe Earl, and maybe Vera."

Liam was unconvinced. "You know how I feel about these things."

"Come on, Liam. It's a chance for their friends to show off the restaurant."

He stared off at the back of the store. "This is against my better judgment."

42

"My friend, I'm afraid you're going to have to stay home from the ball tonight. I promise I'll bring you some goodies. Will that be okay with you?"

Lady stretched, then walked into the living room and flopped on the floor. Liam took one last glance in the mirror, just to make sure he still looked perfect. Light blue Oxford shirt with a summer blazer, no tie. Satisfied, he patted Lady's head. "I'll see you later. Don't get into any trouble. You hear me?"

The directions to the restaurant were confusing at best, but he stuck it out and finally found the place. A small, nondescript building with a stone front. There was a maroon awning over the front door, with "Chez Ray" in script on it.

When he arrived at the door, a well-dressed young woman opened it and welcomed him. She introduced herself as Genevieve, one of the owners. She led him to a private room adjacent to the main dining room. He looked up to see the welcoming committee of his employees. Jeremy, clapping enthusiastically, was dressed in true Jeremy fashion: red short-shorts, a yellow tank top and a purple sport coat with glitter. He spun around and displayed his ensemble.

"I think it says 'I'm formal, but I'm special'—don't you?" He ran over to greet Liam. "Mister Liam O'Connor, this is your night! We wanted to welcome you home with the finest."

Liam was well past being surprised by Jeremy, so he just went with the flow. "Thank you, Jeremy. You look… swell."

Liam looked around the room, at the familiar cast of characters. Ronaldo was wearing high waisted powder blue trousers, with a white, ruffled silk shirt, and a blue waistcoat that matched his trousers. He stood stoically behind his chair, master of the Torero pose.

To his left, seated, was Mikaela, who apparently felt this was an important enough occasion to come out for the evening. She had on a summery cotton dress in pink. She was wearing a short blonde wig, her collarbone flocked with glitter. She smiled at Liam.

"So very happy to see you."

"And nice to see you, too, Mikaela. I'm so glad you came."

Finally, Marianne stood next to Earl, who looked bored and uncomfortable. She waited for Liam to walk over to her, but he didn't. She gave up and went to him.

"Glad you made it, Boss. We had bets out on it."

Jeremy jumped up and down. "I won! I won! Nobody else bet on you."

Liam shrugged. "Well, at least one of you is loyal. I'll keep that in mind."

Genevieve and a young man came into the room. The young man introduced himself as Ray. He explained that he and Genevieve had graduated from UW a year earlier and had been working hard on the restaurant ever since, getting it ready to open.

"It was a dream of ours ever since we were freshmen."

Liam smiled. "So how did you meet the three amigos over there?" He pointed in the direction of the boys.

Ray started to respond, but Genevieve cut him off.

"We got to know them through some art classes we all took. Ray and I took pity on them because they seemed to always be starving. We saw what they were cooking for themselves and decided they would never survive unless we stepped in. Besides, it was great practice for what we're doing now."

Jeremy was beaming, again. "Yeah. We'd eat just about anything they cooked!"

Genevieve grimaced. "I guess that's not much of a recommendation, is it?"

Liam smiled. "Don't worry. We get it. Thanks for hosting this tonight."

Ray disappeared and returned with a server helping him bring out several bottles of wine. Liam looked at him.

"Who selected the menu? Or should I ask?"

Ray laughed. "Don't worry. We'd never let these guys near the menu. Your manager over there worked with us."

Liam stared at Marianne. "Manager?"

Marianne covered her tracks quickly. "Oh, that's just a loose term he made up."

Ray looked confused. "But you told... ."

Marianne went for the misdirection. "Hey look who's coming?"

Everyone turned toward the door.

Genevieve had left the room and returned accompanied by a remarkable sight. It took a few minutes for it to register with Liam.

"Vera?"

Vera walked into the room with remarkable poise. Her hair was fashionably styled in a short cut, perfectly framing horn-rimmed glasses. Her posture was perfect—straight and tall. She wore a long white pantsuit and looked every bit the sophisticated urban businesswoman.

Liam was stunned. "Holy smoke. Where the hell did you come from? What happened to Vera?"

She smiled and pointed at Jeremy. He seemed bursting with pride, his whole body rocking and swaying side to side.

"Let me present the new Miss Vera."

Liam looked at him. "How on earth did you pull that off?"

Marianne jumped in. "You told me to make Jeremy fix it. I would say he did quite the job, wouldn't you?"

274

Jeremy couldn't contain himself. "You want gorgeous? You want spectacular? Just look at me! Who else would you call? Isn't she just dynamite?"

Another figure stepped into the room, taking Vera's hand. Vera looked around and smiled.

"Everyone—- I'd like to introduce you to Mort."

Mort had spiked blonde hair and wore a black tux with a bow tie. Liam sidled over to Marianne and whispered in her ear.

"Who is this guy?"

"Not a guy, Boss. A woman."

"What?"

"A woman, Liam. Mort is short for Morticia. Get it?"

"Well I'll be damned."

Marianne turned him back around and whispered to him.

"Say hello, Liam."

"Vera, you look ravishing! And very pleased to meet you, Mort. Welcome to the world of the Owl's Eyes."

Vera blushed and lowered her head. Mort reached out and with a firm grip shook Liam's hand.

"Nice to meet you too. You're not at all what I pictured from Vera's description."

Liam was still trying to figure out what the hell she meant when Genevieve ushered him to the table.

Liam sat down, and everyone else followed suit.. The wine was poured, and Marianne clinked her glass. "Quiet folks! Jeremy wants to make a toast."

Jeremy's eyes grew large and he turned red. "Oh no. No. Marianne. Don't make me do it! Pleeeeeaase!"

Marianne sighed and grabbed his arm. "Speak!"

Jeremy started to shake, then steadied himself. "All right. I hope you all noticed just how ravishing Vera looks tonight." He found his stride. "She's had the Jeremy Touch. FABULOUS... RIGHT? And MISTER Liam O'Connor is here… " He turned to Liam and winked. "Not so fabulous, Liam. I think you could use some Jeremy as well!" Blowing a kiss to Liam, he looked back at the room. "Just kidding, folks! I just LOVE this handsome man. Don't you? Who wouldn't? Anyhoooo! Let's have a glittery, sparkly time tonight!"

Marianne stood up. "And there you have it. Let's get this party started." She pointed at Liam and raised her glass. "Cheers Boss!"

Liam looked around in satisfaction. He felt it incumbent on him to speak, to give words to the gratitude he felt. All these people came together to celebrate his return to town. He caught Genevieve's eye and called her over.

"Can you bring out your best champagne and spread it around?"

"Absolutely. Just give me a few minutes."

As she retreated from the room, he gathered his thoughts. In a little while, Genevieve and Ray came back with bottles of champagne and glasses. As they were pouring, Liam clinked a fork on his glass.

"Before we get into dinner, I want to take a few minutes to speak to you all. I'm absolutely honored, and very much humbled, by all of this. I know I can be an asshole from time to time at work."

Vera raised her glass. "Here! Here!"

Liam glared at her, and she looked down at the table, clearly embarrassed.

"But obviously, I must have been doing something right to have such wonderful and loyal employees and friends as you all. I can't say enough for all that you've done, and all that you've come to mean to me. As you know, my new book is nearing publication. I suspect you also know that I couldn't have pulled it off without the work and support you've given me over the last year. You're remarkable. I consider you all my friends."

276

He paused and looked around before starting up again. "You all mean so much to me. Just the thought that you've gathered together to honor me is so emotionally gratifying."

Marianne started to applaud. The others all joined in. The applause got louder and louder as Liam was talking. He was overwhelmed, brought to tears.

"Thank you! Thank you all so much!"

They seemed to be looking past him. Maybe they were transfixed by his handsomeness and didn't want to seem awkward. He cut quite a figure tonight, that's for sure. Then Marianne stood, held her hand to her mouth and let out a loud whistle. She wasn't looking at him at all. None of them were. He turned around and gasped.

Helen. Standing not three feet behind him. Smiling. Beautiful. Wearing the same outfit she wore the night he met her at Madeline's—the silk bandana, the linen skirt, the tunic, the camisole.

Oh my God.

He didn't know what to do. He was paralyzed. Was it real or an apparition? She moved toward him and held out her arms. No, it was real. Liam stood up, tripping over his chair as he tried to get to her. Everyone around the table was standing, holding up their champagne glasses in tribute. He steadied himself. Slowly, carefully, as if in a dream, he walked to her. He spread his arms to meet hers. They embraced as the room broke into wild applause.

As Liam and Helen stood, embracing, music started to fill in the room.

The *Flashdance* theme. Liam turned around and pointed at Jeremy. Jeremy grinned and pointed back as he swayed to the music.

"Kiss her!!!"

Liam turned back to Helen, leaned down, and they kissed. Not a peck on the lips. A full-on, passionate, go for it and put-on-a-show kiss. Then it hit Liam. This wasn't a

277

welcome-home party honoring him. No, this was a carefully orchestrated plot.

Those bastards. They pulled it off.

Helen looked into his eyes. "I've missed you, you ridiculous man."

"I've missed you too. So much. I'm an asshole."

"Yes you are." She motioned to the door. "Let's get out of here for a minute."

Liam turned to the assembly. "We'll be back. Carry on."

They weren't even looking at him. They were standing around, congratulating each other. Only Vera was looking his way. With a big smile on her face, she held her arm up and saluted him. He pointed at her and smiled back.

When they got outside the restaurant, Helen looked into Liam's eyes.

"Whatcha doing tonight, Big Guy? You got plans?"

"Not a one. You have something in mind?"

"You know, I believe I have a nice Benedictine at home that might go well as a nightcap. What do you say?"

"I could go for that. Yes. I'd like that."

There was a lot they were going to have to discuss, but for now they seemed content to take in the moment. They hugged again and kissed passionately and long. Then Liam lovingly held her face in his hands.

"So this party wasn't about me after all, was it?"

"No. Apparently it was about us, which is really sweet of them. I didn't know whether to do it. Lots of pain still in here." She pointed to her heart.

"I know. I know that. But I'm so glad you did."

She motioned to the restaurant. "We really should get back in there. They went to a lot of trouble for us. And I understand the food is really something."

Liam hugged her one more time, then took her hand. They walked back into the room as the servers were starting

to bring the food in. The applause started up again, but Liam
motioned to hold it down.

"Let's eat!"

43

Helen was still asleep. Liam reached over and touched her shoulder. Opening her eyes, she moaned and moved closer to him. Just as he was starting to climb on her, there was a knock at her door. She looked at him.

"I have no idea…."

Liam put his finger to his lips. "Let me handle this."

He stood up and grabbed a towel to hide his nakedness. He walked through her living room, which was filled with a path of discarded clothing leading to the bedroom. He got to the door, took a breath, and opened it. Stephen. Liam shook his head in amazement.

Stephen stood there, stunned, mouth open. "Just what the hell are you doing here?" He almost spit the words.

Liam paused for a second before responding. "Let me give you a hint." He let the towel drop. Stephen looked down and gasped.

"Ohhhh…"

"Get my drift?"

"You—you, you—wouldn't."

"Oh, I would. And I did."

"But she's—I mean, I—Oh shit. You're ruining everything." Stephen turned, started to walk away, turned back around, mumbled "Damn you", then stormed down the hall and up the stairs.

Liam waited until the upstairs door slammed shut. Grinning, he walked back into the bedroom. Helen was still sitting in bed.

"Don't tell me. Let me guess!"

Liam nodded. "I suspect he couldn't handle the sight of a real man!"

Helen bit her lip. "Well, I guess we won't be hearing from him again. At least not today." Then she looked at

Liam and held her arm out, wiggling her finger. "Come here, you…Come on in!"

Liam pounced on the bed. "I think I've got a little something…. Let me rephrase that. A big something… just for you."

She held her arms out and smiled as she stared at him. "Oh yes. Yes, you do."

"Say… You got any of that fondue?"

***

"What's for breakfast?"

Helen threw a pillow at him. "Is that all you can think of?"

"Why no, it's not, but that other thing may have to wait for at least a few minutes for us to recover."

She shook her head. "Unfortunately, big guy, I forgot to shop yesterday. How about we get cleaned up and head over to the Union to pick something up? We can sit out on the terrace and enjoy this lovely day."

Liam cocked his head as if thinking it over. "Okay. I guess we could do that. Shall we shower together?"

"I don't know. We've only just gotten just back together. Don't you think that's a bit forward?"

He threw the pillow back at her.

***

As they sat overlooking Lake Mendota, Liam looked into Helen's eyes. "So. Stephen."

"You're an idiot, O'Connor. I get that you don't like the man, but can you explain why you thought I had any interest in him? Wasn't I clear about that?"

"Look, Helen. The guy made sure he was at your place and in my face every time I came to see you. He acted like he lived there. And then you were going to go out with him to dinner."

"Liam, we've been through this. Seems to me it comes down to you didn't believe me, didn't trust me. Has that changed now? If it hasn't we have a bigger problem."

Liam looked at the ground. "I'm sorry, Helen. We haven't talked about it, but I didn't just move here from New York to find my inner self in the Midwest."

"I've wondered about that. New York's the center of the literary universe, and you were right in the midst of it all."

"I know. But I was in a relationship that was annihilated by betrayal. It's taken me years of very expensive therapy to work through it, and I'm afraid its effects were still lingering until very recently."

"I'm sorry, Liam. Do you want to talk about it?"

"Nah. You'd have to talk to my therapist if you wanted to know more."

"Would you like me to do that?"

"Do what?"

"Talk to your therapist."

"Oh hell no!"

"You said 'until very recently'. What's changed?"

"I guess I have. You've come into my life. You and a little girl who taught me about honesty and the fragility of life. I can't carry the ghosts of my past forever."

Helen put her arm around Liam as they looked out over the lake. Liam leaned in and kissed her. Afterward, she held his face and looked into his eyes.

"Don't ever doubt me. I love you."

He was caught off guard. She had said the word. The word he'd neither heard from nor uttered to any woman since Marguerite's betrayal all those years ago.

"I love you too."

There. He said it. Words he didn't think would ever pass through his lips again.

She hugged him, looking up at him. "And one more thing?"

He was overcome with emotion. "Yes?"

"We should eat our food before it gets cold."

Something else was weighing on Liam's mind. "I hesitate to ask, but where are you jobwise?"

"I don't know, honestly. I don't have any decision from Wisconsin. The Dean has told me they're very interested in having me here, but there are internal discussions going on and he hasn't given me any indication of when there might be an answer. Right now, Wesleyan's expecting me to be there for the start of classes in August. My landlord here has agreed to let me stay on through the end of July."

Liam looked out over the water. "That's cutting it tight, isn't it? Where does that leave us? You and me?"

"I don't know. Where would you like it to leave us? Can you handle a long-distance relationship?"

"I've never tried. I guess I don't know. I do know I want to be with you."

She took his hand. "And I want to be with you. But there are practicalities involved. How would you feel about moving to Ohio? Is that something you might consider?"

"I don't know. My life's here now. I'm not sure what I would do in Ohio."

"Maybe you could teach at Wesleyan?"

Liam shook his head. "I'm a writer, Helen. I don't think I could tolerate having to deal with kids. And I know I couldn't put up with the bullshit of academic politics. Bunch of pretenders and pompous assholes."

She smiled. "Yeah. But you can be a pompous asshole too. Maybe you'd fit right in?"

"Real funny, Helen. I may be an asshole, but at least I can get out of my own way."

She laughed. "Really?"

"Hey! I thought you loved me?"

She squeezed his hand. "I do. I do love you. But you are what you are."

Liam pointed out to the lake. "Look. We're not going to resolve those questions today. See the water sparkling in the sun? That's how I feel sitting here with you. I want to take it all in. Last night and this morning have been a whirlwind. I'm happy being with you. I'm even happier making love with you."

Helen looked at him. "If I could have my wish, it would be that we sit here together forever. What could be better than a bright summer day with you?"

Liam smiled. "You know, as much as I would love to grant your wish, I'm thinking we should put this day in motion. Would you be willing to pack up and come home with me for a couple of days? I need to tend to some things, but I also want very much to be with you. Do you have any commitments that would keep you here?"

Helen cocked her head. "You know, that's not much of a rosy invitation, but then it's coming from a curmudgeon. An adorable, sexy curmudgeon, but nevertheless—"

He held his hand to his chest. "What do you mean? I thought it was perfectly said. I'm a famous author, you know."

"Oh, I know. But sometimes the author of pure bullshit." She reached up and kissed him on the cheek. "But I'd be happy to come with you. I have nothing keeping me here."

44

Liam woke to a foul smell. Helen's breath was awful. He didn't know how to give her the news. He opened his eyes, just a bit. A large tongue licked his face.

"Ugh!"

Lady was wedged between them, her head on Liam's pillow, her tail thumping on the duvet.

Helen opened her eyes and startled. Then she started to laugh. "Well, I guess she's got your attention!!"

Liam, propped up on one elbow, reached over Lady to caress Helen. Lady re-inserted herself between them. First, she licked Liam, then she turned and licked Helen. Liam gave in to a smile.

"I guess you've made it into the pack." He moved Lady out of the way. "I'm thinking this probably isn't going to be the best time to put my spectacular moves on you?"

"Probably not. But just so I know, what kinda moves didya have in mind?"

"Well, remember that night I had your pie?"

She moaned. "Oh yes. And you liked my pie as I recall."

"I sure did. So what would you say if I told you I had a little treat lined up for you right here?"

"I would say that'd be… special. What've you got?"

"Mayonnaise!"

"Really… and what special treat can you make with it?"

"A big."

"Yes."

"Juicy."

"Oh yes!"

"Baloney sandwich."

"What?"

"Yeah. A baloney sandwich. Pretty much all I've got in the fridge."

She chased him out of the room. "You're pathetic, O'Connor."

Liam went to the kitchen, followed in close order by Lady, then Helen. As he was filling Lady's food dish, he turned to Helen.

"Uh... I forgot that I had an appointment set with Sharon for this morning. Would I be an awful companion if I kept it?"

Helen smiled. "After the mayonnaise, I don't know. But no, you wouldn't. I can hang here with Lady. Maybe I'll take her for a walk. We can catch up with you after. How's that?"

"You're the best."

"I know."

***

"Wait a minute. You're back with Helen? Last time you and I spoke, you were never going to see her again, because she done you wrong." Sharon smiled. "Am I right?"

Liam had to chuckle. "Yeah, she done me wrong. Or so I felt at the time. Turns out she didn't. Anyway, my faithful employees pulled a trick on me Saturday night."

Sharon cocked her head. "And how's that?"

He leaned forward in his chair, as if to emphasize the importance of the tale he was about to tell. He took a deep breath.

"Well, they tricked me into going to a dinner party at a fancy restaurant in Madison. It was ostensibly to honor me for getting my new book done and welcoming me back from Milwaukee. They pulled it off. I was touched and impressed that they were so excited for me, and more so that they were picking up the tab at an expensive place."

286

Sharon leaned in, mimicking him. "And then? And then what?"

"I don't know if I should tell you or not."

"But you're going to, aren't you?"

"Well, okay. I guess. If you insist. They pulled some surprises to distract me."

"Like what?"

"Like, my bookkeeper Vera. You know—the crazy, stinky one? Anyway, Vera showed up all glammed by Jeremy, and she came with a guy named Mort, only Mort wasn't Mort, but Morticia. Damn, who knew she was a lesbian?"

"Whoa. Focus, Liam. Focus. What about Helen?"

"Oh yeah. They hid her and had her show up behind me just as I was giving my speech."

Sharon scribbled something in her notebook, then looked up. "How'd that make you feel?"

He sat up straight. "Shocked the hell out of me."

"But how did it make you feel?"

"Good! I mean, how do you think I would feel? She came back to me. After all the shit I gave her. We embraced. We kissed. We—"

Sharon held up her hand. "Stop. I get the picture. But let me back up. What about 'all the shit I gave her'? So you're saying you admit you were wrong?"

Damn.

"Wait a minute. She went out on me."

"Liam. Listen to yourself. I'm going to make this simple. We don't have time for you to go through your usual denial and enlightenment phase today. Admit that your alleged reason for breaking up with Helen was pure bullshit. Can you do that?"

"I guess so. But at the time—"

"Forget 'at the time'— it was bullshit, right?"

"Okay, okay. Right. It was bullshit."

"And yet she forgave you, didn't she?"

287

Liam hadn't exactly thought in those terms yet. "Wow. You think so?"

Sharon sighed. "Uh-huh. I think so. No. I know so. And you?"

Liam paused to consider. "I guess I do. So does that mean I owe her now?"

Sharon dropped her pen. "Oh for God's sake Liam. It's not a zero-sum game. Neither of you owes the other. It's a relationship. And while we're on that subject, where do you both stand now?"

He was afraid this was coming. "Helen told me she loves me."

"And?"

Now he was uncomfortable. "And what?"

He looked away from her and mumbled. "Me too."

Sharon stood, walked over and leaned down, staring directly into his eyes from very close range, like a detective closing in for the kill. "You too what?"

He was dead meat. "I told her I loved her."

She didn't move. "And do you?"

Checkmate. "Yes. Yes I do."

"Do what?"

"I do love her. There! Satisfied? I love Helen Woodson."

"Thank God. Oh, and I hesitate to ask, but just to be sure, where's your head with Sylvia?"

"Nowhere. My head's nowhere with Sylvia. As far as I'm concerned, she doesn't exist. That was the old Liam—before he grew up and fell in love for real."

"And Marguerite?"

"Dead to me."

Sharon smiled. "Well okay. We're out of time. We can pick up with the new Liam again next week."

Liam went to hug her, but she pulled back. "Keep it professional."

"Okay. I get it. But thanks."

288

He stood up to leave. Just as he reached the door she called out.

"One more thing, Liam."

"Yes?"

"Don't screw it up. Got me?"

"Yes Ma'am. Got you."

***

Liam decided to walk to the boardwalk at the riverfront. It was a great place to let go of everything and take in the peaceful flow of the river. He looked up to see Helen and Lady coming toward him. Helen looked amazing. The tan she'd picked up over the summer gave depth to her complexion, and the sun glistened on her hair. She was beautiful and he was transfixed. Lady saw him first and pulled Helen over to Liam. Helen held him tight, then pulled back a little to look at him.

"Did you have a good session?"

He was unused to talking about his sessions with Sharon. For one thing, there was never anyone to tell, or who would even care, for that matter. Yet here was Helen, asking the question. He took a deep breath. "It was good. Much of what she brings to me is just common sense. Something she often reminds me I lack."

"Sometimes common sense is overrated, Liam. Ask any artist. It can hold you back from greatness."

Liam took her hand and they started walking, Lady trailing behind. "How so? You're a great artist, and you have common sense."

She looked up at him and smiled. "Yes, but I know the difference, and I know when to suspend common sense. How do you think I ended up with you?"

***

289

Liam wanted to stop by the store to see how things were going, and to pick up some papers he'd left in his office the last time he was there. He left Helen to chat with Marianne and Vera, who had returned to work, no longer relegated to isolation. Liam went to his office and started to pull things together. The phone rang.

Marianne buzzed him. "It's your agent."

Liam looked at the phone. He paused before picking it up.

The voice on the other end was remarkably cheery. "Liam, darling. It's your favorite agent! I have some good news for you. Very good news."

"And what's that, pray tell?"

He knew she was counting to ten, for effect. He cut her off at six. "Out with it, Janice. I'm busy."

"Oh, you silly boy. Janice has great news for you. I've done my thing." Silence. "Liam. *Darby's Gift* hits on September 15. You can thank me now."

45

"Madeline was certainly surprised when I picked up the phone!" Helen was smiling.

Liam looked at her and grinned. They were on their way back to Madison, with Lady perched between them, panting.

"That's funny! Last time I spoke with her you and I were on the outs."

Helen slapped the back of his head. "No. *You* were on the outs. I hadn't gone anywhere."

Liam blew her a Bronx cheer. Lady licked his face, and Helen laughed.

"Anyway, she was happy— really happy-- to hear the news."

Liam nodded. "So. What's up?"

"Susan and Sara are home and doing pretty well. They're going to come up to the cottages two weeks from now, and Madeline asked if we could as well. She's not going to say anything to them until we commit."

He thought for a few moments before responding. "We've got a lot going on, but I wouldn't want to miss the opportunity to see them. I've also been wanting to do something special for Sara. I'm not sure what it would be, but I want to make it really memorable. I don't want her to forget me."

"Oh, I don't think that's a risk, big boy. You're her hero. But I do think it would do us both a lot of good to get away. Let's do it."

"You sure? What about your job situation?"

"My job's going to play out however it plays out. Taking a few days away from things isn't going to get in its way."

They rode in silence for a while. Finally, Helen looked over at Liam.

291

"While we're at it, what about you? Your book's about to be released. What's next? Where's your life headed?"

"I'm a writer. It's what I do. I have a few ideas, but nothing for certain. Maybe I write some new stories. Maybe poems. It's both a frightening time and an exciting time."

Helen nodded, then went silent again. She stared straight ahead. "So here's the big one. Where would you want to be, ideally?"

He didn't skip a beat. "With you, Ms. Woodson. With you. Other than that, it doesn't really matter. I could write in a phone booth if I had to."

She smiled. "And I want to be with you. But the reality is I may well be back in Ohio. Could you see yourself living there?"

Liam stared at the road ahead. She pressed further. "Look at me, Liam. Would you live in Ohio if that's where I end up?"

"Honestly, I'm struggling with that. I've been comfortable here in Wisconsin, so that's the easy choice. I don't know if I can handle a long-distance relationship. That's a tough one. So, can I say I'm still thinking?"

"Of course you can. At this point, we really don't know the options, do we? Right now, the only job I have is waiting for me at Wesleyan. UW's completely up in the air."

Liam looked over at her, but Lady's face was in the way. There was that big tongue again. A huge lick later, he wiped off his face. He pushed Lady away for the moment and looked directly at Helen.

"I love you. You know that don't you?"

Helen nodded. "Yes, I do. And I love you. I just want what's best for both of us. That may be a challenge."

It was raining when they got to Helen's flat. They parked and ran inside, a very wet Lady leading the charge. Helen grabbed the mail on the way in. She threw it on the table and grabbed towels. She caught Lady out of the corner of her eye, making a beeline for the sofa. Helen called out as she ran toward the soaked dog.

"Hey you! Oh, no you don't!"

She dove on Lady with a towel held out in front of her, grabbed the dog and wrapped her in it. Liam was looking on, eyes wide and grinning.

"Wow! I didn't know you were so quick!"

Helen looked over at him and rolled her eyes. "Well, now you know. You try sitting on my sofa wet and I'll have your head, too, big boy."

Liam helped Helen dry Lady, then dried himself off. Helen looked at them. "You two are trouble. What a pair."

Liam smiled. "But you love us both, don't you?"

She looked up at him and smiled.

"You don't deserve this, but I made a reservation at Chez Ray for tonight. I thought it might be nice to revisit the site of our reunion for a quiet evening. Just the two of us. Sound good?"

"You are totally ravishing, Ms. Woodson."

"Don't try sucking up to me, O'Connor. It's not gonna work."

Helen asked Liam to take their bags to the bedroom. While he was gone, she picked up the mail. There was an envelope with a University of Wisconsin return address. When Liam came back into the room, she held it up for him to see.

Liam froze. "Aren't you going to open it?"

She didn't move. She was staring straight ahead. "You know, Liam, this may answer what my future will be. And maybe our future."

"You want me to leave the room?"

"No. Stay here. Please."

She opened the envelope, slowly and deliberately. She held the letter in front of her and started to read out loud. "Dear Professor Woodson: We are pleased to inform you…"

293

Liam let out a huge sigh of relief as Helen read the balance of the letter. They were offering her a position as an associate professor in the art department. They asked that she contact the Dean to discuss compensation and other details. Helen walked over to the sofa and sat down. Liam was overjoyed.

"This is great. I can't tell you how excited I am for you. For us. You don't have to move. We'll be together. Wow!"

Helen didn't respond. Finally, she looked up and smiled. "I'm glad you're happy." She looked back down.

Confused, Liam put his arms around her. "What's up? I thought you'd be happy. This is what you've been waiting for. It validates everything about you and your work. It's a prestigious position at a great institution."

It was obvious she was uncomfortable. "I'm not sure I can accept it."

"I don't understand. Why?"

She said nothing for what seemed to Liam like an eternity, then took a deep breath.

"I don't know where to start. First, I don't know whether the offer is genuine, and secondly, if it comes with strings attached."

"What?"

"Do you recall when I first came here, I was supposed to have dinner with the department chair and other new faculty?"

"Maybe. I don't really remember."

"When I got there, there were only two seats at the table, and one was occupied by the chair— Stan."

It started to ring a bell. "Oh, yeah. Now I remember. You said the others couldn't make it."

Helen nodded. "Yes. Only I learned after that they weren't invited."

"Why?"

She glanced away. "Think about it Liam. Why do you suppose he would do that?"

"Wait! You mean... ."

She nodded again. "I didn't realize it in the moment, but he was hitting on me."

"What? That fucker!"

Helen took his arm. "I need you to stay calm. He started slowly, but it became more and more obvious as the term went on. The comments, the glances, the innuendos. He asked me out. I said no, but he kept it up."

"And did you?"

"Hell no, Liam. But that's not the point. The point is he's been pursuing me ever since I walked in the door in January. He makes comments to others in the department. Implying."

"Implying what?"

Helen started to cry, something new for Liam. She had always been so... strong. She looked up at him.

"You figure it out. It's been humiliating. So, now you see why I don't know if the offer is genuine, or if he pushed it for his own reasons."

Liam started to pace. "Have you spoken to anyone about all this?"

"A couple of the other faculty members, but no one wants to come forward. Stan's too powerful. He controls everyone's future."

"I think I need to pay this asshole a visit."

Helen's eyes widened in horror. "Oh no. Please no, Liam. You need to stay out of it. It's my battle, not yours. I don't want you getting into it and making things worse. It's all academic politics. I have a decision to make."

Liam was beside himself. "I don't see any way in hell you take this job. Unless they get rid of this asshole."

"The fact is we don't know if he's going to remain chair. He's been there quite a few years, and there are a number of faculty who want him out. So, the question becomes, do I walk away from an otherwise great offer, or take it and wait to see what happens to Stan?"

"I say you walk."

"And I say it's not your decision. I'm a big girl. I have to sort this out. I don't have to decide today. I have time. We have time."

Liam held her tight, and she melted into him. Instinct told him he should turn the fucker in. But then for once, he recognized his instinct was likely a bad one. Really bad. He was going to have to let this play out. He stroked her face and kissed her.

"Let's make our dinner tonight a landmark event. Just you and me."

Helen looked at him and smiled. "And Lady makes three?"

They sat together, holding each other, for a long, long time. Lady slept at their feet.

***

Ray was waiting at the front door as they approached. "So glad to see you two again. I guess we didn't drive you off the last time?"

Helen hugged Ray and smiled. "It was delightful. We couldn't wait to come back!"

After they were settled in, Ray brought over a bottle of wine. "I think you'll find this the perfect note for the evening. Let me know if you disagree!"

Helen held her glass up and tipped it toward Liam. "Thank you so much for walking me back from the cliff this afternoon. I thought I was ready to address that issue, but apparently, I wasn't."

Liam clinked glasses with her. "The only thing I don't understand is why you didn't tell me all this sooner?"

Helen held her finger up to her lips. "Shhhh. We said we wouldn't talk about it."

Liam nodded. "I know. Sorry."

She shook it off. "No, no. I didn't tell you because I was embarrassed. I'm the tough, independent woman artist. I didn't want to admit that I was dealing with a serial predator. Also, I saw how you reacted to Stephen. I couldn't afford to have you going off on my department chair. But never mind. Tonight isn't about any of that. Tonight's about us."

Liam reached across the table and touched her face. "Yes. Us. If someone told me even a week ago I would be sitting here with the love of my life tonight, I would've laughed them out of the room. I still can't believe you came here Saturday night. I figured you were lost forever."

"I wouldn't have missed it."

He thought for a moment, wanting to savor the scene. "Let me ask you something. What would you have done if I had ignored you, or blown you off? Wouldn't that have been awkward?"

She smiled. "I thought about that. My first thought was that, if you did, I could walk away and say I'd had more important assholes blow me off, so what the hell? Second, and probably more importantly, I knew you wouldn't. I just had to have confidence in myself, and in my feeling that you knew full well what a fool you had been, whether you admitted it to yourself or not."

"Oh, you're good. And I was an asshole."

"Yep, a giant one. But I still love you."

46

Not far out of Madison, Liam became bored with the interstate. "I'm thinkin' we do the back-roads thing. You okay with that? We're not in any rush, and it's a lot more interesting."

They drove through long rows of tall trees, past lakes and streams, and got to see small towns up close. Liam was in his element. By and large, he had only a vague sense of where they were, but he had traveled these roads before, and at least knew the route numbers.

Helen pointed at the empty middle of the dashboard. "So Liam, my dear. You've never explained to me how it is that you bought a truck without a radio. Isn't that kind of unusual?"

"Uh…It was Madeline's fault."

Helen laughed out loud. "Really. And how's that?"

"She took me truck shopping after my accident. I didn't want to take up too much of her time. I'm considerate like that, you know. So I rushed the process just a bit. This was the best truck I could find in a short time."

"Hmmm. That's not what she told me."

Damn.

He hadn't counted on that. "What? When did you talk? What did she tell you?"

Helen bit her lip. "You really don't know much about cars and trucks, do you? Madeline said that your truck shopping and negotiating skills were entertaining to watch. Tell me this—without looking, what kind of truck is this?"

Liam responded without hesitation. "Blue. It's a blue truck."

Helen whistled. "And there you have it."

***

298

"Hey. What's that up there?" Helen pointed toward the side of the road, about a quarter mile ahead of them.

Liam strained a bit. "Looks like someone's broken down."

"We're in the middle of nowhere. Maybe we should stop and help them."

He grimaced. "I don't know. Maybe they're just fine."

"Really? They don't look fine. What would you think if it were you by the side of the road? Would you want someone to help?"

Knowing he was trapped, Liam slowed and pulled over. The car's hood was up, and there was a figure next to it, leaning over into the engine compartment. Liam motioned to Helen to stay in the truck, then got out and walked over to the figure. "I see you're broken down. Is there something I can do to help?"

The figure stood upright and turned toward him. They both gasped at the same time.

Oh Shit!

"Sylvia?" He could see the anger in her face.

"What the fuck are you doing here? Are you fucking following me? Jesus."

For the first time, Liam had a clear conscience and zero interest in the outcome. "You're the one who's broken down. I did what any decent human being would do. But apparently you're not so much in need that you want help, so I'll just be going." He turned to leave.

"Wait. Dammit. I think I'm out of gas."

Liam turned back and grinned. "Really! I guess you're also out of luck."

Helen got out of the truck and approached. "Liam. Are you okay?"

Sylvia was glaring at them both now. "What the fuck?"

Liam looked directly at Sylvia. "Sylvia. I'd like you to meet my wife. Her name's Helen." He turned toward Helen, who was looking at him with a perplexed expression. "Helen. This young lady's name is Sylvia. Apparently she doesn't need our help."

Sylvia looked confused and desperate. "Oh no, I didn't say that. I do need help."

Helen looked at her. "Well, Sylvia. We're on our honeymoon." She turned to Liam, eyebrows arched. "Aren't we, sweetie? I guess we could take some time away from us to help this young woman. What do you say?"

Liam wanted nothing more than to get away, but Helen had scotched that option. "Well. I guess we could do that." He turned to Sylvia. "Follow me."

The three of them returned to the truck. Lady was sitting in the middle of the seat. Liam helped Helen into the passenger seat and closed her door.

Sylvia stood, expectantly. Liam motioned her to the back of the truck and lowered the tailgate. She looked at him with daggers in her eyes. He smiled. "Hop in. We'll take you to the nearest gas station."

"Oh no. I'm not riding in the bed."

He shrugged. "Okay. Have it your way. I hope someone else stops for you. Could be a long, lonely day out here in the middle of nowhere."

Sylvia looked defeated. "Fuck you. Fuck you and your… your bride. Why can't the dog be in the back?"

Liam laughed. "Funny you should ask. Just so we're clear, the dog's well-mannered and loyal. She wouldn't think of running off. So she's earned that seat. You, on the other hand—" He shook his head. "You're lucky to get any seat. Let me give you a boost." He helped her up onto the tailgate and she crawled, scowling, into the truck's bed. He slammed the gate and walked around to the driver's side.

Helen gave him a quizzical look. "Should I even ask?"

He grinned. "Probably not."

Liam took great pleasure watching Sylvia through the rearview mirror. She was bouncing around the back of the truck, lunging and grasping at the sides and trying to stay seated. He made sure to take the turns a little faster than he should and chuckled with every pothole they hit along the way. Finally, they came upon a small town and pulled into a gas station on its outskirts. Liam got out of the truck as the attendant, who looked to be about eighteen at the most, came out of the building.

"What can I do for you mister?"

Liam pointed at Sylvia, who was still clinging to the side of the truck's bed, her hair pointed in all directions. "I think this young lady needs some gas. Could you take care of her?"

The attendant nodded. Liam dropped the tailgate and helped a totally pissed off Sylvia to the ground. The attendant looked at her. "You need a can, or do you have your own?"

"Of course I need a can. What do I look like?"

The attendant looked at her blankly. "Well, honestly ma'am, if you'll excuse me for saying this, you kinda look like a sheep that got too close to the electric fence. But we'll fix you up with some gas."

Liam handed the guy ten bucks and walked back to the truck. As he was climbing in, Helen looked back at Sylvia.

"Are we going to take her back to her car?"

"Oh hell no. That nice young man will take care of her." He started the truck and gunned the engine as they pulled out. He looked in the rearview mirror and saw a crimson-faced Sylvia with one foot on a gas can and waving middle fingers raised high. It was easy to read the single syllable words on her lips.

Helen was shaking her head. "Okay. Fill me in. Bride? Honeymoon? Who is she?"

Liam smiled. "Oh, I don't know. Just an old score that needed settling."

***

It was late afternoon when they drove past the Windward sign and turned into the resort. The summer breeze in the air drove sun-glistened whitecaps on the lake. Liam pulled up in front of the cottage and parked. As they got out of the truck, Lady jumped down and trotted toward the lake. She ran back and forth along the shoreline, barking at the waves, then turned and ran back to them. Liam dropped to his knees as she approached and hugged her as she nestled up to him. "Pretty neat, huh girl? I told you we had a surprise for you."

He stood back up and hugged Helen. She looked up at him and smiled. "I see where I stand in the pecking order."

He kissed her. "Does that help ease the pain?"

She looked at him and sighed. "I'll take that as a down payment. How's that?"

As they unloaded the truck and carried their bags into the cottage, they saw Madeline approaching along the drive. As she got closer, she held out her arms wide in a welcoming gesture.

"I'm so glad to see you. Both of you. This just makes my day!"

Liam and Helen moved into her embrace. Lady ran over and jumped up on the three of them. Liam grinned. "Looks like the gang's all here! You sure you're ready for us?"

Madeline shook her head. "Well, it's a pretty rag-tag group, but I couldn't be more prepared if I tried." She took Helen's hands in hers. "My God it's good to see you. And thank God this one finally got his senses back." She pointed at Liam and turned toward him. "I think I did a decent job of keeping silent, but you really were a jackass, weren't you?"

He took a step back, looking incredulous. "I beg your pardon?"

She shook her head. "Jackass. You know the term. In fact, sometimes I think you define it. But never mind. You came around. Good for you."

Helen looked down the drive as Liam returned to the truck to unload. "Anyone else here yet?"

Madeline shook her head. "No. You guys are it for now. I think Jack and Susan are coming at some point tomorrow. I thought maybe the three of us could get together for a quiet dinner tonight at my house. Does that work for you?"

Helen laughed. "Are you kidding? Do you think Mr. Gourmand over there is in the slightest way prepared? Do you think he made any plans?"

Madeline chuckled. "You know, there was a time when he really did pay attention to those things, and even knew what he was doing. Too many years on his own, I'm afraid. He's lost sight of some of the finer things."

Helen shrugged. "You think maybe there's hope for him?"

Madeline took her hands again. "Hey! He found you, didn't he? So he's still capable of excellent taste. You have your work cut out for you, but I think you'll manage just fine."

Helen sighed. "I guess that's encouraging. Of course we'll join you. Should we bring anything?"

Madeline shook her head. "Oh no, not a thing. Just bring yourselves. That in itself is the best gift you could give me."

***

303

As Helen was cleaning up and getting dressed for dinner, Liam came into the room. He had on a grease-stained Wisconsin T-shirt and cut-off denim shorts. She took one look at him and scowled. "Oh no, my friend. You're gonna get cleaned up. Madeline's making us a nice dinner and you're going to show some class."

"Hey! We're at a resort."

Helen pushed him toward the clothes she had just hung up for him. "Nope. That's bullshit. You know better. Remember that lovely night we met? If you had looked like this…" She pointed at his chest. "We never would've happened. Got it?"

He'd lost the battle before it even began. "Oh, all right. Give me some time and you won't believe what you'll see."

Helen shook her head in resignation. "That's what I'm afraid of. But have at it."

Madeline was waiting for them at her front door, holding a drink in each hand. "I thought you might be ready for cocktails after your long drive. Did I guess right?" She handed Helen a Manhattan, and Liam a whiskey. They each smiled and bowed as they took the drinks, nodding an affirmation. Madeline gestured toward her living room. "Come on in. I think you'll find the evening most enjoyable. I know I will."

Helen looked around as they sat down. Before them was an enormous charcuterie board overflowing with prosciutto, various cuts of salami, a plethora of cheeses and crackers. Next to the board was a large bowl of mussels in a white wine sauce. In the background, Chopin filled the air. "My goodness, Madeline. You've outdone yourself. I'm not sure we're worthy!"

"Nonsense! I'm so honored to have the two of you in my home again. A famous author and a renowned artist. And two of the nicest people I know." She winked. "Okay, one of the nicest people I know, plus a guy who tries sometimes."

Helen laughed, and Liam winced. Madeline reached out and touched his arm. "You know I'm kidding, Liam. I'm proud and only occasionally embarrassed to call you my friend."

"Thanks. I think."

Later, with Liam and Helen seated at the dining room table, Madeline retreated to the kitchen. She came back with a bottle of champagne and three flutes.

"It's been almost a year since you two met, here in this very house. I think we should celebrate. Particularly since we don't know when you'll be back here again."

Helen's eyes glistened. "This means a lot to us. You mean a lot to us. I don't want to spend tonight thinking about where we might end up. Let's just be together now. Okay?"

Liam saw they were both in tears. "Awww... come on ladies. Lighten up! Old Liam's in the house. It's party time!" He looked at Madeline. "Here. Give me that bottle. Let's get this show on the road!"

Madeline looked at Liam and Helen. "I love you two so much!" Before they could respond, she sniffed the air. "Oh crap. Dinner! I need to get it out of the oven. I'll be right back."

47

Helen was looking at him as he woke up, a beckoning smile on her face. He slithered under the covers.

"DOG!!!"

Oh no. Nooo— Maybe he was mistaken.

"DOG!!!"

Helen lifted her head as Liam poked his out from under the covers, peering around the room. There she was, standing in the doorway. One arm in a sling, the other pointing at Lady, who was lying on her back, tail swishing on the floor. Liam sat up, grabbing a towel and putting it around his waist as he stood.

"Sara! You're here! How are you?"

Sara pointed in his direction. "LIAM."

"Yes. Yes! Liam. So good to see you!"

Sara turned and pointed at Helen. As she pointed, she cocked her head and shrugged her shoulders. It took Liam a few seconds for it to register. She didn't know Helen. He pointed at Helen as well, and slowly spoke her name. "Helen." Sara was still pointing, so he repeated himself. "Helen. That is Helen." He turned to Helen. "Helen— I'd like to introduce you to Sara."

Helen had wrapped herself in the sheet and sat up. "Well hello, Sara. It's so good to meet you. I've heard all about you!"

Sara shrugged her shoulders again. She sat down with Lady. Liam ran to the bathroom and threw on some clothes. When he got back, Helen did the same. Liam sat on the floor with Sara.

"So Sara, Did you just get here?"

Sara nodded her head as she stroked Lady. She looked up at Liam.

"Dog. Lady."

Liam smiled. "Yes. Lady."

Sara looked back down at Lady. "I LOVE LADY."

Liam reached out and touched her on the shoulder. "I know. I know you love Lady. Where are your parents?"

She pointed in the general direction of their cottage. Helen returned to the room. She looked down at Sara. "How about we go say hi to your parents, Sara?"

Sara nodded, nonchalantly. Liam stood up. After a few minutes, Sara stood, and took his hand. Lady got up as well. The little group left the cottage together and walked down the drive. As they got closer to Sara's cottage, Liam saw Jack standing by their car, unloading their bags. Sara let go of Liam's hand and ran to her father. He looked at her, then at Liam and Helen approaching.

"Oh Sara. Did you do it again?"

Sara shrugged. Liam called out. "It's okay Jack. It was fine. We're so happy to see her."

As they came together, Jack pulled Liam into an embrace. "Thank you so much for being here, Liam. It means a lot to us."

Liam patted him on the back. As he released, Liam motioned to Helen, who stepped forward. "Jack, this is Helen. Helen— Jack."

Helen walked over to Jack and embraced him as well. "It's so good to finally meet you. I've heard so much about you folks. I'm so very, very sorry about all you've been through."

Jack took a few moments to compose himself. "I'm sorry. It's just that it's been a really tough time for us. But look at Sara. She's doing so well. We're blessed."

Liam looked around. "Where's Susan?"

Jack held up a finger. "Just give me a minute." He pulled a walker out of the car and helped Susan into it. She turned toward Liam and Helen, raising an arm in greeting.

"Hi Liam. I'm sorry, but I'm just a little slow with this thing."

Jack helped steady her as she walked on the uneven ground to Liam and Helen. She looked at Liam and smiled. "I'm better than it looks. The healing process is just taking a little longer than we hoped. But I'm going to be fine."

Liam held her eyes. "Susan. You look great." She shook her head, but he persisted. "No, really. I'm happy to see your progress." He motioned toward Helen. "This is Helen Woodson. I don't know if you two met last year up here."

Helen reached over and touched Susan's arm as it rested on the walker. "It's so nice to meet you Susan."

Susan nodded. "Thank you, Helen."

Helen looked at Liam. "Maybe you could help Susan get somewhere to rest?"

Jack stepped forward. "It's okay, Helen. It was her choice to present with the walker. We have backup with us." He walked back to the car and retrieved a folded wheelchair. He moved it over to Susan and helped her sit in it.

Susan smiled but looked uncomfortable being the center of attention. "Oh, let's not make a big deal of this. Why don't you all come into the cottage with us?"

Sara and Lady were already inside, snuggled together on the floor. Liam looked at Sara and smiled. "Are you glad to see Lady again? I think she's really excited you're here!"

"DOG!"

Liam reached down and tussled her hair, then stepped back. Jack had helped Susan into an armchair next to the sofa. He motioned toward the sofa. "Please have a seat, Helen. I have to say we were pleased to hear you'd be here with this guy." He pointed to Liam. "He's pretty special to us, but he sure needs guidance sometimes."

Liam held his hand to his chest in mock surprise. "Hey! How do you know it isn't Helen who needs the guidance?"

Jack shook his head. "Powers of observation. We love you just the same, but you've been known to do some—shall we say—impulsive things?"

"Like what?"

Jack grinned. "Like telling a priest to f… ."

Susan cut him off, pointing to Sara.

Helen turned to Liam. "Really? You did that?"

"Well, maybe once."

Susan chimed in. "And reading James Joyce to a little girl?"

"Well, in fairness, she was in a coma."

Helen shook her head. "Oh Liam… you didn't… ."

"Madeline told us about how you two reunited. What a great story!" Jack looked at Helen. "Do you know yet what you're going to be doing for next term?"

"I really don't. I have two options—an offer from UW and my old position at Wesleyan. I have a couple weeks to make the choice. Lots of considerations."

Jack looked at Liam. "What's your next step?"

"I'm completely up in the air. My new book is coming out in September. Other than that, I'm waiting to hear where Helen's going to be."

Jack smiled. "So are congratulations in order? Maybe an engagement?"

Liam overreacted immediately. "Oh hell no." Sensing he'd made a huge mistake, he scrambled to find a way out of it. "That didn't sound right, did it? I meant to say that we're still thinking about what we're going to do, and where we might be."

Madeline went for the save. "I think what Liam is inartfully trying to say is that until they know where Helen's going to end up in September, he's just waiting. I think they're just perfect for each other, but then I'm biased…aren't I Helen?"

Helen showed a hint of a smile but didn't make eye contact. Liam knew he was in deep shit. He noticed Sara was standing at the window, pointing outside. A perfect chance to change the subject. "Hey Sara! What's out there?" He quickly strode over to her. "Look everyone! There's a deer in the side yard. Cool!"

No one bought the ruse, but at least the tension was broken. Madeline looked around the circle. "Now. I'm inviting all of you to dinner at my house tonight. Are you game for that?"

***

That evening, Madeline looked around the table and smiled. "I've hoped and prayed we could gather under my roof again, and here we are. The outside forces that threatened to snatch some of you from me." She looked at Susan and Sara, and bowed her head. "And the inexplicable inner forces that bedeviled and threatened others of you." She turned and looked straight at Liam, smiling mischievously. "None of these were enough to stop our reunion tonight." She held up her wine glass in a salute. "Here's to all of you. May life smile upon you and may you all prosper. May the gales that threatened to scatter us be forever calmed."

The others held up their glasses in response. Susan started to speak, but her voice caught. Jack put his arm around her. "Let me just say Susan and I are so very grateful for the love and support you all have shown to us and to Sara through a very difficult time. We feel extraordinarily blessed."

Susan nodded in agreement and hugged Jack. By then, Sara had gotten up from the table and wandered over to Lady. They sat together on the floor of the living room, in silent conversation.

Liam watched Sara and Lady for a while, lost in thought. An idea started to percolate, slowly at first but accelerating as he took a gulp of his wine.

Whether it was Liam or the wine speaking would be subject to much discussion later. "I have an announcement." All eyes were on him. "As I think you all know, I'm not known for my tolerance of children. At least I wasn't before I met this little girl. I've no idea what she saw in me, but she's changed my life in the short time I've known her. She's such a gift. I've been struggling to figure out what I can do for her in return, but it's been staring me in the face since the day I met her. I want to give her something that's really precious to me. The most precious thing, actually— my special companion, this beautiful animal. Lady."

Helen glanced over at Madeline, who gasped softly and put her face in her hands. Helen looked at Liam and quietly shook her head no. Too late. He was on a roll.

"So. If it's all right with Jack and Susan—" Liam paused for effect. "Sara and Lady are destined to be together."

Bathed in shock, the room was dead still, except Sara, who clearly comprehended none of this and just carried on playing with Lady. Finally, Jack pulled himself together.

"Liam. That's an incredible gesture, but no. Sara's just fine. She enjoys being with Lady, but then she enjoys being with all animals. They pose no threat to her."

Helen squeezed Liam's knee under the table and looked pleadingly into his eyes. It was no use. His instinct was in full flight, fueled by way too much wine.

"No, no. I insist. It would be the highest honor you could give me."

Madeline stood up. "I need to pull dessert together. Can you help me in the kitchen Liam?"

He looked up. "Oh, you should probably have Helen do that."

Madeline locked her eyes on his. "No, you. Follow me."

He did as instructed. She shut the door behind them and turned to him. "Are you out of your mind?"

311

He was shocked. "What do you mean?"

"Oh Liam. That dog is your child. You wouldn't give your child away. Would you?"

He put his hand on her shoulder. "Now Madeline. Have you seen how Sara and Lady have bonded?"

She stood, shaking her head in exasperation. "One day. One day, Liam. Every kid and every dog can play together for a day. What are you thinking?"

"Look. I have no idea where Helen and I are going to end up. Jack, Susan and Sara are a loving family who will give Lady a wonderful home. My mind's made up. It's the right thing to do. I can feel it."

She gave it one last try. "First of all, wherever you end up, Lady belongs with you. Also, you might recall how you could 'feel it' when you thought Helen was cheating on you?"

Liam shook his head. "Totally different."

She closed her eyes. "You're hopeless."

48

It was odd waking up in the morning with no Lady in the room. She'd slept over with Sara at Jack's and Susan's cottage. Liam was jittery and restless. Helen held him closely and spoke with a calm deliberateness. "You know, sometimes we get caught up in a moment of enthusiasm and do things that on reflection may have gone way beyond what we intended."

"What are you talking about?"

"Please let me finish. This may be even more so when the enthusiasm is heightened by a few glasses of wine. No one's going to hold you accountable, Liam. Everyone understands how you feel about Sara, and how much you want to do something special for her. But you know what? You spending time with her, and just being here with her, is clearly something she treasures. It's like Susan's told you—Sara loves Lady because Lady's part of you. If you think it's the other way around, you've got it all wrong."

"I can't talk about it, Helen. Not now."

"If not now, when?"

"The subject's closed."

Liam tried his best to be upbeat as he and Helen packed for the return trip. They carried their bags out to the truck and loaded them in. Madeline came down to say goodbye. As she approached, Helen walked over to her. They hugged.

Madeline pointed at Liam. "How's he doing?"

Helen hugged her again. "I don't think very well, but I'll leave that to him to tell you. It's been so nice seeing you, Madeline. I don't know when we'll be together again. My life's just too much up in the air now."

Madeline wiped away a stray tear. "I love you, Helen. And I love Liam. You take good care of that guy, will you? You're both special."

Helen stepped back to look at her. "I'll do what I can. I love him a whole lot. I really don't know what's coming next, though. Only time will tell."

Madeline nodded. "I wish you only the best. We've been friends a long, long time—haven't we? Please let me know what's going on." She walked with Helen over to Liam, who was still loading up and securing their baggage.

He reached out to Madeline and embraced her. "I'm gonna miss you, lady. We'll be back. I promise you. Just don't know when."

Madeline held both their hands. "I want you to promise me that you'll be good to each other. Can you do that?"

Liam sniffed but caught himself. "Absolutely. You know old Liam will be right there for Helen."

Helen looked away. Ultimately, the three of them hugged one last time. Liam opened the door to the truck. As he did, he saw a flash of red running toward him. Lady arrived at full gallop and jumped up into the truck cab, sitting in the middle of the seat, looking ahead and panting. Liam tried to stop her but failed. "No, no Lady! You can't come. You've got to go back." He got up into the truck and started to pull on her collar, but stopped and collapsed on her, holding her tight. He was shaking.

Helen climbed into the passenger seat and started to stroke him and Lady simultaneously. "Oh Liam. She's your dog. Don't do this. Don't give your precious friend away. She belongs with you. She doesn't understand."

He didn't move, but just remained hunched over Lady, without saying anything. Helen looked up and saw a small form standing next to the truck on the driver's side.

"LIAM'S DOG!" Sara was pointing, arm stiff in front of her.

Jack had run over and stood behind Sara. "Oh Liam. She's yours. We're so grateful for you, but you can't do this. Look—Sara's fine."

Sara looked up at her father and pointed again inside the truck.

"LIAM'S DOG. LOVE."

Helen got out of the truck and came around to Sara, taking her in her arms. "Oh, sweet girl. You know Liam loves you. Lady loves you too, but she's with her daddy now."

Sara kissed Helen. She mouthed something, practicing, then spoke. "HELEN. LOVE."

Helen was full on crying now. "Oh, and I love you too Sara. You're the most special little girl."

Helen climbed up into the driver's seat and rubbed Liam's shoulders. "It's okay, Liam. Sara's okay. It's going to be just fine. Lady's where she belongs. Why don't you come out now and say goodbye to everyone?" She helped him out of the truck.

Madeline had gone to get Susan and was wheeling her over to the truck as well. Liam swept up Sara in his arms.

"Goodbye, little girl. You're my angel—you know that?"

Sara hugged him tight. "Liam. Bye-Bye."

Liam nodded. "Yes. Bye-Bye. I'll see you again real soon. You be good, you hear?"

When Madeline and Susan arrived at the truck, Liam went to Susan and, leaning down, touched her shoulder and gave her a kiss on the forehead. "You take care of yourself. Get well soon—those students need you back in the saddle at school. When you teach *In the Realm of One,* that is, assuming you teach it again, tell the kids you know the writer personally, and he expects them to read every damn word! God bless you, Susan."

After embraces all around, Liam and Helen got back into the truck with Lady and drove down the drive and out onto the road. Liam looked in the rearview mirror and saw

Susan waving from her wheelchair. He kept his eyes on the road as long as he could. He looked over at Helen.

"I think I'm gonna need to stop. Maybe get some coffee. I'm kind of a wreck."

Helen smiled back. "Really? Could've fooled me."

The stop was brief. Helen put her hand on his arm. "You want to just take a few minutes to compose yourself?"

He shrugged her off. "Nope. We're on a mission. To find our future."

She didn't respond. They got back on the road, driving for some time in silence. Finally, she looked over at him.

"You know, Liam, we need to get real here. Why in the world did you try to give Lady away?"

He took some time to put his thoughts together. Not well, but together. "I'm afraid, Helen."

"Afraid of what?"

"Afraid of not being with you. I have to prepare to move to Ohio."

She looked straight ahead. "That's what we need to talk about, Liam. First, you don't need to give up your dog to move, and you know that. Second, I'm feeling that you really don't want to go to Ohio. Am I missing something?"

He didn't look at her. "I'm hoping you stay in Madison."

She exhaled. "Okay. Here's the deal, Liam. I've been thinking about this a lot. I've decided—and I am completely at peace with this—that I will not take the UW job if Stan is still chair. Period. I'm not going to compromise myself."

Liam broke his stare and glanced over at her. "So where does that leave me?"

She turned to him. "That's entirely up to you. At this point, and unless something happens real soon, I am assuming I'm headed back to Ohio. But let me say that the last thing I want is to pressure you. I want to be with you, but not at the expense of either of our happiness. Do you understand that? If you're not going to be happy in Ohio, then you need to stay put where you are. I won't love you any less for that. I hope you won't love me any less for my decision."

Liam swallowed hard. "But. What about us?"

It was Helen's turn to sit silently.

He tried again. "Are we done?"

She turned to him. He could see that she was crying but trying very hard not to show it. "I don't know. I really don't know. I think we need to take it one day at a time. You mean more to me than anyone I've ever known. I want to spend my life with you. But not if you're going to be miserable. I hope you feel the same about me. Do you?"

He nodded but couldn't look her in the eye. "I do. I want to be with you. I also don't want you to be unhappy, and I know you would be miserable if you stayed in Madison and had to put up with that asshole calling your shots. Can we have a long-distance life together?"

"I honestly don't know. I've never tried it."

He tried smiling, but it seemed forced. "I haven't either."

Helen thought for a moment. "You know, it's not all that far. Wisconsin and Ohio? Practically neighbors."

"But I want to be physically with you. That's the best part of being a couple, isn't it?" She said nothing. He realized he was on thin ice. "Can we just put a hold on this discussion until you hear from the Dean?"

"Liam. Get real. We're talking a very short time before school starts. Kind of hard not to talk about it now."

They settled into an uncomfortable period of quiet reflection. Suddenly, out of nowhere, an inspired thought popped into Liam's head. One he couldn't contain.

"Say! Why don't you just not take any of the positions? You don't need to teach... you're an artist. Be an artist!"

317

As soon as the words left his mouth, he knew he was in trouble. Helen glared at him without speaking. He said a little prayer to the gods of forgiveness. Maybe she hadn't heard him.

"Are you mad? Let me get this straight. You want me to give up a big part of my career? And do what?"

Desperate, he panicked. "Why, we could be together! Think of all the extra time you would have for painting. No more students. No more faculty crap."

He had never seen her this close to exploding. She continued to glare, her head slowly shaking back and forth in disbelief. "Right. I give up my career, not to mention my primary source of income, to bask in your radiant presence? Could you think of anything more selfish if you tried?"

He threw a hail Mary. "Why, just to show you that this can be a mutual thing, what if I sell the bookstore?" Mary crashed in flames, rolling like a fiery ball into the abyss.

"Oh my God, Liam. Are you listening to yourself?" Helen's teeth were clenched as she spoke. "Are you equating my academic career with your—how shall I put this—escapist diversion?"

His eyes bulging, sweat pouring off his forehead, Liam knew this might just have been the dumbest conversation he'd ever started. "Why, no. No, not at all. But think about it. Think about how nice it would be to be able to spend all of our time together?" No. That was perhaps the worst argument he could make. He wanted to rescind it, but it was too late.

"No way, pal. I love you, but the very last thing I would ever want to do is give up my life and my own independence to sit around and twiddle my thumbs with you. Give me a break."

The battle was over. Liam had lost in the most outrageous way possible. Time to concede, but of course that wasn't the Liam way. "Okay, it was just a suggestion. Maybe you can think on it and we pick it up later?"

He'd never seen Helen's face red like this. She stared off, out the side window. A strained silence overcame the truck's cab for the balance of the drive to Madison. Even Lady moved away from him, putting her head in Helen's lap.

49

"I think I've done it this time."

Sharon looked at Liam and sighed. "If I had a nickel... ."

Even he had to smile. "I know. I know. But this time was a doozy."

"I might as well ask. You're going to tell me whether I do or not. What happened?"

"Well, first, Helen and I had a wonderful time at Madeline's. Susan and Sara are healing well, and—."

"Focus, Liam. Focus. I don't need the rest of the story."

"Okay. If you insist. We're struggling with what comes next in our relationship. Helen has an offer from Wisconsin, but there's an issue with this guy."

Sharon started taking notes. "What guy?"

"The department chair. He's got the hots for Helen and he's been pursuing her since she got there."

Sharon jotted a few lines, then looked up. "Is it mutual?"

"No, no. Of course not."

Sharon exhaled. "Okay. So what's she going to do?"

Liam started to rock in his chair, clearly uncomfortable but wanting to let it all out. "She's waiting to hear if the guy's going to step down. Apparently there's some thought he will. She's told me she won't come here if he doesn't."

Sharon nodded. "Okay. So far, so good. What happens if she doesn't take the job?"

Liam was rocking harder now. "Well, it looks like her only option is to return to Wesleyan."

Sharon reached over and put her hand on his knee. He stopped rocking. "And how do you feel about that?"

"I'm not sure."

"Not sure of what?"

"Not sure if I want to go to Ohio with her."

Sharon jotted some more. "Do you have to go with her?" Silence. She repeated herself. "Liam. Do you have to go with her?"

He stood and walked to the window. "No. But if I don't, I'm afraid that'll be the end."

"Okay. Has she told you that? That it'll be the end?"

"No. But neither of us know if we can do a long-distance thing."

She looked up at him. "Liam. Please sit down. Take your time. This is important stuff. You know that, don't you?"

He sat. Finally, she spoke. Quietly and with empathy. "Do you love Helen?"

He nodded. "Yes. Yes, I do. And I know I have to give her the freedom to make her own career choice."

Sharon held his eyes. "And do you feel that she's giving you the same choice for yours?"

"Of course. That's the problem. What if each of us does what's best for ourself, and as a result we can't be together?"

"Isn't that the ultimate test of love?"

"I don't know, Sharon."

It was her turn to stand and go to the window. "I think you do, Liam. You've come a long, long way in the last year. A year ago you would've just blown her off if you were faced with the same circumstance. I'm proud of you."

Liam didn't know what to say. He didn't feel very proud of himself. "Can I tell you what I did that was a problem?"

She turned around to face him. "Oh yeah. I forgot about that. What did you do?"

"I suggested that she give up teaching so that she could be with me. I guess that wasn't so smart?"

Sharon closed her eyes and sighed. "Maybe you haven't come so far. What possessed you to say that?"

"I don't know, it seemed like a good compromise in the moment. Kind of on instinct."

Sharon walked back and plopped into her chair. She put her face in her hands. "Oh Liam. What have we discussed about your instincts?"

"I know. I know. My instincts are awful."

She looked up. "And what did we decide was the solution?"

"Never to act on an instinct in the moment. Take my time. Think it through. If in doubt, shut up."

She patted him on the knee. "Exactly."

"So how do I fix this?"

"I think you need to go back to her and admit what you did. I suspect she knows you well enough by now to understand. And pray. Pray for forgiveness."

"Yeah, I guess you're right."

"Okay. Now we should get back to the larger question. Are you willing, under any scenario, to move to Ohio to be with Helen?"

"Honestly?"

"No. Lie to me. Of course honestly."

Liam sat silently, lost in thought.

"And your answer is?"

He stood up, stretched, and looked down at her. There was the slightest grin on his face.

"Yes. Yes, I am. I want to be with her. I can write anywhere."

Sharon didn't look up but took her time writing notes. Finally, she smiled. "Congratulations Liam. Welcome to adulthood." She stood up and walked him to the door. "Let me know how things go."

"Oh you'll be the first to know."

As he walked down the hall, she called out to him. "Hey Liam."

He turned. "Yes, Sharon?"

"Good luck."

***

Liam left Sharon's office much lighter than when he'd arrived. He still had to fix the mess he'd made with Helen, but at least Sharon had confirmed for him the best way to approach it. He was going to have to hope that Helen would forgive him for his stupidity. God knows she had forgiven him for other idiot moves he had made, but then this was the mother lode of mistakes. More importantly, he'd finally been able to admit that moving to Ohio was a viable option. Not because Ohio was any great shakes, because in his view it wasn't. But rather because he was finally in a relationship that was worth holding on to. He loved Helen. He wanted to be with her. But there was another remaining complication. The store. What was he going to do with it if he left town? Totally disregarding the discussion about instincts he had just carried on with Sharon, he had an instinct that required he go sit down with Marianne. Right now. What better time to work that one out? He lengthened his strides as he walked down the street on that lovely late summer morning.

The store was bustling when he arrived. Apparently he had approved a sale, and it was in full swing. Or had he? He shook it off. He motioned to Marianne to follow him as he walked in the door. She was at the counter and there was already a line waiting to check out. She shook her head and pointed at the people waiting. He signaled to Jeremy, who came running over.

"LIAMMMM! YOU'RE HERE!"

Liam held his finger to his mouth. "Shhh…. Use your inside voice, Jeremy."

"Silly Liam. That IS my inside voice!"

Liam exhaled. "Okay. Jeremy, can you spell Marianne at the register? I need to see her."

Jeremy looked puzzled. "Well okay, but you can see her. Look—She's right there."

"Figure of speech. It was a figure of speech. I need to speak with her."

Jeremy nodded, still looking puzzled. "Oh. Okay." He walked behind the counter and up to Marianne. Liam could see a brief argument, but finally Marianne left the register and walked into Liam's office. Liam followed.

She looked suspicious. "Uh-oh. Now what?"

Liam took some time to assemble his thoughts and his words. Apparently not enough, however.

"So Marianne. What would you think if I sold the store?"

"And why would you do that?"

The wheels were turning in his head, but again, not very smoothly. "Well. Uh. I. Oh—"

"What's going on? Out with it!"

Trapped, he had to give an answer. "I'm tired of it."

She looked at him through narrowing eyes. "Bullshit."

Well, that didn't work. "Truth?"

"Of course truth. What's going on?"

He tried to slow his thinking down, just like Sharon had advised. "There's a chance. Now, I'm not going to say for certain, but there's a chance."

Marianne was still staring at him.

"There's a chance I might be moving to Ohio with Helen."

Marianne didn't flinch. "So? What's that got to do with owning the store?"

He hadn't expected this line of questioning. "Well, what else could I do? How are you guys going to run this place if I'm not here?"

324

Marianne laughed out loud. "I would think the same way we've always run it when you're not around. Better than when you're here. You know you just get in the way."

He was taken aback. "Well, maybe you can handle it. But what about Jeremy and Vera?"

"Get real, Liam. They love it when you're not here. Like I said, you just get in the way. Why don't you ask them?"

Now he was hurt. "You don't think I bring something to the table? Look at all the notoriety from having my name associated with it? How many people come here hoping to meet me and talk with me?"

She chuckled. "Yeah. Notoriety is just the right word. Not sure that's a positive, Boss."

He was getting flustered. "So maybe a new owner would bring new ideas and energy. Have you thought of that?"

"Liam. A new owner would fire us. How's that helpful? You'd put us all out of work."

That hadn't occurred to him. "Why would they do that? You guys are the glue that holds this place together."

"Look at us. Picture someone interviewing Jeremy. Or Vera. Or me, for that matter. Come on."

Liam was grasping for straws now. "Okay. Call them in here. Let's all chat."

Marianne shook her head. "Have you noticed that there are exactly three employees here? If we're all in your office, who minds the store?"

She had him. "Okay. You go tend the register, and send them both in. I have your input."

"Knock, knock… ." Jeremy stuck his head in the door, a worried look on his face. Vera was right behind him.

Liam looked up and attempted a casual smile. "Come in! Come in! So glad to see you both."

They walked in with hesitation, glancing around the room.

"Please sit down!" Liam got up and closed the door as they slowly seated themselves.

Jeremy was wide-eyed. "Please don't fire us, Liam! We promise not to do it again!"

"Do what?"

Jeremy and Vera looked at each other and shrugged. "Oh, nothing. Never mind!"

Liam shook it off. "I just told Marianne that I'm thinking of selling the store. I wanted to get your input as well."

Jeremy's jaw dropped. "Nooooooo! Nooooooo! You can't sell it! Oh my god, oh my god... ."

Vera stared straight ahead. A small tick developed on the left side of her face, and she started to tremble. "But Boss. Why?"

Liam, completely unprepared, stammered and tried to find words. "I... I'm sorry. Sometimes things happen that look bad in the moment, but ultimately are for the best."

Jeremy and Vera sat in silence. Liam could detect just a hint of Vera's former odor. The one that Jeremy had eradicated. He knew he had to do something. Quickly.

"Look. It's not the end of the world. And I haven't decided to sell. I just said I'm thinking of it. Can I tell you why?"

Jeremy and Vera nodded nervously. Liam wasn't sure if they really wanted to hear or were just being polite.

"There's a chance, and I'm not saying it's for certain, that I might be leaving town and moving to Ohio to be with Helen."

Jeremy looked confused. "But—Helen's in Madison. Why would you go to Ohio? She's not there!"

Vera reached over and touched his arm. "No, no Jeremy. Helen is in Madison now, but she may have to go back to her school in Ohio." She looked at Liam. "When would this happen, Liam?"

"Soon. Before Fall term starts."

Jeremy still looked puzzled. "But we don't want her to go!"

Vera patted him. "Of course we don't, but that's her decision, isn't it?"

Jeremy nodded. In comforting Jeremy, Vera seemed to be finding her own strength. "Liam. You've been gone before. Sometimes for several months, when you did your book tours. You're going to be doing those again no matter what happens with Helen, aren't you?"

Liam had to admit she had a point. "Yes. So go on?"

Vera took a deep breath. "The store has gotten along just fine when you're not here. So why mess with something that works? I do your books. It's not like you're making a lot of money from this place. Do you really have to sell?"

Liam was concerned because Vera was starting to make sense. How could that be? "No, but I've always been the face of the Owl's Eyes."

Vera and Jeremy both giggled. Vera caught herself. "Why does that have to change, Liam? As we see it, the store does benefit from being associated with your name, but you're not here enough in person to make a difference. If you live somewhere else, there's really no change."

Liam was still trying to absorb the concept of listening to Vera and Jeremy for advice. Well, at least Vera. He looked at them.

"So. What do you propose?"

Vera held her hand up. Liam smiled. "Yes, Vera?"

She stood up. "May I go speak with Marianne?"

By now, Liam had lost control of the discussion. "Sure. Might's well."

She left the room. Jeremy was still looking confused. "But Helen lives in Madison."

Liam put his head on the desk. There was no hope. After an uncomfortably long break, Vera returned. Marianne stood in the doorway. She was the first to speak.

327

"I'll let Vera talk for us. I may have to go back to the register."

Vera kept standing. Liam was clearly outnumbered now.

"So, Boss. Here's what we think."

Liam was not only outnumbered but trapped in his chair.

"Whatever happens with you and Helen. If you stay here, fine. If you go to Ohio, fine. Don't do anything with the store. Leave it in our hands. You can visit from time to time if you want. We'll report to you, but since we'll be here, we'll be in charge. Give us six months. If you aren't satisfied with the way things are going after that time, you can make the determination to sell it. But until then, you do nothing."

Liam stroked his beard in contemplation, saying nothing. Finally, he looked up and put both hands on the desk.

"Interesting proposal. But what if I say no?"

Vera started to speak but Marianne cut her off. "If you say no? We'll all resign, effective in two weeks."

The tick reappeared on Vera's face. Jeremy's jaw fell as he gasped. Marianne looked at them both. "Do I speak for all of us?"

Vera and Jeremy stood and turned to Marianne. The three embraced, then turned to Liam. "Yes. That's the deal."

Liam was still trying to figure out how he had completely lost control of the conversation, not to mention how he had been out-negotiated by his employees. He stood up.

Marianne looked directly at him. "Well?"

He swallowed, hard. "Yes. Deal."

The three nodded and smiled. As they walked out of the office, Liam could hear Jeremy's voice. "What just happened? Anybody?"

***

When he arrived home, Liam was greeted by Lady in the living room, green tennis ball in her mouth. She ran over and jumped up on him. Normally, he would have pushed her down, telling her to mind her manners. This time, he just gave her a bear hug. Best friend in the world. The only one with no demands and no complaints. He looked around the house, his home for the last five years. He wasn't sure how he'd feel to leave it. There was still the faintest hope he wouldn't have to, but he knew he belonged with Helen, wherever she ended up. And Lady would be with them. He set about straightening the place. He walked into his study and sat down at the typewriter. The events of the last couple of days finally had their way with him. He put his head in his arms on the typewriter and drifted off to sleep.

Startled awake by the phone ringing, Liam raised his head and realized the room was dark. He must've been out for quite a while. He stumbled into the kitchen, flipped on a light, and picked up.

"Hello?" It was Helen's voice on the other end. "Did I wake you up? You sound out of it. Are you okay, Liam?"

"Yes, yes. I guess I fell asleep. I need…. I need to talk with you. Tell you I'm sorry."

"It's okay, Liam."

"But I need to tell you…"

"Tell me what? That you were a jerk, again? I know that. But I also get that you were, in your own ridiculous way, trying to be helpful."

Liam was waking up. "So, you're okay with it?"

"Of course not. But I forgive you. We've both been under a lot of stress."

Now he was both awake and with a mission to carry out. "Helen?"

"Yes, Liam."

329

He took a deep breath and exhaled slowly. He heard Sharon's words:

"Welcome to adulthood."

"I'm ready to go to Ohio with you."

There was a long silence. He thought he heard a sniffle but wasn't sure. Finally she spoke, clearly. "Well, that's a good thing. Because the Dean called. Stan will remain chairman. I'm leaving Madison."

For the first time, Liam was prepared for this news. "I'm proud of you, Helen."

She responded without hesitation. "I'm kind of proud of me too. Doesn't mean I'm not disappointed. I had really hoped that I wouldn't have to return to Ohio. I didn't want to admit that to you, but I'm ready now to do it. I'm thrilled you'll be with me."

He took a moment to let it all sink in. He had actually committed to a relationship that was mutual, with a loving woman who cared about him as much as he cared about her. He was going to pick up and go into uncharted waters. "So. I'm thinkin' I should get over there tomorrow to help you start packing."

She chuckled. "You'd better. Otherwise, I'm going to have to ask Stephen to help."

50

"I guess someone's in a good mood today!" Helen smiled as she opened the door.

Liam was grinning from ear to ear. Lady pushed past him and ran into the living room, where she circled, panting and, he could swear, smiling. Liam swept Helen up in his arms and kissed her long and hard, their tongues touching and intertwining. He walked her toward the bedroom as she protested.

"Uh—Liam? We've got work to do—."

He ignored the plea. She gave in, as he threw her onto the bed. "Well okay now!"

When they finally emerged from the bedroom, exhausted but laughing, they nearly tripped over Lady, who was stretched out in the doorway, sound asleep.

Helen kissed Liam one more time. "As I was saying, we've got some serious packing to do. Let's get at it."

***

Later, Helen walked into the kitchen, where Liam was engrossed in trying to fit a few too many pieces into a single box. She put her hand on his shoulder.

"Why don't we take a break? I don't have anything in the house to feed you, but maybe we can walk over by campus and get a bite."

Liam stood up and wiped his forehead. "Sounds like a plan, Ma'am. I could use a break."

She laughed at him. "Seems to me you could always use a break. But in this case, you probably deserve one."

They closed Lady into the bedroom and left the house. Liam looked back as they walked away. There he was. That little nitwit Stephen. Staring from the upstairs window. Liam leaned over and whispered in Helen's ear.

331

"Look what we have here--the Captain's Widow staring out to sea."

"Give it up, Liam."

They walked into the first bar that didn't look overrun with students and found a quiet booth in a corner away from the crowd. With drinks in hand, he smiled at her and spoke the words he never thought he'd be saying.

"Here's to new adventures in Ohio!"

"Shhhhh. I haven't told the Dean I'm not taking the job here yet."

"Ooops! Sorry."

She took a sip of wine and spoke quietly. "Yes. Here's to Ohio. And to us!"

Liam noticed she was glancing at a table on the other side of the bar. He let it go for a while but saw that she was not focused on their conversation.

"What's going on?"

"That's Stan over there. He's looking this way."

"Where?"

"Don't be obvious. He's at that table directly across. In the cowboy shirt."

"Who the fuck wears a cowboy shirt?"

"Cowboys. And Stan. Stan wears a cowboy shirt. Don't ask."

Just as Liam started to respond, she closed her eyes.

"Shit! He's headed this way."

"Don't let him get to you."

Stan walked up and stood uncomfortably close to Helen. "Oh hi Helen—so glad to see you. Welcome to the faculty! I'm looking forward to continuing our collaboration."

Helen looked away, without speaking. Liam stood up.

Helen looked up at him. "Liam. Don't."

"Don't worry. I won't."

He put his hand on Stan's shoulder and smiled.

"So you must be Stanley. I've heard a lot about you. Listen, I'd like to get to know you better. Let's get out of the path of traffic so we can chat." Liam gripped his shoulder and ushered him away from the table to an empty spot in the bar.

Stan looked up at him, coldly but with a hint of uncertainty in his demeanor. "Who the hell are you?"

"Oh excuse me, Stanley. I haven't introduced myself. I'm Liam, and I might just become your worst nightmare."

"Don't call me Stanley."

"I'm so sorry—Stanley. Look, I know who you are, and what you've been pulling."

"I don't know what you're talking about. Let go of me."

"I'm going to say this just once. You're going to leave Helen alone. If you so much as look at her sideways, let alone make any more propositions to her, I will find you. You got me?"

"Let me go. You're out of your mind."

"I asked you a question. You got me, Stanley?" He squeezed harder.

"Yes, I've got you. Now let me go."

Liam released him. Stan started to walk away but turned and glared. "You're a jackass."

"Bingo. And one I don't think you want to run into again."

"Please tell me you didn't threaten the man." Helen had a pleading look in her eyes when Liam returned to the table.

"Of course not. We just had a pleasant little conversation about literature and the arts. A swell little man, that Stanley."

"Am I going to need to call the Dean right away when we get back to my apartment?"

"Yeah. I think that might be a good idea."

333

***

Liam and Helen took their time returning to her place. When they walked in, they heard scratching at the bedroom door. Liam looked up.

"Oh shit—Lady. She's not gonna be happy." As he opened the door, Lady came flying out as if shot from a cannon. She ran to the front door. Liam opened it and looked back. "I'll be just a few minutes. Someone's got some business to do."

Helen watched out the front window as Liam and Lady frolicked around the yard. She spoke to herself. "Two kids. I've got two kids to deal with. What am I getting myself into?"

When Liam returned, they settled back into the rhythm of packing, each working in their own space. Liam heard the phone ring, and saw Helen walk to the back of the house to pick it up. She was gone a long time. Finally, she came into the kitchen and tapped him on the shoulder.

"Can you come into the other room?"

Liam stood up and followed her. She pointed to a chair in the living room. "Why don't you have a seat? We need to chat."

Liam was confused but followed directions. "What's up? Did the Dean call? Am I in trouble?"

"No, the Dean didn't call, although that reminds me I need to call him. And no, you're not in trouble."

Liam relaxed but remained puzzled. "You look kind of serious. Is this bad news?"

"No. Not bad news. But news nevertheless."

Liam smiled. "So out with it!"

"Well. I'm not sure how to present this since I'm still trying to process it myself."

Liam stopped smiling. "Was it Wesleyan?" He was scrambling to figure out what was going on.

334

"No. Not Wesleyan. NYU."

"What do you mean, 'NYU'?" Now he was really lost.

Helen had a bemused look on her face. "NYU just called. They're offering me a position."

Liam was racking his brain, trying to make a connection, but nothing was making sense. Where the hell did NYU come from? "Okay. I'll bite. How and why would NYU be offering you a position?"

"Well, I applied to several schools last year before I took the position here. NYU was interested, and interviewed me several times, but said they didn't have any openings. They gave me the usual 'we'll keep your CV in our files' assurance. I never heard anything from them. Until now. A faculty member died suddenly last week. So now they have an immediate need, and apparently my name was at the top of their list."

"Wait. So what're you saying?"

"They want me to come in and meet with them. The job's there if I want it, and if I'm prepared to start immediately for Fall term."

Liam stood up and walked over to the front window. Lady ran and stood next to him. He looked out at nothing in particular, while he assembled his thoughts. Finally, he turned back to Helen. "You mean—."

Helen stood up and joined him at the window. "Yep. How would you feel about New York?"

"Now?"

"No time like the present."

He blinked his eyes, as if turning on the windshield wipers to clear away the rain blocking his view. "How long do we have to think about it?"

"They gave me a week. If I'm not going to take it, they said they have to move on. They need to fill the position before classes start."

"What do you want to do?"

She put her head on his chest. "It's the opportunity of a lifetime. It would put me right smack in the middle of the art world. And it would bring you back to New York."

Liam dropped his head into hers. He reached down and stroked Lady's head, then looked straight out the window. For Helen, it must have seemed like an eternity as she waited for his response. Finally, he smiled.

"Let's go!"

51

"You do know we have an hour and a half before the plane boards?" Helen rolled her eyes as she stood by while the driver took their bags from the taxi.

"You can never be too early to the airport. Besides, the plane's going to be full. I want to get positioned at the gate to be first in line."

"We're in first class. There's not going to be a big line."

He grinned. "Oh ye of little faith. You've got to trust old Liam, the savvy world traveler."

Helen looked at the cabbie, who shrugged. She took Liam by the arm and looked up at him like a swooning teenager. But only for a second. "Bullshit. You're so full of it!"

He winked at the cabbie and turned to Helen. "You'll thank me for this."

They entered the terminal and waited to clear security. The line wasn't long. As they pulled their bags down the concourse toward the gate, Liam stopped to pick up some coffee for them, and a *New York Times*. They arrived at their gate before the aircraft. Liam picked out seats near the agent's stand.

Helen smiled. "It's a good thing I love you, O'Connor. Now just promise me you won't embarrass me in New York?"

"Ha! You're talking to Mr. New York himself. I'm the smoothest operator out there, don't you know?"

Helen fanned herself with the paper. "It's getting pretty hot and heavy in here, don't you think?"

Passengers slowly filed into the gate area. Liam looked over at Helen and pointed. "I told you it would fill up."

She ignored him and opened the *Times* while he watched the gate agent arrive and start going through her paperwork. Liam was drifting off into his own world when Helen reached out and touched him to get his attention.

"Do you know a writer named Marguerite Fairfield?"

A chill ran through him like a bolt of lightning coursing down an antenna, striking deep in the pit of his stomach. He tried to be casual, but his hands were trembling as he thought through what his response might be. He looked up in panic. Helen was still reading, so hopefully she didn't see it.

"Maybe. I'm not sure. Why do you ask?" There. Maybe that worked.

She passed the open section to him. He grabbed and scanned it. There it was. Big as life. A headline, top left column. **"NOTED AUTHOR IN PLAGIARISM SCANDAL--She Stole His Heart, Then His Book".**

Holy shit. He started to read, his hands shaking.

"When literary agent George Tomassini opened Marguerite Fairfield's highly anticipated new novel, The High Priestess Relents, its words caught his eye. They looked familiar. Too familiar."

Oh man.... Here we go.

Liam tried to look nonchalant. The article went on to explain that Marguerite had lifted, nearly verbatim, almost her entire book from an as-yet unpublished work by a young writer with whom she'd had a brief affair.

God, she has balls as big as all outdoors.

At the bottom of the article, on the last page of the section, was an unflattering photo of Marguerite walking out of her lawyer's office.

Liam thought briefly of trying to pull together the evidence of his own run-in with her stealing his work, to finally get his measure of revenge, but he looked at Helen and knew there was no point. He had dealt with Marguerite once and for all. She was broken when he walked down the

338

hall and out of her life, so what did he care now? His life was now with Helen. He shook it off and took her hand.

"I may have met her at some point along the line. I can tell you she's in a boat load of shit now."

***

They could hear (actually, anyone within a hundred feet of them could hear) a commotion coming down the concourse. Liam strained to listen to the sound. As it got closer, there was no denying it. Gloria Gaynor, blasting at full volume from a boombox. He looked at Helen apprehensively.

She peered down the concourse and started to grin. Then she pointed, laughing. A parade was slowly but steadily approaching, led by a slight figure dressed head to toe in gold lame', a boombox on one shoulder, an "I HEART NYC" balloon in the other hand. Several others followed behind, like a poorly coordinated conga line. As they got closer, the gold lame' figure became, not surprisingly, Jeremy. He looked like a gay Elvis, but he was dancing in his own signature style. No mistaking that. He was followed by Ronaldo, dressed in his bullfighter garb, holding hands with Mikaela, who was wearing tight red capri pants and a white halter top, trying in vain to balance on black patent stiletto heels. Vera followed them, in a navy pantsuit, with Marianne trailing, trying hard not to be part of the group. Liam and Helen stood up as they arrived at the gate. Some passengers were staring, others laughing, and yet others applauding. The gate agent was waving her hands, trying to get everyone's attention to her boarding announcements.

The little *bon voyage* party encircled Liam and Helen. Helen hugged each of them in turn. Liam tried to shake hands with Jeremy, but to no avail. Jeremy jumped up into his arms, Liam protesting but laughing as he did. Liam looked at him.

339

"Why are you all here? You know we have to come back to town to finish packing and pick up Lady."

Jeremy jumped down. "Well of course we do, but we wanted to give you the very best send-off! We couldn't let our favorite people—well, our favorite person plus you—leave town without us all being here to celebrate with you." He looked around at the others and raised his hands. "Everybody! Hip-Hip-Hooray!" The others stood, silently, looking the other way. He tried again. "Come on guys!" They ignored him.

Liam walked over to Vera. She was sniveling and sniffing, tears running down her cheeks. "I'm going to miss you Boss. You're the best person I ever worked for." She grabbed him in a bear-hug, in full sob mode.

"Vera. I'm not gone forever. I'll be back. And you're still working for me."

She sobbed on. "It's not going to be the same."

Liam patted her on the back. As he did, he caught that familiar scent, and moved on a little quicker than he had intended. Ronaldo thrust his hand forward to shake, then bowed deeply. Liam nodded. "Thank you, Ronaldo."

"Please call me Ronnie. That's my name." Then he too fell into Liam's arms. Liam patted his back as well.

"That's quite an honor, Ronnie." He turned to Mikaela. "You're looking pretty hot there, Mikaela. Thanks for coming by to see us."

Mikaela hugged him. "I'm going to miss you, Liam. You're okay."

Liam was moved. "Thanks!"

"For an old guy." Mikaela kissed him on the cheek and laughed as Liam wiped the lipstick off.

Liam looked over and saw Marianne, standing by herself. She was staring out the window at the airplane sitting at the gate. He walked over to her.

"Marianne. What can I say? You're what's kept my little shop going. I'm really proud of you and all you've

340

done." She wouldn't look at him, so he walked around to be face to face with her. "Hey."

Marianne looked down, then finally met his eyes. "Don't fuck up New York, Liam. And let Helen shine. She deserves it."

Liam nodded. Now he was becoming emotional but wasn't about to show it. "I promise. Don't you fuck up my store."

She nodded in return. He went to hug her, but she stuck out her hand to shake.

"First class passengers may now board." The announcement broke the spell. Liam and Helen waved to their assembled well-wishers and got into line. When they boarded and took their seats, they could see into the terminal. All but a single figure were walking away. Marianne stood, exactly where she had been, still looking out the window at the airplane. Liam waved, but she didn't see him, or if she saw him, she didn't respond.

As the plane pushed back from the gate, Liam took a final glance at the terminal. Marianne was still standing there. Finally, she looked up and he saw the slightest hint of a wave, or at least he wanted it to be. He had no idea if she had seen him or not.

Liam and Helen held hands as they started the takeoff roll and didn't let go until the plane had turned from the airport and pointed toward New York. When they got to altitude and the pilot turned off the seatbelts lights, Liam reached under the seat and grabbed his briefcase. He opened it and took out a book, which he slipped to Helen. An advance copy of *Darby's Gift*.

She looked at him with surprise. "You didn't tell me you had this."

"You're right. I didn't." He smiled and reclined his seat.

She held the book lovingly in her hands. She just wanted to touch it, feel it, smell it. She looked at the cover page, the publishing information, then got to the dedication. "For my Lady... ." She read the next line of the dedication, put the book down, and smiled. She leaned over to kiss Liam, but he was already asleep.

Helen sat quietly for a while, watching out the window as the plane broke out over the clouds. The sun was brilliant, the sky a spectacular azure blue. She watched Liam as he slept. "I love you, Liam O'Connor." She thought he may have grunted a little.

She sat back and read the first chapter of the book, then reclined her seat and snuggled close to Liam. She kissed him on the forehead, then whispered in his ear.

"And I'm pregnant."

THE END

Made in United States
Cleveland, OH
25 April 2025

16406088R00188